the Healer

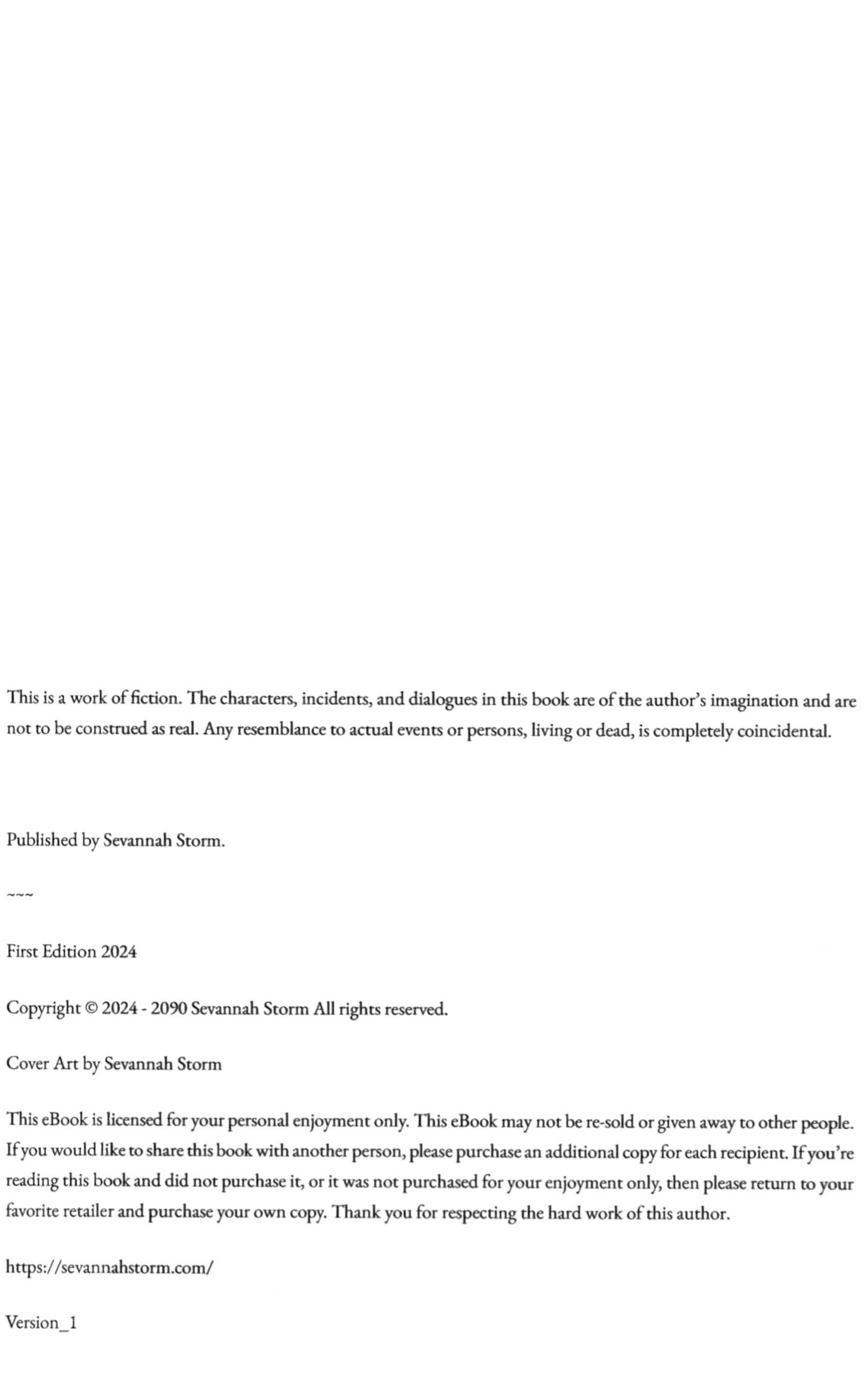

This is a work of fiction. The characters, incidents, and dialogues in this book are of the author's imagination and are not to be construed as real. Any resemblance to actual events or persons, living or dead, is completely coincidental.

Published by Sevannah Storm.

~~~

First Edition 2024

Cover Art by Sevannah Storm

https://sevannahstorm.com/

Version_1
~~~

ALSO BY SEVANNAH STORM

The Blood of Legends Series

The Huntress

The Healer

*

The Gifting Series

Soul Forged

Fate Forged

Sun Forged

War Forged

Star Forged

Shadow Forged

Earth Forged

Lust Forged

Fire Forged

*

The Qaldreth Warriors

Sol Survivor

Dark Survivor (Coming soon)

*

The Space Hunter Chronicles

The Shikari

The Justisaar (Coming soon)

*

Standalones

Xiaxan Fox

Ire of Silver

The Crucible of the Eternals

*

Plump Playwright Series

Plump Jane

Seducing Amelia

Loving Finley

Keeping Tessa

Kissing Navy

CHAPTER ONE

A MEAN BASTARD

WHEN RHYS STEPPED ONTO the splintered wooden porch, the familiar stench of blood hit him—salty, tangy, but with a wealth of wet fur and fish. He stilled and sniffed, allowing the miasma of colors to saturate his nose. The sharper the odor or emotion the brighter the color.

A sunlight yellow 'smoke' trail slipped under the door. Blood laced with bear meant one thing. Roaring, he burst into the cabin he shared with his brother, tearing the door off the hinges.

"Aiden!" Bounding up the stairs leading to their bedrooms, he jerked on the balustrade, almost ripping it from its base.

"He's fine." Noah, Rhys's best friend and beta, filled Aiden's bedroom doorway, blocking the path.

"Move, Noah." Rhys tried to shove past, but Noah stood firm. Short of shoving him against the wall and injuring a brother-in-pack, Rhys spun away to pace. His bear snarled, threatening to take over and bowl Noah out of the way.

"Calm your bear, Rhys. He'll agitate Aiden, and we just got him to relax."

His vision tinged with red, focused, blurred, then sharpened. "What the fuck happened?"

"We think Alrik sent you out on a food run for this reason." His brother-in-pack Jase peered over Noah's shoulder, his dirty-blond hair disheveled, with blood smeared across his temple. "Aiden's usual disrespect didn't help the situation."

"Might have been the trigger." Noah dipped his head. "With a little tact, he might have avoided this."

"Fuck." Rhys yanked his bun loose to run his fingers through his hair, hoping to calm his bear and ease the tension tightening the muscles in his neck. "Go on. Tell me what happened."

"It wasn't a fair fight, but Aiden should have seen this coming. You know how much he wants you to lead." Noah held out his hands, palms out to prevent Rhys from barreling him over. "Alrik and his sycophants cornered Aiden in the gym."

Rhys's breath caught and seared his lungs. Gym equipment could kill if used with brute force. "Is he...?" The lump in his throat strangled his voice. Ice drenched his scalp, sliding down his spine to his fingertips. He shoved them into his pockets, hoping to hide their trembling. "Can I see him now?"

Noah studied him for a long-drawn-out moment. "Don't mention his face."

Rhys halted mid-stride. "Why?" He gripped the door frame and splintered the wood beneath his fingers, fear and fury pummeling his thoughts, his senses. "I'm going to fucking kill Alrik."

"You could take him on, Rhys, but winning means becoming the alpha."

Rhys shot Jase a sharp glare. "Like I don't fucking know that."

"It's just a reminder, brother-in-pack." Noah thumped his back, trying to calm Rhys.

He was far from it. His bear paced inside him, whining for release. Rhys snorted and flicked his head side-to-side, cracking his neck.

"I'll see Aiden first. Alrik's death can wait." One step into the room petrified his muscles. His bones locked, and his bear clawed at the walls, roaring in despair. The stench of antiseptic, blood, and the burned ozone of pain hit him.

The man in the bed wasn't the Aiden Rhys had seen at breakfast. The youthful skin molded over his features was blue, black, swollen, and mottled. Both eyes were sealed shut, his eyelashes like the legs of a squashed spider. His nose was broken, and his lips split and bleeding.

Sure, shifters healed fast, but in the meantime, he would be in fiery agony while his muscles and bones reknitted. Aiden lay like an ironing board, his arms bandaged in place, and one leg in a worn orthopedic boot.

"Sans was here?"

" He is our doctor." Jase nudged his chin at Aiden. "Sans snuck in to tend to Aiden. Said he saw it go down. I asked my brother to escort him home."

"Good." Rhys grunted. Jase and his brother Sawyer were the best trackers in the pack.

At least, Rhys had one ally from Alrik's camp. Taking their alpha on wouldn't be easy, and despite knowing it was the right decision, Rhys didn't like the risks if he failed. The Knights Ridge pack would continue to suffer without him to shield them. Cast out, exiled, he would have to head north to Dane's pack. That wasn't fair on his old college friend. An alpha shouldn't have to tolerate another alpha in his pack, and Rhys wasn't designed to be a beta.

He slumped. "Alrik has to know what this means."

Noah spun a chair and squatted on it, folding his arms across the back. "He was tired of waiting for you to make your move, Rhys."

"Well, by attacking the 'last' member of my family, he made sure I would react." He smiled, but it was nothing more than a tightness across his mouth. There was no mirth, no eagerness behind it. "I won't give in to him."

Jase gaped, but after a glance at Noah's knowing smirk, he quit looking like a fish out of water. "What do you intend to do?"

"I'll wait, bide my time, gather the elders and the strongest pack members eager for new leadership. Let Alrik stew, raise his paranoia to a new level."

"We must bow but not shy from him." Noah grinned. "Spur on rumors of attacks, of allies outside of Knights Ridge. Giving Colt a call might be wise. Might as well do the same for Travis. Having Fenneg's Rabidhide and Suddale's Dawnguard packs on your side would bolster your authority. Dane's already on your side, but Coedwig is smallish and won't hold any sway against Alrik."

Rhys smirked. "I'll tell Dane you said so."

Noah chuckled and flicked a dismissive hand.

"Everything must fail. We'll create a leak in the water towers, cut the power supply, drain the food stores, and cut off the pack's finances." Jase ticked these off on his fingers. "Not so bad we can't repair them when you're in power, of course."

"A battle strategy," Rhys said while brushing Aiden's hair off his temple.

"I love that idea; except we need to challenge him soon." Noah dipped his head. "I can't keep silent for much longer."

Rhys studied Noah's face, familiar with the sadness in his eyes. They had all suffered at Alrik's hands as expected of a cruel alpha. "All right. How much can we organize by sunset?"

Jase's whoop startled Aiden awake who tried to rise, groaned, then slumped.

"Rhys?" His hoarse voice tore through Rhys who had vowed to protect his brother when their parents were killed and Uncle Sean left the pack. Finding Aiden sprawled, bloodied, and bandaged, lashed at the guilt encasing Rhys's heart.

"I'm here, baby bear." He patted Aiden's bicep.

Aiden's brow furrowed. "Argh, quit calling me that."

"Quit trying to get me killed. I'll take on Alrik when I'm ready. Your shit-stirring is to blame for this."

Aiden fell silent before he mumbled, "You're right. I'm sorry."

"Rest, Aiden, heal." Rhys pushed off the bed. "If you're a good little patient, I'll take you for ice cream in the morning."

"Ass." Aiden chuckled, then coughed. Blood dewed on his split lip.

Rhys nudged his head at the door. Striding out, he didn't check whether Jase and Noah followed. Their boots thumping on the wooden floor and their wolf and tiger scents were all he needed. "Make it happen."

Noah jerked, then beamed. "Are you sure?"

"Now you doubt me?" Rhys harrumphed. "I'll set up a barbecue closest to the club-house. I want you two, and any of our pack mates, to come and go. Spend some time with me laughing and drinking beer. If I can't have Jase's sweet strategy, then let's go for the element of surprise."

Jase bounded down the stairs, banging cupboard doors as he gathered the makings of a barbecue. "The meat you brought from town hasn't frozen yet. I'll grab a few steaks."

Noah yanked the door off its one hinge and leaned it against a wall. "I'll round up who I can, then tag Jase. A crowd will gather before sunset."

An impromptu barbecue wasn't unheard of, and it would lead Alrik into a false sense of security. "Send someone to gather the elders. This can't go down without their attendance."

Rhys sighed at the reminder of how old and neglected their elders were. Anyone strong enough to challenge Alrik's reign found a swift death. Their eldest was Sans, and that old lion wouldn't last many more winters.

Gritting his teeth, Rhys swept up a pile of logs and carried it to the firepit. He didn't choose the one closest to the clubhouse, but the largest. Tonight, there would be a show for everyone, with minimum damage to the dilapidated clubhouse and surrounding cabins.

With a hand in his pocket, he nursed the fire, sipping on his beer. Noah arrived with his arm across Willow's shoulder. His younger sister was adorable with her blonde hair in pigtails. Her wide-eyed gaze darting to Rhys's cabin hinted that she would rather be with Aiden.

He offered her a soda. "Drink half of this, then stroll to my cabin." What would happen between him and Alrik wouldn't be pretty, and casualties were possible. Willow out of sight with Aiden meant one less soul for Rhys to worry about.

She forced a smile. "Kick ass tonight."

"Language." Noah chuckled at her glare. "The elders are on their way. They'll trickle in along with their kin."

"Sawyer is rounding up the others." Jase rocked on his heels, cradling a beer can to his chest.

Rhys released a slow breath. Adrenaline pumped through his veins while the excitement and a healthy dose of fear raised the hairs on the back of his neck.

"He's watching from his lofty perch." Noah tipped his beer to his lips.

"Wondering why he wasn't invited?" Jase laughed, a little too loudly. "Let him hear how much fun we're having, how much we care for his brutality."

The urge to look tugged at Rhys. His bear roared, willing him to give Alrik the middle finger. Rhys grinned at the idea. No, he wanted him to join the party. The older male would do so unafraid, bringing Dyl and Vik as his only protection.

Rhys snorted. An alpha shouldn't need bodyguards, and Alrik's security detail said it all. The challenge match would be between Rhys and Alrik. Taking down his bodyguards would weaken Rhys, and that was exactly how it would play out, breaking the challenge laws.

Folks trickled in, each stopping by to offer their support. Fear lingered in their eyes, in their broken spirits, yet they had ventured out with hope the driving force. The weight of their suffering settled on his chest like an anchor, bolstering his determination.

They feasted. The aroma of charred meat added to the pseudo joy in the air. While he nursed one beer and was desperate for another, the chill of midnight approaching tested his patience.

"What are we celebrating?" Alrik's bombastic voice grated on Rhys's last nerve.

The fool smirked, as if everyone's silence was a mark of respect. In an expensive jacket and a crisp white shirt, he had the air of a gentleman at leisure.

Behind him stood Vik, all muscle with no hair. Rhys had never liked the kid growing up. His bullying of others less fortunate or weaker than him wasn't an admirable trait. No matter what Rhys said to him, it had ended in brawling. To be fair, Rhys had Vik to thank for his fighting skills.

Dyl hovered farther away, his gaze vigilant. Not originally from the Knights Ridge pack meant no blood ties to the folks there, no history. A stranger was easier to manipulate, easier to pay off.

The temptation to lunge, to snap Alrik's neck was strong. Eager for a fight, Rhys's bear banged against the restraints. Yet, to assume the alpha role, he had to challenge and win.

"No reason." Shrugging, he met Alrik's gaze, not backing down, not glancing away in submission.

The older male bristled, squaring his shoulders. "Where's Aiden?" He chuckled, but his focus didn't shift from Rhys's face.

He didn't rise to the bait. "I believe he and Willow asked for alone time."

Alrik's attempts to keep the bloodlines pure was pointless. Species with species was his motto despite the mix each pack sported. Rhys hadn't heard of pure bear packs or wolf packs except from fables told around the campfires. Those days were long gone. And besides, love didn't care about blood, gender, age, or status, and Alrik thinking he could control or deny it was proof the old male was an idiot.

He whipped his head to stare at Noah, a pulse ticking at the base of his jaw. "And you condone the dilution of your bloodline?" Alrik growled. "Impure blood weakens our connection to the Lunar goddess."

"Maybe, but from where I'm standing, I'd say the goddess has long abandoned you."

Alrik roared, his face mottling. "You challenge me?"

Noah laughed. "No, not I, old cat."

"I suggest you remove that jacket. When we're done, I'll sell it to pay for repairs. And you better pray I kill you before we find out what you've wasted our money on." Rhys peeled off his T-shirt, draping it across a tree stump.

The problem was the moment he bent to undo his boots Alrik would charge. It was in his nature, and a tiger never changed their stripes.

Rhys loved these jeans, and releasing his bear would shred the well-worn denim. Sighing, he rested his hands on his hips as he studied his alpha.

Surprising him, Jase kneeled and undid Rhys's laces. Fuck, right then, he loved his brother-in-pack. Alrik growled, lunging forward to nudge Jase aside, but Sawyer and Noah leaped in front to shield him.

Vik loomed behind Alrik, attempting to warn them off without shifting into his bear. Made sense, since his hairless bear was a laughable sight. He had the claws and teeth of a polar bear, just not the intimidation factor. Vik was evidence Alrik's "beliefs" were subjective. The last person to mention that had died.

During their posturing, Rhys removed his boots and shimmied out of his jeans. "Thanks, Jase." He nudged his head to the crowd, asking him to guard the innocent.

Noah and Sawyer settled behind Rhys, mimicking Vik and Dyl.

"You have a choice before you." Rhys folded his arms across his chest and met Vik and Dyl's gazes. "Stay, and you die for this male. I sure as fuck think that would be a waste of life."

Without eyebrows, the only way to measure Vik's surprise was by the furrowing of his forehead.

"You know me, Vik, you know my history, my stance, my honor."

The male nodded.

"We may not have seen eye-to-eye, but you're welcome at Knights Ridge, no judgment, a free bear."

Vik settled his gaze on Alrik, before bowing his head. "I prefer to walk away with my life."

Relief flooded Rhys at not having to kill someone he had known for so long.

Alrik spat and faced Vik. "You piece of shit."

Before Rhys could stop him, Alrik swung out a clawed hand, slicing across Vik's face. Rhys took Alrik down, releasing his bear just as they hit the compacted ground. They rolled, scrambling for dominance, claws and teeth connecting when Alrik assumed his ragged tiger form.

Rhys roared as Alrik bit into his shoulder, his incisors sinking deep. Unable to shake the old tiger off, he flipped onto his back and threw Alrik over his head, tossing him far. Ignoring the throbbing numbness working its way down his front limb, Rhys lumbered over to the tiger, tackling him again. The crowds scattered, then regathered like a shifting shoal of sardines.

A wolf pounced on Rhys's back and clenched his teeth around Rhys's fur-lined bicep. As the pain registered, the wolf flew off, sliding along the ground and into the tree stump. Noah's wolf growled, keeping Dyl at bay. He broke the challenge laws by interfering, but then again, so had Dyl.

Rhys settled his bear's full weight onto the tiger, hoping to force him to submit. It took all his control not to slice his claws across Alrik's throat. His bear roared for blood and justice.

"Submit," Rhys grated, the words barely audible when spoken through his bear.

"Never." Alrik's tongue lolled out as he fought for air.

"Submit," Rhys roared, baring his teeth an inch from Alrik's cheek. Rhys didn't want the other's death on his hands, even though the certainty of it pierced his jagged thoughts.

When Alrik met Rhys's gaze with blatant challenge, he leaned back to swipe his claws.

Seconds before he sliced the soft flesh of Alrik's throat, the crowd sucked in a collective breath. Clambering to his feet, Rhys receded his bear to stare at Alrik's lifeless human body. The pooling blood glowed in the flickering light of the dying fire. The stench was as sharp and as yellow as Aiden's. The purer the lineage didn't alter the smell.

Rhys's sweat-drenched chest rose and fell as the sounds of night settled on him, and his aches registered. Flicking off the blood dripping from his fingertips, he stumbled back then faced his...pack.

He met each person's gaze. "Any challenger?" As part of the law, he had to ask.

In a wave of obeisance, they dipped their heads, submitting to their new alpha. Noah and Jase holding Dyl in place, also bowed, despite the grins morphing their faces. They released Dyl who took off into the night. Sawyer broke away to chase after him—the determined set of his jaw assured Rhys this loose end would be settled this night.

Rhys threw his arms wide and laughed, success melting the tension from his body. "I need a beer."

Chapter Two

WELL, THAT EXPLAINS IT

ILONA TRACED A RIVULET of water with a fingertip, smudging the pristine glass on the car's side window. The scent of polished leather filled her nostrils, mingling with Dad's spicy cologne and Mom's subtle perfume. Ilona sat in the back seat, not needing to see their faces as they argued over who spent the most time in surgery. "Moonlight Sonata" by Beethoven played in the background—one of Dad's favorites.

"You know, I will always win." Mom smirked calling forth a grin from Ilona. "I gave birth too."

Dad laughed. "Nice try, sweetheart."

"It counts." Mom pouted, then winked at Ilona, reaching back to pat her hand as it rested on the satin of her black cocktail dress. "How's our new doctor feeling?" She squealed in delight, shaking her fists in front of her, ruffling the dark pink cowl at her neckline. She had coiled her auburn hair into a thick chignon and painted her lips a deep red. As always, Mom looked beautiful.

"We're so proud of you, honey." Mom glanced at Dad. "Aren't we, Gerard?"

Dad met Ilona's gaze in the rearview mirror. "I sure as hell am. At first, I thought using your grandmother's last name was foolhardy when our names carry such weight, but I understand now, pumpkin, I do."

"Thanks, Dad." She squeezed their shoulders.

They were almost at the restaurant to celebrate completing her residency at Amity Community Hospital. She interviewed at eight hospitals, specifically in cities close to Fenneg. Her hospital of choice was Indes Pediatrics, and she had just yesterday received the email confirming her successful application. Other offers had begun to pour in, and more flooded in after Dad announced on his forums who his daughter was. As her proud daddy, she couldn't fault him for it.

She could have met them at the restaurant, but she had dropped by their home instead, hoping to enjoy a pre-dinner coffee with her father while Mom dressed.

"Have you thought about your fellowship?" Mom twisted to look at her at the same time Dad met Ilona's gaze in the rearview mirror. He flashed her a wink before focusing on the road.

Smothering her smile, she readied to reveal her good news. "Oncology." She blinked at the bright lights penetrating the windscreen as Dad stopped at a red traffic light.

Mom beamed. "That's amaz—"

"Shit," Dad bit out.

Ilona screamed, throwing out a hand like she could stop the semi when it plowed into them head-on. A moving wall of metal scrunched the front of the car. The force shoved them back, shoving them into the car behind. Time slowed. Glass shattered and sprayed. Streetlights glimmered off shards tearing through obstacles. Mom's blood-streaked arms rose as if floating underwater before snapping back in recoil. Dad lurched, his head whipping forward into the white airbags exploding to life.

Ilona's vision filled with the floor, then the ceiling, her breath seizing in her lungs. Phones, house keys, pens, and coins shot around the cab.

When the car settled, metal tinkled, and the stench of gasoline burned her nose. Groaning, she unfolded her body, peeling her face off the back of Dad's seat. Her cheek throbbed and burned as if on fire. She pressed her palm there then drew it back to study the blood smeared across her hand.

Silence reigned from the front.

She raised her gaze and blinked, unable to process what she was seeing.

Her door opened. A stranger unclipped her and dragged her out, his grip firm despite her squirming. A pleading wail penetrated her ears. Who is crying like that?

"My mom..." she rasped, wiggling for freedom.

"The ambulance is on its way," the man gritted out, holding her in place on the sidewalk and away from the devastation.

Ambulance? Yes! Hope, warm, bright, blinding engulfed her. She stilled. "I'm...I'm a doctor."

He blinked at her, studied her face for a second, then released her. With her knees weak, her muscles trembling, she staggered and crumpled to the tarmac.

Splaying her bloodied hands, she tried to push herself up, dazed as the cold rain trickled down her face and saturated her dress. The stench of blood and the rain hitting tarmac assaulted her. Across shattered glass and twisted metal pieces she couldn't identify, she studied the wreckage. The full realization was slow to form. Their car was a crumpled mess. The driver of the semi was being lifted out of his cab.

"Dad! Mom!" Tears mingled with the rain, and Ilona whimpered, unable to hear a groan above the patter of the raindrops and the cooling metal.

She rocked to her knees, then onto her feet to stumble to the car. Running her hand along the dented roof, she slid down as she collapsed beside Mom's shattered window.

One look contorted Ilona's mouth into a wail, the sound she made unrecognizable. Her beautiful mother, her neck twisted, her lips smeared with blood, and her lifeless eyes staring at nothing.

Ilona fell onto her backside, raising her face to the dark sky, letting the rain pelt her. The agony cinching her chest stole her ability to breathe. Her vision spun, but instead of calming her breathing, she squeezed her eyes shut.

"Mom... I love you. I'm sorry I never told you enough." Dizziness assailed Ilona, and she bumped her head on the side of the car. She stayed there, allowing the cold metal to comfort her. Her temple pulsed, her face itched and burned—she might be concussed.

She gripped the door, inching herself to her feet. People milled around, gathering on Dad's side. Someone had opened his door and was speaking to him. She held her breath, hoping to hear his warm baritone. He didn't respond.

Crying out, she weaved through the carnage, one destination in mind. The man from earlier tried to stop her, but she shook him off. She rested a hand on the buckled rear of the car, needing its solidity to ground her. Dad could be fine, he had to be. Hand over hand, she pushed herself to hurry, but every step drained her with her limbs threatening to fail her, her body complaining at the abuse.

He slumped over the steering wheel with his face in the deflated airbag. She sucked in a deep breath and peeked between those trying to help. Blood trickled from an injury on his temple, but air misted with each gasp he took.

She nudged and tugged people aside, eager to reach him. When they tried to stop her, she screamed she was a doctor.

On a whimper, she stilled, and stared at Dad, forcing herself to calm, to think. What would he do? Mom was...dead. Her throat constricted, almost cutting off her breathing. She had to focus on the living.

Kneeling beside him, she feathered her hands over parts of him she could reach, starting at the back of his neck. Nothing felt out of place, but moving someone with broken vertebrae wasn't wise. His airway was clear. His wrist and his leg were broken. Tiny cuts marred his skin.

While head wounds bled a lot and sometimes looked worse than they were, the deep laceration worried her because of the potential hidden damage to his brain.

The shrill of sirens piercing the rain's hush was sweet. She wept amid chants of gratitude.

Pressing her palm to his head wound, applying direct pressure, she took his warm hand in her other hand. "I got you, Dad. I got you."

Familiar beeps, trolley wheels on linoleum, and the sharp sting of antiseptic dragged Ilona from her sleep. Had she caught a nap between shifts? She frowned, unable to remember or to think past her throbbing head. Even her ears rang as if she suffered from tinnitus.

She shifted in the bed, and stinging barbs of fire lanced through her, skittering across her skin. Groaning, she tried to touch something obscuring her vision on the left side of her face but couldn't, not with a drip in her wrist.

"What the...?" Her garbled words mimicked her confusion.

"Oh, thank God."

"Gran?" Ilona whipped her head in the direction of the voice, all sounds merging to pulse a pounding headache behind her left eye.

In a chair sat her petite grandmother. Her skin had a parchment appearance, pale and brittle. The bright spots on her cheeks didn't detract from the tears shimmering in her hazel eyes.

"What's the matter? Where am I? Is this Amity?"

"There was an accident. A truck driver had a heart attack…" Gran shivered, then staggered to her feet, her gnarled hands gripping the armrests. "My Elise didn't make it."

"Mom?" Memories flooded Ilona of her mom's lifeless eyes. She whimpered, agony sharper than her injuries squeezed her chest, her ribs, then her heart. "D…Dad?"

"He's in a coma in ICU."

Like sunlight on a cold day, warmth poured into every dark corner of her soul. Ilona melted into the bed with relief. "Good."

"He's stable, but there's no brain activity." Gran pinched her lips. "Living will, sweetheart."

Ilona gasped and chanted a denial, "No. Please, no." Sorrow strangled her voice. She wailed in silence as tears poured free, burning her cheeks.

"I didn't need to convince them to let you say goodbye." Gran's smile was tremulous. "You know these doctors, nurses. Their hearts are…" She cupped her mouth, muffling a sob.

Ilona unstrapped her drip, slipped the needle out, and tossed it aside. "Have they run all the tests? CT? MRI?"

She flipped the blankets aside and grimaced. Bandages crisscrossed her legs, only then did she register the sting of grazed skin over the rest of her body, as if a thousand fire ants feasted on her flesh.

Gran straightened to her full height of five-foot-three and cupped Ilona's hand. "You'll have scars, and a modeling career is no longer an option." She forced a smile. Ilona grabbed her hand, needing her touch and her core of strength to ground her. "Wearing your seatbelt saved you."

"Saved me?" Ilona mouthed in disbelief. Swinging her legs over the side of the bed flooded her with weakness, and she swayed where she sat. "Concussion?" She ran her hand along the bandage across her face.

"And a nasty scar from temple to chin."

"What are you doing, Dr. Devereaux?" Nurse Maddie crossed the room, placed a chart and a stainless steel kidney dish on the table, and crowded Ilona, preventing her from standing. "In you go, my dear."

"My dad—"

"Isn't going anywhere. Dr. Fernandez is on his way to chat with you." She gathered Ilona's legs by the ankles and tucked her under the blankets. As she worked, her gray bun bobbed, with escaped tendrils swaying across her ears. "I brought you Dr. Strickland's chart."

Ilona snatched it, running her bruised finger with its splintered fingernail down the results. Each one confirmed the worst, settling icy dread in the pit of her stomach. She slumped, sliding deeper under the blankets as reality sank in.

"It's true?" Gran shuffled to the opposite side of the bed.

Maddie reconnected the drip, slipping a filled syringe from a kidney dish to insert into the injection port.

"Yes." Ilona's limbs warmed as the analgesics flushed her system, numbing her pain receptors but not the dark hole in her heart.

Time buzzed past. She didn't stir until Gran kissed her goodbye. Gray shadows tarnished her porcelain skin, and exhaustion slumped her narrow shoulders. Ilona didn't know what she could say to ease the sorrow twisting Gran's lips.

She shuffled out of the private suite as Dr. Fernandez strode in. The wind his sharp movements generated whipped his coattails and tousled his salt-and-pepper ebony hair.

"Ah, Ilona, my dear, I'm so sorry." By far her favorite mentor, his sympathy struck a chord.

An undulating wave of despair curled her fingers into fists—a pointless attempt to hold back the burning in her nostrils. She shouldn't cry. Tears wouldn't save her dad. Nothing in known medicine could.

"Let's have a look at your injuries." He peeled the bandage away from her face and smiled.

She twisted her lips in wry amusement. "That bad, huh?"

"It will scar, but you didn't lose your eyesight. That's a good thing, right?" His 'patient' smile remained in place.

Having to experience his bedside manner gripped her tongue, and she snapped, "Don't make me read my damn chart."

He huffed. "You're going to do it anyway. Besides, I'm on my best behavior." Taping the bandage in place, he lifted her gaze to meet his with a fingertip at her chin. "The laceration cut to the zygomatic bone. Thankfully, you were unconscious when we scrubbed it."

She winced, having done that to burn and accident victims, hoping to save the patient pain at a later stage. An infection could occur if pieces of rock, sand, glass, and other matter remained in the wound.

"Did you task Kelly?" Of all the nurses, Kelly was the most thorough at scrubbing wounds.

Dr. Fernandez chuckled. "Only the best for you."

Ilona sighed as he scanned her arms and legs before tucking the blankets around her. "I'll survive."

Against the influx of swarming emotions, she clenched her jaw. She had wanted to live, to suck the marrow from life, so to speak. Now survival was her only option.

Dr. Fernandez wrapped his darker fingers around hers. "As a doctor and a daughter, there was nothing you could have done, Ilona. Wrong place, wrong time."

Not what she wanted or needed to hear. "Thank you, Dr. Fernandez."

"Max." He tapped her nose with his finger. "You're one of us now."

After he left her, Ilona stared at the door for a while. Was she one of them? A doctor, someone who could save lives and had the blessing of the medical board to do so? What was the point of eleven years spent studying, practicing, only to fail when those skills mattered the most?

No, she wasn't a doctor, and certainly not one capable of handling the most precious gifts life could offer...children. Curling into a ball, she allowed the tears to saturate her pillow because her future, her injuries—none of that mattered against Dad's impending death.

Twisting to smother a scream in the pillow, she lay there until the need for oxygen drove her to breathe. One thought circled, formed, dissolved then formed again, forcing her to decide. Dad's living will was her responsibility. She couldn't let Gran carry the burden.

Not now, though. Flipping the blankets back, Ilona slid off the bed, wheeling her drip stand beside her. The night nurses hurried about their tasks, smiling at her as she inched past. A few of Amity's staff greeted her, and she bit her inner cheek, wanting to scream she wasn't worthy of being called a doctor. Had Dad survived, he would have saved her and Mom.

The ICU doors opened as Ilona neared. She didn't give them a chance to close on her, increasing her pace no matter how stiff her legs were. In the far corner surrounded by machines was her dad. They had thrown the works at him—bedside monitors, ventilators, endotracheal tube, and an indwelling urinary catheter—to name a few. Her steps faltered, and the drip stand screeched as she dragged it behind her.

"Dad?" Releasing the stand, she gripped the side of the bed, assessing his visible injuries.

A contusion darkened his temple, nose, and eyes, with swelling contorting his familiar features. His wrist and leg were in orthopedic braces.

"It's me, Ilona. Gran says you signed a stupid living will. Why the fuck would you do this to me?" She pinched her lips to smother the rage boiling up her throat, pushing her to spew her sorrow, anger at the world and God for this unfairness.

Drawing in a deep breath, she laced her fingers through his. Crimson scratches marred his pale skin. The ventilator made rhythmic breathing sounds, and his heartbeat beeped. All looked good, except for the brain scans.

The ICU doors opened with a swish. The squeak of sneakers followed. "Dr. Fernandez ran the tests multiple times, Dr. Devereaux." Nurse Maddie checked Dad's blood pressure cuff, then fidgeted as if she didn't know what to do with her hands. She worked Trauma and not ICU. "Time to head back?"

Ilona nodded. This wasn't her dad. This was a vessel, a husk of the great man she had known. Dad was already with Mom, and even if there had been a hope, he'd signed a living will. "I understand now, Dad, I do."

She kissed his fingers, ignoring her tears splashing onto his knuckles. Then with a final glance, she trudged out of the ICU trailing her drip stand.

She would kill her dad in the morning.

Chapter Three

HONOR AMONG BEASTS

Rhys, the new and improved alpha of the Knights Ridge pack, trudged through the forest, choosing his steps with care. He wasn't in his bear form despite him nagging to change. The sweet scent of pine called forth a need to roam free, to hunt, to breathe in unpolluted air. His thoughts spun like a dervish. Within this month, the alliance with the vamps, finding out Alrik had failed the pack twice, and on top of it, meeting the woman of his dreams.

Callista Devereaux.

Glorious molten hair, green eyes, and an attitude to match.

His bear grumbled, still furious at him for not taking her and saving her from a vamp. Rhys released a long sigh. He'd explained, over and over, that she wasn't their mate. She was Gabriel's. Blood didn't lie. Hers called to Rhys's bear. Yet her and Gabriel's bond had formed on a telepathic level. They'd conversed, expressions crossing their faces even as words remained unspoken.

Missing a chance at Callie had doomed Rhys to a life of loneliness, unmated and unloved, and because of this, many would challenge him for the role as alpha. He needed a mate to solidify his reign. There was still time before his pack would demand he choose. Until then, he'd enjoy spending time with Callie as they built the paranormal unit.

He'd suspected she'd fall for that. Asking the vamps to test her was necessary to prove her strength and his neutrality. He was far from impartial though when it came to her. He had considered Callie's sister Valerie as a possible wife since she had the same blood in her veins, but she was more reserved than he liked. His pack needed a huntress or someone with a similar disposition. Now he'd have to choose from the city packs and perhaps form alliances to strengthen his position.

Drawing in a deep breath, he squared his shoulders and focused on the task at hand. He was there, in the middle of the forest on Knight Ridge soil, to deal with Alrik's first failure. For fear of his retribution, pack members had tossed aside children who weren't the same species—wolf with wolf, bear with bear. Which was the dumbest thing Rhys had heard of, like humans discarding children born with brown eyes.

Alrik had had a disregard for shifters and specifically children that churned Rhys's stomach. They were the pack's future, no matter the species. A polymorph, able to change into any number of animals, would have been a death sentence to a child.

Which was why he was there. This was little George's home. The polymorph child had transformed into a rat and saved a vamp's life. And in doing so, had highlighted Alrik's sin.

The tampered chemicals in the canister had been the second failure, forcing Rhys to make amends with the vamps by breaking with tradition and centuries of animosity. He now had an alliance with the vamp holds. But unlike the vamps who had the Drimari council to answer to, shifters kept to their packs and didn't interfere. He'd mourned that for a while. A shifter council might have stopped Alrik's tyrannical reign years ago.

Rhys raised his chin and sniffed. No aroma of cooked food greeted him as he entered the clearing. Broken chairs littered the unkempt yard, and the stench of garbage wrinkled his nose. It had his bear grumbling, but that wasn't what shot iced fury through his veins. The roar that tore from him was animalistic, his bear's voice shredding his human vocal cords.

George's brothers, four wolf pups, whined from within an iron cage. Their own feces stained their paws. Each child would undergo training depending on when they transitioned as a toddler. No one had taught these pups how to shift into human form. If they had, they wouldn't have remained in the cage. And the condition of their coats revealed they lacked nourishment.

Rhys ripped the door off the cage, tossing it to the side. It scarred the hardpacked dirt with deep grooves and narrowly missed Noah. Since Noah shifted into a wolf, Rhys gestured to the frightened pups in a silent command to take care of the little ones.

He stormed the dilapidated house, his steps vibrating the porch's rotten floorboards. He thrust the door open, breaking it off its hinges, then shielded his nose and entered, uninvited. Colors merged to burn his nostrils—shades of yellow for blood, urine, and vomit. Unwashed bodies, decayed food, and stale air assaulted him. What kind of a person lived like this? Raised children in this filth and tossed out George to survive on her own?

Along with the disgust was the self-directed anger. How had he not known of this? Noah's face twisted in shock, so this was as much a surprise to him. How many pack members lived in such squalor? The scowl that tugged on Rhys's lips was severe, clenching his teeth until his jaw ached. Make that three failures he needed to attend to.

He marched along the narrow passage, his shoulders brushing the thin walls. Mold grew on sections under the peeling wallpaper, and the cold dampness didn't make him shiver. The squalid desperation did. He peered into each room, finding the same conditions—a few unlivable—until he broke into the kitchen.

A woman—in nothing but a tattered dressing gown—sprawled on the floor. Discarded needles littered the filth around her. He raised his nose to the ceiling and sniffed, picking up the tale-tell scent of narcotics in a sharp mustard yellow. Empty bottles of beer painted a larger picture. No food littered the counters or were stacked in the gaping cupboards which meant she hunted and only for herself if he judged the state of her children.

He spun on his heel, exiting the lopsided house with a determination stiffening his shoulders. Noah arched a brow as he tried to hold onto the scrambling four pups. Fear echoed in their yelps. Their distrust of anyone was clear.

"Burn it to the ground, and if she manages to survive that, kill her." He scooped two pups into his arms, and with a low growl from him, they quietened. "I want all houses documented—their location, condition, and occupants. This shit ends now."

"As you command." Noah handed Rhys another pup to make a call.

Once done, he gathered a few pups, and they stood there, waiting for their pack members. The first to arrive was Jase. He took one look, carried the pups to his truck, and was on his phone when he returned.

Rhys nodded. He had good men, and many were friends he'd grown up with. They were like brothers, having endured under the former alpha Alrik's reign. Never had Rhys imagined things were this bad.

And he should have. After all, he and Aiden had been victims too, losing their parents for some imagined slight. They weren't alone, with many being orphaned and taken in and raised by family or friends.

His pack arrived, some having run there in their were forms. They helped pour gasoline on the house, and minutes later, the blaze had him sweating. As a bear, he ran at a hotter temperature and didn't need fireplaces or heaters to keep warm. Despite the discomfort, he didn't move away.

Other men kept the ground around the house wet to ensure the fire didn't spread to the surrounding wilderness. A forest fire would call attention to their land, and despite having no beef with humans since shifters were part-human, shifters tended to be wary of outsiders. As a pack, they watched the house burn to the ground. Smoldering embers glowed into the darkness of night, but no one left.

"I will take the pups," Reade said. "We lost our child. The little ones might ease Miriam's pain." The agony lingering in his gaze meant he too suffered.

"Thank you, Reade." Rhys acknowledged his offer with a nod. He faced his men, a few disgusted or horrified at this discovery. "Spread the word. If you hunger, ask. If you need diapers, we'll find the money, but if I learn you're abusing a child, your life ends."

They grunted their agreement, and thus a new law was formed.

Chapter Four

The Early Vampire Catches the Mate

One month later

Rhys stared into the upturned face of Captain Johanna Metcalfe. Her fury pulsed through her body, in her stiff shoulders, clenched fists, pinched lips, and darkened cheeks. He smothered a grin, loving riling her. She was such an easy target.

"If you think for one moment I will let your beasts order my policemen around, you have another think coming." She shoved her face closer, almost burying it in his chest.

Beasts? This time he did smile, despite looming over the pint-sized human. "Trying to charm me with Callie's terminology won't alter the validity of my point."

Johanna flopped into a nearby chair. Her crisp gray pantsuit didn't crease, it dared not.

"It's about trust, Jo-jo." He lowered his bulk into the leather Queen Anne chair beside her, despite its proximity to a roaring fire.

His bear pushed him to move, skittering goosebumps along his skin, but he resisted, enduring the discomfort for now.

Ignoring his ever-miserable inner beast, he gathered her hand in his massive one, dwarfing hers, and ran a large digit along the delicate vein running from middle finger to her wrist. "You are weaker than us yet hold more power than you realize. Your men can take down a beast, just not during a full moon."

"He has a point, Captain," Callie said from the doorway.

Rhys's head whipped up, and he sucked in a deep breath even as his bear's attention focused on the one woman he couldn't have. Mate, his bear roared. He shook his head, trying to displace the urge to toss the gorgeous redhead over his shoulder. Her scent invaded his nose, his lungs, filling him with this driving need to fuck. Crossing his denim-encased legs to hide his growing reaction, he dampened his roaring bear, unable to deal with his continued castigation.

"Morning." One glance was all he needed.

Her jeans hugged her hips and muscled thighs. Her T-shirt clung to curves and indents he dreamed of running his lips over. She wasn't his. Gabriel de Winter had claimed her before Rhys knew she existed.

He focused on Johanna, needing to break the mesmerizing lure of Callie's delicate features and pulsing strength. As a newborn vamp, or suckblood as she called it, she oozed power. For shifters, there was nothing as seductive nor addictive as an alpha female.

"My men won't follow someone they don't respect." Johanna sighed. "That's true, no matter the species."

"I'm not saying my men lead, Jo-jo. I'm suggesting my team work alongside yours. What they encounter out in the field will require various skill sets."

"I like that." Callie sank into a materialized chair she summoned out of the ether.

Rhys smothered a grimace. Since she had befriended then adopted a polymorph shifter she called George, suckbloods and beasts had formed some sort of truce. He'd learned way more about vampires and their capabilities than any alpha before him. And what they had known hadn't scraped the iceberg.

"If they're stumbling on two arguing beasts, let Rhys's unit handle it and vice versa," said Callie, now the voice of reason.

Johanna stared at Callie for a while, her brow remaining furrowed. "We'll do a trial period. So, where have you been, Devereaux? How do you manage to sneak out when Rhys and I are in the middle of an argument?"

Callie's eyes sparkled as a cheeky smile flared to life. "Gabe had a growing ache I needed to—"

"Nice try, Devereaux. Quit running away." Johanna's lips twitched before she morphed them into a scowl.

She chuckled. "Yes, ma'am." She rested her emerald gaze on Rhys. "George's en route."

Rhys nodded. Convincing the new parents that George needed interaction with shifter-children—now that had been an exhilarating argument. Callie hadn't backed down, her actions that of a defensive mama bear. He had won, but he suspected killing little George's birth mother and saving her siblings might have played a role in Callie and Gabe's agreement.

Rhys wanted George to meet with her brothers. She hadn't seen them since her mom kicked her out of the house. But he didn't know if she was ready, whether they were after the condition he had found them in. When he returned to the lodge, he would talk to their new father, Reade.

Callie stilled and tilted her head as a shadow entered the luxurious lounge. Not a flame on a candle or in a sconce flickered at the intrusion. A stoic man in black formed in front of them. He was one of a booth of assassins. They served the neighboring vampire hold and had been instrumental in the pseudo battle between vamps and shifters that had brought down a corrupted politician. All at her instigation.

Rhys gritted his teeth, not appreciating the man's presence and the distrust that came with him, as if Rhys would harm a child. Seconds later, six-year-old George skipped across the Persian rug with her pigtails swinging behind her. She spotted Rhys and ducked behind the man's leg.

Rhys forced a smile as he sucked in some of his alpha, trying to minimize the dominating effect it would have on a young shifter. "Hey, George. Ready to play?"

"Play?" She peeked around the man. "Hide and seek? Tea parties? Hopscotch?"

He laughed. With each question, she ventured closer, and excitement swished in her unbearably pink skirt. "I wouldn't know, little one. As far as the children know, a polymorph is coming to visit who has the powers of a goddess." He tucked a black curl behind her ear, then leaned in to whisper. "I think they're more excited to see one of the pal'tsy."

He nudged his head at the assassin who belonged to Dimitri Vasiliev, head of the Vasiliev Hold—one of five vamp holds in the city. Unlike shifters who had one pack per city or town, the vamps shared territory.

Her pale blue eyes crinkled, and a giggle slipped out, which she covered with her tiny hand. "I think so too."

He grinned, unable to help it. "Shall we, cupcake?"

When she slipped her hand into his, he stared at it for a moment, at how fragile it was, weighing nothing. Something intense swept through him, and his bear whimpered, cubs.

After raising his gaze to meet Callie's, she wore a sweet smile. "Now don't terrorize those poor kids, George, and remember, they don't all have what you have."

Rhys frowned.

Callie pressed a kiss to George's cheek. "Some of them need shoes and clothes. Some have nice toys, and some don't."

"Can I share?" She twirled on the spot, swirling her skirt, while trusting Rhys to spin her like a ballerina.

He did so instinctively. When she stopped, she swayed with dizziness but raised her arms, asking for him to pick her up. He did so without forethought then blinked at the sweet-scented bundle in his arms.

Not minding that she had him wrapped around her pinky, he tweaked her nose. Rising to his full height, he towered over the pal'tsy who didn't flinch or blink but held his stance. Rhys would drive them to the lodge, and a Vasiliev SUV would collect them after lunchtime. Deviation from this brought Dimitri—self-appointed guardian—to the lodge, and his presence alone raised the hackles on any shifter present.

Rhys hoped to avoid a scene today and had scheduled a tea party for the children away from worried parents. "You look pretty in your picnic dress, cupcake."

She smiled and looped her arm around his neck for an impromptu hug. His heart leaped to choke him. This had been a while coming. She had been so frightened of him when they had first met. His bear roared. His potent fury fired Rhys's blood and demanded freedom to shift. Calm the fuck down. His bear grumbled but settled. They placed the blame for the shitstorm they were in on Alrik's shoulders. Rhys was still mopping up his messes while discovering new ones.

Striding out the Italian-style De Winter hold, he didn't spare the fine architecture much attention. The volutes, overly tall pillars, the rich gold sconces, and framed portraits done by famous artists didn't suit him. He preferred the rustic charm of the lodge with its thick rugs, solid furniture strong enough to handle his bulk, and the large kitchen that dominated the space. Shifters loved food.

Alrik had drained the pack's coffers, but through careful strategizing, they were on their way to recovering, now able to provide for each shifter family. Investments were Rhys's current focus. The money they had wouldn't last. He needed to ensure what they did have would remain consistent for generations to come.

"I'm blind." Jase threw an arm across his face. "So much pink. My powers...they're leaking...I'm melting."

George giggled, burying her face in Rhys's neck.

"He's just jealous, cupcake." He nuzzled her hair with his chin. "Ask Callie to make Jase a pink T-shirt for next time."

George held a finger to her lips. "Our secret." She raised her arms for Jase to take her.

He did, swinging her before buckling her in. They kept up a steady chat, their heads dipped together. Jase sitting in the back forced the pal'tsy into the front passenger seat. The man didn't show his opinion in any way. Still, as big as Rhys was, he wouldn't test the vamp's skills. Restrained power, that of a coiled snake, poured off the man.

As soon as Rhys steered onto the road, the man lowered the window, flooding the SUV with fresh air. His twitching nose said it all. To suckbloods, shifters stank like wet fur as Callie had tried to explain.

Rhys grimaced at yet another reason why she wasn't his mate, not anymore. She had survived the vamp conversion and had come out of it more powerful than expected. All he could hope for was friendship, trust, but that wasn't why he went to so much effort for George. Her situation was at Alrik's hands, and therefore, Rhys's responsibility to deal with. If he could reunite her with her brothers, he would chalk that up to a success.

The pack lodges were on the outskirts of the city. They relocated every fifty years or so when the expanding city boundaries began to encroach on their privacy. Hiding their abilities had been harder when superstition ruled men's hearts. Three years ago their existence became public knowledge. Rhys had considered not relocating and perhaps ring-fencing their properties. Rebuilding cost money, and it meant starting fresh.

As it was, he had men on patrol since snapping a photo of them shifting was a sought-after commodity for the local media. A few armed weirdos had trespassed on their land intent on doing them harm. Other 'visitors' were desperate women hoping to become shifters especially around the Lunar Festivals each month. The mutation gene was in the blood at birth, no human or vamp could be converted to shifter without it. There were stories told of attempts made. All failed. Callie becoming a suckblood was for the best. She would have remained human as Rhys's mate despite the frequent biting during sex, despite his blood flowing through hers, despite the primal connection between their souls. She would have been his mate until her natural death which would be decades before he could follow. And those decades would have been in solitude. Shifters mated for life.

The human police had too much on their plates to deal with these trespassers. It had taken this long for the government to agree to draft laws with the old alpha, Silas

McDermott, who'd volunteered as spokesman. He'd stepped down from his position of alpha, an unheard of occurrence, with his pack's new alpha voted in—also unusual. Colt, Rabidhide's alpha, had done well since then.

There was talk of allowing shifters to manage their security. Any trespassers or crimes committed against a shifter would be dealt with internally. The problem was with the alpha. If he was like Alrik, the punishment would be death, no matter the crime.

Stopping in front of the lodge, Rhys leaped out of the car to open George's door. Jase had unbuckled her, but she didn't move, peeking around Rhys at the waiting children. Her pale blue eyes widened, and the sickly stench of fear tainted the air with an orange blue.

He dipped his head to meet her gaze. "Cupcake, Callie told me how brave you were when that nasty suckblood captured her. Are the cubs scarier than him?"

She shook her head, flinging her curls wild. "Oh, no, Uncle Rhys." Still, she hesitated. "What if they don't like me?"

"Sugarplum, everyone will love you. Besides, I'm invited to the picnic too." Jase grinned, holding out his hand. "You can sit next to me."

She giggled and placed her hands in his. "You can't. You'll eat all the cake."

"Only a little. Okay, no cake for me." He drew her from the car, tossed her into the air, and caught her. As a brown bear, he had the strength to. He carried her to the strewn blankets with the cubs and pups chasing each other.

"Wonderful." Brianne, the resident kindergarten teacher, skipped across the lawn.

Rhys blinked and hid a smirk. He'd never seen Brianne do that, and he supposed she did so now to charm George. His heart swelled with pride, that Brianne would go to this much effort to welcome George. As a member of the Knights Ridge pack, she had heard of George's tragic situation. As a cub minder, she had brought to Rhys's attention that George needed interaction with children, shifter or human.

Rhys's nail in the coffin had been along those lines, and as new parents, Callie and Gabe had caved. Dimitri had been harder to convince. Hence the presence of his pal'tsy. No one knew how many he had trained, but they moved like panthers—merging with the shadows, lethal in their strikes, and silent.

Jase lowered George to the grass, but she kept a white-knuckled grip on his denims. When George shuffled forward, so did the pal'tsy.

Brianne ignored him and dipped to whisper in the girl's ear. "We're so excited to meet you, Georgy. Rhys said I could go crazy, so there's cake, cookies, tea, soda, and tons of sweets."

George squealed. "Pizza? Hotdogs? Candy?" She clapped her hands and lunged for Brianne's offered hand.

The children engulfed her, asking too many questions as they touched her clothes with their grubby paws.

"I'll stay here, Rhys." Jase folded his arms across his chest. "Noah's handling alpha business. Why don't you take a nap or something?"

"As my beta, he can handle only so much before he too will be overwhelmed." Rhys chuckled. "But thanks, grandma, for urging me to nap."

"Rhys, look at you. You're exhausted. Noah worries you don't rest enough, and over-doing it isn't helping the pack. We need you at your best."

Rhys's bear grumbled, skittering goosebumps along his skin and raising the hair at the back of his neck. *He's not saying we're not capable of doing the job, bear. Neither is he challenging us for alpha. What the fuck has gotten into you?*

"…just for a few days, is all," Jase continued, unaware his alpha almost shredded his throat.

"Days?" Rhys faced him, aware he loomed.

Bending backward, Jase threw up his hands. "Take a break, visit Aiden in Coedwig, run through the forests, and give your bear free rein."

Shit, that did sound amazing. To not worry Rhys might be photographed or shot, to sleep in without having to deal with pack business, and to visit with his carefree brother working in another town?

He sighed. Exhaustion saturated every cell as his human bones bore the weight of his bear. "Whose idea was this?"

"Noah's, but to breach the subject with you, I drew the short straw." Jase grimaced. "Don't kill the messenger."

"Organize it, and I'll go."

A bright grin split Jase's cheeks. "You mean, I don't die today?"

Noah slipped from the shadowed porch into the sunlight, nodding at Rhys.

"Maybe next time." Chuckling, he swiped a cookie, dropped a kiss onto George's dark head then joined Noah to attend to pack business.

CHAPTER FIVE

THE BLACK BOX

"I MEAN IT, ILONA. Call if you need anything." Evie's furrowed brow, concern etched into her polite smile, and her outrageous black-and-white, flower print dress couldn't warm Ilona's heart.

"Thanks." She accepted the fragrant hug, smashed her face in her best friend's unbound tight curls, and returned the squeeze with more effort than she had shown any other guest.

"Now, if you want to feel alive and jump out of a plane or off a bridge with nothing but strings as a lifeline, I'm not your girl."

Ilona laughed as expected of her. "Right, I'll ask Kelly."

Evie hugged her again. "Call me, or text. I can do texts."

"Go." Ilona nudged her onto the porch. She stood there, waving, a fake smile cracking her lips, denting her stiff cheeks, and making her scar itch.

The afternoon sky glowed the blue of the Caribbean Sea, soft cotton-ball clouds and a cool breeze added to the cacophony of cheerful birds mocking her sorrow. Shutting the front door, she scanned the chaos with the wake and funeral over. Gran waltzed through the lounge and dining room, gathering dirty glasses and abandoned plates.

Everyone offered to help, but Ilona wanted the silence without pitying gazes and condescending shoulder pats. In the kitchen, Gran rinsed the glasses for the dishwasher.

The house wasn't the one Ilona had grown up in. She didn't have to deal with childhood memories. This was a newer home, but it still smelled like her parents. Mom had a weakness for vanilla candles, and Dad's orchids perfumed the hallway. A shopping list on the fridge would never see closure. Magnets held onto brochures of possible vacation destinations. Ilona on her prom night sat centerstage, the photo curled at the edges. How was she supposed to go through their things? She couldn't sift through their lives as if they no longer mattered.

"Evie gone?" Gran glanced her way before closing the dishwasher door with a flick of her ballet-slippered foot. "Wipe the counters down for me, sweet pea. I need to fetch something from the car."

Seconds ticked past as Ilona stared out the kitchen window, the wet cloth gripped in her hand. The sun was beginning to set, and the colors splashed across the deepening blue took her breath away. Or was that her smothered sobbing?

"Ilona, please come into the dining room," Gran called.

After dabbing her cheeks with the cloth, Ilona draped it over the sink and peeked into the dining room. On the table sat a black box with antique brass butterfly brackets in detailed filigree. In the diminishing light, the polished black wood shimmered.

"What's this?" She ran a finger along the smooth wood.

"A box." Gran's lips twisted before she chuckled. "Made in African Blackwood and was a gift from your grandfather."

"Gramps gave you this?" She furrowed her brow in confusion. Gramps wasn't a sentimental man, and this little chest looked like it would hold something precious.

"No, not your gramps, your biological grandfather."

Ice drenched Ilona's scalp, spreading tingles down to her toes. "What?"

"Before I met Henry, I fell in love."

She clasped her hands over her ears. "Oh, no, you don't."

"I was young and stupid. I didn't know I was pregnant when I left him. Henry loved Elise as if she was his own."

Ilona blinked, ice and fire taking turns to rack her body. Her heart thumped so hard it vibrated in her chest, fluttering butterflies in the pit of her stomach. "Did...Mom know?"

Gran stiffened, her fingers twitching where they rested on the dining room table. "No, I never told her."

"Then why tell me?" Ilona thumped her chest, finding comfort in the familiar ache her fist inflicted. "Why now?"

"His name is Amos Denton. I need you to take this box to him and—"

"Introduce myself to an absolute stranger?" Ilona shook her head, sending her gold earrings swirling. "Hi, I'm your granddaughter. Oh, you want evidence? Here are my DNA test results."

"Don't get sassy with me, Ilona Strickland."

"You can't just spring this on me, Gran. Now? After everything?" She slumped into a chair, holding a palm to her cheek. Her wound itched around the dissolvable stitches, which was a good sign, and touching it soothed the urge to scratch.

"You need time away from all this." Gran swirled a finger, indicating the house. "I'm locking this up. You can deal with it when you're ready. Go to Coedwig, deliver this to Amos, and stay there for a while. Take a break, a vacation. Do it for me, sweet pea."

Time away did sound blissful, and with nothing to do but sleep, Ilona couldn't think of something she wanted more. Her body, mind, and soul held no more life and purpose. She was lost and exhausted. Time alone where no one knew her, knew about her parents...

More than this, a trip would delay the Great Cleanse she dreaded. This house was hers now, as well as the fortune her parents had left her. She didn't need to sort through their things anytime soon.

She rolled her stiff shoulders, trying to ease the tension. "I'll clear out the perishables."

Gran beamed, darting around the table to crush her in a tight embrace. "You'll love it there."

She returned the hug, inhaling Gran's sweet lavender fragrance that she hadn't changed since Ilona was a little girl. "Why don't you come with? Speak to Amos yourself?"

"Hell, no." Gran shuddered. "These bones can't handle the cold."

"Cold?" Ilona smiled. "As in snow-covered hills and pine trees?"

"Icy winds slipping through gaps in your clothing, sludge underfoot, flurries and snowflakes stinging your cheeks? Yes, that cold."

"Where is Coedwig?" Ilona had never heard of it. Fenneg's warm clime and mild winters with not a snowflake in sight confirmed Coedwig was nowhere near this city.

"It's a fourteen-hour drive east. Take a flight to Inner City, then rent a car and head north for a few hours."

"Whoa. When were you east?"

Gran tried to shrug away the question, but Ilona maintained eye contact. "The Devereauxs are from Inner City or thereabouts."

"Right, thanks for the history lesson." Ilona huffed. "I'll just ask Amos then?"

"Don't you dare." Gran slapped her hand on the table then stormed off with a "Just take the damn box, Ilona."

She darted after her gran, crowding her. "What if he volunteers information without me asking?" Grinning and bouncing on her toes, she teased her, enjoying flustering her and the reddening of her cheeks. "I'll get all the gory details."

Gran raised her face to the ceiling as if she prayed for patience. "What was I thinking, Henry?"

"Gramps would snort and arch an imperious brow." Puffing on an invisible pipe, Ilona deepened her voice, hoping to mimic his mannerisms. "This is of your doing, my queen."

Gran giggled then cupped her mouth. "Fair enough. Knowing Amos, he'll be as tightlipped as I am."

"So, you think he's still alive?"

Her hazel gaze turned dreamy. "Oh, yes, he's well and kicking. I remember a man so vibrant death wouldn't dare take him."

"If I may ask, what happened? Did you leave him?"

Tears shimmered, and Gran removed her eyeglasses to dab with a tissue she had produced from the sleeve of her cardigan. "I loved him so much, but he had to marry someone else. When I found out, I took the first bus out of Coedwig, not knowing I carried Elise. I told everyone who asked that my husband was a policeman killed in the line of duty. No one doubted me, not even Henry."

"Did you love Gramps?" Memories rose, of summers spent with her grandparents, how doting they were and such sweethearts to each other. Ilona couldn't believe for a minute Gran hadn't loved him.

"I did. Henry was like your favorite blanket, warm, comfortable, and reliable. He proved in the little things how he cherished me. With Amos, there was no blanket, he was all I needed. He was grand gestures with a volatile temper, but then, so was I." She wrapped her arms around her waist, clutching the crushed tissue between trembling fingers. "I like to console myself with the thought our love would have consumed us, leaving nothing but an ember of something so beautiful and precious."

She patted Ilona's hand. "Promise me, sweet pea. If you meet a man whose passion dominates your senses, propels you to be a better person, inspires you to spread your wings with the full knowledge he's beside you and will never forsake you, you'll hold onto him. Don't let silly fears stop you from embracing such a love." Gran scrunched up her tissue and tucked it into her sleeve. "You fight to keep him. You promise me."

"All right, if such a pillar of masculinity should appear before me..."

"Ilona." Gran rested her hands on her hips, her warning clear.

"Fine." She grinned, unrepentant, then wiggled her pinky finger. "Want me to pinky swear?"

Gran slapped her hand away. "You get your sass from your father."

Ilona dragged her into her arms, gently crushing her in a squeeze. "I get it from you."

Gran's response was a muffled snort, just like Gramps.

CHAPTER SIX

DON'T BE STUPID

"I DON'T KNOW HOW I feel about this, alpha." Madison pressed four fingers to her mouth. "I mean, he just stands there, doesn't say a word."

At fifty-four, she was still a beautiful woman with two pencils pinning her chestnut-colored hair in place. The laugh lines around her eyes softened her 'sternness' and made her more approachable.

"The pal'tsy are part of the deal, Maddy. Each child and their future are my responsibility, and I can't abandon George—"

"No, your decision to include her in cub-play was a wise one. I just... He doesn't talk to me." She buried her fingers into her hair, wobbling the pencils. "Just yesterday, I offered him my blood, for lunar's sake."

Rhys chuckled. "He's there to protect George. Who knows for how long."

"After Alrik's despotic rule, I can understand." Maddy tucked her escaping tendrils into the chignon. The action raised her shirt, exposing a sliver of her ribbed stomach.

"Just endure. Ignore him as he does you."

A sensual smile twitched her lips. "Mm." She ran her hand over her hip in a gesture as old as time. "Let me turn my full charm on him."

Rhys laughed. "You can try. Is there anything you or the children need?"

"We'll make do with what we have, although, there is a broken faucet in one of the bathrooms. I told Noah about it."

"School supplies?" If he didn't ask, she wouldn't tell him.

"I asked for donations from the Inner City Educational Board, and they delivered a few boxes."

Donations? He grimaced, not liking the bitter taste of its implications.

She darted around the couch and threw her arms over his shoulders, smacking a wet kiss on his cheek. "Quit worrying. I got this, and Brianna and I will come to you or Noah if we need something we can't organize."

He patted her arm, huffing at her silliness. Noah strode into the lodge; his blond hair still damp from a shower. He carried two coffees from their local café. Rhys accepted one with a nod, having skipped his morning ritual to repair his leaking roof.

Madison bumped her hip against Noah's as she left.

"Heard the ruckus this morning. You okay?" He dropped into a chair but leaned forward to cradle his coffee between his knees.

"My leaky roof." Rubbing the back of his neck, Rhys relished the lingering twang of worked muscles. "What has you up so early?"

"Sawyer stopped by on his way to the Inner City precinct." Noah sipped his coffee as if he had news to share but wasn't sure how. "Callie's planning on running with the teams tonight."

"She what?" Rhys jerked, then bolted to his feet, pushing his bulk off the creaking sofa. He placed his half-drunk coffee on the desk and swiped his keys.

"Callie wants to patrol to see how our units are operating." Noah trailed him, shoving one hand deep into his chino pocket while he sipped his coffee.

"Is she fucking insane?" Rhys ran a hand over his face. "I can't allow the Huntress to disrupt everything."

It was madness to have agreed to this idea in the first place. But he had wanted to be close to her, to try to understand why her blood had triggered the mating call. Now that the units were rolling out and continuing on its own steam, they didn't need to involve themselves. She didn't need to.

"She has a right to be there with the pal'tsy as much as you do with our unit." Noah leaned on the porch's wooden pillar, crossing his ankles like he didn't have a care in the world.

"Dimitri shouldn't have put her in charge of his assassins. Gabe shouldn't have let her out of his sight." Rhys paced on the lawn in front of the porch.

"And you shouldn't have imprinted on her." Noah's soft words sliced through the ozone-scented tension.

Air whooshed out of Rhys's lungs, and he slumped against the side of the SUV. Just like that, Noah cut to the heart of the matter. "I didn't, but it was a close thing."

Noah crossed the lawn to him. "Blood doesn't lie." He held out his palm, waiting for the keys.

Rhys grumbled under his breath, ignoring his bear's tantrum, and dropped the keys into Noah's hand. "I swear, that woman will be the death of me."

"I'll drive. Let's head to Dimitri's and have him resolve this. She, at least, listens to him."

Rhys in the front passenger seat, gripped his knees as Noah drove along the winding driveway to the main road. He wanted to drive, to have something to hold onto. Bruising his knees was his only option. Tension pinged off every muscle, intensified by his lack of sleep.

If it wasn't for the loss of a potential mate haunting him, it was discovering all their cubs and pups caged and in danger or stumbling on something Alrik had done. Not every secret had been revealed. The unknown plagued Rhys.

Noah snuck glances at him, his knuckles white where he clasped the steering wheel. Rhys tried to calm his bear and his alpha essence pulsing outward, conveying his heightened emotions and stress levels.

"Did Jase talk to you?" Noah's soft question spiked Rhys's heart rate.

"Yes, and I agreed, just not now."

"I'll set a date, and you'll fucking stick to it, Rhys. Take care of yourself before taking care of us."

Rhys harrumphed. "That was Alrik's attitude, and look where that landed us."

"I'm talking emotionally and physically, not financially. You're not power-hungry, so quit comparing yourself to Alrik, but if you keep up this pace, you'll burn out." Noah stopped at a traffic light. "A weak alpha is worthless to the pack."

"Weak?" Rhys roared, throwing a swing.

Noah caught his fist then tossed it at him. "Stop it. I'm your best friend. Listen to what I'm saying, brother-in-pack." He sighed, put the car in gear, and accelerated when the light changed to green. "After we deal with Callie, head to the cabin and let your bear out. Some fresh air might calm you a little, buy you time until you can go on vacation."

Rhys grunted. Noah spoke the truth, but Rhys's sight still pulsed red with pent-up fury. He wanted to rip off limbs, to sink his teeth into flesh, preferably a deer's haunches. Biting a woman's shoulder during sex claimed her, and he didn't want to be stuck with a lifetime mate because he couldn't control himself.

So relieving the stress with sex was a no. "Is the lake restocked?"

Noah's shoulders slumped, and he flicked Rhys a grin. "Always. Imported salmon for our delectation."

"The full moon's near. It might be best if I made myself scarce."

"I wish I could." Noah smirked. "You'll have to peruse the hopefuls at some point, Rhys. One of them might be—"

"I know. I just don't need to deal with that now. Let's get the pack settled, cared for, and maintain what we have before I bring a woman into this."

"If Gabe died?"

Rhys laughed, but it lacked humor, as if his life had taken on the dull grays of monochromatic cinematography. "How does an ancient vamp die?" He shook his head. "She loves him, and his death won't mean she'd seek comfort in my arms. Callie is a fighter. She would stand on her own. And besides, her blood is at the center of this. I just need to find a woman with the same lineage."

"Easier said than done." Noah stopped the car in front of an eight-foot brick wall. Barbed wire and electric fencing along with patrolling men in black would have any passerby think this was a military base.

He lowered the window, and Rhys dipped his head to glare at the guard.

He waved them in, no expression marring his features.

Rhys frowned. "How do they live like that? Emotionless."

In a pack world, everything was emotional, the more intense the better. His initial reaction to Callie had been a bombardment of lust, admiration, and awe. One sniff of her essence and his bear had roared, demanding he claim her.

"They're vamps. We're only now beginning to understand them." Noah drove along the paved driveway, and the rolling green hills on either side had impeccable gardening. Both screamed money. The mansion ahead was in stark contrast to their lodge.

"We don't live as long as them, but fuck, surely we can make wise investments." Rhys shifted in his chair, trying to calm his frustration. Money would help his people and ease their lives.

"Well, maybe aligning with the suckbloods was a good strategic decision." Noah grinned. "Maybe meeting Callie was the best thing for Knights Ridge."

"Let's just deal with the now before you start congratulating me on future successes." Rhys slid his bulk out of the SUV, raising his gaze to the towering mansion's façade.

The architecture was Greek with a bit of Russian thrown in. Bronze domes serving as lookout points glittered in the sunlight. The de Winter hold was a sprawling Italian structure, with two levels and dungeons below. Dimitri's was three levels of breathtaking architecture. There were other buildings on either side. The doors of one said garages, but it seemed too small for the number of vehicles Rhys suspected they owned.

"Well, well, to what do I owe the honor?" Dimitri Vasiliev danced down the steps, greeting them with a hug and handshake as if they were old acquaintances. His white-buttoned shirt was crisp and his dark-gray slacks tailored.

Rhys grimaced at his dirty denims and a plain T-shirt that had permanently stretched into the shape of his shoulders and chest.

Ebony curls cascaded over Dimi's piercing green eyes. A deep inhale revealed his species with old blood, money, and power resonating off him. Yet, along his throat ran an intriguing, jagged scar. Sunlight didn't kill a suckblood, only weakened them. And they healed like shifters. So what would leave a scar? Rhys pondered this each time he saw Dimi, and one day, when he could gather his balls in hand, he would ask.

Not that Rhys feared the suckblood. No, but something like a jagged scar tended to have a matching emotional one. At the moment, if Dimi decided to take offense at his probing, Rhys wasn't energized enough to fight him off.

George had played a role in solidifying their alliance. She had taken to Dimi, and since children were impossible for suckbloods, protecting her had become a serious matter for him. He had tasked his pal'tsy to guard her despite Callie and Gabe adopting her. Who was more skillful than the Huntress? Rhys snorted, drawing a startled look from Noah.

"We're here to discuss...Callie." He leaned his backside against the fender.

"What's to fear?" Dimi gestured with his chin for them to follow.

Rhys trailed him inside. A three-level atrium with marbled flooring and a dual staircase dominated the foyer. Doors led off on both sides and down the center was a passage with more doors.

Dimi strode through the first door on the left, into a parlor with large leather couches, wall-to-wall bookshelves, and a roaring fire. The dark wooden panels added to the welcoming warmth of the room, along with the thick Persian rug and sturdy antique coffee tables. Everything looked new but smelled old. Shit, Rhys would be happy with furniture not threatening to splinter.

"Beer, whisky, cognac?" Dimi offered.

"Anything." Rhys shrugged and sank into a chair that didn't squeak under his weight. He rubbed the smooth brown leather and inhaled the sweet fragrances of smoke and cherries.

On the table beside him, a chilled glass of beer appeared out of nowhere. He hated that they could summon shit out of the ether.

"Thanks," he grumbled. He took a long pull from his beer. The smoky, bitter flavor, and the lingering after taste, hinted at imported. Go figure.

Dimi faced the room, with the fireplace behind him. He'd slid his hands deep into his pockets and rocked on his toes. "I'm glad you came over. Callie raised a few concerns about the state of your pack."

"What?" Rhys jerked, spilling beer down his T-shirt. He didn't care that the cold liquid saturated his jeans or pooled onto the leather. "Why the fuck would you discuss my pack?"

How dare they? He shifted to put the glass down, but it filled, just as his T-shirt dried and the beer mess vanished. Fuck, cleaning up after him like he was a cub? He gritted his teeth, willing his agitated bear to calm.

"Our alliance is long-term. She wants a contract drawn up so alphas after you for generations to come adhere to the agreement. This includes investment capital to build your infrastructure, schools, and such."

Rhys blinked, torn between the warm pleasure at her concern and forethought and the fiery anger at her implication he was incapable of seeing to his people.

"An amount will be transferred to your account, matched by the Vasiliev Hold."

Rhys stiffened and sliced a glance at Noah, wishing he had a moment to confer with his beta. "I don't like handouts."

Dimi closed his eyes for a second. "It's for George, her future, and her pack's stability." Exploding into action, he blurred and appeared in the chair beside Rhys. "Wealth means nothing to vamps, Rhys. We've accumulated so much property, investments, bonds, shares, masterpieces, it's like oxygen to us. There to use but not necessary to survive." A tumbler of burnished liquid formed in his hand from which he sipped. "Callie has made a sizable donation to the Inner City precinct, as well."

Noah laughed, cutting through Rhys's tension. "She's spending her husband's money."

Dimi grinned. "True, but to be fair, neither of us will feel it."

Rhys frowned. Money was money, and it held its own power over people. "Who receives the status reports on what I spend it on?" He swallowed past the lump in his throat, tightening his shoulders as if he negotiated with the devil.

"No one." Dimi swirled the golden liquid in his tumbler. "The other holds think we're foolish to boost the shifters, our mortal enemies, but I agree with Callie. Those are antiquated thoughts, mired in tradition, and silly superstition. Just like we donate to human charities, why can't we invest in shifters too?"

"Charity?' Rhys thumped his empty glass onto the polished wooden table. "We don't need charity."

Dimi sighed, pinching his brow like he held back a headache.

Rhys grimaced. "I'll talk to my pack and let them decide." They did need the money, and it could fill holes Alrik's neglect had created. But it shouldn't be at the cost of Rhys's soul, and it certainly shouldn't make him or the pack beholden to suckbloods. "What are we going to do with Callie?"

"I'd suggest you go with her, and take Johanna along. Like a formal survey of the teams' performance." Dimi's lips curled into a wicked grin. "If there is anyone who can calm, manipulate, or reason with Callie, it's her old captain."

Rhys frowned at having not thought to include Jo-jo. How tired was he? His eyes burned with grit. Exhaustion saturated every inch of him. His bear didn't rear his head as much as he used to unless enraged, which he was, pacing across Rhys's nerves, getting his point across.

"I have plans to take a few days off and head north." He sighed, taking a leap of faith his beta could handle this. "Noah or Sawyer will escort the ladies."

Noah grinned, squaring his shoulders. "Happy to."

Dimi rose and offered Rhys a hand up. He hesitated but accepted the suckblood's assistance. "You have my number. Call if you need anything. I mean it, Rhys. Anything."

On the drive out the complex, Noah's features wavered between concern and joyful hope. "Shit, Rhys, if the money has no strings attached, we could do so much. All those repairs, build better roads, upgrade the schools, and the lodge. Not to mention our digital infrastructure."

"And start that skill-share training you mentioned?" Rhys couldn't help but wallow in Noah's excitement at the holes they could plug.

"I'd have our people slot in with the contractors we hire, make their tuition part of the contracts." Noah laughed, slapping the steering wheel as they drove through the massive gate. "Imagine being able to do our repairs without having to pay an outsider."

"Depending on how much money it is, we might be able to afford proper equipment for our clinic." The research lab Alrik had started took care of itself, earning funding as well as hiring human staff. But this money could give them the boost they needed. The possibilities were endless. "Let's discuss the donations first before we spend it all."

"Investments."

Rhys shook his head. "No, donations. Investments imply they're expecting something in return. Either way, I don't like owing anyone."

"Then let's take a portion, invest it somewhere else, and repay their donation. We only need the initial capital to get started." Noah changed gears and floored it, a grin brightening his face.

"It's your baby, then." Rhys was happy to assign it to him. "We have enough cash to eke out a normal life. If more and more shifters find work outside the pack, then that cash will grow with their tithing, and we've survived with the slow progress we've made so far on our infrastructure."

"I just don't want to offend the suckbloods, Rhys. We've formed a tenuous alliance, and if we outright reject their donations, they might see us as too proud to bend, to forgive, and to build a future where this omnipresent animosity no longer divides us."

"Can you imagine shifter and vamps merging?" Dreams of merging with Callie hadn't once touched on her as a suckblood. Rhys hadn't cared what species she was. But if he had a choice, he'd want his mate to be a shifter.

"Hybrids would be more powerful, something Alrik hadn't considered, or perhaps he knew and feared. We're not even sure if children are possible from such matings. Is it the suckblood as a species that makes them infertile, or does the problem lie with the female or male biologically?"

"At least our lab is helping them solve this." He grimaced.

As per Alrik's instructions, the lab focused on gene-splicing, for lunar's sake. The 'generous' politician with his hidden agenda behind the chemical concoction purported to improve the suckbloods' fertility had been arrested. The initial batch had promised to do just that. Once the vamps had bought into the formula, Alrik and the politician had altered the mix.

To make amends for Knights Ridge's involvement in the human politician's goal to trigger a war between the vamps and shifters, Rhys had offered the lab's assistance in ensuring the chemical was safe and as viable as initially tested. It was the least he could have done.

An image of little Callies running around and playing with pack children sent a wave of warmth through him. She might not be his mate, but he did hold her in high regard. He wanted her in his life, even if it was on the peripheral.

"Need me to call Callie and Jo-Jo?" He didn't want to overburden his beta. It wouldn't be good if they were both exhausted.

Noah veered onto their gravel road leading deeper into their land. "Nope, I've got this. You let your bear free, go fishing, sleep in."

"Sounds like bliss." Trees closed around them, cutting off their houses and buildings from the public's prying eyes. Still, despite the dense vegetation, some folks got through. Perhaps Rhys should build a wall with electrical fencing as Dimi had done?

"Then go visit your brother for a proper vacation."

Rhys opened his mouth to argue.

Noah settled a look on him, silencing him. "You agreed, and the word of an alpha is law."

Rhys gritted his teeth. "Task Jase to organize more patrols. Alternate the volunteers. Let them train alongside Callie's units."

"Done." Noah stopped the car and climbed out, leaving the engine running. While he undressed, stripped, and tossed his clothes onto the backseat, he grinned at Rhys. "Enjoy."

Noah snapped and popped as his limbs and muscles morphed. His eyes changed first into yellow slits, then his ears and his nose to a snout. Limb by limb blurred and reformed until a pale-gold wolf peered at Rhys through the open door. After a chaff, he loped off.

Rhys slid across the gearstick to the driver's seat. He closed the door and steered the SUV left. Excitement built inside until the rearview mirror reflected the grin claiming his lips, cheeks, and face.

His bear leaped to life, bouncing around in his eagerness for freedom.

Guilt struck Rhys at his neglect. Noah and been right to remind him.

"Sorry, bear, give us a few minutes, and you'll taste sweet air, cool water, and a salty salmon."

Chapter Seven

PACK MENTALITY

When the wooden porch creaked, Rhys glanced up from the paperback he was reading. He wasn't expecting visitors. This cabin was so far away from the city and too deep into their property, which meant the intruder couldn't be someone trespassing. Nor had Noah, Jase, or Sawyer phoned or texted Rhys, so this wasn't pack business.

Sighing, he placed his paperback face down, using the couch as a bookmark. On bare feet, he padded to the front door and wrapped his fingers around the door handle as a shadow rippled past the window. He raised his chin to sniff the air and slumped at the familiar scent.

Whipping the door open, he faced Willow, Noah's younger sister.

"Rhys, you scared me." She pressed her hand to her heaving bosom.

He doubted that. Shifters didn't startle easily with their heightened senses. In a tight skirt and a transparent blouse, her reasons for being there must have dampened her senses. She should have sniffed his proximity through the door.

"What are you doing here, Will?" He spun on a heel and picked up the T-shirt he had slung over the back of the couch, donning it under her vigilant gaze.

She scented of arousal, wafting off her in pale peach and sky-blue, hinting at her nervousness. He grimaced at the impending conversation. Flexing his alpha, he pulsed power, adding to her anxiety. She stiffened with her fingers plucking the hem of her shirt.

"I..." She paused, leaning against the door frame, almost as if she second-guessed her reasons for being there.

"I can remember when you used to tear around this lake with Noah's car keys or jeans in your jaw." Rhys forced a chuckle, hoping to remind her he had known her since she was a cub.

"Um, yes, happier times." She lowered her chin, trying to hide her flushed cheeks.

"Did Noah send you?" He knew damn well Noah hadn't.

Since her purpose there was blatant, Rhys needed a way to extricate them both from a potentially embarrassing situation. She'd never shown interest in him. It had to be the lure of being an alpha's mate. Yup, he couldn't be there during the Lunar Fest, just in case. But then again, he couldn't avoid the mating festival every damn month.

"No, I came here to...check on the cabin. To make sure it's clean and usable." She spread her red lips on a deep, relieved sigh, before flicking her blonde hair off her shoulders. Despite her beauty rivaling any suckblood, she wasn't for him.

"Coffee?" What he wanted to do was roar at her to leave, to get the fuck away from him, but he cared about her, saw her as a sister when he'd never had the luxury of one. At Rhys's suggestion, Aiden had left for Coedwig the moment he'd healed from Alrik's bullying.

And Uncle Sean lived in Suddale with his human mate. He'd dated Miriam in secret, knowing how Alrik would react but also not wanting to abandon Rhys and Aiden until they could defend themselves. The wife joined her mate's pack as per protocol, but Alrik would have killed Miriam on sight.

Rhys didn't begrudge Uncle Sean his happiness even though he'd outlive a human. What Rhys missed was Sean's wise counsel which had been his salvation since his parents' died. He gritted his teeth at the reminder of their mysterious deaths. Something else he needed to add to his to-do list. Find their killers, although, it wouldn't surprise him if Alrik had orchestrated the midnight attack. He'd done so before. Killing anyone who opposed his despotic rule. Still, Rhys needed to know without doubt.

"Thanks, I'm good." She stumbled back, throwing out her trembling hands. "Let Noah know if there's anything needing repairs." And with a whiff of perfume mingled with her sweet youthful scent, she was gone.

He sighed, letting his relief sag his shoulders. That was a close call. It could have gone south with him rejecting Willow and breaking her spirit. This stilted interaction hadn't dissuaded her. He had no doubt she would return with more courage, hoping to use her feminine wiles to seduce him. An alpha's mate held too much power.

Shit. If little Willow thought he was an easy target, then all the unmated women under his protection would visit him in the near future.

He needed a wife.

Time away would help. Perhaps he would find a suitable woman not from Inner City. Putting the kettle on, he video-called his brother, tapping the teaspoon on the ancient hardwood counter, swaying his hips to the beat he created. No tune came to mind, but there was something primal about the rhythm, as if tribes summoned their warriors to war.

War? He wanted a vacation, but if his damned brother didn't answer the phone soon, there would be a battle of note.

"Some of us work nights, y'know." Aiden groaned, muffling his words when he ran his hand over his face. He squinted into the camera, waiting even as his eyelids drooped.

Rhys chuckled. Just seeing his younger brother was like a vise no longer limited his ability to breathe. "Some of us don't care." He tried to peer around Aiden crowding the video cam. "Got any space for your brother?"

"Shit, you've been ousted?" He scanned his room, giving Rhys a full view of his unshaven jaw. "My studio is too small. You're going to have to squat with Dane, and he ain't going to like it."

"Relax, baby bear. I'm just visiting. I'll check into your bed and breakfast." Rhys spooned instant coffee into a mug, then poured in the boiling water, giving it a good stir.

Aiden grinned. "You are squatting with Dane. He lives there. Mrs. Cromwell still serves a mean breakfast. When will you be up? Tonight?"

"Yeah, am thinking about leaving as soon as I pack a few things." Excitement had his bear pacing, and Rhys didn't bother calming him. He hadn't had a break in ages, and for once, he looked forward to time alone.

So, leaving for Coedwig was an easy decision.

"I'll let Dane know you're on your way." Aiden tapped two fingers to his temple.

Rhys ended the call and sipped his coffee, savoring the bitterness, as he stared across the rippling silver lake reflecting the afternoon sky. After rinsing the mug, he donned his socks and boots. He grabbed the car keys, closed the cabin door behind him, then climbed into the SUV. En route to the lodge, he dialed Noah, informing him of the decision. He didn't mention Willow's visit, preferring to pretend it didn't happen.

"It's the Lunar Festival soon, Rhys." Noah hesitated. "Be careful."

No one needed to tell a shifter when the full moon was near. Attending a mating festival promised him a good time, or at least, a little relaxation. Still, he'd prefer one not so close to his pack. "Yes, Dad. I promise to use protection."

"Ass." Noah chuckled. "Want me to pack you a bag?"

"No, thanks. Knowing you, I'll arrive there with a week's supply of boxers and nothing else."

Noah laughed. "Fair enough. I'll call ahead and reserve you a room."

"Thanks."

Silence settled on the other end, and for a second, Rhys thought the call had dropped. "This is a good idea, Rhys. I miss my friend, the one who laughed and found enjoyment in everything life threw at him. Find him and bring him back with you."

Rhys frowned. Responsibility had dampened his spirits, but he hadn't realized how bad it was. "I'll try." That was all he could promise.

"Good. Jase is packing your bag, and you can check it before you leave, grumpy."

At his childhood nickname, Rhys grinned. "I will check." He ended the call with his heart lighter than it had been in months.

Jase and Noah waited on the lawn with Rhys's bag in hand. Both males beamed with restrained energy, looking like eager teenagers whose parents were going away for the weekend.

Rhys stopped beside them and slid his window down. "Why do I feel as if my lodge will be covered with toilet paper, my rugs stained with something sticky, and a police report pinned to my door?"

Jase chuckled. "Very funny." He popped the trunk and tossed in the bag.

Rhys winced and put the SUV in park before darting around to unzip the bag. Jeans, T-shirts, socks, toiletries, his phone charger, and a roll of cash were thrown in haphazardly.

Grinning, he slapped Jase on the shoulder. Stress drained from Rhys's body, and his blood bubbled with excitement. In three hours, he would be sipping a beer with his brother. He waved out the window as he drove off, picking something jazzy on the radio while he merged with traffic heading north out of Inner City. With the city's skyline behind him, a cool breeze toying with his hair, he scratched his beard and allowed his thoughts to drift.

By the time he drove along Coedwig's main road, the sun had set, a chill penetrated the car's exterior, and he had suffered through too much jazz and gas station coffee. He hadn't visited in years, but nothing much had changed. The white lights of Mo's Diner shone like a beacon, and he suspected Mo slept on the premises. Tuesdays was to his right, and Cozy Cromwell's was a little past Mo's.

After parking his SUV, Rhys climbed out, inhaling a deep breath of crisp air with drifting snow flurries glowing in the streetlights. He tugged his jacket closed but didn't zip up. His bear generated enough heat for the cold weather not to bother him. Slamming the car door, he strode across the busy parking lot, raucous laughter and blues calling him.

As he approached the front door, it opened, and a cuddling couple stumbled past him. He sniffed and chuckled. A pair of wolves were finding companionship before the festival, and he couldn't fault them for it. Shifters were sexual creatures, needing affection and sex often. Which didn't explain why he hadn't had either in a while.

He threw out his hand to slow the door's journey, then let it click shut behind him. Warmth engulfed him. He hurried to remove his jacket, hooking it between many others. The bar sprawled on either side with the pool tables left and the tables and chairs to the right. To the rear, a mirrored shelf held a variety of liquors, rums, whiskeys, and brandies. Filling beer glass after glass was his brother, tall and lanky with matching brown hair and blue eyes. He had more of their mom in him with his devil-may-care charm.

Aiden had lived under Rhys's shadow for most of his life. When he had suggested Aiden leave Inner City for an indefinite stay in Coedwig, he had snatched the opportunity, preferring the less stressful life in the wilds.

"Rhys." He leaped over the counter and bolted across the crowded room to throw his arms around Rhys. In the months apart, Aiden had grown, filling out across his shoulders and chest.

"Hey, cub, miss me?" He hugged Aiden, lifting him off the floor.

Warmth from his happy bear and love for his brother swelled his chest. How he had missed him and his wise counsel. Noah was a wonderful beta and brother-in-pack, but Aiden was blood.

"Come, have a beer." He thumped Rhys on the shoulder and slipped behind the bar. Within seconds, he placed a chilled bottle of beer on a coaster while Rhys claimed a bar stool. He grinned, delighted Aiden remembered how he liked his beer.

"How're things? You happy?" Rhys took a long drag from the bottle and sighed. The smoky bitterness coated his tongue and stripped the remnants of tension from his body. His bear hummed with contentment. "The occasional texts from you don't say much."

Aiden shrugged. "I like it here."

Rhys scanned the bar and the friendly faces. "I gathered as much since you didn't come home."

"Why the visit, though?" Aiden threw up a palm. "Not that I'm complaining."

"Needed a break. Life's been a little...crazy." Rhys clenched his jaw against mentioning he'd almost found his mate.

He was hoping a woman might tempt him during the festival. Even better, trigger the mating bond. Twisting on the barstool, he scanned the room with purpose, resting his attention on a few potentials. When he realized they had variations of red hair, he faced Aiden to sip his beer, keeping his scowl hidden. His next lover would be a blonde, dammit.

His bear chuffed, mocking him.

"Told Dane you were heading up." Aiden laughed, and the sound, so similar to Dad's, twisted a dagger in Rhys's heart. "He said seeing is believing."

"Well, here I am." Rhys ran his thumb down the bottle, rubbing off the condensation.

The exhaustion that had hounded him for who knew how long softened him until he expected his ass to swallow the bar stool. He downed his beer and declined another.

"I'm off to bed," he called, dropping notes on the counter. "Will pop in to see you tomorrow."

He slid his jacket off and hooked it over his arm before striding out of the bar. A warm bed, a good night's sleep, then he would reveal all to Dane in the morning. Perhaps his old friend could steer him along a sane path.

Mrs. Cromwell opened the door to Cozy Cromwell's Bed and Breakfast. Rhys swept her into a spinning hug. She giggled like a girl but returned the hug, patting him on the shoulder like she always did.

"The prodigal son returns." She tucked in the gray tendrils escaping her bun. Pink splashed across her cheeks, and she was a little breathless.

"When will you come to your senses and marry me, Harriet?" He adored teasing her, and she loved his charm.

"Stuff that. Just glad you're visiting, Rhys-my-boy."

"Same." He rocked on his heels while savoring the aromas of fresh baked bread and coffee. "Thought it high time I spent a few days with my bear."

"True, the city can be restrictive." She gestured to the bag he had dropped when he hugged her. "Cocoa or straight to bed?"

"Bed, please." He hoisted his bag and crossed the threshold, closing the door behind him. "If I can put off speaking to Dane until after a night's rest, that would be wonderful."

He stomped up the stairs, trailing her. She opened a door and stepped aside, letting him slide past her. In dark blues and grays, the room had a masculine ambience, along with the massive television mounted to one wall.

"Sweet dreams, Rhys, and it's wonderful to have you here." She shut the door.

Silence settled upon him.

Unpacking his bag took minutes. He enjoyed a leisurely shower, leaving the en suite in his towel. Once he dried himself, he hung up the towel and sprawled naked on the bed, flipping through the available channels on the television. What he wanted was a movie, something old, or a comedy.

Not bothering to light a fire in the hearth, he climbed under the sheet. He texted Noah that he had arrived, and with his hands behind his head, stared at the ceiling. His thoughts drifted to memories of Callie, but Rhys shoved them aside, choosing to focus on the muted sports channel, instead.

He would leave Coedwig cured of his Callie obsession, or he wasn't fit to be the Knight Ridge's alpha.

Chapter Eight

Memories Are Made of These

WHEN THE SOFT FLURRIES began to fall, Ilona pulled over. White coated the land until it reached the shadowed forests about a mile out on either side of the road. Icing sugar capped the pine trees, and gray clouds churned, warning of a fresh batch of snow on its way. Warmth from the heater blasted her face and filled her with a false sense of comfort. If she stepped outside, she would remain toasty yet enjoy the crisp beauty of winter.

Opening the door should have altered her plans, but despite the slap of icy air burning her cheeks, she exited the car. Her foot sank into the snow. The pristine blanket was deeper than she expected. With a firm grip on the car door's frame, she tugged herself up and out, only for her to stumble forward. Said foot didn't budge. Crying out, she splayed out face first in the snow like a child with an urge to do a snow angel. There wasn't a soul within miles to witness her antics. Despite her lodged foot, she grinned, biting into the snow while she waved her arms.

Laughter struck at her silliness.

White powder covered her from her jeans to her jacket. Cold seeped into her clothing, chilling the warm skin beneath. She had forgotten snow was crystallized water with a level of danger to it. Pushing herself onto her knees, she flipped onto her backside to scoop the snow away from her boot.

As snowflakes snuck between her collar and braids, she shivered. Her fingertips were burning, and with reason since her new gloves rested on the passenger seat. Whatever pinned her might cost her the boot because she wasn't about to freeze to death to keep it.

As quickly as the flurries started, it stopped. Silence settled over the world. Peace saturated her. She raised her face to the patches of dark sky scattered with innumerable stars. The vise squeezing her chest eased, and for the first time since waking up in Amity, she could breathe and feel.

Emotions assaulted her, denial, grief, guilt, acceptance, hysteria. In and out, over and under until they merged into one roiling mass. She arched her back and screamed, cursed, sobbed with her tears plopping into the fresh snow. Thrashing like a toddler throwing a tantrum, she fluffed clouds of snow when she slapped the ground around her.

Drained, she stilled, staring into the distance at the blinding white snow, the dark trees, yet focusing on nothing. She didn't know how long she lay there, but her chattering teeth drew her back to her situation. Undoing her boot laces was a struggle with her numb fingers, but she managed it, sliding her foot free. In one last attempt, she wrestled with the boot as the cold penetrated her sock.

Gathering all her strength, she wrapped her fingers around the leather and tugged. She flew backward, sprawling once more in the snow and without the boot. Determination gripped her. She crawled to the boot, but a gust of snow snagged her attention. Standing there, staring at her was a grizzly bear, not twenty yards away. Her heart leaped to choke her, and her limbs sank with fear slithering down her spine as cold as her fingers and nose.

"Move, Ilona." But she didn't. She just sat there.

The bear sniffed the air, proving it was real and not a figment of her imagination. With a squeal, she scrambled to her feet and dove through the gaping car door, shutting it behind her.

She righted herself, arranging her long limbs beneath her before scanning the surroundings, wiping her bangs off her face to do so. She couldn't see the bear. Her mind must be playing tricks on her. Gripping the steering wheel, she fumbled for the wipers.

And yelped, thrusting her back into the chair. Ten yards away, the bear watched her from the verge, tilting its head with curiosity before sniffing her boot. A shiver racked her body. Her nose and cheeks burned.

As soon as she started the car, a gust of residual warm air hit her. She moaned. Another shiver tore through her. She couldn't stay here all night, not for a boot, and she sure as hell wouldn't try to get it again with a grizzly bear out there.

"Fuck it, damn snow, you can keep the boot."

She started the engine, clenching her frozen fingers around the steering wheel before reversing the rental. Taking a wide berth, she crawled past the bear, her gaze fixed on it, watching for any indication it might charge. She released a long sigh, slumping her shoulders as she drove off, flicking glances at her rearview mirror showing the bear chewing on her boot.

"Great. Next time, buy two pairs of boots, dumbass." She cranked the heater. If she didn't lose her fingers over this foolishness, it would be a miracle.

With the grizzly bear no longer a threat and her appendages thawing, she thought on her lunacy, climbing out the car in the middle of nowhere, frolicking in the snow like a child. She smiled. Excitement bubbled up like a slow-boiling kettle, and she let the warmth rise through her. A new beginning, an adventure hovered on the horizon.

As she took one last peek in the mirror, the squeal of the skidding brakes drowned out her scream. Standing in the middle of the road was a naked man...holding her boot.

She closed her eyes, questioning her sanity.

"No way would there be a naked man out in this weather." Chewing on her bottom lip, she stared at him. "Fuck me, James."

Evie's saying slipped from Ilona's lips, and the intense longing for her friend to be there gripped Ilona. Sliding into gear, she reversed, slowly, half expecting the man to be a mirage. He waited until she stopped the car before strolling balls to the wind to the passenger side.

When the door opened, she gaped. Tall, broad-shouldered with brown hair to his collarbone, his muscles rippled across his massive chest, catching the light.

He settled his blue gaze on her with the frame of the door hiding a certain part of his anatomy she shouldn't be eager to see. "Your boot, ma'am."

His voice, like liquid caramel, brushed over her senses, setting them ablaze. Something hot slithered into her core. She shifted her ass, trying to ease the dense ache. "Um, thanks?"

He placed the boot on the seat then closed the door.

She blinked, then leaped from the car, limping to where he walked away. Trying not to focus on his tight gluteus maximus or the tense and release of his bicep femoris muscles in his thighs, she hurried after him like a groupie. Shit, if Evie could see her now.

"Sir?" Ilona called after him, wincing as snow seeped into her sock. "You can't be out in this...as you are. May I take you somewhere?" Spinning on the spot, she squinted at their surroundings, seeing no broken down vehicles, no footprints other than the bear's. Where the hell was it? She peered into the distant forests hoping to catch a brown smear galumphing between the trees.

The man paused and stared at her. "You want to rescue me?" He arched a brow then chuckled. His good humor hit her innards like a shot of whisky. "That's a first."

"You'll catch hypothermia out here." Willing her gaze not to dip lower than his shoulders, she shrugged off her jacket and shivered, but offered him the too-small garment anyway. "I don't have a blanket, but I do have a heater. Please. I'm going to Coedwig. Someone there will be able to help you..." She scanned the rolling white hills. "Find your car."

"I'm not cold."

Shit. Looking past his...um, penis, she focused on his unfidgeting hands. He was in the late stages of hypothermia. If he curled up now, he would die. "Do you feel tired?" He wasn't shivering, either. "Do you know who you are?"

He laughed, leaning his head back to do so. His deep rumble washed over her, filling her with unexpected warmth again. She had to fight to hold back a smile.

"I know who I am, and no, I'm not tired."

She closed the distance between them, taking cautious steps to not alarm him. "I...can't abandon you. Please don't ask me to." If he fainted, there was no way she could lift him into the rental.

He studied her, his gaze like a caress, resting for a while on her eyebrows. "You have red hair?"

She nodded. Was he delirious?

He strolled toward her, unphased by his manly attributes so on display, which were textbook perfect if not on the big side. "And green eyes?"

She shrugged. "More hazel than emerald, but yes."

He caught her chin in a gentle pinch and tilted her face.

Heat stung her wind-chapped cheeks. He couldn't miss her scar, and he didn't, his focus shifting. Pinching his lips, he released her. "I'm sorry."

Tears stung her eyes. "Sorry?" She was breathless, her lungs struggling to deal with the freezing air and the rising wave of sorrow.

"For the pain you've endured." His voice cut through to her heart.

She blinked, forcing the tears back. Such understanding and kindness from a stranger? "Life is pain, isn't it?" She willed herself to shut up. "Please." Shivering, she gestured to the car. "Come with me, and take my woolen hat too." Whipping it off, she offered it to him.

He ignored her outstretched cap and jacket and caught a curl between his fingers. His gaze locked onto hers and dark blue swirled in his eyes. "I'll find you in Coedwig." With a grip on her elbow, he ushered her to the car.

Stunned, she allowed him to slip her inside and shut the door. Her heart pounded in her ears, and where he touched, tingled. Spinning in her seat, she searched for him, finding him crossing the snow-covered fields...barefoot.

She squeaked. There was nothing she could do. The man was huge, so forcing him to get in the car was impossible. Shoving her foot inside the boot, she tugged her cap on, and scrambled out of the car, sliding her jacket on too.

"Sir!" Running after him, she puffed air like a smoker.

He paused again, a slow sensual smile forming.

She trembled for another reason she was ashamed to analyze. "I can't abandon you. I swore an oath," she cried out, stumbling to a halt beside him.

"Are you always this stubborn?" He cupped her shoulders with his massive hands and spun her. "My car is just over the rise. I'm snow bathing." His eye twitched.

She snorted at that blatant lie. "Right."

He ran a gaze over her, lingering on the rapid rise and fall of her breasts in her T-shirt. "Undress and join me." His voice deepened, hoarse and sexy.

Amazed at the heat shooting along her nerve endings, she gasped. Aware he waited for her response, she shook her head.

He shrugged. "Until later, ma'am."

This time, she let him walk away. Watched him do it with the avid eye of an artist. Hell. He was gorgeous, beautiful, something Michelangelo would drool over. Hiking to her car, she slid in and palmed the steering wheel. Warm air blasted her from the still-running engine.

Drawing in a deep breath, she released it on a moan. A giggle escaped. She banged the door shut. Now that was an encounter of note. Pity she didn't have it in her to sneak a photo. Evie would just have to believe her without evidence.

Driving off took all Ilona's concentration. She wanted to look back, to search for her mysterious man. She crested a hill, and sprawling before her in the dip of the valley was Coedwig. It had one winding main road, with many capillaries reaching out to tiny cabins, their lights flickering gold in the darkness.

The nearer she traveled, the larger things became, with the pines trees towering above the road, the capillaries wide enough for trucks. Civilization came to life in a ramshackle bar, well-lit diner, a doctor's practice, and a mercantile store. The farther she drove, she passed homes alongside the road and one double-story with 'Cozy Cromwell's' in neon lights on the siding.

She chose an available parking bay, her snow tires crunching. The installation of those delayed her departure from Inner City, but she was there now. Smiling, she texted Gran and Evie, letting them know she had arrived safe but not sound. Marching along the salted path, she lugged her bag up to the large wooden door. It opened as she raised her hand to knock.

"Well, well, what do we have here?" A tall man blocked the light and warmth pouring through the door.

He was wrestling-huge, with bulging muscles and a barrel chest. His mocha skin contrasted with the shock of white hair flopping over a face God took a hand in creating.

She gaped, wishing she had loosened her hair to hide her scar. People stared at it, as fresh as it was, throwing pitying expressions at her. She hadn't minded, uncaring what they thought, only aware of what it meant to her. Her survival. Her parents' death. Now, with his ice-blue gaze trailing her like Mr. Nude had done, her scar itched under his perusal.

"We have here a freezing woman. Mind moving?" She arched a brow.

He jerked back, surprise widening his eyes, but he leaped aside. "Harriet, your guest has arrived."

His boom rattled Ilona's bones, and she glared at him, huffing past him with her heavy luggage. He hadn't asked to carry it, and she wasn't about to demand he help. What an ass.

A wide staircase curled upward to the left of the foyer with a room leading off on either side. Wooden flooring and colorful rugs trapped the warmth. The ceilings were high, with cream-painted wainscotting and brass wall lights adding an inviting glow. A glance to the right showed a formal dining room, with an antique dark wood dining table and chairs with burgundy brocade. To the left was a living room with deep floral couches and a roaring fire in the fireplace. Down the hallway, just past the stairs was a white and cream kitchen, bright light pouring through the arched doorway.

"Dane, leave the poor girl." A woman adorable as her gran appeared. Her gray hair was unraveling from her chignon, and her eyeglasses kept sliding down her nose.

Ilona beamed. "Hi, my gran made a reservation."

The woman hurried past Ilona. The essence of rose trailed her with the ties of her apron whipping around her. She tugged a book along a side table and ran a gnarled finger down a page. "Ms. Strickland?"

Ilona winced. "Call me Ilona."

The elder woman frowned. "Are you all right?"

"I'm fine." Ilona pinched her lips and glared at the man, despite the heat of the ass's stare burning her. "Quit staring," she whispered.

His eyes widened again, then he chuckled and continued to stare.

"Oh, all right. Dane, take Ms. Strick—"

"Ilona, please." She unzipped her jacket, wondering if the spike in her temperature was due to Dane's curiosity or Mr. Balls-to-the-wind. She hoped it was the latter's fault. Smirking, she handed her jacket to Dane.

The older woman smiled. "If you call me Harriet. Quit standing around, Dane, and make yourself useful. Take Ilona's bag upstairs." Her grip on Ilona's elbow was surprisingly strong for such a tiny woman. "Would you like a cup of cocoa?"

Ilona nodded. Dane lifted her bag like it weighed nothing, then jogged up the staircase, highlighting an ass she had to admit was exquisite. His denims rode low and cupped his gluteus maximus to perfection.

"We don't get guests often." Harriet's voice faded down the passage, and Ilona hurried to catch up, the aroma of roast beef urging her to follow. "What brings you to Coedwig?"

"My grandmother sent me. I'm supposed to find Amos Denton." She hoped revealing her purpose meant a quick in and out of Coedwig. For such a smallish town, everyone had to know everyone.

"Why would you want to find him?" While pouring boiling milk into cups, Harriet frowned. A delicate rose pink splashed across her cheeks. "Sorry, I don't mean to pry."

Ilona shrugged and climbed onto a barstool, leaning her elbow on the kitchen's island. "Gran claims he's my grandfather."

"What? That mean old bastard?" Dane grumbled something under his breath before sliding onto a barstool beside her, bringing with him the fragrance of pine needles, cold wind, and snow. "Sorry to hear that."

"Don't scare her, Dane. Amos is a sweetheart."

He grunted. "To you, maybe. He's a pain in my ass." Dipping his head, he sipped from the mug Harriet placed before him. "Planning on staying long?"

Ilona wrapped her fingers around the mug and raised it to her lips. The sweet, addictive aroma of chocolate greeted her, and floating on the surface were pink mini marshmallows. Dane had all the white. She looked away to hide a smile.

"I don't know." When the cocoa warmed her belly, she flashed Harriet a grateful smile. "I have this box I'm supposed to give him."

"Twenty-something years ago?" Harriet tapped her chin, her gaze unfocused. "The only woman... Would your gran be Monique Devereaux?"

"Yup, the one and only. She's a little bundle of sassiness. Thankfully, I take after my dad." Ilona winced as fresh pain rose out of the ceaseless dull ache circling her heart. Tears pressed against her eyes like she hadn't just railed at the stars. "Um, if you don't mind, I would like to turn in."

"Yes, of course. Dane?"

He grunted and slid off the stool, but it was too late. Tears won out and ran like rivulets down Ilona's cheeks. She hurried to wipe them away, embarrassment flushing her face. Then he did the stupidest thing. He wrapped his bulky arms around her and crushed her against solid muscle.

The floodgates opened. She drenched his T-shirt in seconds.

When Harriet slapped his arm, he released Ilona. "She hasn't been here fifteen minutes and you have her crying."

"It wasn't me," he growled, but he kept his hands on Ilona's shoulders. He dipped to meet her gaze, his ice-blue eyes startling. "Sweetheart, I'm sorry for your pain or how life treated you before coming to Coedwig, but you're welcome to stay here as long as you need to."

Another kind and understanding stranger? Did Coedwig breed them big and sweet? Ilona chuckled through her tears. "Thanks."

With a tissue Harriet took from her cardigan sleeve, he dabbed Ilona's face, his finger under her chin keeping her in place. He was gentle for such a lummox, gentler around her scar. "I'll show you to your room. Dinner's in about an hour or so."

Ilona shook her head. As delicious as the beef smelled, her stomach churned. "I'm to bed if you don't mind."

Dane studied her. "Fair enough. Tomorrow morning, after one of Harriet's epic breakfasts, I'll take you to Amos."

Harriet harumphed. "I'll show her upstairs while you fetch more firewood."

"Yes, ma'am." He grinned, dropped a kiss on Harriet's cheek, then jogged out the back door into the night. Going outside without a coat reminded Ilona of her naked Neanderthal.

"Wow, Ilona, for Dane to invite you to stay?" Harriet's eyes twinkled, and Ilona would swear in front of the medical board, Harriet planned a matchmaking.

"Dane's your grandson?" Her chance to pry.

"No, he owns most of Coedwig." Harriet hung up her apron and gestured to the passage. "He's what you would call our mayor."

Ilona gaped, now seeing her sobbing in his arms as a tanktastic faux pas. "Oh."

"He lets me run this bed and breakfast, even named it after me, just so I feel useful." She climbed the stairs. Ilona trailed her, gripping the balustrade to drag her exhausted body up to the landing. Her knees trembled on each step. "Breakfast is when you wake up, dearie."

"That's not fair on—"

"I always have something on the fry. Dane and Rhys eat like bears." She grinned and opened a door into a bedroom in creams and rouge.

A quilt adorned the bed, florals in shades of pinks and puce assaulted Ilona's eyes. As long as it was clean, which it was, she wouldn't complain about the décor. Dane had placed her bag on an antique armchair. Through a door was a modern en suite in beige and pink.

In one corner of the room was a cast iron fireplace, and beside it, a small bundle of wood. "This is wonderful, Harriet."

The woman beamed. "I hoped you'd like it." She patted Ilona on the forearm. "Good-night, and sleep well." She closed the door with a click.

Ilona took a calming breath, embarrassment warring with anger at her silly breakdown. And the hug? She had burrowed into his embrace, a wealth of comfort flowing through her as if he truly cared.

Unzipping her bag, she unpacked what she needed and disappeared into the bathroom. A hot shower thawed every inch of her. She winked at her reflection in the mirror. The scar puckered, and her smile faltered at the reminder of her loss. It would always be there, a red flag taking her back to that night and the following days.

With her back to the mirror, she rubbed her hair. In a shaggy bob brushing past her shoulders, it was easy to care for without taking up too much time. She wrapped a towel around her head, then used the bath towel to dry the rest of her.

Tying it with a knot between her breasts, she opened the bathroom door. A roaring fire burned in the fireplace, and a fresh stack of chopped wood sat on the tiles beside it.

"I did knock."

She yelped, but a grinning Dane shut the bedroom door. His rumbled goodnight penetrated the thin walls, along with his chuckle and thundering steps down the stairs.

She smiled. The mayor? Huh.

Chapter Nine

COEDWIG'S SURPRISE

Coming north meant snow and lots of it. Surrounded by forests, solitude made shifting easier, more private. Few amateur photographers or gun-toting madmen lingered in this weather. Rhys had left Cozy Cromwell's, circled the house and marched into the nearby forest, then stripped in the shadow of the trees. His bear took the lead. The pristine snow coating the hills had urged him to leave his mark. He had zigzagged across it, rolling and pouncing until tiny flurries rose from his snow-dusted paws.

Then he'd spotted the woman, laughing and crying in the snow. Everything about her had called to him. Her heart was broken, as torn as her cheek. Yet she had begged him to come with her, vowing not to abandon him.

Please don't ask me to.

I swore an oath.

Intriguing. Still, a blanket of sorrow had coated her despite her antics seeming innocent and amusing, at first. Stubbornness she had in spades. Was he interested because of her red hair, her hazel eyes, the pain trembling her cheeks? Or was it her elusive fragrance that teased his senses, aroused him? It had taken thoughts of George and her brothers living in squalor to dampen Rhys's ardor. Yet the woman hadn't once lowered her gaze to his exposed and hardening cock.

With his thoughts dazed, his bear whining to chase after her car, he had forced himself to walk away. He chuckled. Now, that would be a fool's errant. He wasn't a bloodhound. With her cap off, he'd caught a red curl, touched her pale chin, and ogled her curves. He sniffed the air, catching a hint of her fragrance. The wind was furious, whipping across his nose before he could take a deep inhale. Sure, he was grizzly, but he didn't have the olfactory power of a polar.

He laughed. She hadn't believed his snow-bathing claim. Her disbelief was made more delicious when she pursed her plump lips.

She was a beautiful woman, one he decided to search out when he returned to Coedwig. Outside Cromwell's, as he paused onto the porch, Rhys spied the woman's rental parked out front. Logical since there wasn't another bed and breakfast or hotel available. She had to be staying at Harriet's.

After yanking on the door, he bounded up the stairs, disappearing into his room for a quick shower. Dressed in jeans and a T-shirt, his boots on, he clambered downstairs, following his nose to the dining room. No redhead's scent lingered.

"How was your evening run?" Harriet smiled, sliding a cocoa in front of a plate piled high with cookies.

Rhys patted his chest and sat. He chose a cookie, bit into it, and beamed when the moist, chocolate gooeyness filled his mouth. "Where's Dane?" Putting off chatting to Coedwig's alpha wasn't wise. Rhys didn't want to delay it further.

"Taking care of things." She refilled his cocoa, then claimed a chair. "Are you staying for the Lunar Fest?"

Understanding Harriet's curiosity, he grunted something noncommittal, but yes, he might pursue a woman if he took a liking to her. Hell, any warm body would do, if they didn't mind him calling out 'Callie' in mid-orgasm. Damn, now that had been embarrassing. And pitiful. Thankfully, only his hand had witnessed his shame. He didn't tell Harriet any of that. Or that a certain redhead-not-Callie had sparked his interest. Until he found the woman, his sex life was up in the air.

He wanted to ask about other guests, but the opening front door interrupted him.

"Hey, anything left for me?" Aiden poked his head in, then stepped through the door. He scanned the cookie plate and sighed. "Any cake?"

Harriet chuckled and hurried to pack Aiden a slice. He leaned against the door frame and eyed Rhys cradling his mug. "Thought I would walk you to the bar."

Just the distraction Rhys needed. Draining his cocoa, he lowered the cup, then hurried to slip on his jacket.

Harriet held out a container with dark chocolate showing through the semi-transparent sides. "I'll keep your dinner in the warming drawer." She trailed them onto the porch, tugging her cardigan around her, then with a wave, returned to the house.

"How's Noah and Jase?" Aiden met Rhys's gaze briefly. "How's Willow?"

"Will?" Rhys grinned. So, that's the lay of the land. He hadn't known Aiden was interested in her. "She tried to seduce me this morning."

Color splashed across Aiden's cheeks. He pinched his lips as if he wanted to say something but thought better of it.

"It's why I decided to visit." Rhys peeked at Aiden. "I've got to find a mate before my brother's women try to seduce me."

"Women?" Aiden gaped. "None, well, maybe a few, and Will isn't...wasn't...we didn't—"

Rhys laughed, slapping Aiden on the shoulder. "Relax, pup."

"Not funny, bro." He glared.

Arching his brow, Rhys met Aiden's matching eyes. "Yeah, well, if you like Will, then pursue her."

"Shut up." He stomped into the bar and disappeared through a hidden door behind the counter.

Rhys sighed, removed his jacket, and headed for a bar stool, planning on sitting for a while. His ears twitched, proving he heard the random conversations, the shot-down come-ons, and the swindling at the pool table his brother kept in the back. He didn't listen in, preferring to sip his beer, savoring the bitter flavor coating his tongue. Bitter? That made him think of the suckbloods' inability to taste human food. Suckbloods? He shook his head, loving how Callie's terminology had snuck into his vocab.

Callie. Lunar help him, if only he could get over the damn woman. She wasn't meant for him, but his bear disagreed. If only Rhys had met her first. If and maybes had plagued him for months.

Grumbling, he took a long pull from his beer.

"I can't tell you how glad I am to see you, Rhys." Aiden broke the silence between them as he wiped down the bar counter. "I mean, I asked you to visit but never expected you to come."

Rhys pursed his lips, the chilled swig of beer pooling on his tongue. "Needed time away to clear my thoughts. How are folks treating you here?"

"Your call to Dane helped. He took one look at me and realized I wasn't planning on challenging him for alpha." Aiden pushed his pseudo-glasses up his nose. He didn't suffer from poor eyesight, but it did make him look timid. The Whitakers had the same brown hair and blue eyes, but where Rhys was a mountain of a man, a grizzly, Aiden was more of a black bear. "So, what's the real reason behind the visit? You know, we do hear things, what you city-folk get up to."

"Yeah, there's talk you formed an alliance with the de Winter hold. My gramps is rolling in his grave," said an old cougar to the left of Rhys.

"But I hear some vamp wanted to start a war?" asked an old wolf who sipped her white wine spritzer, raising it at the old cougar in greeting.

"We're always at war," the cougar grumbled. "But you've done well, son. Alrik was a mean bastard."

"That he was." Rhys couldn't agree more. The fight for supremacy had been easier than he had expected. He only wished he had challenged for alpha sooner.

"Is this about a woman?" Aiden asked, still intent on finding out the reason behind Rhys's visit.

So much for an evening in company. He grunted and pushed his empty beer bottle aside. Before he spilled his failure, he rose, tossed a few bills on the table, then saluted Aiden. Rhys wasn't running. It was a strategic retreat until he could gather his thoughts and intentions.

Tugging on his jacket, he savored the chilled wind as it slashed across his cheeks. He squared his shoulders and strolled to Cromwell's. As he meandered up the road while the late sun set behind the towering pine peaks, his stomach growled. The possibility of one of Harriet's roast beef dinners fueled his stride.

Chapter Ten

Get It Done

In her ballet flats, Ilona scampered down the stairs, the aroma of bacon calling her. She peeked into the dining room, and like a king at a banquet, Dane sat at the head of the table with platters of food spread out before him.

"Morning, how did you sleep?" He grinned and gestured with a fork for her to join him.

"Like a baby." Ilona slipped into a chair and reached for the bacon platter.

He scooped a pile of pancakes onto his plate and drizzled a ton of maple syrup over them. "When you're done eating, I'll take you to Amos. He's at Tuesdays for the annual pool tournament."

"On a weekday?" She frowned.

"It's a standing event, and everyone treats it as an off day." Dane shrugged. "As long as they get their work done, I don't care either way." He sucked in a deep breath that expanded his chest like a puffed-up pigeon. "As the mayor, I have to show my face, of course."

"Oh, good morning, Ilona. Coffee?" Harriet hurried into the dining room carrying a pot of coffee.

Ilona nodded, her mouth too full to talk. Within seconds, she was stirring in sugar and cream. She groaned after a sip of the strong, smoky heat layering her tongue. "Nectar." After four strips of bacon, a slice of toasted ciabatta smeared with fresh butter and homemade marmalade, she was replete. But there was space for another coffee.

"That was scrumptious, as always, Harriet." Dane rubbed his flat stomach through his dark-blue T-shirt, flashing his mocha skin rippling with muscle. Satisfaction was in the bright smile he bestowed on the older woman.

"I'll make more for Rhys." She waved her hand over the leftovers.

"And whatever he doesn't eat, just pop in the warmer. Ilona's nibbled like a freaking bird. I expect her Coedwig appetite to kick in soon." Dane pushed away from the table to rise. "We'll leave in five minutes?" He arched a brow at Ilona's empty mug then at her ballet flats. "I want to find Amos before the lunchtime crowd. Hopefully, we'll catch him in a good mood."

Fair enough since she had slept in. "Thank you for breakfast, Harriet."

Upstairs, Ilona stared at her nibbled-on boot from last night. Not finding where the bear's teeth had scoured the leather, she sat on the bed to don socks then boots. After brushing her teeth, she tugged on a thick fleece-lined jacket, fluffed her hair over the collar and grabbed the black box.

Dane waited for her at the front door, wearing a massive parka in hunter green that would have drowned her. His short hair curled over the collar, implying it needed a trim. It had the look of fresh snow. "Ready?"

She took a deep breath. "As ready as I'll ever be."

"Gloves? A scarf?"

She groaned, darting up the stairs to grab them. Returning to him, she tucked the box under her arm as she peeled the gloves on, with the scarf looped around her neck. He captured the ends and tried to strangle her, flicking it a few times around her until she felt like a giraffe with a goiter.

"If I fall, it's on you." Her scarf muffled her words and obscured her vision.

Opening the front door blasted a gust of icy wind into her. She gasped, dipping her nose into the scarf.

"Stay close to me. I'll warm you."

Her cheeks caught on fire at the suggested proximity. She fiddled with her zipper, tilting her face away hoping to hide her scar. But when he waited for her response, she scrambled for one. "That's the best pick up line I've heard to date."

He blinked at her. So, she huddled behind his great bulk, which shielded her enough for her to close the door behind them.

He laughed and loped ahead, leaving her at the mercy of the elements. The sky was a pale turquoise, the snow blinding against the graveled tarmac and sludge. He held the door open on his red SUV. She hurried to dip under his arm and slide in. Warmth was instant when he shut the door, cutting off the chilling wind. She clamped the box between her denim-encased knees to buckle up.

He slid into the driver's seat and started the engine.

"Seatbelt." She wiggled her fingers, asking him to tug it across, so she could buckle him in.

"Not necessary, Mom. Tuesdays is a minute away."

Ilona stilled, tormented by the memories of the accident. It was silly to wonder if not wearing their seatbelts would have saved them. She bit her inner cheek to keep the tears at bay.

Dane stared at her. "Care to talk about it?" The gentleness in his deep baritone cut through the silence between them.

"No, but thanks."

"I'll listen when you're ready." He accelerated out of the parking spot and turned the SUV around. His tires crunched as they found traction.

The townsfolk meandered on the sidewalks like it wasn't below freezing. Children played in the snow, building animal-shaped snowmen and making snow angels. The many cars parked outside Mo's Diner and Jameson's Mercantile said they did good business. Coedwig was the image of a bustling town, a charming place to raise children. Pine and tradition scented the air, implying generation after generation had lived here.

Within minutes, Dane parked outside a single-story log cabin with neon signage on its fascia boards—the bar she had seen when she had driven into town. Tuesdays was open and crowded if she judged the packed parking lot.

"Shit," Dane muttered. "Lunchtime's early."

She climbed out before Dane could open the door for her. Now that she was here, she twitched with barely restrained energy. What would she do if Amos hated her on sight? She sighed, castigating herself for her doubts and silly fears. If her dear old grandfather didn't want her, that was fine too. She would return to Fenneg having lost nothing.

She raised her chin, uncaring that the action allowed the wind access to her throat. With a yank of the scarf, she tossed it on the seat then closed the car door. Time to face this task, to finish it, and head home.

Not that she knew what she would do when she returned to Fenneg. Waiting for her was the Great Cleanse and her new job at Indes Pediatrics. As a doctor, as a healer of children, she wasn't sure she could do anymore. A doctor had to have heart, drive, passion…

Dane held the cabin door until she ducked under his arm and inside the warm interior. He peeled off his jacket and hung it on a hook buried among many other coats and jackets. After he helped her out of hers, he did the same, shoving her gloves inside her jacket pockets. Waiting for him granted her a few moments to scan the packed bar.

The stench of beer filled the air, but no smoke rose toward the ceiling, as if no one in the town smoked. How odd. Regardless, the floor was clean, the counter at the back long with sturdy stools and a young, brown-haired bartender serving drinks. With the crowds blocking her view, the pool tables had to be toward the rear.

Silence descended, and one by one, women and men stared at her, raising their chins to sniff the air. She restrained herself from asking Dane if she reeked of skunk. Blues played on the speakers, but not loud enough to hinder conversation.

"Come." He wrapped his fingers around her elbow and ushered her toward the bar, cutting a fine swathe through the crowd.

He tapped a barstool with his boot. She slipped onto it, cupping the box in front of her. He dropped onto the stool beside her and waved two fingers at the bartender. Conversation resumed, and the volume rose to an almost deafening roar.

Woman after woman, gorgeous enough to be models, draped themselves over Dane, casting heated glares at Ilona. Blonde or brunette, slender and tall made her think Coedwig was a fashion capital. She caught snippets of their whisperings.

"…found a woman to warm you yet?"

"…you can do better than her."

"…the full moon is almost upon us, and I was hoping…"

Ilona smothered a chuckle. Make that the porn capital with so many horny women in one place. Big man, big feet, big penis? Despite knowing the statistics, the adage had her coughing to cover her laughter.

Dane handled them with skill, whispering something in their ears to send them away with hopeful smiles.

"Two beers." The bartender flicked coasters onto the counter before placing the bottles on them.

She blinked. Beer so soon?

"Name's Aiden." The bartender winked at her, and his dark blue eyes warmed when he ran his gaze over her.

She tilted her head to better display her scar, hoping to deter any advances. Not that he wasn't attractive. She scanned the room again and frowned. Most of the men were built like athletes or bodybuilders, and they all had this tension around them like coiled snakes.

Dane chugged his beer like he hadn't just eaten a mountain of food. "Where's Amos?" He gestured to the room at large with a twirl of his bottle.

"Here somewhere." Aiden shrugged. "Nothing noteworthy has happened...yet." He polished a glass, studied it in the dim lighting, then polished it again. "Why are you looking for him?"

"I need to speak to him." Ilona sipped her beer, letting the bitterness cut through her nervousness.

"Figured as much." Aiden blessed her with a sensual smile. "Hey, Jillie, have you seen Amos?"

The elderly woman to the right of Ilona nursed a white wine. She hitched her thumb behind her and raised her glass to her lips, her assessing gaze resting on Ilona.

"Amos!"

Ilona jerked at Dane's boom, and the crowds quietened.

"Quit your hollering." A tall man fiddled with his belt when he shuffled through the men's bathroom door. "Can't a man piss in peace?"

No, this couldn't be him. He looked too young, late forties, early fifties max. Black hair peppered with gray fell to his shoulders, so long he could have tied it into a man bun. His eyes were a dark brown, and with that square jaw enhanced by his thick yet trimmed beard, Ilona could see why Gran had found him attractive. His nose was the deciding factor. A masculine version of hers and Mom's.

Shit. She faced Aiden, but the mirror behind him showed Amos's progress across the bar. Her heart pumped blood along her arteries with too much force. Flutters claimed her chest. The air was too thin. She struggled to inhale.

"Breathe." Dane rested his hand between her shoulder blades.

His strength poured into her. She nodded, taking in slow controlled breaths until her heartbeat returned to a semi-normal pace.

"So, what do you want?" Amos's voice behind her stiffened her back and tightened the grip she had on the beer.

"Care to explain?" Dane nudged her.

She squared her shoulders then spun on the barstool to face her grandfather. He towered over her with his intimidation factor not aided by her seated position nor his glower. There was nothing to do but tell him.

"Hey, it turns out we're related." She closed her eyes for a second, gritting her teeth at her tactless words. "You're my grandaddy." In for a penny and all that.

"What?" Amos ran his dark gaze over her face and lingered on her scar.

She raised her chin, letting him see she was damaged goods. He would find out soon enough, anyway. She twisted to grab the box and shoved it into his hands. "Monique asked me to deliver this."

"Mona?" He gasped, clutching the box tighter. "You're Mona's granddaughter?" He didn't wait for an answer but focused on the box in his hands. "I...gave her this." He clenched his jaw, flicked a glance at their attentive audience then at Ilona. "Meet me at Mo's. Now."

He unhooked his coat, slipped it on, then stormed outside, the door banging shut behind him.

"Your grandmother should have at least warned you about him." Jillie sipped her wine. "He's a mean bastard."

Ilona sighed. "So everyone tells me." She leaped off the stool, slid money onto the bar while ignoring Aiden, and bolted after Amos. The sooner she got this sorted, the faster she'd be on a plane home. A glance over her shoulder confirmed Dane trailed her.

The wall of muscle she walked into sucked the breath out of her. She clung to massive biceps while catching her balance. Raising her face to mumble "Oh, I'm so sorry" catapulted her heartbeat. Heat burned across her cheeks. She knew this man. Dipping her chin, she darted around Mr. Naked Neanderthal and snatched her jacket off the hook.

One traumatic event at a time, thank you very much.

She marched out of the bar without a backward glance. Standing on the sidewalk, she rocked on her feet and hunched her shoulders against the biting wind while waiting for Dane. When she realized he might not be coming, something slithered down her spine she would admit was fear. She couldn't face Amos alone, could she?

She opened the door and peeked inside. Of all times to be chatting to her handsome stranger, did it have to be now? And of course, she had to linger on his many attributes she had vivid recollection of. She settled her gaze on Dane. "Is this going to take long?

Want me to fetch you afterward?" She put enough impatience in her tone that he hurried to don his jacket.

Hiding a smile, she ducked outside and waited, trying not to imagine how this thing with Amos would play out. Her breathing became ragged.

Chapter Eleven

TRAPPED

After another asphyxiation attempt with a borrowed scarf that stank of dog, Dane walked Ilona up the gentle hill to Mo's Diner. She suspected he hadn't driven her because he thought she might faint. The crisp air did help hold back the dark spots circling her vision, so she sucked in great gulps of it. Fainting upon meeting her granddaddy would sure power the rumor mill. She blamed her fluttery state on coming face to face with Mr. Naked. He was as gorgeous in jeans and a T-shirt as he was naked, holding her boot. Who was she kidding? She much preferred him in his birthday suit. Raising her face to catch the chilling breeze helped smother a giggle at the image of him with a red ribbon twirled around his golden body.

"Not the way I would have gone." Dane rumbled with barely suppressed laughter.

"Oh, and what would you have done or said?" She flicked an arched brow at him, irritated at his condescension. "Been in this situation before? How many unknown grandparents do you have?"

"Touché." He threw his arm across her shoulder and tugged her into the curve of his body, shielding her from the wind.

She wanted to struggle, to reject his familiarity like he had known her for long and had the right to intrude on her personal space. But then, she would freeze. Grand gestures of offense would gain her nothing.

He shrugged. "Still, I would have given him the box and let him reach his own conclusions."

"Right, that a woman he once knew sent him a box he'd given her?" She shook her head. "First conclusion would be…she died." Raising her gaze to the sky, she let the chilling wind dry the tears forming. No more talk of death. "He looked furious, though."

"Wouldn't you be if you found out you had a child, and no one told you?" Dane tightened his arm to halt her, spinning her to face him. "We're family orientated, Ilona. Not telling him cut out a large chunk of his soul."

She blinked, wondering if Amos would force his way into her life. She couldn't bear to lose someone again... No more thoughts of loss. "I'm staying longer than I thought?"

Dane nodded and guided her into a stroll, neatly dodging a woman with an ingratitude of children in tow. Amos watched from the booth closest to the entrance with one hand resting on the box centerstage of the table. Dane held the door open for her, allowing her to duck in before he followed.

The aroma of roasted coffee, cinnamon sugar, and toasted cheese greeted her. She inhaled deeply.

"Hey, Mo." Dane kissed the cheek of an elderly woman in a waitress uniform. He gestured to Ilona to slide in first before he trapped her in the booth, taking up a large section of the seat with his great bulk. "I'll have a coffee and a donut."

She blinked at him. A massive breakfast, a beer, and now a donut? "Where do you put it all?"

When he grinned, she dropped her gaze, not needing his charm to melt her resolve. She wasn't looking for sex, love, or forever after, and by the number of women seeking his particular companionship, he wasn't the type of man she could afford to lose her heart to.

"I'm a growing boy." He rubbed his taut abdomen.

"Welcome to Coedwig, Ilona. What will you have?" Mo chewed gum as expected, and she had two pencils sticking out of her grey chignon. So cliché.

"Just a coffee, thanks, Mo." Everyone knowing Ilona's name shouldn't surprise her. Small towns tended to spread news fast. A new person in town searching for grumpy Amos and claiming to be his granddaughter? Yup, that would be news worthy of a good spreading.

"Where's Mona? Is she well?" Amos rested his dark gaze on Ilona, pinning her to the spot.

"She's as sassy as always. Said she couldn't come on account of the damn cold." Ilona was starting to agree with her.

Icy fingers seeped through any gaps in her clothing, and heaven forbid, she left a part of her body exposed. Snow was pretty on television and somewhere far away. Underfoot, it was nothing but a death trap.

Amos's eyes shimmered with unshed tears. "And where is she? Which city?"

"Fenneg."

He nodded, sucking in a shuddering breath. "Damn fool woman just left me in the middle of the night, no explanation, not even a fare thee well."

"She said something about you intending to marry another." Ilona smiled her thanks as Mo slid a coffee in front of her.

Dane bit off half of his donut.

Amos jerked back, tightened his fingers around the box, and dragged it closer. "Shit. That's why she left?" He threw back his head and guffawed, sounding like a longtime smoker. "I ought to find her and whip her ass. All these years wasted..." He retrieved a letter from his jacket pocket, tossing it onto the table.

Scrawled across it in Gran's familiar penmanship was Amos's name.

"She explained what happened to my daughter." His jaw tightened, and fury slithered across his features. "My...daughter." He shook his head. A single tear slid down his weathered cheek. "She says you're a doctor?"

"Wow, I never pegged you as one of those." Dane ran his ice-blue gaze over her face. Both eyebrows almost touched his hairline, despite his slow smirk and relaxed posture. Sure, that's why Ilona had studied for so many years. To impress people.

She ignored him, tapping the torn envelope instead. "Where was this?" She had tried to open the box, but the brackets and lock hadn't budged.

"In the box." He slipped a chain from around his neck on which hung a tiny key. "Now answer the damn question, granddaughter."

"I studied medicine." She glared at him, meeting his dark gaze without fear. If they were to have a relationship, she wasn't going to let him intimidate her, or worse, bully her.

"Residency?" He waited, but she didn't answer, choosing to sip her coffee. "Answer me." He slapped the table, trembling the plates and cutlery on its speckled linoleum surface.

She lowered her cup to its saucer. "I don't need to answer you, especially when you raise your voice at me. It's not endearing yourself to me, Grandfather. I don't need to be here. I've delivered the box, task done." She turned on Dane. "Move."

The damn man didn't, just smiled at her as he ate his second donut.

"I loved her with every breath in my body. I still do." Amos's husky voice stilled Ilona's half-climbing over Dane.

She sank onto the seat, blinking at the broken man before her.

"I never married and had no intention of doing so unless it was to her." He lunged across the table and gripped Ilona's hand. "I'm leaving on the first flight to Fenneg, but I can't abandon this town during the Lunar Festival."

"Abandon?" She frowned.

Dane threw back his coffee. "Amos is our resident doctor."

"He's a what?" A spark ran up her scar, throbbing it. Black and red spots tainted her vision. If Gran stood before her, she would receive such a tongue lashing. "That conniving traitor."

Gran hadn't wanted to accept Ilona's decision to not practice medicine anymore. She didn't want Ilona to mourn, to take a few weeks, months, hell, even years, to come to terms with her limitations. Instead, she had to visit her unknown grandfather under pretense.

Dane bit into his third donut. "Does she expect you to chase after her, Amos?"

"No, she thinks I'm married and bouncing my grandkids on my knee." He rose to his full height to lean across the table, cupping Ilona's unscarred cheek. "I could have experienced that with you. Please, stay, just for a few days."

"I don't know if that's wise." Dane wiggled his eyebrows trying to imply something.

Amos scowled, lowering himself into the chair with a few cracks and pops of his joints. "I'm going, and there ain't a damn thing you can do, Dane. I'm old, and each second alive is precious. I want Mona in my arms, my life, and I have every intention of luring her here to stay."

"What?" Ilona squeaked.

Not have Gran with her in Fenneg? No, that was out of the question. Where would her home be? The tempestuous emotion in Amos's eyes told another story. She slumped into the seat. Gran would reject him again, so Ilona had nothing to worry about. A few days on duty in a small town, how busy could she get? It would be like working at Amity, one last hoorah.

"Fine." She folded her arms across her chest, glaring at the man.

"I don't like this," Dane growled under his breath.

The rumbling deep from within him raised the hairs on her neck. She shivered and tightened her jacket.

Amos stiffened but shook his head. "Challenge me if you must, but I'm leaving."

Ilona thumped Dane on the arm, stinging her knuckles when she hit solid flesh. "Are you implying I'm incapable of handling a small town? I'll have you know, Mr. Mayor, I've worked trauma, for pity's sake."

He captured her fist, holding it in place. Heat poured from him, hotter than a newly filled water bottle. "I didn't say that. It's just... Some folks are picky about who doctors them."

"They can damn well get over themselves, or they can heal on their own." She tugged her hand free, aware he let her, before facing her grandfather. "Amos, how long? I'm not staying here so you and Gran can...y'know, get naked."

His cheeks darkened, but she couldn't say if it was from embarrassment or fury. "You'll stay as long as it takes." He rose to his feet, tossed a few notes on the table, slapped a set of keys into Dane's hand, then stormed off.

Ilona scrambled across Dane's lap to follow.

Then bumped into Amos's chest who had halted his exit. "Where does she live? Give me the address."

Ilona pinched her lips as she shoved her face in his, showing her defiance. He could have at least said please.

"You're as infuriating as she was." He waved his hands into the air. "Fine, I'll find her without you. How many Monique Devereauxs can there be?"

She laughed. "It's not Devereaux anymore."

He gasped. "She married?" His gaping mouth slipped into a grimace.

"Is it Strickland?" Dane leaned his elbows on the back of the bench, watching them.

"My daughter was Dr. Elise Strickland?" Amos paled. He threw out a hand to grip the door handle. "I knew of her, of her husband...your parents." He charged at Ilona to cup her shoulders. "Tell me, where's Mona?"

Dane leaped off the bench, his chest warming Ilona's back. Was he complicit in this nonsense? Or did he think Amos would hit her?

She slumped, unable to handle whatever this was with any emotional integrity. This shitstorm was of Gran's doing. Ilona rattled off the address. Amos left the diner with the door banging behind him, climbed into his truck, then sped off. As if she waded through quicksand, she flopped onto the bench opposite Dane, who had returned to his donut.

"I guess I'm your new doctor for the foreseeable future." She dabbed her eyes with a paper towel. "Anything I should know about?"

Dane pushed away his empty plate. "Shit, this isn't going to end well."

Rhys couldn't move. His bear shook its head, whining for release. Slapping him down, he grabbed his coat and slipped it on as he strolled out. Seeing Callie in other women wasn't fair to himself or the women. Gritting his teeth, he strode up the hill, and paused, watching through Mo's windows as Dane, Rhys's redhead, and Amos chatted. Her expressions were easy to read, her shock, her pale face, her anger and flushed cheeks, her dismay and resignation, and ending in her slumping across the table.

He shoved his fists deep into the pockets of his jacket. Dane would have to explain what was going on. The woman stomped out of Mo's, leaving a bemused Dane seated in the booth. She hesitated when she saw Rhys standing there.

He didn't know what to say. Asking if she was all right was lame, even as a thought. She marched up the hill to Cromwell's.

Rhys didn't hesitate. Besides taking a second to stare after her swinging ass, he opened the door and slid into the spot she vacated. "What the fuck is going on?"

Dane grunted. "Where do I start? Ilona is Amos's granddaughter."

Ilona. Rhys tested her name on his tongue. He shivered, relishing the skitter of excitement brushing across his senses.

"Amos hadn't known she existed until now. But instead of getting to know her, he's hying off to Fenneg to find Mona, her grandmother." Dane swiped his finger over the sugar dusting the empty plate. He sucked on his finger. "Now, I have a new doctor for the fest."

"She's a doctor?" Rhys grinned. *I swore an oath.*

Dane half-chuckled. "So she claims."

"Just…" Rhys rubbed a hand over his face. "Go easy on her, Dane. She's suffering."

He locked gazes with Rhys. "I know, and she won't say why. Cried on my shoulder yesterday."

Rhys's heart twanged, though why he cared, he couldn't say.

"So, what brings you to Coedwig?" Dane finished his donut and gestured to Mo for another round of coffee.

"I needed a break. I've so much going on. Trying to repair what Alrik destroyed, rebuilding my pack's morale. And on top of it all, I'm working closely with the humans and vamps to form a policing unit. Devereaux thinks we can…" Rhys didn't want to discuss any of that, didn't want to rehash the emotions Callie invoked.

"Devereaux?" Dane frowned.

"Callista Devereaux. Although, I suspect she's de Winter now." Pain cinched his chest, and his bear roared, deafening his internal hearing. Threatening tears stung his eyes. Dammit, an alpha never cried. Get it together.

"Ah, for a moment there, I thought you knew our Devereaux."

Rhys shook his head. What were the odds of stumbling on a descendent of the Devereaux line right here in Coedwig. Could it be Callie's lineage? He almost grumbled at his staccato heartbeat. Not all Devereauxs came from the same melting pot. And he couldn't swap his infatuation from one woman to another.

"Amos's Mona was a Devereaux."

Everything within Rhys stilled, and for once, that included his bear. "So her granddaughter is…?" He struggled to swallow. The one woman he found attractive since meeting Callie turned out to be related to her?

Dane nodded, a mischievous smile splitting his face. "She's new to Coedwig, but if I was you, I'd steer clear."

"What? Why?" Warning him off had the opposite effect. Now he had to see her again.

"She's under my protection, Rhys. Alpha to alpha, stay away from her. Like you said, she's been hurt. Whatever happened, she needs time, space, for however long it takes to heal."

Dane had the right of it. Rhys grunted. Still, she intrigued him, and it wouldn't hurt to get to know her better. "Two alphas protecting her is better than one."

Dane leveled an unflinching stare on Rhys. "You've changed."

He grimaced. "I have." Having tasted what love could feel like, he was more than determined to find it. And in doing so, break the hold a non-mate Callie had over him.

Dane sipped his coffee. "I might be howling at the wrong moon. We'll touch on this after you've met Ilona and she's chewed you a new one."

Not for all the moons in the universe would Rhys reveal he'd met her already. He drained his cup and rose. "I look forward to it." At Dane's furrowed brow, he laughed. "See you at Cromwell's."

Chapter Twelve

MAGIC

Dane steered into a narrow road, following its zigzagging as it meandered around large pine trees that had to be centuries old. He drove around a corner, and before Ilona nestled a cabin against a grove of trees. Sunlight spilled across the clearing. He jerked the car to a halt in front of a salted walkway leading up to a wraparound porch.

The door was a pretty sky blue, and everything looked well-maintained.

"This is yours."

"What?" she squeaked, twisting in her seat to face him.

"This was your grandmother's, and Amos kept it pristine in the hopes she'd return. Giving me the keys was his way of saying it's yours now."

"But...if Gran returns with him, won't she want it back?" Ilona scanned the pretty house with its chimney and shuttered windows. She could imagine herself enjoying her morning coffee on the porch swing built on one side.

"She'll move in with him if I judged his determination correctly." Dane grinned and wiggled his eyebrows suggestively.

"And you're the mayor?" Ilona chuckled while exiting the SUV.

She strolled along the path. The cold wind whipped her hair as the sun warmed the crown of her head. When she crept up the few steps onto the porch, she paused at the door.

"It's unlocked," Dane called. "We don't have crime here."

Nodding as if no crime wasn't phenomenal, she parted the door on silent hinges. The scent of lavender tantalized her, and she inhaled.

"How is this possible? It smells like my gran." She scanned the rooms searching for the fragrance.

In the small dining room on the left, a potted lavender took centerstage on a polished wooden table. The open-plan kitchen, in bright whites and grays, nestled at the rear of the dining room.

"Amos modernized the kitchen." Dane peeked his head through the archway. "Living room over there, bedrooms to the rear of the house, and a garage tucked at the back. But I have another plan to while away the afternoon."

"What?" She faced him as a car door thumped from the front of the house. Over his shoulder and through the sheer curtains, she narrowed her gaze on a man crossing the snow to the porch.

"That should be Sheriff Jake Dunn, our local law enforcement." Dane swung the door wide. "Good timing, Jake. Come meet our new doctor."

"Temporary doctor." She slipped around Dane's bulk to offer the sheriff her hand.

In jeans, a T-shirt, and a thick jacket, he didn't look like a policeman. Not to mention the shoulder-length hair peppered with gray. He had piercings in his left ear and tattoos climbing his throat, hinting at something intricate beneath his clothes.

"Welcome." He rocked on his heels, hooking his thumbs into his pockets. "Ready to taste snow?"

"What?" Ilona gritted her teeth at her monosyllabic response.

"Dane's got a hankering for some board time. Ever skied, boarded, tobogganed?"

She shook her head. "No, just sandboarding on the Dunes of Sashan, east of Fenneg."

"Close enough." Dane patted her back, and she stumbled into Jake's arms. She tossed a glare at Dane while rolling her throbbing shoulder.

"Milligan's Research Tower is on the south face of Echon Mountain. The scientists haven't messaged that they need anything, but we should prepare you for an emergency. I've asked Dane to let you drive to Lover's Point. Each day while you're in Coedwig, I need you to practice the drive as many times as you can. Text me or Dane before you go and when you return, just in case I need to gather a search team. Doc's used to the drive, but now he ain't here..." Jake grinned, flashing a gold tooth.

"Might as well board a little, get you started on that too." Dane nudged her with his shoulder, almost toppling her.

She waved her hands, fear sliding down her spine at the thought of all that snow. Hell, the snow had won her boot. How was she supposed to show the snow who was boss? "I'm not dressed. I mean, I don't have the equipment, the gear—"

"Got you covered." Jake hitched his thumb behind him. "We keep a supply, so help yourself. Best stash it in your trunk, y'know, for—"

"Just in case." Ilona grumbled under her breath about high-handed men.

With another nudge from Dane, she hurried to the rear of Jake's SUV, popping it to stare at the mountain of stacked equipment. The men removed snowboards, helmets, goggles, stretching around her to take what they needed.

She must have hesitated too long because Jake chose a pair of snow boots for her, kneeling to check if they would fit.

Dane hooked goggles over her face, resting them with care on her forehead. He ran a gentle touch along her scar. "You'll tell me about this one day, Ilona."

She pinched her lips against the violent bombardment of grief that snatched her breath away and spun her vision. It had been dormant since Mo's. Instead of answering, she regulated her breathing, trying to hold back the sorrow.

He lowered the goggles over her eyes, then tugged a helmet on, adjusting the straps despite the tears pooling on her eyelashes.

"I have the portable medkit in my backpack." Jake hooked a bag over his shoulder, then grabbed her board and his. "I chose a one-fifty board. Should be a good fit." He climbed into Dane's SUV, choosing the backseat.

Dane shoved her toward the driver's side.

"I feel railroaded." She glowered at him over the hood of his car.

"Got to be done." He grinned. "No rest for the wicked doctor, right?"

She snorted but slid in, hoping she didn't break her leg boarding. She said as much.

Jake shrugged. "No worries. I'll carry you back."

"To what? I'm the only damn doctor in this town."

His laughter was husky and peppered with snorts. "There's a hospital fifty miles north, and we can get Rebel to air-lift you. Though, I'd prefer to crawl to the hospital than fly with that maniac."

"Jake's scared of heights," Dane whispered with a chuckle.

"I heard that." Jake punched Dane's shoulder.

"Of course, you did." He laughed. "Shifters have super sensitive hearing."

"Wait. What?" she squeaked, blinking at him. She had heard of shifters and vampires revealing their existence, but saving the lives of children had come first. When she had wanted to know about it, it was old news and of no interest to her busy colleagues. "You're a shifter?"

"Yup, who do you think chewed on your boot." His laughter rang loud.

What? How had Dane known... Never mind, what mattered more was that Mr. Naked was a shifter. Well, it explained so much. She struggled to swallow past the lump in her throat. Typical her, having tried to save a man not needing her help.

"Let's just get one thing clear," Jake growled. "I ain't scared of heights. Rebel just thinks he's some sort of hero."

Over his shoulder, Dane smirked at Jake. "You're law enforcement, Sheriff. You can't be lying in front of our new doctor."

He snorted.

Their back-and-forth banter eased her grip on the steering wheel. She settled into the driver's seat, taking in calming breaths at yet another adventure she could thank Gran for. How the hell was Ilona supposed to doctor shifters? Despite their human-like appearance, there had to be something biologically or physiologically different about them.

Speaking of maniacs, Dane directed her along a road no one would find if they had a GPS, a compass, and floodlights. Every time she lifted her foot off the gas pedal, he urged her to speed up. Tension petrified her shoulders when the car slid around corners with tree trunks inches from the side mirrors. Sneaking glances at the relaxed passengers, she studied the fear teasing the edges of her mind. Not once had she lost control careening along the snow-covered road. Exhilaration had her laughing as adrenaline flooded her arteries and blurred her perception of danger.

"We're here." Dane gestured to her to hit the brakes, and she did slowly, assuming hitting them on snow worked the same on sand.

She released the steering wheel with a sigh. For miles ahead of her lay a blanket of white snow, crisp and unmarred by human presence. Soft winds twirled clouds of white powder, and in the shadow of the mountain was a tower in grays and blacks, bold against the white. Lights shone from within the two-level structure high above the deep green and brown forests skirting the sides of the mountain.

"That's Echon Mountain, and he's a fickle bastard. Last winter, he toppled the research tower, and we had to reinforce it during summer. An avalanche buckled its frame." Jake whipped out his phone to show her the photos.

"What are they researching?" She met his gray eyes then zoomed into the photos, marveling at the crumpled metal, twisted like ropes of licorice.

"Climate change." Jake slipped his phone into his back pocket. "They bring in revenue and keep to themselves mostly. Bad weather grounded them last week. Poor Mo bitched about them running her off her feet."

Ilona chuckled. "I wish I was here to see that." She zipped her jacket closed and climbed out of the SUV, joining Dane at the cliff's edge. He dropped the snow boots beside her and helped her lace the inner boot and both zones. After slapping on the goggles, he buckled her helmet. Jake adjusted her highback on the board's binding to a three then clipped her onto the snowboard.

"Close enough?" She laughed then yelped when Dane tugged her jacket tight over her ass, touching where he shouldn't.

Not that his touch was suggestive, and his posture remained business-like, so he wasn't hitting on her. Relief flooded her with wonderful warmth. She wasn't ready for romance, not yet.

As he velcroed her sleeves over her gloves, he gestured to the cliff's edge with his chin. "We leap off here and carve the slopes, then trudge uphill to reach the tower. But today, I want you to try boarding, nothing fancy."

She laced her hands and tugged, tightening the gloves as she peered off the edge at a fifteen-foot drop. Her excited gasps became puffs of condensation. "Anything I need to know about the scientists?"

"We're not visiting them today, but if you run into them in town, they're desperate for female companionship. Don't be fooled by their sweet smiles."

She laughed, wondering what had made Dane warn her off. "I'm not worried." She gestured to her scar. "Still learning to live with this, and it has its benefits."

His blue eyes narrowed, then he tucked a curl behind her ear. "You're stunning, Ilona. No scar can detract from that."

"Right." Tempted to snort and roll her eyes like a teenager, she bent to check the clips on her boots, flipped the hoodie over her helmet, then yanked on the cord stopper. Then, with a brave grin she was far from feeling, she threw herself off the edge. Anything to escape the intensity in his gaze.

She swallowed her scream as she plummeted, the drop rushing wind past her face and threatening to tear off her hoodie. Seconds before her board touched down, she bent her knees to absorb the impact. The wind lashed her cheeks, inflamed her scar, but the exhilaration won out.

She carved through the snow, veering from left to right, squealing, and laughing as she headed for the tower in the distance. The sounds of slapping snow behind her said she wasn't alone and could enjoy this moment without fear of abandonment.

The chilling wind, the warm sunlight, the bright snow, and the crisp air elevated her out of her sorrow, freed her to soar like an eagle. The snow was harder than the sand but easy to work with when she knew the techniques. When she aligned with the tower, she rested her weight on her heels and whipped to a halt, spraying a cloud of white powder. She grinned at an approaching Dane who glided like a graceful ballerina on creatine.

Jake trailed him by a few seconds. "You're a natural."

She shrugged, unclipped the board, and tucked it under her arm. "Now what?"

He nodded to the sheer rock wall hundreds of yards away. "We trudge back to the car."

Each step felt like a mountain rested on her shoulders and her legs like cooked spaghetti, but it brought them closer to the cliff she had leaped off. Sadness struck at the scars they had left in the pristine snow. In the shadows beneath the cliff, Jake pointed north, so up the mountain she went, curving around until the jagged rockface dominated her view but shielded her from some of the chilling wind.

"Do you think the tower is strong enough to handle an avalanche?" She rasped the words, proving her fitness level needed work. Shifts, sleep, shifts, and more sleep had summed up her life for the last three years.

"Dr. Ferguson, who leads the research team, said there'd been a little rumbling which implies tectonic activity below." Dane nudged his chin at the face of the mountain. "There's been a gentle shift of snow. If the two combine, they could be in for an avalanche."

"They need to stay inside the tower if it happens." Jake dug into his back pocket for his buzzing phone. He grunted his name as they hiked higher, nearing the top of Lover's Point. "On our way." He shoved his phone into his pocket and hiked past Ilona with renewed vigor.

"Jake, what's up?" Dane followed him, grabbing her hand to drag her with him. Her thigh muscles protested the abuse.

Jake didn't pause, just kept moving. "Edison got into the catnip again."

"Shit." Dane peeked at Ilona. "Why do we keep that stuff?"

"I've tried confiscating his stash, but they grow their own." Jake removed his gear, tossed his board in the trunk, and the medkit on the backseat before sliding in.

Ilona sliced glances between the two men. "Catnip?" She stacked the board on top of Jake's, the goggles and helmet beside it, then hurried to the front passenger side.

Jake met her gaze. "It's like a drug to cat shifters."

"Drive, Doc. There's no time for your fish-out-of-water impression." Dane guided her around the hood and lifted her into the driver's seat as if she weighed nothing. He leaped over the hood of the car and climbed in, closing the door behind him.

"Hurry, Doc, catnip tends to drive Edison wild, and he starts challenging the younger shifters." Jake patted her shoulder.

She hurried to start the engine with trembling fingers.

Careening to town was easier with the tire tracks dark sludges and ruts, showing her the way. "Um, does Amos know?" She peeked at Dane and hesitated, studying his profile for signs of a polar bear. For a man of his size, he had to be a big animal. Or was that not how it worked?

"Of course, he's half shifter."

She closed her eyes for a second then whipped them open, having forgotten she was driving. "I'm a human doctor. I don't know how to treat...shifters." Animals was what she was thinking. Hell, she couldn't even treat someone's pet pig. Cat shifter? Like in lion, panther, puma? She bit her lip to smother a squeak.

"Relax, we have phenomenal healing properties." Jake patted her shoulder. "Now and then, an injury might be too much for our blood to deal with. That's where you come in."

"What am I supposed to do for a catnip overdose?" When the car jumped a hidden bump, her eyes widened, but she managed to land the SUV on the tarred main road with a jerk. After veering onto the verge, she hit the brakes but kept the engine running. She twisted to face the men. Were they still called men? Were they like a morphing artificial intelligent robot, or was it magic that helped them transform?

She shook her head at the concept of magic and leveled a glare on them, the same look Mom had used on her when her teenage sass had crossed a boundary. "Listen, I don't know what the fuck you two are expecting, but I'm sure as shit not a vet."

"Just drive, Ilona. Head straight for Tuesdays." Jake pointed at the building down the road past Mo's, like she didn't know where the hell it was.

"Fuck. We'll talk about this later, Dane." She floored it, fishtailing the SUV's ass on the road. When she steered into the parking lot in front of the door, she switched off the engine. She didn't move when Dane and Jake leaped out of the SUV and bolted into the bar.

Sighing, she palmed the steering wheel, debating whether to head to Cozy Cromwell's and pack her bags. Dane tucked his head out and waved at her to hurry.

Thunderous crashes from inside the bar mimicked the urgency in his wild gestures. She laughed as hysteria rose to choke her.

Yanking off her gloves, she dropped them onto the seat. She closed the door and ducked under his arm and into the bar.

Chapter Thirteen

PROOF IN THE CLAWS

Among the debris of splintered tables and chairs in Tuesdays, Jake sat on top of a man—Edison, Ilona presumed—whose scrambling feet shifted broken glass on the floor. Jake tried to grab the man's legs but received knee butts in the chest and face for his efforts. The bartender, Aiden, held Edison's arms, pinning them with his weight.

Dane joined the fray, throwing his body across the legs. Jake flipped over and swung a fist. The sound of it striking Edison's jaw echoed in the silence.

Drawing in ragged breaths, Jake relaxed, flashing Ilona a pleased smile. "And no, we don't expect you to handle this."

Aiden peeled himself off the floor, freeing Edison's hands. Ilona blinked at a human limb morphed into a cat's paw. She knelt beside the unconscious man and gathered his hand in hers, marveling at the thick fur and man-sized paw. It twitched as claws extended in slow motion.

"Lona, move." A roar whipped her head up.

Mr. Naked launched himself at her as claws raked across her shoulder. Fire tore through her, summoning tears, then hundreds of pounds landed on top of her, crushing her to the tiled floor.

Air rushed out of her lungs. She gasped, unable to breathe with a man on her chest. He lifted himself off her. She sucked in beer-stench, delicious-man-scented air, sweeter than the first breath of spring. Her swift enjoyment of her ability to live was overshadowed by the hot liquid on her shoulder, and the agony numbing her left arm.

She snuck a glance at Edison to find him unconscious again with Jake sprawled across him. Shoving Mr. Naked back with her good hand, she got to her feet, fury stiffening her body as her wound burned.

"What the fuck?" She threw her good hand in the air while she paced, uncaring that she had an audience. "I'm the fucking doctor here. Who's helping me?" She clenched her jaw. "I could kill Gran and Amos. You too." She pointed at Dane, then Jake, and ignored the sensual blue eyes of the stranger she had no right to ogle. Tightness gripped her chest when her vision spun. She shivered. "I'm not capable of handling this. Not now, maybe not ever. What was Gran thinking?" Tears welled and flowed down her cheeks, but she tossed her head back on a hysterical laugh, sounding like a hyena. "I'm cursed. I'm living evidence magic exists. Cursed, I tell you."

"Come, Lona, let's get you to the clinic." Mr. Naked cupped her cheeks, forcing her to focus on his handsome face, the sharp angle of his jaw, his sensual lips, the softness of his beard.

She giggled. "What, are you going to stitch and bandage me?"

"I can do it." Aiden raised a hand. "I have a little first aid training."

Dane nodded. "I'll drive."

The warmth of Mr. Naked standing so near to her penetrated her jacket. She sighed, leaning into his confident strength as he escorted her outside. He lifted her into the back of the SUV, spreading her across the seat before joining her. When he tucked her against his warmth, she slumped, fighting the ebb and flow of the pain lashing at her.

Her turn to stare. She tightened her fingers on her thighs against the silly urge to stroke his beard. "And you are?"

He arched a brow.

"Well, I can keep calling you Neanderthal, Mr. Naked, Mr. Balls-to-the-wind, but I have a feeling you might prefer your name."

His chuckle rumbled from his belly, vibrating along her side. "Rhys."

"Reece?" She tested his name on her tongue, nodded, and snuggled into him, needing his solid body to prop her up.

Dane pulled off, but the trip was short, not that she tried to look at the wound. There wasn't enough light anyway. Like she weighed nothing, Rhys lifted her into his arms and marched into a dark, dank building. She clung to him, unused to being carried. Burying her nose into the curve of his neck, she squeezed her eyes shut and tried not to savor his mesmerizing cologne.

The flickering lights bathed a cozy yet dusty waiting room, a built-for-one reception counter, and wide-swinging doors. Four doors led off the short passage. After navigating through one into a consultation room, he lowered her onto the bed but kept his hand on her back as if she might faint.

Despite shivering at his touch warming her through the thin fabric of her clothes, she snorted. A Strickland was made of sturdy stock. No fainting here despite the spots circling her vision. That was shock.

Aiden rifled through the cupboards and banged the doors. She smiled at him like she was high. Sharp movements exploded a kaleidoscope of colors across her vision, and parts of her face numbed.

"Edison's fur was mottled, is that normal?" She glanced at Dane, trying to ignore Rhys staring at her. "Mange?" She giggled. "Not that I'm a vet."

Aiden returned with a pile of medical supplies, dumped it on the bed, and gestured to the Mr. Naked to step back.

"Wait, help me remove the jacket." She bit the sleeve and tugged, entangling her right arm.

Rhys peeled the jacket off her, using a snail's caution on her left side. Blood saturated the inner lining and had drenched her shredded white T-shirt.

She grimaced at the thought of raising her arm to peel off the T-shirt. "Cut it off me."

Aiden hesitated. She cursed while twisting and wiggling until she could slide the shirt over her head, grunting and whimpering when each movement bolted fire down her chest. The T-shirt gathered at her neck. She raised an expectant gaze to Rhys. He clenched his jaw, his focus intense as he peeled it off her, his touch surprisingly gentle for his size.

Her white bra was blood-stained, and the strap hung on by a thread. Two lacerations from her shoulder to below her collarbone pumped blood. "Stop the bleeding first. Rhys, apply direct pressure. Aiden, find an analgesic, lidocaine or morphine will do. I don't want to feel anything when you start cleaning."

"Found a vial of morphine." Aiden waved a bottle with clear liquid in it.

"Give me ten milligrams." Fifteen was the standard amount, and even though it was tempting to take more, she wanted to remain awake for whatever the hell this was.

Aiden fumbled as he filled the syringe before hesitating again, unsure where to inject her. She held out her palm, her body trembling from the shock, and her mind taking trips to escape the fire consuming the left side of her chest.

Freaking hell, that hurt. She winced as she injected herself around the lacerations. Minutes later, the burn of morphine added to the agony before dousing it. She sighed, offering a timid smile. "You can clean me now."

"Fuck this shit." Dane removed a dagger from his boot and sliced his palm.

"What the hell are you doing?" She stared at the pooling blood, unable to grasp his motives. "Do you think I can treat you in my condition?"

He curled his fingers into a fist. "Aiden, hold her still."

Rhys slid his hand across her back then lunged toward Dane with a deafening roar. "Don't you fucking dare."

Dane's blue gaze met Rhys's, and a silent power struggle played out. "Protect, Rhys, and last time I checked, I'm the alpha here."

Rhys cursed and ran his hand through his hair. "Ask first...please." He glanced at her, his brow furrowed. Stepping aside, he mouthed, "I'm sorry."

He caught her elbow and stroked a path to her wrist, sending a wave of goosebumps along her skin. Lacing his fingers through hers, he squeezed.

"What's going on?" She sliced glances between them.

But instead of answering her, Dane dribbled his blood into her wounds.

"What the fuck—?" She screamed as shards of electric fire ignored the morphine and tore through her, shuddering and convulsing her body.

As exhaustion drained her petrified muscles, she slumped in Rhys's arms. He guided her to lie down seconds before her vision darkened. Her ears rung, reverberating their words and merging with her untamed heartbeat.

"I'm going to kill you, Dane." As threats went and in her croaking voice, he had to be quaking in his boots. "Why the fuck did you do that?" Whether her strength returned or not, she sat up, slapping Aiden's hands away where he cleaned the wounds.

"Shifter blood heals, Doc." Dane dried his hands then tossed the paper towels into the trash can. As if he understood what she needed, he showed her his palm.

Gasping, she scooted off the bed to hold his hand still as she ran her thumb across his unmarred palm. She grabbed his other hand in case he deceived her by showing her the wrong palm. "And you knew giving me your blood would heal me?"

At his shrug, she thumped him on the arm, bruising her knuckles then reared back.

Chuckling, he caught her swinging fist. "Get back on the bed, Doc. Let Aiden clean your wounds, and I'll treat you to a slice of Mo's apple pie."

"Apple pie?" Like that could make up for his mistreatment of her, using her as a test subject. Didn't he know that blood carried diseases? Probably not, the idiot.

Rhys lifted her onto the bed before she could kick Dane. Her leg swung wild.

Dane grinned. "Now, now, Doc. Wounds first, then pie."

Furious anger pulsed the morphine and Dane's fucking blood through her. She grumbled under her breath, planning on heading to Cozy Cromwell's and packing her bags. Jake mentioned a hospital north of Coedwig. She would request a full analysis of her blood.

First, she had to eat pie. There was no way Dane would let her leave with the bloody Lunar Festival coming up. To escape, she would have to sneak out.

She glared at Rhys. He'd apologized, had tried to stop Dumb Dane from doing this. Tears stung her eyes, and she hurried to dip her chin to her chest, the stench of her bloodied wound twitching her nose. She was far beyond her comfort zone. With these three men running roughshod over her, she didn't stand a chance. Rhys kept a hand on her elbow, its warmth strengthening her. She clasped his other hand, offering him a squeeze in thanks before glaring at Dane again.

"Traitor," she whispered to Aiden when he leaned closer.

He winced, but his continued silence sliced guilt through her. What was a young male supposed to do against Dane? Alpha? Fuck.

With her drowning in Rhys's jacket, he bundled her into the SUV, her hand trapped in his. She wasn't foolish enough to open the door and throw herself from a moving vehicle. Despite her mumbling she could walk, he carried her into the diner and sat her beside him like she was an energetic toddler.

Dane and Aiden slid into the booth and watched her, waiting. She stared at the plate before her. A generous portion of apple pie with a dollop of whipped cream tempted her to dive in. Hunger pangs twisted her insides, and perhaps she was hangry too.

"Don't you like pie?" Mo served fresh coffee, with Aiden drawing a bubblegum milkshake toward him.

What was he, a four-year-old? The aroma of coffee, bubblegum, and cinnamon gurgled Ilona's stomach.

"Extra cream, please, Mo." Ilona forced a smile and gripped the fork with her right hand.

Aiden had bandaged her despite the awkward placement of the wound, showing his first aid experience. She couldn't be angry with him since he hadn't lied. The morphine would wear off soon, and she dreaded the waves of crippling agony made worse by the thought of stitches. She'd examine it later to check whether she needed a few.

Edison's claws had sliced from her deltoid muscle, across the clavicular head to the sternocostal head and missed, by some miracle, her cephalic vein. He hadn't punctured her lung since her breathing was easy with no bubbling. Nor had he cut through a ligament, evidenced by her ability to use her shoulder and arm. The only pain she had suffered was from the attack and when Dane's blood had dripped into her wounds.

More whipped cream arrived, and she hurried to eat the pie under Mo's vigilance. Ilona hummed at the sweet, spicy, cinnamon flavor coating her tongue. Rhys shifted beside her, where he toyed with his untouched coffee. Licking her spoon, she snuck a glance at him and sighed.

Wow. With the diner's lighting catching the gold streaks in his hair and the deep blue in his eyes swirling with something hot and intense, she was lost, staring at him like a pubescent teen ogling the male models in a men's sports magazine.

"Good?" Aiden grinned with blue-stained teeth. "Mo's chicken soup is better."

"Why would you need chicken soup? Do shifters get colds?" She tried to ignore Rhys's fingers wrapped around hers, his thumb stroking across her knuckles. Removing her hand from his was something she should do, but she couldn't bring herself to. Nor did she meet Dane's gaze. Anger simmered at his irresponsible behavior. And he called himself a mayor? She snorted. Safest person to chat to was sweet Aiden.

Jake stamped snow off his boots as he entered the diner, slid into the booth next to Dane, and squeezed Aiden against the window. "How are you feeling, Doc?" He gestured to the pie. Mo hurried to fill his order.

Ilona gritted her teeth and flicked a glance at Jake. "Ask Mayor Ass."

Dane winced and grumbled something under his breath.

Jake jerked and twisted to gape at him. "You didn't." He ran a hand through his gray hair with light flickering off his earring. "Sorry, Ilona, his intentions were good."

"Intentions?" she squeaked, and instead of ranting at poor Jake, she shoveled more pie into her mouth.

She was hungry, and the pie was amazing—hot and sweet against the cool whipped cream. No matter what she decided tonight, she would enjoy this treat.

"How's Edison?" Aiden steered her focus to him.

In that second, she loved him. Her emotions rollercoastered out of control. She wanted to crawl into a hole and not show her face for weeks.

"In jail." Jake sighed. "Come, Doc, I'll drive you to Harriet's."

Ilona dropped her fork onto the plate and froze. Rhys blocked her way. Her breath caught when she raised her wide eyes. "Um, I'd like to leave...please." Squaring her shoulders, she waited until he climbed out. With a mumbled 'thank you,' she scrambled to her feet. She circled the booth to squeeze Aiden's shoulder in thanks and ignored Dane.

The trip to the bed and breakfast was in silence until Jake stopped outside the house. "Monitor your wounds, Doc, and if it heals, think about going easy on a panicking polar bear." He winked and left her standing on the pathway.

Dane was a polar bear? She shook her head, trying to focus on the important things like what the hell had just happened. Harriet ushered Ilona up the stairs, clucking under her breath. She must have heard about the incident and somehow understood Ilona didn't have the energy to talk about it.

As soon as she stood in her en suite, she peeled off Rhys's jacket, pausing to shove her face into the lining. Fuck me, James, he smelled good, like freedom, and sex, and her deepest longing. Careful, she draped it across the chair, then stripped the rest of her clothing, piece by piece. The reflection in the mirror wasn't the excited med student she once was. This woman had deep sorrow-filled green eyes, messy auburn hair, too pale skin, and a puckered red scar running from eyebrow to chin, tugging her facial muscles down.

Now a white bandage crossed her chest.

She didn't recognize this woman even though there were elements of her parents in her features. Whatever prettiness she had before the accident, she used it to charm unhappy or distressed patients.

She forced her lips into a smile, but it made her grotesque, like something out of a horror movie. Smothering a sob, she focused on what she could control. The sting of the tapes clinging to her skin proved the morphine was wearing off sooner than it should have. She frowned, not feeling anything but stiffness in her shoulder like she had played a squash tournament.

A cry escaped her lips at the red scratches where the lacerations had been. She stumbled, bumping into the shower door before leaping forward to bring her shoulder into focus. No, this was impossible. Her wounds looked weeks instead of hours old.

Electric excitement warred with cold fear at this discovery. Did other doctors know, or was she the first? She gasped. Amos knew. Stepping into the shower, she raised her face to the warm spray as possibilities fired across her mind. What else could their blood do? What could it cure? Cancer? Leukemia? Trauma victims? Brain inactivity?

Ice tingled her scalp, slithered down the back of her neck to trickle into her hair. She whimpered at the realization her dad might have been healed if the hospital had shifter blood in storage.

Washing her hair and body was easier than she had expected, with her injured shoulder not hindering her movements. As she slipped into bed with her hair in a towel, she tried to think of a way to pump Dane for information about shifter abilities without having to forgive him.

In the end, she succumbed to sleep with the phantom sensation of Rhys's warm hands caressing her hair and holding her hand.

Rhys sprawled on his bed, unable to silence his bear and the fire scorching his veins. The excitement thrumming his nerve endings were all thanks to one woman. Lona. He grinned. She hadn't tarred him with Dane's brush, and for that, he was grateful. To stop Dane, Rhys would have had to challenge him for leadership. One of them might have died, and if not, then their friendship would forever be altered.

Rhys had been tempted. The fear darkening the brown of her hazel eyes had wrenched his heart, urging him to toss caution to the wind. He rubbed his chest, hoping to calm his bear. Somewhere in the house was Ilona, and he longed to find her room, to sneak in, and to watch her sleep. Perhaps his bear would find peace in knowing she was well.

Grunting, he rolled onto his side. She was only one woman, but more than that, she wasn't Callie. Hope flared like an unfolding blossom bathed in sunlight. He would pursue whatever wove between them, and even if—he growled—he never saw her again, he had moved on from his silly suckblood infatuation.

An argument broke out in the hall, but he tried to ignore it, despite his advanced hearing.

"You fucking bled on me without asking me first or warning me. Humans can't mix blood types, idiot. Not to mention the diseases transmitted via blood. But if you'd bothered to ask..." Lona's voice was husky.

Her passionate fury poured molten desire through Rhys, raising the hairs on his arms and snagging the rhythm of his heart. What was she doing awake at this late hour?

"It healed you, though," Dane mumbled.

She had the balls to argue with the alpha. Rhys admired that.

Palm hitting flesh followed. He grinned, not the slightest bit sorry for Dane.

"Feel better?" Silence met Dane's question.

"A little."

He chuckled. "Come here, Doc."

"I don't want a hug." She squealed then grumbled, "Bloody bear."

"Here I was hoping you were developing a crush on me."

"Hardly. I would like nothing more than to rip your balls out through your throat. As a doctor, despite knowing it's physically impossible, the thought of trying fills me with wicked joy."

Rhys winced at the mental image but laughed anyway. Feisty, Dane had called her. Rhys couldn't agree more.

Dane growled, "What the hell? I thought I was forgiven?"

"You are, but that doesn't mean you can get all lovey-dovey with me. The number of women clinging to your impressive biceps leaves me cold, Mayor Ass. Besides, I'm temporary, remember."

"Fine, but I'll wear you down."

A pause followed. "Why? To what end?" Curiosity filled Lona's voice. "Y'know, never mind. I'm not interested for...reasons."

"I'll ask your gran—"

"Night, Dane." A door banged shut.

Dane whispered to his bear, unaware Rhys listened in.

So, his friend liked the doctor? Rhys smothered a chuckle lest Dane heard him and intruded. Things had become interesting. Despite Dane warning Rhys away from the woman, he had no intention of stepping aside for his dear old friend to sweep her out from under him.

He growled and squeezed his eyes shut, recalling her pinned beneath him, moaning at each bite of her apple pie, and climbing over him like he was nothing but a hay barrel. Fuck. He threw himself onto his back and splayed his arms out wide.

The way his blood pulsed through his body, ignoring this attraction wasn't possible. And all was fair in love and war, right?

CHAPTER FOURTEEN

VILLAGE DOCTOR

POUNDING ON HER DOOR dragged Ilona from sleep. Growling at the intrusion, she flopped over, feeling like she had been drawn and quartered through the snow backward. She yanked the pillow over her head, praying the person would go away.

"Doc, two kids broke their arms. Coedwig needs you." Dane's voice was muffled as if he stood to close to the door.

Two? At the same time? "They can heal." Guilt pinged through her heart. She had sworn an oath to do no harm. Her circumstances didn't mean her vow no longer mattered.

"Broken bones work the same on shifters. If they're not aligned properly—"

"So help me, Dane." She sucked in a shuddering breath. But he was right, and her not going was harming the children, wasn't it?

Silence rang out, deep rumbles followed, and a thump jerked her fully awake.

"I have coffee." That was Rhys's voice, right?

No, Dane waited at the door. No point in getting wishful and dragging her dreams into reality. That way led to disappointment.

She flipped onto her back and threw a pillow at the door. "Come in."

In her boy shorts and a baggy T-shirt, she was more than decent. Her hair was a mess, but she didn't care. Taking the time to brush it would only encourage Dane. Developing a crush on him would never happen. She was a one-man kind of woman. Not to mention the eager hopefuls flirting with him were striking, beautiful, and unscarred.

The door banged open, and he crept in, balancing a tray. The aromas of coffee, waffles, bacon, and sausage filled her bedroom.

"You're wonderful." She sighed, smoothing a spot on her duvet.

He lowered the tray, his tongue sticking out in concentration. Then he sat on the edge of the bed and almost spilled the coffee.

"Jake's warming the clinic and trying to find out how it happened." Dane ran a hand over his face which didn't lighten the dark circles under his eyes. "If you hurry, we can be there in fifteen minutes. I've asked Harriet to pack your things, assuming you're moving into your house when we return from the clinic?"

Ilona cupped the coffee mug to her chest between sips and nibbles of bacon. Did she want to stay? To discover the possibilities of his blood? "Yes, thanks." She studied his cheek for any sign of the slap she had given him the previous night. Grimacing, she ran her thumb along the edge of her cup. "Sorry about..." She nudged her chin at his cheek.

"I should apologize. I wanted you well, and as an alpha, I don't ask first before I do something." He captured her hand holding the last bite of a waffle. "Dr. Ilona, please may I have your permission to share my blood should any harm befall you?" Those big ice-blue eyes, those pouting lips...shit, the man was a natural lady killer.

She smiled despite her best intentions. "Charmer."

He grinned. "I'll take that as a yes."

When he released her hand, she popped the piece of waffle into her mouth, chewing as she assessed this virile man in his jeans and T-shirt. She sucked on her thumb before gesturing to the door, asking him to leave. Then froze. Rhys filled the space, his shoulders almost brushing the door frame.

"Morning." She gulped and clasped her hands on her lap. Fussing with her hair would accomplish what?

"How are you feeling?" His deep voice caressed her ears, sparking goosebumps along her skin.

She shivered, relishing the tingles sliding down her back. Her nipples pebbled under the T-shirt but covering them would bring attention to her reaction.

When conversation turns awkward, take control of the situation. She lifted her coffee for another sip. "Dane, give me ten minutes. I'll meet you out front."

He glowered, scooped up the tray, then rose.

Rhys stepped aside to let him pass, entered her room, then closed the door behind him. Her breath caught at having him alone. Right, like she knew how to seduce. Not that she wanted to. No, of course not.

"So?" He grinned and scattered her heartbeat

That wasn't possible, medically. She pinched her lips and dipped her chin, hoping to hide her burning cheeks behind the fall of her hair.

"How do you feel?" He crossed the room to stand at the foot of the bed.

His black jeans hugged thick thighs; his white T-shirt clung to his ripped chest and torso. But more than running her hands over his indents and hard edges, she longed to bury her fingers in his hair, to rub her thumb over his beard and bottom lip.

"Good." At her rasp, she cleared her throat.

"I'm sorry. I couldn't stop Dane." Rhys's blue gaze rested on her wounded shoulder. "Politics and pack boundaries play a part."

She shrugged. "I won't lie. I was super pissed at him. The worst is that his crazy antics worked." Tugging on her collar, she revealed the red streaks.

Rhys kneeled beside her bed and ran his fingertips along the scars. She didn't dare breathe, expecting herself to wheeze. Not that she could recall when last a man had touched her with such ease. And how much she liked his fingers on her would be suppressed until she could analyze it on lonely nights.

Flipping the blankets aside, she swung her legs off the bed, expecting him to step back. He didn't. Instead, he caught her fingers and helped her up. An inch separated them, but he didn't release her. He toyed with her hands, gliding and sliding his over hers. His breathing shuddered, and he raised trembling fingers to brush away a curl covering her eye.

"What are your plans for the day?" His voice thrummed through her like the soft roar of a steep waterfall, promising a cool swim but with devastating consequences.

"Mend broken arms, clean the clinic, move into my gran's old home, and drive to Lover's Point a few times." Peaceful by trauma standards. The weight on her chest eased. She could do this.

"Need help?"

She stilled and met his gaze, drowning in the blue depths while the intensity in them promised sweaty nights and ecstasy. "No, but thanks." Placing her palms on his chest, she tried to slip past, brushing a hip across something incredibly hard.

He hissed and gripped her elbows for a second.

"Rhys?" She smiled. "I have to get ready."

"I know." Closing his eyes, he sucked in a sharp breath then crossed to the door. "If you need anything—?"

"Thank you." She followed him, but his gaze dipped to her bare legs.

He groaned, stepped backward through the door and shut it with a decided snap.

Blinking at the door, she took a few moments to slow her breathing before dressing. She tugged on jeans, clipped on a bra, slipped on a forest-green T-shirt, then a jacket, before dropping onto the edge of the bed to don socks and boots. A quick brush of her hair and teeth, and with a minute to spare, she threw her things into her bag. She didn't want to overburden Harriet.

Rhys's deep voice rumbled a greeting from the passage. Harriet laughed at something he said. When Ilona left her room, Harriet had her hand on the doorknob to the room across the passage. If that was Rhys's room, Ilona was wise to move out—temptation and all that.

"Morning, did you sleep well?" Harriet's parchment cheeks were bright pink, and her gray eyes sparkled.

"Of course." Ilona wrapped an arm around Harriet's fragile shoulders for a gentle hug.

Dane appeared at the bottom of the stairs. "Will you two quit gossiping? I have two cubs—"

"I'm coming." Ilona hurried down the stairs, leaped the last two steps, and nudged him out of the way. That wasn't easy to do with his great bulk, but she managed to budge him an inch.

"How's the shoulder?" He narrowed his mischievous eyes, a dimple appearing in his cheek.

"Good, like you need to ask, Mayor Ass."

"Hey, am I still not forgiven?" He grumbled under his breath as he trailed her to his SUV.

"Forgiven, not forgotten." She climbed into the passenger side, hoping he didn't demand she drive.

A few minutes later, he steered into a parking spot in front of the brick building she didn't have fond memories of. They could have walked to it, but the wind had teeth this morning, nipping at any exposed part.

"Morning, Doc. How ya feeling?" Jake fell into step beside her.

"Good. Dane and I need to talk about the impact of shifter blood on human diseases and whether someone's researching this. Is it common knowledge?" She spun on her heel and walked backward, meeting Dane's gaze.

He shrugged. "Over the last few decades, scientists showed interest in certain townsfolk and their healing abilities. They chalked it up to the fresh air and healthy food sparking many diet fads."

She nodded. "Mediterranean?"

He grinned. "As a polar bear, I see nothing wrong with living off fish."

"No, thanks, give me beef, elk, or bison, and I'm happy." Jake held the door open for her.

Dane leaned in to whisper, though why he bothered when Jake could hear him, she didn't know. "Lion."

She gasped. "But...how's that possible? Lions don't roam these lands."

"Over the centuries, shifters migrated to safe harbors, so to speak. Now we're a mismatch of species, our genes blurring. The odds of all your cubs shifting into the same animal have more to do with luck than anything else." Jake grinned. "But my genes are dominant. All my cubs are lions."

"Does the purity of those genes matter? I assume, as an alpha, your polar bear must be strong."

Dane beamed, rubbing his chest like she'd complimented him.

She pushed through the swinging doors, heading for the faint voices in conversation.

He shrugged. "Works the same as humans, Doc. In a family of brown eyes, a kid with blue eyes is born."

She pursed her lips, surprised at his insight. With a sigh, she nudged the consulting room door open. Two boys sat on the bed scrapping and swinging punches even as they nursed their injured arms.

With no overprotective furrowing of their brows, two women chatted, their shoulders relaxed. When Dane squeezed past Ilona into the room, they unfolded their arms, sharing smiles in greeting—neither were flirtatious.

"All right, who do we have here?" Ilona paused in front of the fighting boys.

In torn jeans, grubby shirts, dirty fingernails, and their hair standing on end, they were the poster image of rambunctious boys.

"I'm Cammy." The blond raised his gaze to meet hers, nudging the brown-haired boy beside him.

"I'm Jonny." He waved with his good hand.

"So, what happened?" She smiled to soften the question.

They snuck glances at each other. Barely suppressed laughter brightened their eyes and split their cheeks with mischievous grins. When neither explained, Ilona couldn't help but smother a smile. They must have been doing something they weren't supposed to.

"We've broken bones before. This time, Mommy noticed." Cammy rolled his eyes. "She damn near lost her shit."

"Language." A woman behind Ilona grumbled something, and Cammy stilled his fidgeting.

"Who's first?" Ilona schooled her features into a stoic expression, hoping she appeared professional behind her chuckling.

"Me." Cammy offered a cheeky smile and held out his arm, not bothering to suppress a wince.

"Let me see." To assess the damage, she clasped his arm with a gentle touch.

It had begun to heal. Yellow and green bruises along his ulnaris and minimi muscles didn't prove he had broken his radius or ulna. She assessed Jonny's arm, which had similar bruising, almost like they had clamped their left arms in a vise.

"X-rays?" She arched a brow at Dane.

In a small town, she wasn't sure what technology was available. At Amity, the best and latest machines and techniques helped her treat the sick and injured children in her care. Then again, despite having all the equipment and knowledge at her disposal, she couldn't save her father.

"We used to have an old one tucked in the storeroom." Dane gestured down the passage. "It died."

She grimaced. No X-rays meant assuming the worst. There was a high probability they weren't compound fractures as evidenced by no bones piercing the skin, but that wasn't a definitive diagnosis. Shit, all she could do was prescribe orthopedic arm guards. No X-rays worried her. She needed to see how the bones had broken, to ensure they would heal aligned.

Facing the mothers, she plastered on a polite smile. "Any idea what caused this?"

One blonde shook her head. She peeked around Ilona at Cammy. "Knowing him, he launched himself from tree to tree believing he could fly."

The other mother nodded. "That was the cause last time, but we only found out afterward." She wrung her hands. "We're shifters, and if our alpha trusts you…" She thrust out a hand. "I'm Denise, Jonny's mother."

The blonde woman blushed. "Sorry, I must have left my manners in the other truck. I'm Beth Dunn, Cammy's mom."

"Dunn?" Ilona flicked a glance at Jake hovering in the doorway.

"Guilty." He grinned. "Beth's my mate, and Cameron's my youngest cub."

Ilona smiled as she lifted each boy off the table. They hurtled out the door and along the passage like nothing was wrong. Dane's grumbles as he chased after them lightened her heart.

"Please tell me you have a pharmacy?" She scowled at Jake's shaking head. "They need orthopedic arm guards. We don't use plaster of paris or fiberglass anymore."

"Write out the prescription, and I'll send someone to Glenfell." He sighed. "Sorry, Doc, that's all I can do."

"They need to be fitted. But they'll probably heal before you have the armguards. Sounds like this happens often, so having them on hand might not be a bad idea." She gestured to the mothers to follow her, escorting them from the consulting room to the reception area. Rifling through the reception desk, she found Amos's prescription pad. "These are standard and should be over the counter."

With ease, Dane held the boys by the scruffs of their T-shirts. "What do you need, Doc?"

"I want a cast, Doc. Can I have one?" Cammy stopped in mid-wrestle as soon as Dane carried them into the reception area.

"Me first." Jonny swung a punch, and they scrapped again.

"Even better, boys, you get to wear a specialized armguard like the knights of old." Ilona ran her hand over her arm then assumed a defensive stance holding an imaginary shield.

Their mouths parted in awe, while their eyes twinkled with excitement.

It was Jonny who asked, "Can we have swords?"

"When sickness or a wound brought a knight low, they stayed inside by the fire demanding roast chicken and mead." Ilona used a stage whisper. "I'd ask for cake and popcorn."

They beamed before dancing around their mothers with their pouting lips and puppy-dog eyes, making loud demands for mead.

"Thank you, Doc." Denise shuffled her son through the front door.

Jake picked up Cammy, and with a nod to Ilona, escorted Beth to their SUV.

"Well done." Dane leaned against the doorframe with his legs crossed at the ankles.

"Thanks. I wanted to do my fellowship in pediatric oncology, but—" She bit her lip to silence her words. No way was she bringing up her parents, not when she'd accomplished something today, even if it was peace of mind for the mothers. "You get coffee. I need to clean this place." She ran her finger along the top of the reception desk and grimaced at the thick layer of dust.

"Ilona—"

She whipped her gaze to his. "I'm not talking about it, Dane. Help or get out."

He stared, a frown marring his brow and twisting his lips. "I'll get the coffee."

She peered at him through the glass doors at his broad back, then with a flick of her hand to wipe away the tears, she searched for the janitorial closet.

Chapter Fifteen

A Good Day

Between dusting, mopping the floors, and chasing a disruptive Dane out the clinic, Ilona hurtled the rental along the road to Lover's Point. Knowing it like the back of her hand might save lives, and if Jake said she needed to prepare herself, then she had to practice. She fishtailed the SUV onto the road, skidding to a halt on the graveled tarmac.

Aiden skipped down the steps at Mo's and headed toward Cozy Cromwell's.

Ilona lowered the window. "Morning, Mr. First-Aid." She blew her hair out of her face, aware she must look a fright in her dust-covered clothing.

"Hey, Doc." He shoved his hands deep into his jeans acting like the freezing wind was but a gentle spring breeze. "How ya feeling?" He bit his lip and looked away.

She switched off the engine and leaped out, darting around the hood to tug his hand out of his pocket to squeeze it. "Aiden, come on, it was an accident. I don't blame you. We all thought Edison was unconscious." His hand was oven hot. She shivered as its warmth penetrated her glove.

"I'm sorry, Doc. If I'd only reacted faster..." He sighed, releasing her fingers to rub up and down her biceps. "Rhys chewed me a new one, and he was right. You're human, and your reflexes aren't as fast as ours."

"Rhys did what?" She gasped. The nerve of the man.

"He's trying to ensure you stay alive, Doc."

She paused, assessing her actions to and from the clinic, or along the road to Lover's Point. "I wasn't aware I was in danger."

"Like you said last night, if you're injured, we're doomed."

"Doomed?" She chuckled. "You could call Rebel or drive a doctor over from Glenfell." She hugged him as she said, "I don't blame you, Aiden." Stepping back, she ruffled his hair as she would do if she had a brother. "Where you off to? Need a lift?"

"Visiting Rhys at Cozy Cromwell's."

Rhys... She'd like to visit him too, maybe sit on his lap, let him loop his muscled arm around her, brush his beard across her chin, press her lips to his lush ones. She cleared her throat. "Want me to drop you off on the way to the clinic?"

"I'm good, thanks, Doc. Come by Tuesdays for a beer tonight, on me."

"I'll text you if I do, but it might be late. I don't want to treat brawlers nor fend off desperate men looking for a partner for the night." She laughed. "Not that a burning STD requires emergency treatment."

With a wave, she climbed into the rental. The truth was, she wasn't in the mood to sip beer and doubted she would be. As she stood there, her muscles throbbed at the abuse she had put them through cleaning the clinic. When Amos returned, she would give him a piece of her mind. Who left a medical facility in such a state? Sure, shifters didn't suffer from human diseases, or so they claimed, but hygiene should matter. What if the next patient was human?

Shaking her head, she parked in the nearest spot to the clinic, hoping to reduce the wind's chances of sneaking into her clothing. Harriet waited in the reception area, humming an indiscernible tune. On the chair beside her sat a basket.

"I brought lunch." She leaped up when Ilona opened and shut the front door with swift movements. The clinic was toasty warm.

Ilona slipped out of her jacket and hang it on the hooks provided. "You shouldn't have, Harriet." Her stomach gurgled on cue. "I'm grateful, though."

"It's nothing much. Just a roast chicken with Dijon mustard and peppers on rye, a slice of chocolate cake, and a flask of my vanilla bean coffee."

"Nothing much?" Ilona grinned. "It sounds heavenly."

She scooped up the basket and gestured to a door leading off the reception area. After discovering Amos's office during her search this morning, she'd tackled it first, wiping the bookshelves and all the medical books he had collected over the years. A stack of papers sat on the corner of the desk, which she would sort through tomorrow.

The mahogany desk gleamed after the polish she gave it, and the Persian rug no longer had a layer of dust on it. The window faced the side of Harriet's house and behind it where the snow-covered fields met the forest stretching to the horizon.

"Did you bring enough for two?" Ilona set the basket centerstage of the desk and flipped it open. Delicious aromas teased her nose, mingling with the crisp spine scent of the polisher.

"Just coffee." Harriet beamed. "I needed a break too."

"I don't know how you do it, cooking so much and managing a bed and breakfast."

She shrugged. "I have someone who helps in the kitchen. Since Dane moved in, I don't feel alone. Although, a little quiet time is never a bad thing."

Ilona plated the sandwiches, then grabbed a coffee mug for a refill, pouring coffee into the lid for Harriet. Biting into the sandwich, she groaned. "I didn't know I was so hungry."

Harriet laughed. "I thought as much. I can't stay long. With two men to feed, I need to ensure the portions are sufficient, and I have a cake waiting for a little love. I finished packing your things after I laundered a few of your items. I hope you don't mind. Dane delivered a bag or two of groceries to your new home. He wanted to warm the house so it would be ready for you when you finished for the day."

Tears pressed behind Ilona's eyes. She struggled to swallow the bite of sandwich past the lump in her throat. None of her neighbors in Fenneg had been this thoughtful. Hell, she couldn't pick them out in a line-up. Dane and Harriet's unexpected kindness squeezed Ilona's chest like a vise.

"Thank you." It wasn't enough to convey how she felt, but it was all she could think to say.

"When you come by to fetch your bag, please take a plate of food with you. You're too thin, my girl." Harriet sipped coffee with grace as if she took tea with a queen. "You know, you're the talk of the town."

"I assumed as much. What with Edison and the two boys this morning—"

"That did liven up conversations at Mo's, along with Rhys carrying you like a knight would a damsel-in-distress." Harriet laughed, but her smile faded. "The talk is about the Devereaux part of Mona's name, Ilona."

"What?" Ilona frowned. "Well, that's odd." She flicked a dismissive hand. "Who's asking?"

"Rhys," Harriet answered.

Ilona's heartrate spiked. Not that she could say if it was from alarm, or just from hearing his name. Though, she sure as hell hoped it was the former. "I'll get to the bottom of this."

Harriet nodded. "What are your plans for the rest of the day? More cleaning?"

"I'm afraid so." Ilona scanned the office, shoving the last bite into her mouth. "And a few more trips to Lover's Point."

Harriet rose, splaying her fingers on the desk to brace herself. "Then I'll be off. I'll have Dane or Rhys deliver your luggage to your house. In case you work late, or I miss seeing you tonight, come for coffee sometime."

Ilona escorted the older woman to the front door. "Will do, and thanks again, Harriet. You've made this trip special for me."

Harriet's smile was sweet, yet her eyes shimmered with unshed tears. "You're a darling, Ilona."

"Don't overwhelm me with flattery. It will go straight to my head." She gripped the handle, snapped the door shut, and sighed. Harriet meandered along the salted walkway in nothing but a cashmere cardigan for warmth.

With a shake of her head, Ilona faced the next section to clean—the reception area. But only after her cake. Grinning, she hurried to the office, slid into the still-warm chair, and flicked a finger through the dark chocolate icing sugar.

She closed her eyes, relishing the sweet, smoky taste before taking a huge bite of the cake. The clinic had been dirty for who knew how long. Half an hour longer wouldn't matter when there was cake to devour.

That was how Dane found her, bent over a slice of cake like a crack addict, with icing on her nose, and a steaming cup of coffee beside her.

"I'm not sharing," she mumbled while sucking on a thumb.

"Come between a woman and chocolate—are you insane? I like my face the way it is, thank you. Harriet has me doing another run to your house. Need anything?"

He was such a great bear of a man with the sweetest of hearts. Ilona put the spoon down with which she butchered the slice of cake and pushed herself out of her chair.

She spread her arms wide. "Gimme a hug, you bear."

Dane threw out his hands to hold her back. "Um, no, not with chocolate all over you."

"What? When I offer a hug, you run? That's not very mayoral of you." She grinned, but it faded. "You have my thanks for making the house occupiable."

"Gotta keep the new doc happy. Just doing my mayoral duty." He winked, wiped her nose, then sauntered out.

She was tempted to watch him leave, but there was cake. Dane was right. Chocolate came first, always.

She'd call him later about a little trip to Edison's.

Fighting a slight case of despondency at finding himself alone at breakfast, Rhys strolled alongside Aiden, trying not to breathe too deeply. The feminine scent clinging to his jacket and Aiden's had his pacing bear in an uproar. Rhys would have preferred Lona to return his jacket personally, but she had asked Harriet. He gritted his teeth, trying to force his tense muscles to relax. With each lashing wind, he caught the familiar scents of lavender and antiseptic.

"Who hugged you?" Unable to stay the question meant he was unable to look away from Aiden's matching gaze. He dreaded the answer, with the vicious bite of jealousy lashing his chest.

"Doc." Aiden grinned. "She didn't want me to feel guilty about last night."

Rhys pursed his lips. Last night, when Lona had been plastered against him, when she had filled his arms and relied on him to care for her. That last night? He forced one foot in front of the other, lest he spun on his heels and hurried to Cromwell's. No, she was at the clinic.

He tilted his head and ended up eyeing the brown building uphill from Harriet's. The urge to visit, to speak to Lona, to tease a smile to her pinched lips and to touch her, halted his footsteps.

"When are you thinking of going home?" Aiden's question snapped Rhys out of his madness.

He shrugged, falling into step alongside him again. "I'm not sure."

"It's early afternoon, but I need a beer or a shot of whisky." Aiden pointed to Tuesday's.

So did Rhys, because how to woo Ilona was beyond him. No matter what approach he thought of, either he or his bear dismissed it. He slid onto the stool after hanging up his jacket and thrummed his fingers on the clean wooden counter.

Two regulars argued to one side, and desperate for the distraction, Rhys narrowed his hearing.

"She's mean," the old cougar said. "Today, she arrived on my doorstep and jabbed me."

"You have mange, you old cat." The wolf chuckled. "You're lucky she cared after last night's fiasco."

"Now, Jillie, I said I was sorry." The cougar growled. "But no, my apology meant nothing. She had Dane pin me to the ground like a common criminal. I had snow up my nose." His cheeks flushed a ruddy red. "It was damn near embarrassing."

Rhys shot a glance at the clock above Aiden's head. Perhaps another run before nighttime? His bear rumbled with eagerness—a feeling Rhys was happy to share. What was Lona doing now? Had she made headway at the clinic? Fuck, he should just succumb to the urge and pop in for a visit.

"She's our doctor now that Amos's chasing tail," Jillie said.

Rhys's attention snapped onto the older shifter. They were talking about Lona. "What do you think of the new doc?"

Jillie sipped her wine spritzer. "I have to admit, I like the way she treated Edison after what he did. Takes a true healer. And that she hasn't gone soft on Dane is impressive." She chuckled. "I'm starting to like her, but if you think she'll give you the time of day, even after last night's heroism, I don't know. She takes after her grandmother, that's for sure."

Rhys clenched his jaw as his bear went berserk, roaring demands he couldn't obey. He didn't need advice from strangers on how to seduce a woman. Well, he did, but no one needed to know that. "I'm not planning on mating the woman," he bellowed, then lowered his voice when the bar stilled. A pissed-off alpha tended to raise hackles. "I'd like to find out if she's family of Callie and Valerie." His eye twitched at that blatant lie. Right.

"Oh, then sure. She might be." Jillie shrugged. "I have a vague recollection of Mona being from this side of the country. Might even harken from Inner City."

His heart danced then settled into a tribal rhythm. Lona was a Devereaux, but how diluted was the connection? Callie had the right blood but was the wrong woman. Perhaps Ilona with the right blood could be the right woman? A woman he could mate.

"Doc said she'd text if she planned to pop by." Aiden grinned, interrupting Rhys's thoughts. "It'll be late if she does stop for a beer. She said something about brawls petering out with most having found a willing partner for the night."

With his bear excited, Rhys agreed to wait. Minutes turned into hours, and she didn't show. Tossing notes onto the counter, he saluted Aiden, then left. In his SUV, Rhys gripped his steering wheel hard enough to bend it. The metal groaned, forcing him to release it. He needed to run, to rid himself and his bear of this restlessness.

His irrational behavior irritated him, making his teeth itch. How desperate was he to see the woman? What, like letting her know he only liked the idea of her because she might have Callie's blood flowing through her veins? Yeah, that would go down well.

He drove to Cozy Cromwell's and parked his SUV in front. Icy snow buffeted his body as he stripped off his clothing, flinging the items onto the seat before shutting the door. It was too late for a naked man jogging around Harriet's house to arouse suspicion. Most would assume he was taking his beast for a run. A minute later, he galumphed through the forest. His heavy tread shook snow off the lower branches and trembled the hardened earth beneath him. His bear rumbled in joy when the wind ruffled their fur.

He had missed this. The moon was almost full, promising an entertaining few days in Coedwig. Perhaps he should corner Ilona under the guise of seeking information on her lineage. He sucked in a breath, wishing her scent filled his lungs. Tomorrow, he would have Noah trace the connection. With that decision made, Rhys gave his bear full rein, again.

Chapter Sixteen

Well-Meaning Intruder

A scraping noise pierced the fog of sleep. Ilona twitched then snuggled deeper under the blankets, dismissing the sound as a branch against a window. But when banging followed, she sat up and shivered. Cold air lashed across her bare arms, pebbling her unprotected nipples in her thin tank. The house had been warmer last night, but in the pre-dawn temperatures, the fireplace and central heating couldn't cope.

She swung her legs off the side of the bed, her knees chilling in seconds. Better pajamas might be a good idea. Ripping the quilt off the bed, she whipped it around her and paused, listening for the direction of the noises.

Something tinkled, like glass touching glass. She spun, searching for a weapon of some sort. A boot? An electric toothbrush? Smothering a groan, she gripped the quilt at her chest and peeled her bedroom door open. Sticking to the side of the passage, she crept forward, one well-placed foot at a time, keeping her breathing shallow and silent despite her deafening heartbeat. The wall against her shoulder offered some comfort.

The closer she came to the kitchen, the more familiar the sounds: the popping of toast, the sizzle of bacon. Its delicious aroma merged with freshly brewed coffee. She peered around the wall and groaned. "Dane!"

The ass didn't jerk in surprise. He must have had heard her approaching. "Good morning, sleepyhead."

He scooped bacon onto a plate of scrambled eggs. Coffee gurgled in the machine, and she sighed, eager for a cup. But succumbing to one meant he won.

"What the hell are you doing in my house?" She tugged the cover tighter, wishing she had taken the time to dress.

"Making you breakfast." His puzzled expression shot frustration through her. "You like bacon. I remember that."

"I also value my privacy." She raised her arm to point at the door, then lowered it. Maybe he'd broken into her home because he needed her medical expertise. "Is someone hurt?"

"Nah, just thought a sweet breakfast and a drive to Lover's Point made sense." He placed two glasses of orange juice on the dining table.

She blinked at him, then at his bare toes like the cold didn't seep through the floorboards. "Did you turn down the heating?"

"Nope, it's set to seventy." He gestured to the panel mounted on the wall. "You must still be sensitive to the cooler temperatures."

"Still?" She chose a chair to slump into. "I doubt I'll ever acclimatize." After a sip of orange juice, she swallowed past a delighted hum. "Freshly squeezed?"

"Only the best for our doctor." He winked, then chose the chair opposite her. "I did knock, but when you didn't answer, I worried."

"Sorry, I was super tired." She flicked a glance outside at the dark blue skies and the bright glow of thick snow. His SUV wasn't out front. "You didn't walk here, did you?"

"Sure did." He grinned, scooping eggs and bacon onto her plate.

"In bear form?" She dished most of the food off her plate—she couldn't eat the mountain he had served.

"Yup." He picked at his T-shirt. "Carried these so you wouldn't be alarmed by my naked self in your kitchen."

She bit her tongue, not wanting to remind him she had been alarmed regardless of the state of his modesty. A bite of bacon kept her mouth occupied, but she glared at him while she chewed. Had he not intruded, she would be dreaming and in blissful warmth.

"What are your plans for the day, Doc?" He sipped his juice with his pinky sticking out.

With a dip of her head, she hid her smile as she rearranged her cutlery. "Where I need to be. At the clinic." She spooned in the fluffiest scrambled eggs she had ever tasted. A pot of marmalade sat on the table, along with butter. Waking up to this was heaven, but if she told him that, he would intrude willy-nilly.

"So, a quick trip to Lover's Point and a bit of snowboarding?" He arched a brow.

"Sounds like a plan." She smiled, smearing butter onto a slice of perfectly toasted ciabatta. "Trying to bribe me to stay?" As she swept a hand across the table, she bit into her toast then licked butter off her bottom lip.

"Maybe." He smirked.

"Got things to do back home, Dane, and a job at Indes Pediatric Hospital." She winced.

A decision needed to be made there. She couldn't keep them hanging on. Dr. Olson had been most understanding when the news of her parents' death reached him. Still, they needed a doctor dedicated to saving lives and to helping children. She didn't fit the mold anymore. Staying in Coedwig, or a place like it, might be the safer option. At least, her medical training wouldn't have gone to waste.

Tears prickled, so she hastily squeezed her eyes shut. This wasn't what her parents would have wanted, but neither had they foreseen their deaths nor Ilona's inability to save them.

Dane didn't speak, just watched her, concern furrowing his brow.

The thump of a car door snapped her out of her daze. Jake strolled across the fresh snow, stomped his boots on the porch, then knocked on the front door.

"Come on in, Jake." Dane's invitation gritted her teeth. This was still her home, for now.

"Good morning." Jake's wide grin dampened her ire.

"Grab some coffee, Sheriff, and help yourself. Dane made it." She gestured to the fast-dwindling food Dane muscled through.

He glared at her but rose to grab Jake a plate.

"Whoa, what a privilege." The scent of snow and wet cat reached her when Jake chose a chair. A sprinkle of white sloughed off his shoulders. "How did you sleep, Doc?" He scooped mountains of egg and bacon onto his plate then buttered a slice of toast.

"Well, just cold." She shivered on cue, then shrugged the quilt in place, not wanting to reveal her barely decent pajamas. "If you'll excuse me, I'll dress for the day."

Not waiting for their replies, she bolted, shutting her bedroom door on a soft click when she was tempted to bang it. Fuck. Sucking in calming breaths didn't steady the staccato of her heartbeat. This was small-town life. Neighbors became friends became family.

With two men in the house, she wasn't about to shower. Thermal underwear, jeans, a long-sleeved shirt, and a jacket would be good for starters. Psyching herself up, she tossed off the quilt, her tank and boy shorts, then yanked on her clothes. On the edge, she sat, donned thick socks and her boots, lacing them tight. In the bathroom, she ran a brush through her hair without looking in the mirror, but when she brushed her teeth, she made the mistake of meeting her gaze.

She gasped then gagged, swallowing toothpaste. Spitting out the remnants, she gargled and rinsed before studying her reflection. Where there had been an angry gash down her cheek, the skin had knitted like the wound was weeks old. Holy fuck. She needed a sample of Dane's blood, pronto. All those kids in car accidents or suffering from leukemia? Didn't he care? Did he know how his blood could save lives?

She had to play nice.

Opening her bedroom door, she called out she was ready before reaching the dining room.

"Talk was wild yesterday about your treatment of Edison," Jake said around a mouthful of buttered ciabatta.

"I had to if he has mange. I wouldn't be able to say for sure without a skin sample." Or blood sample, but she didn't mention that. "I gave him a general antibiotic, even though I don't know how your blood reacts to human meds. Dane said the only way to find out was to inject him and see."

Jake shrugged. "I haven't heard of a shifter dying from antibiotics."

"His mange might be from catnip abuse." Dane drained his coffee and rose to gather the dirty plates.

Jake chuckled. "Yup, you're a doctor, Ilona. After receiving an injury from him, most folks wouldn't want to help him."

"Leave the dishes, Dane, I'll get to it later." She wanted this morning done, and with any luck, a little quiet time before she opened the clinic.

"You didn't eat much," Jake said as he headed for the front door. He held it open for her, along with her woolen cap and gloves.

"Saving myself for Mo's apple pie." The explosive combination of cinnamon, baked apple, and whipped cream made her mouth water. Pausing on the porch, she tugged on the cap and her gloves while her breath condensed.

"The cold burns more calories, Doc. You've got to eat more."

She didn't know whether to find Jake's concern sweet or creepy for checking her out. Snorting, she slid into the driver's seat when he pointed at it. She would go with sweet because he was a loving father and had a wife...no, a mate. "I'll eat my fill of Harriet's chocolate cake too, Jake, don't you worry. She's hellbent on fattening me up."

Dane shut her front door and leaped off the porch in nothing but jeans and a T-shirt. Barefoot, he ran across the snow and climbed in the back, shoving a scarf between the seats for Jake to grab.

"So ready for this. A few inches fell last night which means untouched snow as far as the eye can see." Dane rubbed his palms together and grinned.

Without responding, she started the engine and steered the SUV onto the 'road.' By now, she had the trees memorized since she was unable to rely on road markings or grooves in the snow. Jake and Dane remained silent as she careened around corners, clipping it at a steady pace. Not once did Jake encourage her to speed up nor did Dane warn her of too-sharp bends. She drew the SUV to a gentle halt to not lock the tires and switched off the engine.

"Impressive." Jake smiled before flicking the scarf around her neck. "Let's suit up." He bolted from the cab, circled to the trunk, and flipped it open.

She stared out the window at Echon Mountain, the flickering lights of the tower, the dark green of the forests, and the sunlight creeping across the snow, painting it in golden yellow. From inside the cab warmed by the heater, the world around her was breathtaking.

Shivering in anticipation, she opened the door and stepped out. The wind snuck through the gaps of her clothing. She looped the scarf, zipped the jacket closed, then joined Dane and Jake. After gearing up, Dane checked her goggles and raised her hoodie, before securing it with a tug.

She threw herself off the cliff with more confidence than before, this time eager for the ride. The wind slapped her cheeks, icy cold lashing her face. She bent her knees to absorb the landing. By going first, she carved the untouched snow and chose where to board. But despite the thrill sparking adrenaline through her and summoning a smile, the hike back remained at the forefront of her decisions. The farther she went, the longer the return walk.

Resting her weight on her heels, she skidded to a halt, furrowing the snow, and spraying up a cloud of white powder. She raised her face to the sun's rays, eager to feel the kiss of warmth against her chapped cheeks.

Dane and Jake stopped beside her.

"So beautiful." Dane's breath condensed as he huffed. "I couldn't imagine leaving this for the city."

"Same." Jake twisted and waved at a man on the tower's small balcony.

Unclipping the board, she stomped back, longing for a hot cup of coffee or cocoa. Gripping the nose of the board, she used the tail like a ski pole, dipping into the snow and dragging herself forward. It eased the effort on her thighs, but by the time they reached the SUV, she sucked in ragged breaths, and her arms trembled.

The return drive to her house was in silence.

As soon as she parked, she hopped out with a wave. "See you guys later." With a pointed look at Dane hoping to convey he better give her some space, she disappeared inside.

She shut the door, rested her temple on it, and waited for the rumble of the SUV to fade. A peek outside showed no sign of a polar bear or lion. After a quick shower and a hot cup of coffee on her porch, she headed for the clinic to start the day.

Little Allison had come in covered in burrs, and in her cub form too. That had taken time to untangle. Mrs. Cromwell just wanted to chat to a friendly face about her grandchildren not visiting and the possibility of winning the town's crochet contest this year. Ilona didn't have the patience to learn that skill, and despite the waste of her time, she cherished those Harriet-chats. Not that Ilona charged for them either when the elderly woman brought lunch, cake, and coffee.

The highlight of Ilona's day was a glimpse of Rhys's gorgeous ass as he ran naked into the forest behind Cromwell's. She hadn't blinked, savoring the ripple of muscle along his fine legs and broad shoulders. Holy shit, he was a sexy man.

She fanned herself with medical cards on STDs before snorting. Looking never hurt anybody, and besides, he hadn't known she ogled him. Heat burst across her cheeks anew. If he did know, what could she say?

She hurried away from the window, planning on confronting him soon enough about his not-so-secret interest in her grandmother.

Chapter Seventeen

BEAR-ASS

"Rhys!" Lona hovered at the entrance of the bar.

Silence descended with the patrons turning as one to peer at Rhys.

He admired her in the wall mirror, free to do so without being obvious. The urge to spin on his stool to watch her march toward him gripped him. He tamped it down while he fought his vocal bear. She was taller than Callie. Not something he noticed before. Lona fit him well, though. His arms recalled the weight of her filling them. The tips of her braids brushed each shoulder

He shifted on his seat, hoping to ease the burn of desire pooling in his loins. But he didn't look away.

Meeting his gaze in the mirror, Ilona strode toward him with enough malevolence to raise the hairs on the back of his neck. She challenged his alpha, and the excitement skittering along his nerves meant he liked it. Her actions gave him a semi hard-on. He didn't bother to hide his 'growing' interest. Instead, he smirked into his beer.

With small towns, she would've heard about his interest in her if this morning's intrusion into her room hadn't enlightened her. He remained relaxed despite his eagerness. His senses tuned into her approaching steps, the softness of her breathing, and a deep inhale that screamed her human genetics.

"I hear you're asking about Devereaux?" Her voice was raw, husky, and his bear roared a greeting.

Last night, the pitch had been higher in her distress, and this morning, he had thought she was hoarse from sleep.

Fuck. He tightened his grip on the bottle, almost to breaking point. Make that a full hard-on. With a voice that sexy, distinguishable, as he thrust into her, he would never call Callie's name. He twisted slowly, arching a brow at Lona.

He snagged on a bare belly button exposed by low-riding jeans clinging to wide hips. Last night, when she had asked him to help her undress, he hadn't had the time to ogle. Well, maybe a quick peek at her heaving breasts marred by blood trickling into her cleavage. Leather boots adorned her feet. His gaze shot up, past a tight camo-green T-shirt clinging to her abundant assets.

Her skin looked like toffee.

He grunted at that random thought and let his grunt stand as a greeting. "Not really. Just thought you were family of Callie's. It doesn't make any difference to me either way." Because he wanted Ilona, with or without the Devereaux blood flowing in her veins.

He sipped his beer, ignoring her. But damn, it was hard. He wanted to taste those plump lips, nibble on her pert chin, see lust darken her hazel eyes. The Devereaux traits were there, in her direct gaze and inner strength that sang a siren's call.

"Give me a beer, Aiden." She claimed the stool beside Rhys, bringing with her a mixture of lavender and antiseptic.

He sucked it into his starved lungs, able to do so without alerting Aiden to his interest. His bear rumbled in pleasure.

"Ilona, let me officially introduce you to my older brother, Rhys." Aiden grinned. "He's city folk."

"You were city folk too, you know." Rhys chuckled. "I went for a run last night and have to admit, there's an appeal to living in the wilds."

"Shit, does that mean you'll visit more often?" Aiden faked a shudder, but Rhys recognized that sparkle in his eyes. It was good to see it. Inner City and what Alrik had done to Aiden had all but snuffed it.

"No, Callie keeps me busy. Her ex-captain too, who makes Alrik look downright friendly."

"Didn't you say Callie got married?" Jillie asked, back in her seat with her spritzer.

"Yup, to Gabriel de Winter. Turns out vamps have mates too." Fuck, and he had hated seeing her slip out of his grasp.

"No shit." Aiden gaped.

"But she adopted a shifter girl, so regardless of the alliance, I'd have reason to meet with her."

"And you allowed it?" Ilona's husky voice rubbed across his senses.

Rhys twisted to look at her, grateful for the opportunity. No derision or judgment crossed her eyes.

"I didn't have a choice, believe it or not. George's mother kicked her out, forced the little girl to survive on her own. I dealt with the mother." He grimaced at the memory, of finding neglected pups trapped in a pen, their mother sprawled in the empty kitchen with the stench of drugs filling the house. "Since Gabe thinks of George as his daughter, I can't intervene. All I could do was convince them to let her play with shifter children. Vamps don't have any of their own." Yet.

"It's an unusual situation," Ilona said, sipping her beer.

His gaze lingered on her lips as she wrapped them around the bottle's mouth. "Yes, it ties the Knights Ridge to the de Winter hold. It's complicated." His thoughts settled on Dimitri Vasiliev and his pal'tsy.

"What kind of name is George?" Jillie frowned.

"Her birth name is Tara, but since her mother abused her, she's not partial to it. She'd shifted into a rat when Callie met her, and thinking her a male, Callie named her George."

Jillie coughed on a sip of her spritzer. "The girl's a poly?"

"Yes, and now she's in the hands of vamps." He'd thought himself in love with a vamp, but he didn't say that. Jillie's horrified expression didn't need to petrify. "What kind of a doctor are you?"

He settled his gaze on Ilona, allowing it to trail the scar on her cheek, the indent of her neck, the heaviness of her breasts. Did he ogle her? Hell, yes. And he would continue to do so at every damn opportunity.

She spun the bottle and coaster between long-fingered hands. "By training, a human one, but now I dabble in veterinary." Saluting Edison with her bottle, she offered him a smile.

"That must've been a sharp learning curve." Rhys winced. Was last night her first excursion into the shifter world? Where was she when the news channels had broadcasted their existence a mere three years ago?

"Broken bones healing within days? Legends spoke of such occurrences high up in these mountains and remote towns. Coedwig has been an eye-opener, and now I hope to find the cure to sicknesses plaguing the human world."

"How so?"

"There has to be healing properties in your blood. If I could isolate and replicate it without 'harvesting' shifters, we can eradicate most human diseases, and hopefully, brain damage too." While agony swept across her delicate features, she closed her eyes. Like her false humor could hide her suffering, she offered Aiden a stiff smile before winking at him. "I've had this death-defying crush on Aiden since I met him. He's so talented with his first aid knowledge and piercing blue eyes." She wiggled her eyebrows at his brother, and her genuine smile hinted at a dimple in her cheek. "And the way he polishes a glass..." With the coaster, she fanned herself.

Her teasing made Rhys shift on his stool, trying to ease the restless energy rushing through him. After dropping bills onto the counter, he forced himself to leave before his instincts kicked in. His bear wanted to drag her with him, but he knew better. He had to first gather his control and a plan of approach. Intruding into her bedroom had been foolhardy. She had looked so soft, appealing, and disheveled like she had spent a passionate night—

Almost ripping his jacket off the coat hook, he shrugged it on while heading outside to his SUV. His emotions were in turmoil, more so than with Callie. Ilona...invoked something potent, intimate.

"Rhys!"

Ilona's husky voice forced him to stop with his bear refusing to take another step. She hurried after him, her footfalls growing louder, crunching snow to reach him. As she neared, he spun, grabbed her by the shoulders and pinned her to the side of his SUV.

"It's not wise to follow me, Ilona," he said.

Snow flurries peppered her skin and dissolved. His sharp eyes watched each one in his line of vision. The urge to kiss her gripped him, the puffs of heated air escaping her gaping mouth called to him, begging him to lower his lips to hers.

She shivered beneath his hands, goosebumps forming on the exposed skin her yawning jacket revealed. He fumbled with the zipper and dragged it up, closing it. With seeking fingers, he hooked her hoodie and tugged it over her head, releasing a shuddering breath at not succumbing to her appeal.

"You've been asking around town about my Devereaux lineage, Rhys. Why not ask me outright?" She arched a brow, challenging him. "I might not have the answers, but we could find out together."

He clenched his jaw. Fuck, everything about her set his senses ablaze. He inched closer, eager to feel her skin against his.

"Can I treat you to a coffee?"

He jerked back at her invitation, not certain whether he should spend more time with her with his control non-existent. "Now?"

"Sure. I can meet you at Mo's Diner." She hitched a thumb up the road.

He lessened the gap between them, shielding her with his bulk, sharing the warmth of his bear. She shivered, leaned toward him then stepped away, shoving her hands deep into her jacket pockets.

"Sure."

With a nod, she sidled from under him and headed to her blue rental. After yanking his door open and sliding onto the seat, he gripped the steering wheel, needing it to keep him in the moment.

Claim her.

He ignored his bear and started the engine.

Before we lose another one.

The tires spun before they found traction in the snow-covered gravel. The SUV lurched forward, and he drove out of the parking lot, heading for the diner. Shining like a beacon, the diner's orange glow, between intermittent swipes of his windscreen wipers, guided him.

He parked the SUV, switched it off, and waited. If she didn't pitch, he would go for a run. At his immobility, his bear roared his anger, flushing heat through Rhys's body.

"You'd take her now, bear," Rhys said, his voice guttural. "Doing so without her permission would wound her. Can you accept the consequences?"

His bear grumbled but said no more.

Rhys released a shuddering breath, grateful for the silence.

Ilona stopped beside him and hopped out of her SUV, shutting the door. Shooting him a raised eyebrow, she rushed inside, greeting the staff on duty with a wave. She slid into the booth, placed her order, and waited...for him.

Her solitary figure compelled him to open his door.

"It's been slow tonight, what with the science crew on the hills," Mo said from the kitchen before scurrying out, her waitress outfit snug but crisp.

"Do you think the tower will hold in this storm?" Ilona frowned, peering at the increasing winds revealed by the sweeping flurries of snow in the streetlamp's pale glow.

"Rebel resupplied them this morning, so I suppose I'm just being a worrywart. Maybe this time you can finish your pie." Mo shoved a pencil behind her ear, balancing it on top of the one already there. It pushed her graying hair out in a wild tuft.

"Got any coffee? It's been one hell of a day."

She nodded and gestured out the window. "That buck planning on coming in or what?"

Ilona didn't look and forced a shrug. "It's your guess."

When Mo dashed into the kitchen, Ilona pinched the bridge of her nose. She hadn't lied about her day. The temptation to drop her head in her hands was strong. She just wanted to crawl into bed, read her latest guilty pleasure, and accept a life of loneliness as her fate.

As if out of the woodwork, the town's men and women had flooded the clinic with all manner of pseudo-symptoms, all leading up to a come-on or dinner invitation.

Including Dane, who'd arrogantly assumed she would dine with him. She'd put paid to that suggestion. Despite repeating rejections, he'd persisted. With a snort at the memory of his shocked expression when she'd pretended to knee him in the groin, she rubbed her eyes. She'd driven to Lover's Point more times than yesterday in a desperate attempt to extract herself from whatever scene was thrust upon her. The children...or cubs she saw were a godsend. They hadn't had hidden agendas. Neither had their parents.

None of the offers could compare to the bear of a man sitting in the SUV outside Mo's Diner. That same gorgeous man strolled the snow naked, had rescued her when Edison hurt her, tried to defend her, and yet she sat in Mo's waiting for him, hoping for...

Ilona winced. For what? What a fool she was. Worse, showing him her scars hadn't driven him away. His tentative touch had been hot and evocative. Her reaction to him pulsed hope through her. This was her life now, wondering if a man not disgusted by her scars meant a possible date or did revulsion equal rejection?

The door opened allowing the sneaky frozen fingers of a stiff breeze to sweep across the diner, under the tables, and through gaps in her clothes. She clasped her hands between her thighs and huddled. Rhys slid into the booth in front of her, bringing his mind-altering cologne with him. At the same time, Mo served a slice of pie, a mountain of cream, and a hot coffee.

"I'll have the same, please, Mo," he said.

Muscled forearms came into view when he rested them on the table. Exposing bulging forearms, he pushed up his black T-shirt's long sleeves as if the weather wasn't below freezing. Just like Dane. Bear?

"Tell me all about her," Ilona said by way of greeting, picking up the spoon to dig into the pie.

"Callista Devereaux's in her late twenties and ex-law enforcement. She's a redhead with green eyes, the same as her sister, Valerie. Her blood is supposedly remarkable to the vamps, and I've seen her fight. They call her a huntress, whatever that means. She's sassy and honorable, strong, and stubborn." While Mo served him, he fell silent then palmed his spoon to slice into the pie seconds later.

"Sounds like you care for her." Ilona fought the inevitable heartache.

This man wasn't meant for her either, despite his electrifying touch and the intensity in his blue eyes. The sharp pain mingled with the bitterness of disappointment told her she would have liked him to be hers. Then again, would he find her attractive as scarred and human as she was?

"I do. She's special. When I learned you have Devereaux blood running through your veins, I had to find out more. Once Callie and Val hear about you, they'll be here in a heartbeat."

"Stumbling upon me was a coincidence?" Ilona arched a brow then licked the cream off her spoon. Blue lights swirled outside the diner, drawing her gaze. She stilled, balanced the spoon on the side of the plate and rose to her feet. "Shit, Mo. Is Jake looking for me?"

He rushed in, leaving his SUV running and its door open. Ilona didn't glance at Rhys while she shoveled in another quick bite. Looks like yet another slice of unfinished pie. She cast a forlorn glance at the bowl of cream.

She settled her gaze on Rhys. "Thanks for meeting me. I know you didn't want to." Shit, why did I say that? "Mo, I'll square up later. Have a nice life, Rhys." And that? Heat flushed Ilona's face, but she ignored it, climbing out of the booth as Jake opened the door.

"Of all the nights." He marched into the diner, stamping snow off his boots.

Tugging her jacket closed, she rocked on her toes while zipping up. "I'm ready, Jake. Is it the scientists?"

"Damn weather chose the wrong day." He paused, leveling his brown gaze on her. "Avalanche, Ilona. The team's on their way."

She gasped and darted out the door and into her rental without a second thought. Her side door opened. She gaped at Rhys when he slid in. His bulk consumed the air in the cab, filling it with his scent, his dominating presence.

She so didn't need this distraction. "Get out, Rhys. I don't have time to debate this with you."

His gaze met hers. A pulse ticked at the base of his clenched jaw. "Don't ask me to abandon you."

She winced. Throwing her words back at her was unfair. "Shit. We'll talk about your high-handedness later."

She reversed, spinning the tires, trusting them to find traction. With what confidence she had earned in the past few days, she hurtled down the main road.

Jake trailed her with his blue lights spinning.

Chapter Eighteen

WHO'S IN CONTROL?

Rhys's focus strayed to Lona's hands gripping the steering wheel, spinning out the ass of the rental as she took corners along the mountain path. She handled the SUV with a lover's touch. Her lips pinched white, her breathing calm as she flexed her fingers, spun the steering wheel, caught it then changed gears. They were clipping it, traveling at a speed he found exhilarating, pumping adrenaline and lust through his veins. His bear rumbled in agreement.

"What's the plan?" He looked away from the temptation of her.

"Jake said this happened last year. He had the tower reinforced during the summer. Let's hope it survived."

"If it didn't?" Rhys frowned. What was the worst-case scenario? What would her approach be? By the calm pouring off her, he assumed she had dealt with such an event before.

"Then we let the team find them." Her confidence didn't inspire peace within him.

He was learning who she was and allowing someone else to risk their lives while she stood on the sidelines wasn't in her nature. "The team?"

"Shifters on the force, and dogs for the humans, or so Jake claims. In hindsight, I should've asked for more details." She peeked at Rhys. "This is my first time."

He clenched his jaw, hoping to hide his surprise and fury. When he saw Dane, Rhys would... Do what? This wasn't his pack or town. Still, he hated that they endangered her. His bear paced, testing the confines and bumping the sides with his shoulders.

"There aren't shifters on the science crew, which means getting the injured to the hospital as soon as possible." Her tension came through when she gripped and released the steering wheel. She leaned forward to peer at the churning clouds. "Rebel might struggle with the chopper, but we've got to rely on his skill tonight."

"Is this a normal day for you?" What he wanted to ask her was how often did she endanger herself like this? His bear roared at the thought of her injured again. Rhys didn't need his irascible partner to distract him.

Her self-deprecating laughter hinted at sadness or loneliness. He didn't like the thought of either. "No, but I'll be fine." She slowed to a stop alongside other police vehicles.

Males and their dogs gathered around a small brazier which Rhys doubted cast off much heat. A few peered over the cliff's edge. She jumped out to open the back and stomp on snow boots. He scowled. Her jacket was insufficient for this weather, but the tight grip she had on her jaw said she wouldn't listen to reason.

"What's the latest?" she asked no one in general, sliding on goggles and tapping a helmet in place.

Rhys released a sigh when she looped a scarf around her neck. Still, he'd rather her not be out in this weather.

"They found one, Doc. Leg's busted something fierce." A male faced her before glancing at the opposite side of the mountain.

Gusts of blinding snow obscured, for the most part, a fallen tower submerged under tons of fresh white powder. Dark figures worked around it.

"On it," she said, hooking compact splints onto her backpack. Snapping the SUV's hatch shut, she marched to the ledge and dropped the board on the hardpacked snow. After lacing the zones, she stepped onto the board, clipped her boots in, and tugged gloves onto her hands. Without warning, she launched herself off the edge.

"What the fuck," Rhys roared, storming to the edge of the cliff. As one, the officers spun to gawk at him. "Did you just let her...?" He couldn't believe she would do this despite watching her gear up. She was human, for fuck's sake.

"Listen, Mr. Whitaker, Ilona's a natural. Tested her skills myself," the sheriff said, approaching him from behind to pat him on the shoulder, trying to calm him.

Rhys stared into the distance. Turbulent winds swept snow in all directions, obscuring most of the tower and the folks down below. He couldn't see farther than twenty feet at a time unless the winds quietened for a moment. A sense of helplessness settled upon him. His bear's fury gripped him. He wouldn't lose a Devereaux, not if he could help it.

Tearing off his jacket, he tossed it into the back of her SUV. One by one, he threw his clothes inside, until naked, he let his bear take center stage. Pops, grinding bone, and grunts preceded a muzzle, thick fur, and massive paws. In an instant, he was too warm, his bear thrilled by the freezing temperatures.

Growling, he lumbered toward the males, hints of cat, wolf, and bear twitching his nose. His bear grunted as they dived out the way. A grizzly launching himself off the edge wasn't a grand jeté. He tumbled and slid down the mountain until coming to rest near the bottom. Sprawled in a heap, he stumbled to all fours. With a shake of his head to clear the dizziness, he sniffed the air then ran in the direction of lavender and antiseptic.

Grumbling at her recklessness, he galloped to where she crouched alongside a man enshrouded in yellow smoke. Rhys sniffed—human blood. She showed no signs of injury and judging by her focus, everything was in control.

A man in a thin jacket spoke into his walkie-talkie, and a swaying rope descended. Snow whipped around them, but she wiped her goggles with gloved fingers and hooked the rope to the gurney. After two sharp tugs, it lifted the injured man.

"One down, Lionel, how many more?" she tried to ask above the howling wind.

"Four, but we haven't found them yet, Doc."

"It's a lot of area to cover, and the wind isn't helping. It won't be long before they ground the chopper." She knelt to dig a hole, shoving snow downhill. Minutes later, she spiked the outside of her cave with her snowboard—a red flashing torch cable-tied to its edge—and crawled into the hole.

Rhys moved closer, peering inside.

"Rhys." She glared at him. "Do you never listen?"

His bear growled at her open disrespect while wondering how she knew this grizzly was him. He made a note to ask her. Later.

"Fine, go help the others, and fetch me when they find the next one."

He changed to talk to her, resting his hands on his hips. "You aren't warm enough, woman. You're worth nothing if you're dead."

She blinked at him, her gaze traveling over his naked body. The fact she wiped her goggles to get a better look made him want to laugh.

"I have thermal blankets, you idiot," she said. "I'll wait here."

His bear grunted at her calling them an idiot, but Rhys changed anyway. The quicker they found the scientists, the sooner she would be in front of a fire.

It was slow going sniffing out blood and digging folks up while the falling snow worsened the visibility. One by one, they found the scientists while Dane tore through the tower for those trapped inside. Rhys fetched her each time she was needed then watched her dig new holes. After each rescue, she gave him a pointed look to say, 'get on with it.' He galloped off.

Exhaustion hounded her, and she shivered uncontrollably, but he sensed she was as stubborn as he'd first deduced. With the last man found and airlifted to safety, they turned as one, heading to the parked vehicles.

Dane tried to carry her, but she swatted him away. When she stumbled for the fourth time, Rhys nudged her with his head, telling her to climb on. This time she didn't ignore him, didn't straighten her spine and push forward despite her waning strength. She crawled onto his back, buried her face and hands into his fur, and allowed him to carry her the remainder of the way.

He wanted to roar his joy. Happiness and warmth tore through him. His bear growled at her acceptance of their help, seeing it as a major achievement. When they reached the clearing, the excitement of the team woke her. She slid off him, trailing her hand along his neck. At the last second, she cradled his head against her chest and pressed a kiss to his brow. This simple yet precious gesture silenced him and his bear.

"Thank you," she said and trudged away, joining the men around the brazier.

He changed, then dressed before grabbing a blanket and dropping it over her shoulders. She tugged it closer and flashed him a smile.

"Well done, all of you." Sheriff Dunn nodded in thanks then gestured to the team to call it a night.

Rhys trailed Ilona to the SUV, sliding in as she did. The ride back was in comfortable silence, less rushed, but her brow furrowed as if doubts plagued her. She stopped the SUV alongside his but didn't park, keeping the engine running.

"Thanks for coming with me, and tell Callie about me," she said in farewell.

Her words from earlier haunted him still. *Have a nice life, Rhys.*

"We'll meet for coffee tomorrow, ten o'clock," he said.

"But..." Her hazel eyes narrowed in confusion.

He lowered his gaze to her pink cheeks and parted lips. "My bear knows your scent, Ilona. If you don't pitch, I'll hunt you down."

"Fine, but I don't see the purpose of it," she grumbled. "I don't need to hear more about Callie. You love her and should fight for her."

He jerked back. Love? No, he was no longer sure what he'd felt for Callie was love. What had he said to convince Lona of such?

"Fight an ancient vampire for his mate?" He laughed even though he had considered it many times. "Coffee at Mo's at ten." He closed the door on her arguments and grinned, watching her drive off.

Stubborn woman. Just the way he liked them.

Chapter Nineteen

CONSEQUENCES

"I KNOW YOU'RE INTERESTED in Doc, but she ain't one for dilly-dallying, Rhys."

Rhys removed his arm thrown over his eyes and scowled at Dane sitting in the chair in his room. He hadn't heard him enter, but as exhausted as Rhys was, that didn't surprise him. Groaning, he slapped a pillow over his face, wishing he could sleep for another hour. When Dane continued to suck on his teeth, stamp his feet, and grunt as he shifted in the chair, Rhys tossed the pillow aside.

He sat up. "Glad we can finally chat, Dane."

"Yeah. I see you're well, an alpha, and an even bigger bastard, but why set your sights on Ilona?"

What the hell? As far as he could tell, they weren't dating. That gave Dane as much right to Lona as Rhys. He ran a hand over his face, hoping to rid himself of his exhaustion. "I met her on a snow-covered field south of Coedwig."

Dane snorted. "I know that. Your stench was all over her boot."

"She intrigued me then." Rhys gave him a pointed look. "More so now that I know she's another Devereaux woman."

"Have a fetish for their lineage?"

"No, well, maybe. I can't explain it. If you came down from your mountain every once and a while, you'd know more, see more." Fetish? Did he? Trust Dane to sum up his obsession in one line.

"Why? To see you breaking with tradition and forming alliances with our enemies?" As Dane leaned forward, his pale hair fell across his forehead, and his ice-blue eyes sparkled with humor. "Since I know you, trust your judgment, I assume it was unavoidable." He slapped his thighs and chuckled. "Thanks for helping us saving the scientists?"

"We found them, but Ilona did the saving." Rhys wasn't taking credit for having a good sense of smell.

"Regardless, the Winterclaw pack thanks you. Official business done, want breakfast? I smell bacon on the fry."

Rhys grinned. The aroma of bacon tantalized his nostrils, as well. "Give me ten. I need a shower."

"Damn right you do, but hurry if you want to eat." Dane closed the door as he left.

Rhys hopped into the shower, taking Dane's warning to heart. The bastard had done it before, eaten everything in the dorm room. While they had both studied conservation, Rhys wished he'd changed his major to commerce.

He clambered down the stairs, his jacket in hand and his laces undone. As he burst into the dining room, Harriet laid out a steaming pile of bacon. She flashed him a sweet smile in greeting and gestured to the sideboard groaning under the weight of eggs, sausages, toast, fresh-baked bread rolls, fried onions, sautéed mushrooms, and cherry tomatoes.

"Ma'am, mind moving to Inner City?" Rhys didn't get this treatment in his lodge. He flashed his most charming smile, and despite the blush staining her parchment cheeks, she shook her head.

"Harriet's trying to get Ilona and me together. Wasted breath, but she doesn't want to listen to reason," Dane said around a mouthful of sausage. "I did ask Ilona, but she shot me down."

"She did?" Her rejection jolted pleasure and hope through Rhys.

"Yup, said she wouldn't date a man who broke women's hearts as carelessly and as often as he rutted with them. Damn near swallowed my tongue."

"You took it as a compliment." Rhys smiled at Harriet, who poured him a coffee.

"I did, so when I asked her again, I didn't expect the kick to the nads. Made myself scarce after that."

"And if she'd said yes, would you have mated her?" Harriet hovered with a sugar bowl in hand.

"I would've considered it." He scratched his trim beard.

"That's a no, ma'am." Rhys rose to pile a few more eggs onto his plate.

"Would you?" She waited, with something intense in her gaze as she stared at him.

"Mate Ilona?" he asked even though he understood her question. He weighed whether he could reveal this to her or Dane. It wouldn't hurt to have allies fighting for his cause.

"In a heartbeat." His bear grumbled his approval. Rhys rubbed his chest, with his knife clasped between his pinkie and ring finger.

Happiness warmed Harriet's gray eyes, and fresh pink flushed her cherub face. "Perhaps I'll take you up on the offer to visit your city, Rhys."

"I would be honored by your presence."

"Nonsense. You ain't stealing two of our treasures." Dane waved his fork at him. "As I see it, you ain't said anything to Ilona or else you wouldn't be walking today."

"I have a coffee date with her at ten." Rhys couldn't resist tweaking his friend. The scowl furrowing Dane's brow meant he struck gold.

"Oh, that's wonderful. How did you get her to agree?" Harriet clapped her hands, then snatched the last bacon to place on Rhys's plate.

He received another scowl from Dane for this betrayal. "I didn't give her a choice. Threatened to hunt her down if she didn't show."

"You know where she lives?" Harriet asked.

"I have no doubts I'll find her." Rhys tapped his nose then shoveled in the last mouthful of egg.

She beamed as if he had shared a secret with her then left them to the meal. The continued silence from Dane drew his attention.

"Are you serious?" Dane met his gaze, the alpha in him challenging Rhys's bear. "Are you pursuing her because of your fetish?"

"Blood doesn't lie." Rhys pushed away his empty plate.

Dane pursed his lips. "That's more a vamp thing than shifter."

"Like you won't lose your mind and crave the taste of her blood during the mating ritual? Listen, Dane, I need to mate, and if I can have a woman with Callie's blood running through her veins, then I'm the luckiest S.O.B. Besides, when I met Lona and found her intriguing, I didn't know she was a Devereaux." He held out his hand when his friend made to speak. "I'm not sure I loved Callie, or whether I'm disappointed in a missed opportunity. The way my body and bear react around Ilona tells me it's the latter. Now quit making this harder for me. My intentions are honorable, and if she denies this attraction, then the decision is hers to make."

"You'll take her away, Rhys. We need her."

Rhys frowned. Dane made a valid point. "She's here only until Amos returns. How long could that be? Dane, I've got to try. You know the pressure the packs place on their alphas to mate. I'd like the chance to find mine before someone chooses one for me."

He sighed. "Fair enough."

Rhys left his friend to the waffles Harriet brought out. He needed time alone to understand where Callie rested in his heart. Missing the chance to claim her had pissed him off, but it could be her lineage calling to him. Like when a shifter met the twin sister of his mate. She smelled good but not as mind-bendingly delicious as his mate.

What he admired most about Callie was the strength and power in her veins. Perhaps that wasn't what he wanted, what his pack needed. He paused on the wooden porch to tie his shoelaces and shrug on his jacket. White snow blanketed the world except for the gravel-covered road.

If he told Ilona about the vamp's formula and his pack's involvement, she might volunteer to come home with him. This all rested on the coffee date. If she didn't show, he would know he didn't stand a chance with her. Yes, he had acted high-handed, but her kiss pressed to his bear's forehead had spiked his hope.

The sky was a crisp blue and perfect for a stroll. Since he had the time, he strode to Mo's, enjoying the freedom to do so. There were no pack obligations, no meetings with Jo-jo that always ended with them screaming at each other.

He entered the diner and chose the same booth from last night. Peering outside, he watched people go about their business.

"Coffee? Apple pie?" Mo smiled a welcome.

"Just coffee, thanks, and you might as well add last night's bill to mine."

"Will do, honey. Waiting for someone?" She gestured to the vacant seat opposite him.

"Yes, for Ilona."

Her face fell as she shook her head.

Rhys's hackles rose, and he straightened.

"She's not well. Jake texted me to get a pot of my chicken soup on the boil."

"Not well?" Rhys growled the question, struggling to form the words. "But she looked well yesterday." He grimaced. That sounded lame. "Where does she live? I can sniff her out, but finding her that way would take too long."

Mo flipped open a tourist map and tapped a spot.

Rhys studied it then bolted, using some of his bear's speed to reach Harriet's. He needed his SUV and its GPS. Folks dove out of his way when he sprinted past yelling apologies. Ten minutes later, he slid to a halt outside her home. He raced up the snowed-in walkway and onto the porch to bang on the pale blue door. Each second without a footstep reaching his sensitive hearing ramped the tension between his shoulders. When he knocked again with no response, he tried the handle.

The door swung open on well-oiled hinges, but the house remained silent. Sunlight streamed in through unshuttered windows, but no other lights were on. He shut the door and raised his nose for a sniff. Trailing her scent along the passage, he headed for her room that he assumed sat at the back of the house.

Pushing the door open, he studied the huddled lump in the bed. The acrid stench of sickness filled the room. He shot forward to sit on the bed's edge and peel back her blankets. Sweat drenched her hair, her skin clammy, and she moaned at the cool air touching her shoulders.

"Ilona." He hoped to rouse her. The heat pouring off her was too intense for a human.

She must have dosed herself last night with the bottles of medication on her nightstand. He doubted they had impacted the cold making her nose glow like a traffic cone.

"Rhys?" Her eyes cracked open, and at the sight of him, she groaned, rolled away from him, and slapped her pillow over her head. "Go away."

"What can I get you? What do you need? Are there other doctors in town? At the hospital?" He tugged the pillow out of her hands and her toward him.

"Don't be silly," she said through her clogged nose. "It's just a cold."

"You're burning up." He held his wrist to her forehead.

"Hotter than you for a change," she huffed, then ruined it by sneezing. "I hate being sick. It's so inconvenient." She flipped away from him and fell off the bed. Crawling on all fours, she headed for the bathroom before struggling to her feet. When she swayed, she threw out a hand to stop him. "I've got to pee, and no, I don't need your help." After another stagger and wobble, she shut the bathroom door behind her.

The toilet flushed amid many grumbles about his audacity, his sexiness, parts of his anatomy she liked. The more she spoke to herself, the more he smiled. A squeal had him tapping on the door and lowering his hand to the handle.

"Sorry, just saw my reflection. I'm taking a bath." Running water followed.

"What if you faint?" He pressed his temple to the cool wood of the door.

"Under no circumstances can you enter this bathroom with me naked." She sneezed twice. A thump, a moan, and a few curses peppered the distance between them.

"Ilona? Talk to me, or else I'll come in there."

"I'm fine, dammit." She did sound feistier.

"Can I call a friend, a woman preferably?" He didn't like the idea of another man standing where he was.

"So help me, Rhys." Rippling water accompanied her stepping into the tub.

The urge to open the door was the hardest temptation he had fought in a while. Made harder when her throaty moan that took a one-way path to his groin. She sneezed a few times, each time accompanied by a groan.

She was sick, and all he could think about was bedding her. Releasing a long-drawn-out sigh, he pushed his back against the bathroom door and slid down it, landing on his backside. He folded a leg to rest his elbow on his knee.

"You weren't dressed appropriately yesterday." He tapped a rhythm on his splayed leg.

"Great. Just what I need. A lecture. Well," she huffed, "you can keep your I told-yous to yourself."

"But then again, this could be coming from when you frolicked in the snow because of a boot." He grinned, remembering her childlike joy and debilitating sadness. The memory of her sorrow wiped away his smile.

"You're right. I should have expected this and taken precautions."

Silence fell. He strained his ears to hear water rippling, her breathing, anything.

"What's your favorite color?" He picked at the stitching in his jeans.

"What?"

"It's random questions, or I climb into the bathtub with you." He smiled at her grumbling.

"Sky blue," she said a few minutes later, but only after he rattled the doorknob. "Damn Neanderthal."

He chuckled, enjoying tormenting her. "Favorite movie?"

"Nope, you have to answer your questions too."

"Storm gray," he said.

"You'd look good in that color." Her words warmed his heart, sending shards of joy into the dark recesses of his soul. "Casablanca."

He twitched at hearing her choice. "Why?"

"Bogart was unapologetically male."

"Do you like strong men?" Silence met his question, and he reached up to rattle the doorknob again.

"Yes." She cursed him under her breath.

He grinned. "Shawshank Redemption."

"Because good triumphs in the end?" She splashed.

The imagined imagery of her washing her body dried his mouth, increased the rhythm of his heart, and spiked his temperature with a steady throbbing nestling between his thighs. His bear whined for action. He shifted on his ass.

"Yes. Music of choice?" He cleared his throat hoping to return his hoarse voice to normal.

"I have too many, and it depends on the moment. For now, I'd say Nina Simone."

Sultry, sensual, throaty? Yes, he could hear her singing along. "I'm into Rammstein, but my go-to would be Pink Floyd."

"Both are good choices. I'd have to be in the mood for either, though." She sneezed and groaned. "Pain meds," she said as if dictating to herself.

He glanced at the nightstand. One of those generic bottles might contain an analgesic. Her bed was a mess, and her sheets soaked. One his feet, he browsed through the closets until he found a stack of linen. Within minutes, he remade her bed, and despite the fresh pillowcase, it still scented of her. He buried his face in it, inhaling deeply. His bear grumbled, complaining again.

"Shut up," he said. "I'm working on it." He fluffed the pillow and placed it at the head of the bed.

"Working on what?" She hovered in the bathroom doorway.

The bath flushed her skin pink, and by skin, he meant her bare legs, the robe's small V at her throat, and her face. She swayed and threw out a hand to grip the doorframe.

"Getting to know you." He hurried around the bed to grab her hands. She tried to shake him off, but he held firm. "Just get into the damn bed before you fall over."

"We need to talk about your high-handedness." She climbed between the sheets, moaning as she rested her head on her pillow. "I haven't forgotten."

"You're a terrible patient," he teased, lifting the blankets to tuck her in. "Which meds are for now? Then I'll head out for chicken soup."

A tear slid down her cheek, and her sniffing turned into a sob. "Sorry, I'm miserable when I'm sick."

He clambered onto the bed, resting his head on the pillow beside hers then looped his arm around her to rub her back.

She hummed, her eyes stuttering closed.

"You're just doing it wrong," he said. "You need to see it as a forced vacation. Besides, you have me to order around. Few get that luxury." He flashed her a smile.

Her eyelashes fluttered open, unveiling her hazel eyes. "You don't have to stay." She shook her head and winced. "Pain meds." With a groan, she rolled over.

He found himself rubbing her stomach and froze. Needing space before he did something to jeopardize his seduction, he spun away.

"Mo's for soup. On it." He bolted out the room and beat a hasty retreat.

Chapter Twenty

VACATION

Ilona ogled the sleeping man sprawled on the three-seater. His bedside manner was better than hers. He had brought home tubs and tubs of Mo's chicken noodle soup. But instead of feeding Ilona in the bedroom, he warmed the living room with a roaring fire and carried her to the two-seater couch. After cocooning her within many blankets, he placed a bowl of soup in her hands.

They watched movie after movie, their banter and commentary entertaining. And with each bout of laughter, she felt better, not so sluggish, and the hearty soup calmed the nausea gripping her stomach. The meds had her waxing romantic, but she liked the idea of his company making a difference.

The sun was setting, casting streams of light across his torso and face. Her heart leaped into her throat at the sheer beauty of him. His form dominated the couch, with his long legs crossed at the ankles. He had removed his boots, and dark-gray socks adorned his feet. His T-shirt stretched tight across his chest with the short sleeves cinching his biceps. A bit of brown hair peeked over his shirt collar. She sighed. Her fingers itched to run through it.

No man should look this good, but then again, Dane was as virile. She expected an award for her ability to decline the many offers she had received in the past two days. Rejecting those had been easy. Resisting Rhys wasn't.

He embodied everything she looked for in a man. Strong, muscled, tall, dark, sexy, and kind. She wasn't a fool, though. He wanted her so keeping her company guaranteed him a romp in her bed. She vowed not to succumb because, with him, she would lose her heart.

He stirred, his long lashes fluttering before opening to reveal blue eyes. Blinking at the television mounted on the wall, he asked in a sleep-coated husky voice, "What did I miss?"

"Nothing much." She snuggled deeper into the blankets, her focus on his reflection off the television screen rather than the scrolling credits.

He glanced at her and smiled.

Her breath hitched. She blinked at the seductive curl of his upper lip.

He sat up in one smooth move, declaring a set of strong abs she had excellent memory of. "Your nose isn't as red."

Great. Remind the patient how shitty she looks. She wanted to drop her head into her hands and moan. "Thanks, I think."

"What do you feel like for dinner? Chicken soup?"

"No." She barked her response then grimaced, not that she was hungry. But no dinner might mean Rhys abandoning her for the evening. She wanted him to stay. "Thank you, but no. Pizza?"

"Sure." He chuckled. "I'll tell Mo how her soup made you feel sick to your stomach."

"You do that and I'll kick you out of my house." She smiled, the one that had lingered under the surface since he had entered her home this morning.

"You'd have to escape those blankets first, and I doubt you could outrun me." He bounded off the couch to lean over her, tucking her in tighter.

"I'm hot," she whined, flashing him a pout for good measure.

He brushed the hair off her temple, his touch cool against her flushed skin. "Good, incubate the germs, and show them who's boss."

"You?" She grinned.

His lips twitched, but a full smile didn't form, thank the Lord. "Tonight, you should drink a hot toddy."

"You just want me drunk, and besides, who's the doctor here?" She nudged her head at the television since he had trapped her hands within the blankets. "Let's choose another and order pizza."

His fingers brushing her scarred cheek stilled. Curious, she raised her gaze to meet his. "Your temperature's down." He stroked her jawline instead of releasing her.

"I suppose you'll send me the bill for services rendered?" Instead of turning her head and pressing a kiss to his palm, she forced a laugh. It had to be the meds. No man had ever tempted her like he did, so much her wits scattered and her instincts leaped toward promiscuous. She wanted to do him. The thought alone shot shards of lust and fear through her, proving she was in a sound mind to start something with him.

"Pay for the pizza, and we're even."

She snorted. "The amount shifters eat? You'll bankrupt me." Wiggling, she tried to dislodge the blankets enough to tug her arms free. "I need the bathroom." When nothing loosened, she met his gaze again. "Are you a ninja blanket wrapper of great renown?"

Chuckling at her silly joke, she attempted to squirm free. Exhaustion weakened her arms and rasped her breathing. Sure she was better, but her body hadn't fully recovered. Within seconds, he had her unwrapped.

"I'll take that as a yes." He slid a hand under her bare thighs, an arm around her back, and she was airborne. "I can walk." She clung to him for stability.

"If you say so. What pizza do you want?" he asked as if carrying her was normal for either of them.

"Ham and mushroom with extra olives. The pizza menu's on the fridge."

He lowered her feet to the floor outside the bathroom door but didn't step away. Instead, he closed her robe, his fingers grazing her skin. She glanced away, not wanting to know how much she had exposed herself.

Tapping her nose with a fingertip, he gained her attention. "Call when you're done." He walked to the door. "I mean it, Ilona."

"I mean it," she grumbled under her breath, mimicking his macho attitude.

The door shut on her words and his answering laughter. She had forgotten about their sensitive hearing. A wave of heat bathed her face as if the fever had returned. What had she said when she had taken a bath? She had vague memories of complimenting parts of his anatomy.

"Shit." She rose to flush before leaning over the basin. After she washed her hands, she cupped her cheeks imagining hearing the sizzle as her fingers cooled her humiliation.

She opened the door a crack and peered out. He wasn't waiting for her which meant she could clothe herself with something more than a bathrobe. Panties would be first. With her nethers covered, she might feel less...vulnerable. Whipping off the bathrobe, she slipped a pair on. When she yanked on an oversized T-shirt that fell to mid-thigh, she shivered as the air touched her skin.

"You done?" His hoarse voice from the doorway drew a squeal from her.

His intense gaze traveled her bare legs. How much had he seen? A fresh fever gripped her as her embarrassment burned anew. She had lost count of the number of times she'd exposed herself to this man.

"Do you have to sneak up on me like that?" She held up her arms, expecting he'd insist on carrying her again.

He crossed the distance between them, but instead of lifting her, he gripped her hips and tugged her snug along his length. With nowhere else to go, she draped her raised arms over his shoulders.

"If you weren't sick..." He ran his hands up her spine to press her against his chest.

"What? You'd slow dance with me?" She offered what she hoped was a teasing smile, trying to disarm the moment because, damn, if he kept this up, sick or not, she might seduce him. Then she ruined that thought with a sneeze which bounced her temple off his sculpted chest.

"Definitely." He chuckled.

He glided his hands down, past her hips to grip her backside. Then she was airborne with a garbled squeal. When he threw her over his shoulder, he swatted her butt cheek for good measure. She was so grateful she had panties on despite the thin cloth not hindering the sting of his palm searing her skin.

"I could throw up." She wouldn't, not when she had his tight ass in her line of vision.

"Throw up what? Soup? You digested that hours ago."

He had a point. She scowled. "I'm certain I saved a pea or a carrot."

"Pizza's on the way." He swatted her backside again. But before she could spew the dire threats on the tip of her tongue, he swung her over and caught her in his arms, pinning her to his chest. "Feeling better? Still dizzy?"

"Better, yes. Dizzy? I'll say no, because then I can pee in peace." Maybe revealing her possible lie wasn't wise.

He smirked. "One faint, and you'll pee under strict supervision."

She shuddered, not that it was sexy to watch someone pee, but she liked the intensity of his gaze and his no-nonsense attitude. She hadn't lied about liking masculine men.

"Cold?" He ran his palms up and down her upper arms.

She shrugged, not knowing what else to say. Sliding out of his embrace, she climbed onto the two-seater and tugged the blankets over her. He studied her but said nothing. His focus exploded butterflies in her stomach overriding the shame still lingering. Something sensual and breathtaking skittered across his features. A ball of molten need unfolded in her core. She shifted in her seat.

A knock at her door broke his gaze. He bounded over and on a muted growl, swung the door open with a "what do you want?"

"Hey, my pack, my doc, my responsibility." Dane peeked in and waved. "How are you feeling, Doc?" He shoved Rhys aside with effort and shut the door. "Want my blood?"

At least he was asking first.

"No, thanks, not when we don't know whether it will work on a common cold. I'd prefer to look at it through a microscope." At what lay ahead for her, excitement filled her like an inflated balloon.

"We can do a syringe." He sat on the couch Rhys had napped on. "Shifters don't get sick, Ilona."

As tempted as she was by his offer, she couldn't be the guinea pig to assuage her curiosity. "What if it heals me, but is slowly killing my human cells or converting them into a hybrid?"

He clenched his jaw and rubbed his palms along his thighs. "How's your wound?"

"It doesn't hurt." She rolled her shoulder to prove it.

Dane's brow furrowed as if he didn't believe her. Rhys, still standing with his arms folded across his chest, glowered at Dane. Her breath hitched at the fury pouring off Rhys. Her reaction triggered a dry cough. He hurried to offer her a glass of water. She thanked him with a smile and sipped, enjoying the cold water soothing her throat. After she placed the glass on the coffee table, she faced a doubtful Dane.

"What? Don't want to take my word for it?" She huffed.

Flicking the blanket open, she tugged her shirt's strap off her shoulder, exposing her chest from collarbone to cleavage. Red marks marred her skin where the lacerations had been.

Rhys pinched his lips, gripped Dane by his shirt, and thrust them both out the door.

Ilona gaped then yelped when a bang reverberated through the house as if Rhys had shoved Dane against the siding. She scrambled off the couch, wasting precious seconds to untangle herself before racing onto the porch. The cold hit her, summoning a full-body shiver. She gasped, goosebumps traveling from her toes to her scalp in an instant.

Rhys did have Dane pinned to the wall. He growled at him, making hoarse noises harsh enough to shred a human's vocal cords. She caught a few words like 'protect,' 'mate,' 'disrespect,' and 'claim.'

Dane laughed, unphased by Rhys's words.

Chilled to the bone and lacking the tolerance to deal with whatever this was, she spun on her heel. "That's it. You two can just—"

She stomped into her home. Bolting the door shut, she switched off the lights in the lounge, covered the fire in the hearth, then headed for bed. She popped her meds and crawled between the cold sheets, grumbling to herself about idiot shifters.

Rhys pounded on the door, rattling it in its frame. "Ilona, please, you have my shoes, my car keys."

"Catch a ride with Dane." She didn't yell, assuming he could hear her croaking voice dampened by the thick blankets she burrowed under.

"He left." His voice was pitiful.

She ignored him, lying still, and praying her shivering would stop. It did, but she lay awake, clinging to her blankets, curled into a ball, and listening for any movement.

"Are you still there?" Despite whispering the words, she hoped he would answer but dreaded it. She didn't know what she would do if he hadn't left.

"I'm not going anywhere, Lona, not with you unwell."

Lona? He'd called her that before. She liked the familiarity of it, as if he cared for her. The door thumped, sounding similar to when he'd guarded her while she'd bathed. She couldn't leave him on the porch.

Sighing, she slipped out of bed, wrapped a throw around her shoulders, then padded to the front door. Unbolting it, she opened it. Rhys sat on his ass and peered at her.

"What are you doing?"

If he smiled or was charming in any way, she would close the door in his face. But his expression was serious, with a slight furrow marring his brow.

"Go home, Rhys."

"I...can't." Sadness darkened his eyes. He dipped his chin to his chest. "It's been days of knowing you, Lona. Please don't ask me to abandon you."

Shivering with gusts of wind and snow drifting into her house, she left the door open and climbed onto the couch she had occupied all day. Bundling inside the throw, she waited for him to close the door behind him and settle the pizza boxes onto the coffee table.

He hesitated, then sat next to her to drag her onto his lap. Unable to resist the heat pouring off him, she moaned and burrowed into his warmth. "I'm a shifter, you know this. I figure you're also learning how we mate."

"No, but not that it has anything to do with me. I'm human." She sighed when she shoved her fingers under his shirt.

"For the most part, yes, but shifters can mate with humans."

"What?" As intelligent as she was, sometimes connecting the dots was challenging. Could Amos have mated Gran so many years ago? Could he now? "What does mating mean?"

"It's finding the person who fits your weaknesses and strengths. There's also this deep connection and an instant comfortability like you've known each other forever." He shifted on his feet as if there was more to it, but he remained silent.

"So, what does that have to do with me?"

"I'm comfortable with you, Lona. I want the opportunity for us to get to know each other." He squeezed her against him, burying his face in the curve of her neck. He groaned, nuzzling her and shooting shards of electric desire to her core. "I love the scent of your skin."

At the compliment whispered in his deep voice, her neurons zinged passed her nipples and headed straight to her clitoris. She squirmed on his lap.

His head fell back on a muted moan.

"Get to know me as in date?" Tugging her hands from under his shirt, she rested her palms on his chest to push away, hoping to break the spell he weaved around her senses.

"Yes, as in date." He swept a curl off her temple. "But it means convincing you to move to Inner City. The Knights Ridge pack has a laboratory if that helps you to decide. We're working on creating medicine for the vampires to conceive." He cupped her scarred cheek, tracing a finger along it.

When she tried to jerk away, he caught her chin between forefinger and thumb. Then, as slow as the setting sun, he leaned in and feathered his lips along the scar's ridges. He growled and looped an arm around her to draw her closer. Her heartbeat thumped in her ears and butterflies consumed her chest. She was insane to let him touch her like this.

"You're helping them conceive?" Excitement pulsed through her at the groundbreaking research his scientists were doing. Or was that languid desire when he skimmed his fingers down her throat to trace her collarbone. "Any results?"

"We're close. We've started vamp trials, and the women smell fertile."

Her nipples hardened when he traced his fingers along her T-shirt's collar. "Your olfactory—?"

His thumb tugging on her bottom lip shuddered bold need through her and halted her question.

"I can smell emotions too." Dipping his head, his gaze snagged hers as his lips descended. When they brushed across hers, she gasped. "Anger, fear, arousal."

Her cheeks burned, and despite wishing she could kiss him, she didn't like how he toyed with her.

"Arousal doesn't mean sex." She slipped off his lap and drew the throw around her as she gathered her dignity. A rather large bulge in his jeans snagged her attention. A fever claimed her, and she forced herself to shuffle back, ignoring the throbbing between her legs.

"No, it means attraction." He didn't hide how aroused he was, and the slow perusal he gave her with his intense blue eyes tested her resolve.

"Find a woman not scarred, not an emotional wrec—" She bit the inside of her cheek, spun on her heel, then stomped off.

Climbing into bed, she yanked the blankets over her head. Like a child, she cast her thoughts back to before the crash, as if the universe hadn't messed with her life. No accident happened, she hadn't lost her parents, she wasn't scarred, and she didn't have the sexiest man she had ever met horny as hell in her living room.

"You can't hide from this, Lona."

"Go away." She rolled over, offering her back.

His footsteps neared, and the bed dipped, but before she could scold him, he slid under the covers and tugged her against his bare chest. Shit, he was so deliciously warm.

His voice rumbled as he said, "As an alpha accustomed to scars, bloodshed, death, yours doesn't bother me. It speaks of a woman who has endured much. If your scar healed, would that change who you are?"

She shook her head, too nervous to speak with her ass nestled against something incredibly hard while her heart pounded at the truth in his voice.

"Dimi, it's Rhys. Can you send one of your pal'tsy to Coedwig? I need him to lick someone."

Frowning at the strange request, she twisted to watch Rhys on his mobile. He didn't mean her, right? Like she would let someone lick her. Ew, what the hell was wrong with these people? Then her doctor's mind took over. He had implied they could heal her scar, and just by licking if she took his meaning. She needed samples of their blood and saliva.

Hell, not that she knew what to tackle first: cancer, injuries, blood disorders... The list was endless.

Rhys sprawled on the bed, with his bare chest exposed for her admiration. His gaze traveled to her breasts, then up along her neck to linger on her lips, sparking a tingling trail of sensory overload. He touched where his gaze had, feathering his fingertips over her lips, skimming along her neck to stroke his palm across a nipple.

Fire burst outward, and her breast swelled. She bit her inner cheek and shifted, trying to untangle her legs and slip off the bed. Now he was taking liberties when he had no right. Sure, her body screamed permission, but she hadn't given it. Not yet, anyway.

"Thanks." He hung up, placed his phone on the nightstand, then sat up in a fluid motion, his mouth meeting hers.

She hadn't expected a kiss. His lips were dry, soft, hot, but the moment he slipped in his velvet-like tongue, she melted. The demanding way he conquered her mouth scattered her thoughts. With a sweep of his tongue, he claimed her. She had longed for this and needed to sample his lips. Groaning, she nestled against his chest as his musky flavor burst to life across her tastebuds. Permission granted.

"Kissing you is better than I imagined." He feathered kisses along her jawline then swooped in to claim her lips again.

Fuck me, James. The taste of him, the way he left no part of her untouched, sent waves of lust pulsing through her. She clung to him, kneading his chest beneath her fingers as he dominated the kiss.

Before she could think to join in, he flipped her, tucked her snugly against the front of him, and nipped her exposed shoulder. "Sleep, heal, and in the morning, we'll discuss what this is between us."

Sleep? She wanted to snort, but her mind reeled. He had kissed her. Was he serious about dating her? No, not after days, but she wanted him to be serious, and therein lay her dilemma.

With his hand gripping her hip, his chest warming her back, and his lips pressed to her neck, sleep claimed her, dragging her down to its sweet depths.

Chapter Twenty-One

BLOOD DOESN'T LIE

Ilona awoke with her nose smashed against a pectoral muscle an inch or two away from a nipple. The woodsy scent of Rhys's velvet skin filled her senses as the warmth of him beckoned her to snuggle deeper into his embrace. She had never slept in a man's arms before, and the sense of security it summoned had to be an illusion.

He stirred and rubbed his hand up her back, taking her shirt with it. Groaning when he encountered bare skin, he shifted, tightening his arm around her.

"Morning." His sleep-drenched voice hardened her nipples. It promised sensual delights the world had never seen. "How are you feeling?"

"Better." She drew in a deep breath through her nose, proving her sinuses were clear even as his scent filled her lungs. A cold could last weeks. Dane's blood flowing through her veins had to have played a role in healing her this swiftly.

Rhys flipped her onto her back, pinned her to the bed, and entangled his limbs with hers. "Lunar, I love waking with you in my arms."

Claiming her lips, he sliced his hot mouth across hers. He plunged in, unapologetic, as he conquered her. She fought him with her tongue, which only deepened the kiss. He tore away with a guttural groan.

"You rattle my control, Lona. From the moment you stubbornly refused to get in your car and leave me out in the snow. Your husky voice, your lavender scent." He dipped his face into the curve of her neck and inhaled. "Beautiful."

"I'm not...ready for whatever this is, Rhys. Not by a long shot."

He stilled, pushing himself into a plank position. "What happened, sweetheart?"

She shook her head, not wanting to talk about it, not wanting it to be real as if speaking it confirmed her worst nightmare.

"Is that why you whimper in your sleep?" He lowered himself, his length and weight pinning her again. Instead of trapping or smothering her, his presence melted her resolve.

Cupping her cheeks, he stole short, sweet kisses, between tugging at her bottom lip with his. His persistence didn't piss her off. He made her feel cherished. He didn't deepen the kiss but waited for her to respond. Patience flowed off him. He acted as if he needed to know her thoughts like they mattered to him.

"No screaming, pleading, or wailing?" She expected worse than whimpering.

"Ilona, please, tell me."

She released a shuddering breath and slipped her arms around his waist. "About three weeks ago..." On cue, the tears formed and slipped free. With her hands on him, she couldn't wipe them away, couldn't press her fingertips to her eyes to stem the flow. So, she lowered her gaze, letting the tears fall. "My parents died." Those three words tore through her, and she sobbed. "Me, a doctor, and I couldn't save them."

"Oh, Lona, sweetheart." He rolled over, taking her with him. His arms tightened around her, keeping her close.

His embrace, like Dane's, opened the floodgates, and she cried great shuddering sobs. Rhys whispered sweet nothings but held her for as long as she needed him too.

He rubbed her back or rocked her until her tears dwindled. "Tell me about your folks, Lona. What did you love the most?"

Her heart swelled to bursting, and right then, she knew she was in trouble. As she blurted out her parents' idiosyncrasies, and he listened and laughed with her, she tried to build a wall around her heart. Any man who cared enough to endure her blubbering was a man to avoid. Without a doubt, he would break her heart because loving him meant losing him.

Not if she went with him, if she researched the healing efficacy of shifter blood. As boyfriends went, one who couldn't get sick halved her chances of them dying and breaking her heart. She could only find out by going with him.

"Feel like pancakes, bacon, maple syrup, fresh coffee?" Rubbing his thumb across her bottom lip, he dipped his head and kissed her, moaning when she parted her mouth for his intrusion. He shuddered, his heartbeat thumping through their chest cavities. Power rushed over her, at her ability to affect such a virile man.

He leaned back and brushed the curls off her temple. "I could warm the soup?"

"No leftover pizza?" she teased, suspecting he had eaten it all.

A slow smile crawled across his face, warming the deep blue of his eyes. "I definitely want to date you."

"So you keep saying." She grinned. "But instead of enticing me with your gorgeous body and boyish charm, you're bribing me with your laboratory and your blood." She twisted her lips to imply that was weird but ruined it with a chuckle.

"I didn't think just me would be enough."

His honest answer smothered her laughter, and there before her, was a man as insecure as she was. "Rhys, you're a wonderful man, and you are more than enough. It's just that I can't live through losing someone I love. Not again."

"You choose not to love?" He frowned. "Ilona, that's not how love works. When you don't want it, it will find you."

"I'm doomed to love because I don't want to?" She closed her eyes at the sincerity in his. She could love him, and if he continued to be sweet, kind, considerate, loving him might happen faster. "Be mean to me, no sweet gestures, no typical boyfriend behavior."

"I'm your boyfriend? I'll take that as a win." He laughed, the husky quality of it reverberating through her. "Lunar above, Ilona, love doesn't work like that either. Are you curious about me, my life, my origins? Do you want to spend time with me? Do you find me attractive? How does any non-boyfriend behavior impact any of those questions?"

Her breath hitched. She wanted to know the answers, to learn what had molded such a remarkable man. "Rhys, please, don't make me love you."

"Why not?" He tightened his embrace and snatched a quick kiss. "Do you want to sleep in my arms? To kiss me whenever you want to? To share in my joys, hopes, sorrows, and to have me share your burdens? If you can answer that with honesty, Lona, then you're ready for love."

When he rolled off her and the bed, he took her with him. He gripped her ass, massaging each backside cheek with his large hands. Shards of need were swift to strike, and she trembled under his touch.

He straightened as if he heard something but didn't retreat. "I have every intention of pursuing your kisses, the feel of your ass in my hands, the paradise between your thighs." He stole another too-short kiss. "Let me know when you're ready to love me."

He released her a second before a knock sounded on her front door. She gritted her teeth, torn between relief and irritation at the intrusion. Let him know when she could love him? It was sweet of him to wait, but it added pressure to her chaotic thoughts and emotions.

"Why are you knocking? It's your house." Amos's voice sliced through the sensual tension thrumming between Rhys and Ilona.

Gran huffed. "It's not. It's Ilona's now. Besides, there's a car parked here. She might be...busy."

"What?" Amos's footsteps stomped along the passage, coming closer. "If any of these randy bucks has seduced my granddaughter, there will be hell to pay."

"Should I hide?" Rhys's teasing smile snatched her breath, and she blinked at him, a little dazed by him. "Ilona?" He groaned and captured her mouth with his, tugging on her heart, her soul with a flick of his tongue. No wonder desire was so addictive. "Woman, you were made for kissing."

She released a shuddering sigh. "You won't fit in the closet." After a quick trail of her fingers along his ribbed torso, she hurried to the bedroom door to swing it open. "I can fuck who I want. I owe you no explanations, Amos."

"Fuck me...please." Rhys's plea drew her focus. He adjusted his jeans around an impressive erection.

Despite the rush of arousal flooding her system, she scolded him, "Quit it. You've known me three days."

"Never had a one-night stand?"

She gasped, gripping the door until the wood bit into her palm. "You want one?"

He dragged his heated gaze down her body, thrumming need through hers. "No, I want many."

Right answer. Forcing her gaze away, she bolted into the passage and whacked into Amos. Tumbling back, she bounced off Rhys's chest. He caught her with his arm around her waist, pinning her against him.

"Who the fuck are y—? Rhys?" Amos grinned, thrusting out his hand in greeting. "What brings you to our neck of the woods?" He frowned, slicing glances between Ilona and the man holding her in a far-too-intimate embrace.

"Needed a break." Rhys kissed the crown of her head. "But now I'm babysitting a sick doctor."

"Sick?" Amos's posture changed as he scanned her for symptoms. "Reddish nose, flushed cheeks, hoarse voice...a cold?"

"Rhys plied me with soup and kept me company." She tapped his arm, asking him to release her. Once he did, she slipped around Amos to the lone woman hovering by the front door. "Gran?"

"I'm so sorry, Ilona. I shouldn't have sent you here. I should have come myself." Tears streamed down Gran's cheeks, and she wiped them away with trembling fingers. "I was a coward then and one now." She tugged Ilona into a crushing hug. "You could've died from Edison's claws or when you rescued the scientists."

Ilona stepped back from the hug and dismissed the danger with a flick of her hand. "I could've died from Harriet overfeeding me. My jeans are a little tight." They weren't, but shards of illogical guilt forced her to downplay the last few days.

"I like your curves," Rhys whispered when he kissed her shoulder on the way to the kitchen.

Ilona twisted to glance at Amos. "I can go home, right? With you here, Coedwig doesn't need me anymore."

"Stay, please. Just a few days." Gran pouted in that way that always made Mom laugh...and cave.

"You're leaving?" Rhys hovered in the dining room, holding a bag of ground coffee. "I wanted to ask Monique about the Devereaux line."

Leaving him settled like lead in the pit of her stomach. Between the remnants of sinusitis and unfulfilled sexual tension, she wasn't able to sift through her emotions without bias. He was a sexy-as-hell charmer, determined to woo her, but that didn't mean she had to drop everything and stay with him. She had tasks waiting for her, like sorting through her parents' home and maybe putting it on the market.

"The Devereaux line?" Gran frowned, sliding into the dining room chair to watch Rhys make coffee. Amos busied himself at the stove, starting on breakfast.

"Yes, I recently made the acquaintance of Callista and Valerie Devereaux. Their father was a police officer who died in the line of duty. Callie says he was an orphan." Rhys lined mugs on the counter, gathered the sugar and cream, and carried them to the table.

"Why the interest?"

He settled his gaze on Ilona, his focus intense. "My bear reacted to Callie, but since she's a vamp's mate, my connection to her made no sense."

"You think it's a blood thing?" Amos asked from the kitchen, raising his voice above the sizzling bacon.

Ice drenched Ilona's face, and that lead in her stomach softened and rose in a wave of nausea. "You want me because I might have the same genes as her?"

"No, yes, let me explain." Rhys shortened the distance between them, but she jerked back, shaking her head as tears stung her eyes.

"I'm the substitute?" She wrapped her arms around her waist, coiling away from the sweetness of his duplicitous affection.

Not waiting for his response, she sprinted along the passage to her room and yanked out her bag, dropping it onto her bed. She grabbed her things and threw them in, uncaring in what condition they would arrive in Fenneg.

"Lona." Rhys filled the door with his bulky frame.

Not looking at him, she refused to acknowledge the volatile emotions leaping and dancing in her chest. She had known she could fall for him, had sensed he would break her heart, but no, she had succumbed to his charm and let him kiss her. At least, she hadn't spread her legs for him. Heat burned her face from her cheeks to the tips of her ears at how close she had come to doing that.

"Don't Lona me. Offering me your lab and your body when you only wanted me because of her? That's low, Rhys." She darted into the bathroom and grabbed her toiletries, zipping them into the waterproof bag before tossing them into her luggage.

"Um, Ilona, Rhys, there's a...man here to see you," Gran called down the passage.

Rhys spun at the news and sniffed the air. "If you want to know if vamp saliva can heal, then come." He stormed off, sending more illogical guilt through her like she was to blame for his silly fantasy.

Trailing him, she peered around his bulk blocking the passage. In a casual stance, a tall man with ebony hair and emerald eyes hovered by the door. He was breathtaking, like something out of a men's magazine in his tailored gray slacks and a crisp white button-up shirt. His looming broad shoulders and the seductive smile teasing his lips oozed power. A web of scars marred his throat, but they added to the mystery of him.

"Dimi." Rhys bounded forward to hug him. "When I asked for a pal'tsy, I didn't mean you."

"Asking me to send one of my men to lick someone isn't intriguing? It outright dared me to come." He scanned the lounge and dining room before settling on Ilona. "Prekrasnyy."

His rasping voice sent shivers down her spine, stirring up the sexual tension she had moments ago turned her back on. When he strode between Gran and Amos and slipped around Rhys, Ilona considered fleeing. Fascinated by the allure of his eyes, she rooted her feet to the floorboards.

He captured her chin to raise her face for his perusal. "Mm, the scar is fresh. Be still, my lovely."

Then he licked her, running his tongue from her eye to her jawline. His tongue was hot, wet, and his cologne smelled of something wild and free with a hint of cinnamon. Delicious, coiling, heated tendrils of anticipation sparked every neuron. She was standing there letting this stranger lick her. As she drowned in his eyes, she had no intention of stepping back.

Her life had become a series of bizarre and heartbreaking events. She giggled as hysteria added to the churning emotions she couldn't and didn't know how to deal with.

"Lona," Rhys gestured to the stranger, "this is Dimitri Vasiliev, a vampire."

So, this was what a vampire looked like? She hadn't expected this level of potency. His air of arrogance announced to all he took what he wanted, did as he pleased, and had the talents and authority to back it up.

"You taste incredible." Dimitri paused and inhaled, expanding his chest. "There is power in her blood, Rhys. I sense it." He jerked back.

His eyes widened as if something dawned on him. Tilting her head farther back, he crowded her with his body. He slid his fingers from her elbow to her wrist and raised it to kiss the underside.

His lips warmed where they touched. "May I?"

She frowned, struggling to understand him through her hazy thoughts.

"No," Rhys growled then grumbled, pressing against Dimitri's back.

The vampire didn't move, standing firm against Rhys's bulk. "May I, Ilona?"

She settled her gaze on Rhys's face twisted in agony...and fear? "What does he want to do, Rhys?"

"To taste your blood." Everything about his stance implied she was his and his alone.

Part of her reveled in the emotions crossing his face. That was twice now he'd revealed a little of what he felt for her hidden beneath his handsome exterior. "What will that accomplish, Dimitri?"

His chuckle settled on her senses like melted butterscotch. "I am ancient, little one, and have encountered many curious creatures. History is in the blood. It does not lie. Relax, I only want to taste, not to feast."

History was in the blood, as in the truth was in DNA. "Have you tasted Callie?" She stared at Rhys, at the pulse ticking at his jaw, at his clenched lips, at his dark blue eyes filled with pain.

Dimitri laughed. "That is an intriguing question. No, I haven't."

She raised her wrist with a nod. If his saliva healed her, she had more than shifter blood to research.

He gathered her wrist to his mouth. Scraping his fangs across her skin sent shivers through her, and an insane sensuality claimed her. Her senses exploded, and against her will, she arched her back, offering him her body. Keeping her gaze on Rhys, she hoped she conveyed the offer would have been for him.

Fire burst outward as Dimitri's fangs pierced her skin. In an instant, the sharp pain altered to that of lust, burning need, and anticipation. She moaned. Her knees weakened, and she threw out her hand to splay across the passage's wall. She didn't break eye contact with Rhys, witnessing the shudder running through his body and the harshness of desire darkening his face. On a smothered groan, he parted his mouth as if he couldn't breathe.

The second after Demi bit her, he flicked his tongue across the puncture wounds. "There is shifter in your blood and something older." He ran his thumb across her wrist, wiping away the smears of blood before sucking on his thumb.

Rhys shoved the distracted vampire aside and yanked Ilona into his arms. She whimpered when the heat of his body engulfed her, his scent drenched her lungs, and his erection pressed into the juncture of her thighs. She could fuck him now and to hell with the consequences.

But he didn't take advantage of this. Frustration built alongside gratitude, so she clung to him, suffering through each second as lust consumed her. She hated and loved him for his honor.

"I have tasted this power before." Dimitri sank into the closet couch, staring at nothing as he licked his lips. "Tell me about yourself." He directed his question at Gran. "The bacon is burning, Amos."

Amos yelped and disappeared into the kitchen.

Dimitri patted the couch beside him in a silent request for Gran to join him. Preparing to protect her grandmother if need be, Ilona lurched forward.

"She's safe," Rhys whispered before he sucked on her earlobe.

A frisson of need shot to her core, and she gathered her splintered resolve and thrust him aside. She was packing and heading for Fenneg, a city she thought she would never want to leave. Now it was a pseudo-home. With her parents gone and Gran here, what did Fenneg offer but an escape?

Rhys stilled. "You're still leaving?"

"How did Dimitri's arrival change your motives, Rhys? You need to come to terms with your feelings for Callie." She swallowed past the lump in her throat. "Maybe you should date women who don't look similar..." Shaking her head, she disappeared into the bathroom to don a pair of jeans, a bra, and a shirt. He leaned against the doorframe when she opened the door.

"I didn't stand a chance with her. Gabe got to her first. As a strong woman, she would make a wonderful mate for any alpha." He released a jagged breath. "I came north to find a mate, not caring what she looked like. In our culture, blood doesn't lie, Lona. When we meet the one, it triggers a response in our inner beasts. I've had that response twice. With Callie and with...you. Finding a Devereaux in this town was a surprise."

"I have bad news for you. My name is Ilona Strickland." She hefted her bag and dumped it in the lounge, returning to the room to grab socks and boots.

"Blood doesn't lie. As a doctor, you know this to be true."

Dropping onto the couch, she laced her boots, choosing to focus on the task than to meet Rhys's pleading gaze. He was delusional if he thought a few days was long enough to get to know someone. He was a supreme idiot if he thought humans would agree to their shifter ideas of courting.

And she was the ultimate fool for taking his interest seriously.

After kissing Gran on the cheek and giving Amos an awkward hug, Ilona stomped out of the house, banging the pale blue door behind her. It opened a second later.

"Lona, please..." Rhys hovered in the doorway with Amos frowning over his shoulder.

"Goodbye, Rhys."

As she drove off, his sad face in the rearview mirror tempted her to turn around. She remained firm against whatever these emotions he invoked. They had no basis, no substance. Everything he had said and done had been lies.

Something reached through her innards and shoved her intestines, stomach, pancreas aside to squeeze her heart. She drove from Coedwig as she had arrived, in tears.

CHAPTER TWENTY-TWO

THE MEANING OF HOME

THE DRIVE TO INNER City was a blur. As an ex-doctor, the number of fatalities Ilona had dealt with due to crying while driving was high. It hindered the driver's eyesight and endangered the other road users, but once the city skyline shimmered on the horizon, she couldn't halt the tears. A growing ache urged her to return to Coedwig, but the furious part of her willed her never to set foot on snow again.

The thing was, she liked being in Rhys's arms, liked the way he looked at her, made her feel sensual, alive, worth knowing. Her past paramours had done nothing but demean her. She got it. The medical industry was cutthroat. Limited jobs meant a dog-eat-dog world. From stealing her notes to...drugging her, nothing was off-limits.

Waiting in the terminal, she tried not to make eye contact with fellow passengers. On her luggage pinned between her knees, she tapped the plane ticket, hypnotized by the sound and the puff of air it made.

Despite instigating a glorious revenge, she still couldn't remember what happened that night. One moment she was drinking a latte Connor had bought for their study date, the next she was naked from the waist down in a pool of vomit. A cold dread had slithered down her spine and settled her riotous thoughts. She had yanked on her discarded jeans, then headed to the emergency room.

With the test results, proof of her rape, and the ketamine dregs in her latte cup, she had gone to the dean. She hadn't told her parents about the one time she had used their names. Of course, the dean had to verify her claims. Not for the rape, but that she was the famous daughter of the Stricklands.

As a justice of sorts, Connor lost his scholarship. She hadn't stopped him from doing this to others, but dragging her name through the courts and putting her parents through hell wasn't an option. At least now, Connor couldn't molest his patients.

She shuddered as nausea churned in her gut, hinting at that same sense of dread.

The fiery part of her nature had wanted to drug him and tattoo 'rapist' on his forehead.

Rhys didn't disgust her. His touch was gentle. His charm his own. He had honor and would never drug a woman. Then again, he didn't need to. The crushing pain squeezing her rib cage was disappointment. She would have liked to have known him better.

Maybe if she dyed her hair?

Shaking her head, she stopped the tapping and palmed the ticket. Changing herself for anyone was a superficial attempt to heal what was broken deep inside. The call to board echoed through the gate, bringing her to the knife's edge of her indecision. She pushed herself to her feet, unclipped the handle of her luggage, then wheeled it toward the flight attendant.

Her heart was in pieces. She needed it whole before she considered any kind of relationship. Her medical studies hadn't covered how to heal a broken heart, well, except for psychiatry.

With a tentative smile, she offered her ticket to the smartly dressed man in a blue uniform. She glided past him, through the glass doors, and onto the boarding bridge. Now was when the lead male would force his way through security to confess his undying love, to plead with her to stay. She cast a glance over her shoulder and giggled at her silliness. If Rhys had done that, she'd have boarded the plane anyway. Or, at least, she hoped she would have.

Finding her window seat, she tucked the luggage into the overhead compartment and buckled in. She would head to her apartment first, clean up, then pop in by her parents. Carl would have died by now. Then again, he was a cactus. Settling back, she closed her eyes, leaned her temple against the cold bulkhead, and dozed through the pre-flight instructions.

The plane's wheels touching down jerked her awake. She stretched in the confined space and flashed a smile at the elderly lady squeezed into the middle seat.

Ilona's knees throbbed from the cramped legroom. Usually, she splurged on business class for this reason, but had taken the first flight out. Beggars couldn't be choosy. Now that she was in Fenneg, she didn't need to rush. Rhys and Inner City were behind her, and the elderly lady needed assistance to disembark.

With her chin in her palm, Ilona stared out the window. The airport staff darted everywhere like busy bees, wheeling away luggage, refueling the plane, and restocking the food stores.

"Sorry about this." A twitching smile cracked the old woman's parchment cheeks. Her gnarled fingers trembled where she gripped Ilona's forearm. Late onset of Parkinson's?

"No rush." Ilona patted her cold fingers. "Are you visiting?"

"Yes, my granddaughter gave birth to a beautiful boy." The joy washing off her pricked tears behind Ilona's eyes.

Life for other people went on when her parents' lives had ended. At that moment, she couldn't imagine herself boarding a plane in her frail age to visit a new great-grandchild. Years of aching loneliness and a pointless existence stretched before her.

"That's wonderful. Is anyone meeting you at the airport?" This woman unaccompanied in Fenneg didn't sit well with Ilona. She sliced glances at the smiling flight attendant bidding their customers a good day. Soon, one of them would assist this great grandmother off the plane.

"My grandson is fetching me." Her eyes sparkled with excitement.

Ilona would trail her to ensure she found her family. Alone, in a strange airport, made the woman easy pickings for pickpockets, muggers, and murderers. Grimacing at her dark thoughts, she forced her gaze out the window again.

"Oh, where are my manners. Are you visiting too?"

Air whooshed out of Ilona's lungs. To think her return to Fenneg was temporary bolted a bright warmth through her. She would have to leave at some point, move closer to Gran, but she hadn't given it more thought, hadn't poked her emotions to gauge her reaction.

"Fenneg was my home." She loved this city, its cultural and art festivals, the sandboarding mania, Sunday morning kayaking with Dad, coffee dates in the National Rose Garden with Mom, watching movies while eating salted caramel popcorn with Evie, and sending a child home with cancer in recession. Those were Ilona's Fenneg memories.

And despite the happiness she had known, one car accident overwrote them all. Mom's lifeless eyes and smeared red lipstick, Dad lying in the bed with the machines ticking his life away, and the scar along Ilona's face, flashing nightmarish images every time she caught her reflection.

"Was?"

Ilona forced a smile. How to explain her doctor-not-doctor status? "I just finished my residency. I need to choose which hospital in which city to move to."

The older woman beamed. "You're a doctor?"

Ilona shrugged. Discussing whether that was true anymore wasn't for passing conversation. The flight attendant's appearance was a Godsend. Ilona sighed and rose to help but had to duck her head. The cleaning crew boarded to sweep through the cabin, and once the elderly woman was assisted off the plane, Ilona unstowed her luggage and followed.

The grandson hurried over as soon as they waddled through the boarding bridge. Ilona veered toward the long-term parking lot. The sight of her bright red Jeep her father had given her on her sixteenth birthday shot darts of agony through her. The gift had delighted her; Dad's broad smile with the keys dangling from his fingers, and Mom struggling to fix the massive bow on the hood. Now it served as a reminder of happier, more carefree times. With snow tires fitted, Ilona could use it in Coedwig.

She shook her head. No more snow and no more Dane, Gran, or Rhys by association. So, not Fenneg, and not Inner City. Maybe Tillden or Suddale to the south? But to start the application process again meant accepting failure, her limits, her inability to save everyone. It said much that she hadn't lost a single life during her residency. If she had, maybe her inability to save her parents wouldn't have hit her so hard.

She slumped. It still would. Helplessness had no cure she knew of.

After sliding her luggage into the trunk, she settled into the driving seat and reached for the seatbelt. She swerved onto the freeway, barreling along to her small apartment close to Amity Hospital. The bustle of life highlighted the bleakness of her own. Schools held sports events, shoppers chatted in mall parking lots, and a colorful hot air balloon drifted across the cerulean sky. Tall palms swayed, and folks in shorts and flip flops meandered along the sidewalks.

The warm breeze dewed sweat on her upper lip. She closed the window and switched on the air conditioning. Almost snorting at her low tolerance for the balmy weather, she turned into her dedicated parking bay.

The moment she opened her apartment door on the fifth floor, her shoulders drooped. Carl was fine, glowing lime green with health. He dominated the island in her quaint kitchen. The walls, counter, and tiles were white with the only splash of color her brown corduroy second-hand lounge suite.

Everything was as she had left it in her mad dash to pack for Coedwig. Clothes littered her bed. She gathered her nightgown, a now-dry towel, a discarded sock, and let the tears fall. Cleaning gave her purpose. While she wept, she dusted, mopped, scrubbed until her fingers throbbed, and her lower back ached. Then she collapsed into her overlarge lazy boy and stared at the flickering night lights.

The apartment block across from her played a silent tune, switching window lights off and on in a strange synchronicity. The air flowing through her apartment cooled the sweat on her skin without removing the crisp fragrance of the pine freshener. Savoring it all, she thought of Rhys and how addictive his cologne was.

With a shove, she was off the couch to dig her dead phone out of her bag and plug it in to charge. She switched it on and cringed at the litany of pings. Tons of texts from Evie, colleagues, and the one or two 'friends' she had retained during med school as well as a missed call from Dr. Olson.

Ilona typed quick texts to Gran to tell her she had arrived, and to Evie letting her know she hadn't died from a weird pathogen. Tomorrow, after a 'good' night's rest, Ilona would call Olson and discuss her options.

When the starless night sky offered her no comfort, she played out what she had said to the doctor who had interviewed her. Her naïveté and firm belief that the world was a good, decent place had reflected in her serene composure and bright, eager smile. Perched on the edge of the visitor's chair, she had answered the questions with confidence. What a fool she had been.

With a steaming cup of green tea in hand, she sat on her couch, tucked a leg under her, and stared at the boxes towering in the corner. Since moving in years ago, she had yet to unpack. It made no sense when her choice of hospitals hadn't been confirmed. Either way, staying for long near Amity was never on the cards. Now, she didn't have much to pack. And whatever was in those boxes meant nothing to her if she hadn't touched them. Hell, she couldn't even remember what she had put in them.

Sighing, she unfurled her limbs, and rose. Placing the untouched tea on the scarred coffee table, she popped the top box open. The smell of home hit her, dust with stale popcorn and cotton candy. A scream raced a sob up her throat, and she unfolded her maroon-gold high school scarf, clutched it to her chest, then slid to the floor on a whimper.

Her wail turned silent, as her shoulders shuddered under grief's overpowering heaviness. The pain cinched her chest, faltered her breathing, and with a slow mewling, she crumple to the unforgiving tiles.

Part of her wished she could burn everything, stop the onslaught of memories, and remove anything that could trigger it. But the quiet, calm voice of reason whispered she would regret it.

Cool air washed across her damp cheeks, and while suppressing a shiver, she got to her feet, tossed the scarf into the box, and flipped the lid shut. No, she wasn't ready to deal with any of this. Staying in Coedwig would have been safer but also the coward's route. A long soak and the familiar scent of her bed called to her.

Running the bath, the testing of the water's temperature, the sprinkle of wild orchid bath salts, and the laying out of her nightgown was on autopilot. She rested her phone on the edge of the tub, and sank into the water, sighing as it melted the tension from her muscles. Any remnants of her illness faded, and she sank deeper until her chin submerged.

Her phone rang at eight. The unknown prefix on the number said Coedwig. Tempted to shut it off, she raised a finger, hovered for a few seconds on the red button, then touched the green. Gran could be in trouble.

"Lona?"

Hearing Rhys's baritone comforted her, as if he cared. She tried to shove that down, but it bubbled to the surface. Memories of his blue eyes, broad shoulders, and dimpled smile fluttered her heartbeat.

"I didn't think you would answer." The pain in his voice shouldn't affect her like it did, shouldn't lash guilt across her.

Touching her cheek disturbed the water, but she ignored the surging waves and traced the scar with a gentle finger. She was as much a fool as he was. To think he could shift his affections for Callie to Ilona, or for her to hope he wouldn't see her scar, that he might like her, the ex-doctor, and the wounded woman she now was?

Foolish. "Hello, Rhys."

His breath caught. "Fuck, I love your voice."

His rumbled with a sexual tension her body recognized. Heat infused her cheeks, and she clenched her thighs to ease the new ache burning between them.

He cleared his throat. "You got home all right?"

She nodded, then sighed, realizing he couldn't see her. "Yes, I texted Gran." Trailing an invisible pattern on the porcelain tub, she left the implication unsaid. He meant nothing to her, and therefore, didn't deserve a text.

"She said so. Where are you now?"

So, Gran had chosen sides? Ilona gritted her teeth, ready to phone the woman and lambaste her.

"At my apartment. I've yet to visit my parents' house to deal with the mountain of packing awaiting me. I'll start in the morning, maybe with the kitchen." She shivered. Holding the least amount of memorabilia, it seemed the safest.

"Wise." An awkward silence fell, peppered only by his breathing. Still, she could listen to him all night. "You could get an auction house to pack up what you don't want."

She sat up, splashing water over the sides and smiled at the suggestion. "Good idea. What will I do with two toasters?"

The company could pack up her apartment too. A storage locker somewhere was an option. The expense would be negligible. The thick down blanket, a layer of pink insulation, and several meters of fog surrounded her heart. The thought of navigating that, tearing it open to sift through her parents' stuff and her pre-scar life, drained the energy from every cell in her body.

"Have you eaten?"

It was sweet of him to ask, but whether she had or not, there was nothing he could do about it.

"No, not hungry. I did have a green tea." The untouched, now-cooled tea sat on the coffee table where she had left it.

"You'd be happy to know, the scientists are recovering well."

Shit, she hadn't given them a thought. Though, to be fair, they had a mild case of hypothermia and broken limbs. She hadn't expected any fatalities, other than a possible stroke or heart attack she couldn't have foreseen without full knowledge of their medical history.

"Good. How are the boys doing?"

"Boys?" Rhys shifted, a smothered moan implying he settled into a more comfortable position. "I haven't heard anything, so I assume they're doing well."

Silence stretched with only their breathing traveling the miles between them. The water cooled. Not that she was cold. "Why did you call, Rhys?"

He gasped and shifted again, squeaking whatever he sat on. "I plan to call every night at eight, Lona. You left in a rush, and I know, it's my fault." His words garbled as if he ran his hand over his face.

So, guilt had driven him to call.

"Night and goodbye, Rhys." She swiped her thumb to the left, ready to disconnect.

"Lona!"

Pausing, she waited on bated breath for him to continue.

"Please, don't hang up. You're killing me here, Ilona. Please." The pleading in his voice caught tendrils of longing in her heart and tugged on them. "Keep talking to me until I know you've settled. Until I know you're doing well."

"What will that accomplish, Rhys? A clean break is better. Your affection lies elsewhere, and no amount of conversation will change that. Besides, what did we share other than a few hours of our lives?"

He growled, and the sound shot shards of heat through her. Pebbling nipples aside, the man was mesmerizing. "Tell me spending time with me didn't mean something to you."

Her heart leaped to choke her, and she sat up, splashing more water over the side. No, she couldn't tell him that, and therein lay the problem. She had loved his charisma, his sweet care, as if she mattered. The day and night in his company meant the world to her, too much. Yet, by his own words, she was the substitute.

Her mind scrambled for a plausible lie. His silence pressed on her, forcing her to speak the truth.

"I...can't." While shaking her head and flinging droplets in the process, she croaked the words. "Encouraging you isn't—" She clamped her lips shut.

"So, being truthful about Callie is the only stumbling block?" His voice had roughened. "She's my friend, Ilona, and yes, I was attracted to her. I thought she was my mate lost to a vampire. But my reaction to you far outstrips anything I ever felt for Callie."

Her heart ached, throbbed, shooting flickers of pain to her collarbone. She wished she could believe him.

"I tell you what... Let's take it a day at a time." He sighed. "At least, give me a chance to prove my sincerity."

She smiled, flattered by his persistence. He was there, she was here, would it be that bad to let him in, just a little? Long-distance relationships didn't work, and she didn't have the energy to argue with him.

Either he would win, and she would come to love him, or it would peter out. "All right, Rhys."

He roared a violent yes, the kind of victorious cheer that had to go with a fist pump. "If I was there, I'd kiss your socks off."

She giggled. "Not wearing any."

"Yeah, figured as much with you in the bath." He groaned. "Do me a favor, Lona? Eat something, even if it's just a cracker."

He was right to be concerned. She hadn't eaten since lunch yesterday. Studying her pruny fingers, she nodded. "For you."

"Good. Thanks for taking my call."

After he hung up, she balanced her phone on the side of the bath again and stepped out. Without his breathing and his sexy baritone in her ear, the apartment was too silent. She donned a baggy shirt and padded barefoot to the kitchen. It took minutes to make a bowl of ramen, and despite knowing how devoid of nutrition it was, she slurped the noodles into her mouth while staring out the window.

The city's raucous cries, overhead aircraft, and distant sirens did nothing to ease the loneliness and perpetual sadness in her heart. Cursing, she rose, tossed the remnants of her meal, and headed to bed.

Chapter Twenty-Three

UNWELCOME

"Well?"

Rhys raised his gaze to Mona peeking from the dining room. Harriet's eager face came into view.

"She's giving me a chance." He beamed. Leaping to his feet, he swept both ladies into a hug. They squealed and laughed, their cheeks pinkening.

"Hands off my woman." Amos grinned before popping a forkful of cake into his mouth.

"Coffee?" Harriet offered while patting her hair into place.

"Please." Rhys chose the nearest dining chair.

"Now what?" Mona gripped the back of the chair next to him.

"I head home. I have a pack to lead." He spooned sugar into the coffee Harriet slid before him. "I'll phone Ilona tomorrow night at eight."

"I'll call her every morning then."

He chuckled. "We're using strategy? Duel attacks?"

Mona shrugged. "I'd love nothing more than for her to move closer, Rhys."

He nodded, wanting the same thing. So far, he had made it through the door. His chest swelled with welcome warmth, and his bear rumbled his approval. If he played his cards right, she would move into a cabin on Knights Ridge land, would work in his labs, and would warm his bed.

Fuck, he hoped she would mate him.

His heart danced, spiking a fiery excitement through his veins. Peace descended on his soul. He hadn't thought of Callie as more than a friend since meeting Lona. Chills slid down the back of his neck, and his eyes widened. His need to break the connection to her had been lip service, but with Ilona, the hope pulsing deep within him was boundless.

"I hope you touch her heart, Rhys." Mona's unexpected serious tone snagged everyone's attention. "She thinks her inability to save—" She pinched her lips, and Amos lowered his cake fork long enough to throw an arm across her frail shoulders. Patting him, she met Rhys's gaze. "Being a doctor didn't save my Elise, so why trust herself with children? Why risk their lives?"

His breath caught. What Mona hinted at was a deeper layer to Ilona he hadn't seen yet. No, it was incongruent to the core of steel running through her. The revelation circled, and settled, rose, and churned until he placed himself in her shoes. After spending years studying to save lives, only to fail those dearest to her? It explained her sadness and withdrawal into herself when she thought no one watched her.

Her strength was her shield and mask.

"So, I assume you're leaving?" Dane leaned against the doorframe. "Come in, piss off our doctor, then fuck off?"

Rhys grimaced. "Something like that. I have a pack to manage and need to plan how to fix this."

"You're not staying for the Lunar Festival?" Harriet squeaked.

His body twinged in dismay. His aroused state wasn't due to the waxing of the moon but because of a certain sassy redhead with hazel eyes and a mix of innocence and fire. He hadn't wanted to be in Inner City during the full moon, but now, he had no choice. If something should befall Lona, he needed to be close to the airport. The urge to fly to Fenneg gripped him, with his bear roaring at him to leave now.

He had made too many assumptions, had barreled over her feelings, as if she would fall in line with his. She hadn't as a non-shifter.

"Come, walk with me." Mona looped a scarf around her neck, then reached for her coat. She settled her hazel eyes on Amos. He nodded and didn't follow.

Rhys donned his jacket and hurried to open the door for her. Silence reigned while they strolled on the salted sidewalk. The crisp air slapped his cheeks but didn't reach his bear. He raised his face to the blue sky and sucked in long breaths.

"I forgot how beautiful it is up here." She rubbed her hands together before shoving them in her coat pockets. "Do you love my granddaughter?"

Air rushed out of his lungs like she had sucker-punched him. "I'm attracted to her."

"That's it? No fire and damnation if you can't mate her?"

He smirked. "There is that, but she doesn't believe I care, doesn't understand how shifters love. I'm trying to remember to think like her."

Mona pursed her lips. "Give her time. She's a smart woman who spends too much time mired in her thoughts." She dipped her chin inside her scarf. "I'm trusting you to have her best interests at heart. If you can promise me that, I'll back you up and give you more freedom."

"I can't let her go, Mona, not ever. She's..." His salvation. How to put that level of desperation into words?

She studied him. "So, if you could keep her forever...?"

"I would, in a heartbeat." His chest expanded, cutting off his air. Fuck, he would board a plane now. "What you said earlier confirmed I should grant her a little space. I'll still be there for her, whenever she needs me, even if she doesn't realize it."

Mona smiled. "I've forgotten how passionate and committed shifters can be. We humans tend to hesitate when it comes to matters of the heart." Looping her arm through Rhys's, she nudged him to Harriet's. "I will do what I can when I call her in the mornings. Nothing too obvious, mind you."

He chuckled. "She'll be pissed if she found out we united against her."

"I'd say not to tell her, but honesty is better."

He agreed, not wanting silly misunderstandings and secrets to keep him away from Lona. Spilling his heart on what he had thought Callie meant to him would help. Sure, he'd told Lona, but reiterating it wouldn't hurt.

Amos waited for them on the porch. He opened his arms, and Mona slipped into his embrace, snuggling against his chest. Rhys sighed, admiring how they acted as if they had never been apart. He strode past them and bounded up the stairs to pack. Noah and Jase would be pissed he returned early, but once he explained...

He grimaced.

"Are you going to fix this?" Aiden's voice at his open bedroom door paused Rhys's packing.

He glanced at his brother—whose hair had that disheveled power-socket style—and nodded before zipping his duffel. "I have to."

"Good. I've never seen you act like this, Rhys. Not you. Not my older brother."

Rhys frowned. Everyone criticized him as if they had the right.

"You've behaved like a horny teenager, not thinking things through, charging in, making demands. Ilona's human, can't sense your alpha vibes, doesn't care about pack hierarchy, or suffer under the primal urge to submit to a beast more powerful."

Powerful? Around her, he was the weakling, but he didn't correct Aiden. If Rhys had a chance to do things over, what would he change? Not mentioning Callie would have led to hurt feelings later on, but by then, Ilona may have loved him.

His breath whooshed out in a low rumble.

Love wasn't something he thought much of, had assumed it was automatic when he found his mate. Not once had the idea risen that she might not be a shifter.

And he wanted her love, for if she did choose to love him, it was freely given, not compelled by the shifter dynamics or magic or whatever folks wanted to name the mating call.

"Come home, visit the old pack, see Will." Rhys met Aiden's gaze, hoping not to reveal how much he would appreciate Aiden keeping Willow company during the Knight Ridge's Lunar Festival.

Each pack held their own celebration with permission to pass between territories. Humans would call it an orgy, but shifters didn't like sharing. And though there would be multiple bed partners over the three days, there was never a threesome.

Aiden's shoulders stiffened, and he shuffled from foot to foot. "Will?"

"Yes. You remember her," Rhys teased, slinging his duffel over a shoulder. "Gorgeous, blonde hair, wild, sweet, with just a hint of innocence remaining."

Aiden glowered. "What do you mean? Who would dare—?"

"Enough, cub. She's all woman now, and besides, you know how mating season affects our women the hardest." Fuck. Had Lona been a shifter, she would have submitted to the sexual attraction between them. But he didn't like the thought of multiple men having slept with her. Silly, though, since shifters were a sexual species basing decisions on attraction and instinct. A shifter mate would have had many lovers as was their culture.

Aiden folding his arms across his chest and leaning against the doorframe didn't diminish the anger in his eyes. "Fine. I guess I could take time off."

"Great. I'll settle with Harriet and meet you at Tuesdays." Rhys waited for Aiden to stand aside, then bolted down the stairs.

The company on the return trip would prevent him from wallowing in his thoughts, in replaying his and Lona's past interactions, and from rehearsing future conversations.

After a quick argument he won, he paid for the booking. He swapped numbers with Mona then waited in the parking lot outside Tuesdays. Part of him was eager to head home, another dreaded the trip. He didn't want to discuss his last discussion with Will despite mentioning she'd hit on him. At some point, Aiden had to realize he had feelings for the woman.

While Rhys waited with the engine running, he texted Noah that he was on his way back. He shouldn't have when his phone rang seconds later.

"It's a long story, with no happy ending yet." He didn't bother with a hello.

"Fuck that, Rhys. It's been ages since you had a vacation."

Wincing, Rhys held his phone away from his ear. "I found my mate, Noah."

Silence met his revelation. "Oh, well, this is good. Wait. No, this doesn't make sense. Stay, rest, spend the next week in bed, but you're not coming home."

"He said no happy ending, idiot," proving Jase listened in.

"Shit, well..." Noah sucked in a sharp breath. "Why not?"

Aiden bounding across to the car, opening the back door, and tossing in his bag ended anything Rhys may have wanted to reveal. "Long story, like I said. I'll share when I get back. Oh, and Aiden's visiting for a few days."

"Great. I'll have Will make up a room for him."

Noah hung up, and Rhys slid his phone into its bracket, just as Aiden hauled himself into the passenger seat. "Who's manning the bar?"

"Human students eager to enjoy the festivities." Aiden beamed as he clipped the seatbelt. "Frees me to partake, as well. Dane said he'll send a ride in about four days."

Rhys nodded as he drove off. He stiffened his shoulders against the thought leaving Coedwig left Ilona behind. She wasn't there, he knew this, but it was where they met, where he spent a glorious few days with her. Even sick, she had been adorable and sexy as hell.

Silence consumed the car after it had taken Aiden a while to settle. "Want to brainstorm?"

Rhys jerked back at the question. The thought of doing so was more cold-blooded than the chat he had with Mona. "No."

Aiden huffed. "I could have—"

Snorting, Rhys tossed a smile. "Enough, cub. Lona will be my mate, have no fear."

"Fine, then tell me, what do you plan to do?"

Rhys gritted his teeth, wanting to snap at Aiden. "None of your business."

"But—"

He growled, throwing out his alpha vibes. "One more word and I'll drop you off. You can run back to Coedwig."

Aiden folded his arms across his chest and stared out the window.

Rhys chuckled. Oh, his brother still had a little child in him. "Are you sulking?"

"No, just have nothing else to say."

Rhys wouldn't again mention Will throwing herself at him. Some things were best not discussed. And if he probed Aiden's feelings for Will, Rhys would be expected to reciprocate. That wouldn't do.

Heart to hearts weren't for shifter males, and he wasn't about to start. "Will should have a room ready for you."

Aiden arched his brow at him. "She knows I'm coming?" His arms tightened when his hands flexed into fists.

"I didn't know you wanted to surprise her."

Aiden shook his head. "It doesn't matter."

"You're right. She'll spoil you rotten. Breakfast in bed, waiting on you hand and foot." Rhys grinned. "Or were you hoping for—?"

"You've made your point. Ilona and Will are off-limits." Aiden flicked on the radio, and the mournful notes of a trumpet filled the cab.

At last. Rhys grinned, content to endure a few hours of sultry blues.

CHAPTER TWENTY-FOUR

A MOUNTAIN

IF THE ACCIDENT DIDN'T torment Ilona's dreams, images of Rhys left her breathless and unable to rest. The beating of Dad's pulse under her fingertips, the burning of her scar, the phantom sensation of Rhys slipping his arms around her jerked her awake.

She lay still, staring at a familiar ceiling. The sun's rays just kissed the horizon, but the city's bustling pierced the morning's calm. She swung her legs over the side of the bed and rested her elbows on her knees with her face in her hands. Exhaustion stung her nose and eyes. She sucked in a deep breath, trying to clear her head.

Pushing off the bed, she randomly chose jeans and a T-shirt, along with clean underwear. Clothed and while making coffee, she brushed her hair and planned the day. While cupping her mug until the heat warmed her fingers, she leaned against the windowsill and perused the street. From afar, people looked content, busy, and oblivious at how their lives could change in seconds.

After downing the coffee, she grabbed her phone, keys, and slipped a bank card in her back pocket. The drive to her parents' house was opposite to traffic, and she arrived within minutes. Letting herself in, she strode to the kitchen, not losing her focus. If she could clear out one room, she would consider that a success.

On the dining room table, she placed the fridge photos and memorabilia she wanted to keep. A deep inhale of her father's dark roast prickled tears behind her eyes, but she set the unopened bag aside, along with her mother's variety of teas. When she missed them the most, she would make a cup and savor it, as if they shared the experience with her.

Their favorite mugs joined the small pile.

Then she emptied the food cabinets, stacking what she would donate, tossing what would expire soon. When her phone rang, a glance at the microwave showed the time was eight.

She blinked at the caller's name and answered, "Gran?"

"Good morning, sweetheart. How are you feeling today?"

"Just like that? Like you didn't toss me into the fire while you got it on with Amos? Or chose sides between me and Rhys?" She winced. Not what she had meant to say, but true, nonetheless.

"Don't you take that tone with me, Ilona Strickland." Gran huffed. "Do you truly resent my happiness?"

Ilona pinched the bridge of her nose, fighting the approaching headache. "No, of course not. That's not... I didn't..." Fuck. She gritted her teeth and tapped the sushi menu on the fridge. "Fine. I'm happy for you."

"Now, answer my first question. I worry, y'know."

What did Gran expect from her? "My parents died. I'm sure as shit not miraculously better."

"Ilona. Stop it. This isn't you, my girl."

A tear slipped free, and she flicked it off her cheek. "I miss them, Gran. The house smells like Mom, and I keep expecting the front door to open to their usual banter." She sucked in a shuddering breath. "I'm almost done with the kitchen. Rhys said I should call in an auctioneer. They'll pack everything I don't want."

"That's a brilliant idea. Are you taking care of yourself? Want me to come back for a while, to keep you company?" The tremor in Gran's voice hinted at the deep emotion returning would summon within her.

Ilona shook her head. No, she had decided she would bear this. "I'm fine. Off to Amity today. I'm hoping to see a few familiar faces." And test her blood. "I plan to call Indes to speak to Dr. Olson. So, don't worry, Gran, I've got this."

"Good. I'm proud of you, Ilona. Always have been." She sniffed, which summoned another tear from Ilona. "Should I call tomorrow morning?"

"Please. It's lovely hearing your voice." What she wanted was a hug, engulfed in Gran's spindly arms and lavender fragrance.

Ilona ran her fingertip down the sushi menu, forcing herself to focus on the individual letters. Having used the same technique during the long hours of studying, it helped ward off exhaustion or an anxiety attack. Her heartbeat calmed, and the vise around her chest eased, allowing her to breathe easier.

"I'll call at the same time then. And please, eat something."

Ilona chuckled. "Will do." Rhys and now Gran knowing she wasn't eating? Were they texting each other? She opened her mouth to ask, then bit her tongue. "Love you."

"Love you too, my girl."

After Gran ended the call, Ilona dialed the Chinese takeaway and ordered salmon sashimi. Her mouth salivated as her stomach gurgled. Not one for sushi, she opted for spring rolls when out with friends. Her craving for raw fish made no sense. Regardless, she asked for two portions and rattled off the address.

While she waited, choosing not to think how odd it was to eat sushi for breakfast, she went through the dining room. Mom's expensive china, as beautiful as the pieces were, didn't suit Ilona's non-existent social life, but she would ask Gran tomorrow if she wanted the set. Ilona removed the family photos from the one wall without focusing on the smiling faces. In a few years, then she could chance a proper look. For now, on the dining table they went.

The front doorbell chimed, and she swung it wide open, sliding the delivery man the cash she had taken from Mom's cookie jar. Her fingers trembled when she tore open the packaging and bit into a sliver of salmon. She groaned and swallowed on a delighted hum. The salty, soft texture of the fish was heaven-sent.

Licking her fingers, she tossed the empty container, then washed her hands in the kitchen sink. A glance at the time drove her out the door. Amity wasn't too far, just a little past her apartment. She parked in visiting, then strolled through the swing doors with a forced smile when she nodded at nurses and doctors with whom she had done her residency. Her pace was brisk, and she waved with an air of haste, hoping no one stopped her.

She headed for the labs, needing to speak to Evie. As she pushed the glass door open, the cooler temperatures summoned a sigh when it chilled her sweat-dewed skin. Soon she would acclimate to Fenneg's weather. She rubbed her hands with sanitizer before lunging to the left and right of the aisles, searching for a familiar face.

"Ilona, what are you doing here?" With cornrows and thick bottle-top glasses, her friend beamed, her smile bright against her toffee skin. "Holy shit, girl, your scar looks months old."

With a wince at the reminder, Ilona tucked her face into Evie's hair. "Hey, Evie, I need a favor." She returned the hug, craving it more than she realized. Tightening her arms, she held on for a tad too long. "I suspect my blood is tainted, and I worry I'll lose it before we can study it."

"What?" Evie gasped, shooting her eyebrows to her hairline.

Ilona spilled everything, from the moment Edison injured her to Dane slicing his palm, to Dimitri licking her scar. She tugged her shirt collar to the side, showing healed slashes.

Evie ran her fingers along the faded scars. "You think you could nail down a healing gene?" Around the lab, she hurried to gather alcohol, a tourniquet, tubes, a tube holder, needles, tape, and gauze.

"I'd like to find out, Evie. What if we could heal cancer or mend bones in days?"

Evie popped her head around the cupboard door. "Oh, babe, I know you too well. You're hoping it could heal brain injuries."

Ilona dipped her chin to her chest to hide the sting of tears. "I'm sorry I didn't return your calls or texts."

Evie shrugged as she patted a stool. "I figured you needed time. So much happened to you." While she fastened the tourniquet, she met Ilona's gaze. "How are you doing?"

Ilona's breath caught as a flood of overwhelming emotion threatened to shred her control. "I've been better. Despite my parents...dying, I almost fell in love in Coedwig."

"Oh?" Evie drew blood, so good at it Ilona barely felt the pinch.

The barrel filled with normal-looking blood. She sagged, having hoped there would be a visible change.

"Yeah, but that didn't end so well." By end, she meant her running away like a coward. Her mother used to say running solved nothing. Talking was the only way to resolution, so Rhys calling her was a start.

Hell, the thought of dating him scattered butterflies in the pit of her stomach.

"Shit, Ilona." Evie raised her head from the microscope, having placed a drop of Ilona's blood on the glass slide. "Your blood is like a newborn's."

"What?" Ilona hopped off the stool, and when Evie shifted aside, she peered into the microscope. Her red blood cell count was off the charts. "That makes so much sense. Red blood cells help create collagen for new tissue."

"But not this fast, and all from one man's blood?" Evie frowned. "This happened days ago, right?"

Ilona lifted her head to nod before peering into the microscope again. As a medical student, she knew her blood well. What she saw on the slide wasn't familiar.

"So, if you cut yourself now, you'll heal supernaturally?"

Ilona met her friend's dark-coffee gaze. "What are you thinking, Evie? Another test?" She tapped her chin. "The scientific community will need photographic evidence and regular blood results."

"Something like that." Evie beamed, rubbing her palms together.

"I'm off to see Dr. Fernandez and run a few errands. I'll slice my palm later today and document it."

"Good. Got time for an early lunch?" Evie wiggled her eyebrows.

Ilona's stomach twinged as if hollow, but she brushed it aside. "Sure, meet me in the reception in about fifteen?"

After striding to the nurse's station, Ilona waited, drumming the counter's surface. Switching from the irritation showing in her fingers to her toes, she beat out a steady rhythm, creating a tune she could almost shake her ass to.

"Ilona." Kelly barreled toward her, her hair unraveling from her bun. With her cheeks pink and a slight shimmer at her temple, she looked flustered.

Ilona accepted the hug as air whooshed out of her lungs. Kelly was a great hugger, using her body and strength to engulf the victim with love.

"Oh, my word, look at your scar. How's this possible?" With Ilona's chin in hand, Kelly twisted her face from side-to-side. "It healed so well. I can barely see it."

Overreaction on her part, but Ilona appreciated the enthusiasm anyway. "Testing a new product." And she was, sort of, so not an outright lie. "Is Dr. Fernandez in?"

Kelly released her but rocked on her heels. The woman was never still, and often, Ilona had envied her boundless energy. "Nope, at a conference in Tillden."

Ilona slumped, having wanted to discuss shifter blood and the endless possibilities. "When will he be back?"

"A week at the most. He mentioned seeing the sights."

"Please let him know I stopped by. I'd love to touch base—"

"Ready?" Minus her lab coat, Evie danced beside Ilona. Her rainbow skirt suited her, along with the red-embroidered woven shirt. "What do you feel like? Bacon and eggs? Pizza? Sushi?"

At the mention of Chinese, Ilona expected her stomach to revolt, but it gurgled like she hadn't just fed it a substantial portion of salmon. "You choose."

Kelly squeezed Ilona's forearm in farewell and hurried along the passage, disappearing into the oncology ward.

Evie looped her arm through Ilona's and ushered her out the door. The sun's heat was unforgiving, and a fine sweat dewed on her upper lip. A cool breeze stirred her hair, whipping the ends across her shoulders and collarbone, hinting that she needed a cut. The air was rich with exhaust fumes and the sweet fragrance of the white blossoms on a nearby hedge. Mom would have known their classification.

They strolled along the sidewalk to a nearby diner. Ilona's steps faltered since the diner had the look of Mo's. Memories of Dane biting into donut after donut, Aiden with his bubblegum milkshake, Mo's delicious apple pie, and Rhys sitting opposite her, his forearms bare. Her eyes widened as she recalled the moment. Like a starving man, he had watched her lick cream off the fork. She shivered. The attraction had been there right from the start. He had said as much, but she hadn't believed him.

Sliding into the booth, she smiled at the waitress—a young student. "Apple pie?"

"Sure thing, with cream or ice cream?"

Ilona sighed, her smile lingering. "A double serving of cream, please."

"Straight to the dessert? Make that two." Evie beamed. "And a double-thick chocolate milkshake."

The waitress settled her expectant gaze on Ilona.

"Yeah, might as well." She nodded, and as the waitress scurried off, Ilona studied the red and white décor, the steel-rimmed bar stools, the red booths, the black-and-white checkered flooring. Onions and burgers were on the fry, and she sucked in a deep breath, relishing the aroma.

"What's on the cards for you today?" Evie fiddled with the condiments on the linoleum table. "Need anything?"

Ilona grabbed her friend's hands for a quick squeeze. "I'm fine, and all I needed was a hug."

Evie laughed. "I thought Kelly was going to pop you like a tube of toothpaste."

"I love her hugs, but she's damn strong. You wouldn't think so with her petite frame." Ilona sniffed. "I've missed Amity and the staff there." She offered a weak shrug. "I just need to find my niche, my place in this changed world."

"Your folks wouldn't have wanted you to give up on your dreams, Ilona."

"My folks wouldn't have wanted to die either." She bit her lip, then slumped. "Sorry, Evie, dealing with it has been tough."

"Only time heals, so they say. What no one tells you, is that you never forget." Her brown eyes shimmered, but she forced a smile, one wide enough to dimple her cheek. "I met someone, but that's all I'm going to say."

"Oh?" Ilona grasped the subject change, prepared to pretend to be a teenager without a care in the world. "So did I."

Evie squealed, sending the ends of her braids flying. "Is this the almost-fell-in-love guy?"

Ilona waved a finger. "Oh, no, you don't. Tit for tat."

The waitress slid onto the table two small plates of apple pie drowned in whipped cream, and two sinfully large chocolate milkshakes. Ilona dove in, groaning at the first bite. When next she saw Mo, she would castigate the woman for turning Ilona into a cinnamon-and-baked-apple-pie addict.

"His name's Eric, and he's not in medicine."

Ilona laughed. "I don't know what Rhys does."

Evie clapped with her fork in hand, splattering cream across the table. "Look at us, not pining for a surgeon."

Ilona faked a gasp and placed four fingers across her lips for emphasis. "It's an insult to the tradition."

Content to shove pie into her mouth, Evie nodded with a hum.

"He's in Inner City."

Evie stopped chewing, then swallowed hard. "Oh, dear."

"Not necessarily. Gran moved to Coedwig. I'd either have to do the same or choose a city close to her." Ilona bit the inside of her cheek to smother her squeak. When had she decided on this? Sure, the idea had niggled, but it wasn't concrete. Inner City wasn't the only option. Glenfell had a hospital too.

"Makes sense." Evie took a long drink from her milkshake. "I've heard good things about Heartstone Pediatrics."

Ilona had heard the same, but that would put her firmly in Inner City. Her phoned buzzed in her back pocket. She licked her thumb and forefinger, then extracted it. Grinning, she flashed Evie the screen before answering.

"Dr. Olson, what a pleasure to hear from you." She winced at sounding super happy and unauthentic.

"Good morning, Ilona. So glad to reach you." He chuckled, bringing his appearance to mind—gray-dusted brown hair, wide smile filled with bright teeth, and ruddy cheeks.

"I planned to call you today. I'm in Fenneg sorting out my parents' things. Could I come through to Indes to see you? Do you have time?"

"I'll clear my schedule." His voice settled on her like a thick and comforting blanket.

She glanced at her watch then smiled at Evie. "I'm at Amity. I can leave now and be there in an hour?"

"Perfect. I can't wait to see you, Ilona."

After hanging up, she stared at her phone. He had been at the funeral. She remembered that now. Many people had been. The day had passed in a daze for her, yet her mind had recorded it like any other, right down to the gray suit he had worn.

"Wow, just like that. He's a legend, Ilona, and he called you." Evie bounced in her chair.

"Still, he can't keep the position for me forever. The start date looms."

Evie waved her cake fork before placing it on the unused napkin. "Just remember to cut your hand afterward." She swiped her thumb over the empty plate to gather the last crumbs. After sucking on the digit for a moment, she widened her eyes. "Go. I've got this." She gestured to the disaster zone, mostly her fault, that was their finished meal. "And text me the details."

Ilona lunged across the table to kiss her friend on the temple—the cleanest spot on her face. "I'll chat later."

She jogged out of the diner and along the sidewalk to her car. As soon as she started the engine, a blast of air cooled the sweat on her skin. The drive was relaxing, with blues playing from a radio station she had stumbled across. It belied the tension stiffening her muscles and her fingers gripping the steering wheel.

She was in turmoil, undecided, when she half-knew she was moving, just not to where. Gran would be ecstatic, and Rhys... Ilona's breath caught. Sexy, gorgeous, irresistible Rhys would take her relocation as a sign she would date him. Tormenting her were images of herself dressing for dinner, sitting across from him at a candle-lit table, sipping white wine, with his heated gaze on her lips. Yes, she wanted that and all he made her feel.

Without Callie.

Ilona chose the closest parking spot outside the impressive blue, yellow, and white building. After hopping out, she hurried across the emergency bays to the front doors of Indes Pediatrics. The air conditioning chilled her as she strode across the white tiled floor, past the reception and multi-colored walls depicting superheroes, to the stairs spiraling up the first two levels. She took the steps two at a time, not wanting to waste Dr. Olson's time.

His office door was open, with the delicious aroma of coffee wafting out.

Tapping his door, she peeked inside.

"Ilona. You made good time." He beamed, holding up a coffee mug.

She smiled and nodded, stepping farther into his office. His glass desk against a patchwork carpet was cheerful. Sunlight streamed in from the wide windows, and toys lined one wall. He had discarded his medical coat, which, along with his stethoscope, hung on a coat stand beside the door. In jeans, a pink T-shirt, and sneakers, he didn't look like a doctor. The casual clothes put the kids at ease, and the non-surgical staff dressed for that purpose. Some days they wore pajamas, bunny slippers, and clown noses.

"So," he gestured to the chair then faced the state-of-the-art coffee machine, "how have you been?"

Before she could answer, the machine whirred as it ground beans. He held up a finger, then pressed a button the moment the machine gurgled. Spinning, he rested his backside against the sideboard and folded his arms across his chest.

"I'm okay. Had to help my...grandfather in Coedwig."

Olson arched a brow.

She scratched at a tear in her jeans. "I covered his clinic for a few days."

"Coedwig's north of Inner City, right?"

She accepted the coffee mug, helping herself to the cream and sugar he placed on his desk in front of her. He chose the chair beside her, twisting to face her, and studied her over the brim of his coffee.

"I'm not sure where to start." When the mug almost slipped from her trembling fingers, she set it on the desk and clasped her hands on her lap. "I was unable to save them." Clearing her throat might bolster her dwindling voice, might lessen the impact of his understanding gaze. "The people I loved the most I couldn't save, Dr. Olson. It made me question whether I was capable of saving anyone, and the most precious of all, children."

He opened his mouth to speak, but she shook her head, needing to share her thoughts.

"You know as well as I do, confidence is key. The patients, their family, need to believe I will do my utmost. But even if I sacrifice my soul, I'll have no impact on the outcome."

He released a long sigh. "It's what we have to learn to live with, Ilona. The illusion of control. You might find the cancer early, you might throw the best medicine we have at it, but still, the patient dies." After placing his cup beside hers, he grasped her hands. His were warm and soft, so unlike Rhys's. "I'll let your position go to the next candidate, but you're making a mistake to give up on this, on you." With a squeeze, he leaped to his feet and circled his desk to rummage in his top drawer.

He held out an orange business card.

She took it with trembling fingers and read the white cartoon lettering.

Dr. Sarah Olson

Pediatrician

Heartstone Pediatrics

"Olson?" Ilona arched a brow.

"Ex-wife." He smiled. "Still damn good at what she does. I'll send her your file, my interview notes, so expect a call."

"But Heartstone's in Inner City." Ilona gaped, torn between the flood of relief softening the tension in her back and warming her heart against the stubborn determination not to succumb to Rhys's offer.

He did have a laboratory, and if she shared her plans to research shifter blood, she might have access to an endless supply. How he reacted might be the deciding factor on their compatibility. If her boyfriend was researching human blood, would she react negatively? She hoped, with her medical background, she would be more open-minded. But Rhys wasn't in a medical field.

"It's close to Coedwig."

She knew just how damn close it was. Shit, she wanted to see Rhys's face when she told him about moving to Inner City and her research.

"I'll call her tonight, and text you the details. Get your affairs in order, Ilona. The interview could be within the next three days."

"Three days?" Could she have the house packed by then?

"Sarah's impulsive, relies too much on her instincts. If she decides to see you, then you better be ready."

Ilona released a held breath with a whoosh and rose, running her palms down her denim-encased thighs. "Okay, Dr. Olson. Thank you."

"Don't give up on your dream, on what the medical profession meant to your parents, Ilona. That's all I ask." He circled his desk and cupped her elbow for a squeeze.

"I'll try. Might just follow my grandfather's footsteps and open a clinic." She shrugged. Coedwig had been quiet and undemanding except for the crazy scientists and hopeful suitors.

Dr. Olson grinned. "Or that."

In a daze, she sat in the parking staring at Dr. Sarah Olson's business card. Before she started the engine, a text message came through. True to his word, he had reached out to Sarah, and Ilona was to meet with her as soon as she could.

Shit. Now all she had to do was pack two homes and relocate. No biggie.

CHAPTER TWENTY-FIVE

ENOUGH

"I DON'T GIVE A shit how you feel about this, Callie." Rhys narrowed his gaze on her. "Your presence disrupts the teams."

Jo-jo's head snapped up, and her eyes widened. Gabe pushed off the wall, his shoulders squaring as a scowl skewed his face. Dimitri sniggered where he sat in front of the unlit fireplace in the de Winter hold, sipping cognac.

Callie opened her mouth to speak, but Rhys postured, throwing out his alpha vibes.

"Just because you're a vampire doesn't give you the right to do as you please." He sucked in a calming breath when his bear clawed the walls of his confinement, roaring for release. "You're law enforcement first; everything else is just gravy."

She opened and closed her mouth on a snap. Her cheeks flushed a delicate pink. Gabe chuckled, thumped Rhys on the back before kissing Callie's temple and striding out.

Dimi shrugged and followed, swirling golden liquid in the tumbler.

Rhys arched his brow at Johanna, expecting her to leave too.

She grinned as she leaped to her feet. "You've got this."

Alone with the woman he had crushed on, he sighed and extracted his phone to check the time. Four hours and some change before he could call Ilona.

"You're right." Callie's shoulders slumped. "Thank you for having the balls to confront me, to hold me accountable. I forget I'm a mom, and whatever I do, George watches, learns."

He nodded then lowered his gaze to his phone. One minute had passed since he had last checked. Hours stretched ahead for him. Each second was the slow scratching of nails on a chalkboard.

"What's her name?"

Startled, he met Callie's gaze. "Who?"

"That's the umpteenth time you've looked at your phone." She smiled. "So, who is she?"

He stilled, vacillating between vague responses, an outright lie, or the truth. Since he planned on introducing Ilona to Callie, it left him one path. "Her name is Ilona Devereaux Strickland."

Callie arched a brow. "Devereaux?"

"Lona's grandmother is Monique." The hope that Callie might recognize the name was a slim one. Still, he had to try.

She unraveled her legs to rise. "As in Aunt Mona?" A slow smile dimpled her cheeks.

As a vampire, Callie would always be beautiful. While he studied her green eyes, sensual lips, he poked his emotions with a mental finger. Affection remained, but when he looked at her, he thought of Ilona. Her quiet determination in the face of her parents' death, her strength of will when lives were at stake, and her desperate need to shield herself against further pain.

"Are you saying you not only found an unknown cousin of mine but you're dating?"

He pursed his lips in a grimace. Were they dating? Fuck, he hoped so. "It's complicated." He racked his brain often, needing a solution to emerge from the crush of pent-up lust. Hearing Ilona's husky voice was a sledgehammer pounding at his control. "She's in Fenneg."

Callie gasped. "Shit." Her eyes narrowed while a frown formed on her brow. "Why?"

"She lost her parents within the last month and is questioning her reasons for becoming a doctor." He reeled from Mona's revelations.

The Lona he knew was a healer to the core. Her heart would shrivel and die if she couldn't help people. If he could convince her to choose Inner City, to 'date' him, she would make an amazing mate. She would put the welfare of the pack first.

"Ah, so why monitor the time?"

He grinned, allowing his eagerness to swell his chest with warmth. "I call her every night at eight."

Callie tapped her chin. "You can't woo her from here, Rhys. Get your ass there."

"No. I'm giving her space." His bear growled at his words and hadn't shut up since Lona drove off. Rhys had promised his bear he wouldn't lose her, yet he had failed.

"She's trying to be strong. I had Mike to hug, to talk about my dad into the small hours of the morning. Does she have someone like that?"

Mike? Rhys frowned. "Your partner?"

"Ex. But he's like a dad to me, and he let me cry on his shoulder whenever I needed to. Without too much snark, mind you."

Rhys's breath caught at his double failure. He pressed his phone to his ear, dialing Noah. "Get me a flight to Fenneg," was all he could say through his clenched jaw. Taking long, slow breaths, he calmed his furious bear and the fire in his veins.

Leaping to his feet, he paused when Callie arched a brow. "Can you handle things this side with the least amount of drama?"

She snorted. "Duh."

Stilling, he studied her a moment before sighing. "I'll get Sawyer to babysit."

"Rhys." She folded her arms across her chest.

Instead of speaking, he leveled a pointed look on her.

She harumphed, her manner that of a teenager denied the chance to have fun. "Fine. I'll behave."

"Good, and kisses for George." He chuckled as he made his escape.

With his destination the airport, he strode out the de Winter hold without a backward glance. Whatever he needed, toiletries, clothing, he could purchase in Fenneg.

Cupping and releasing the steering wheel, he navigated through the rush hour traffic, praying he didn't miss the flight, whenever that was. Hell, he didn't know how long he would be in the air, or whether he could call Lona at eight. What would she think if he didn't? Would she think he gave up on her? Darkness settled over his soul like a moonless night. No, he couldn't fail her.

After leaving his SUV in long-term parking, he loped over the pedestrian crossing and jerked to a halt.

"Thought you might need a few things." Noah waited on the sidewalk outside the domestic terminal with Rhys's duffel bag in hand. "Flight's in forty minutes. Checked you in already, and you have time for a quick bite."

Tears burned behind Rhys's eyes. He yanked Noah into a bear hug, thumping him on the back. Smiling, he stepped back. "Eat with me?"

Noah grinned. "Sure."

Over burgers, fries, and an ice-cold beer, they spoke of the upgrades Dimitri and Callie's money was funding. Dimi had put Noah in touch with a suckblood investor. Things were progressing at a steady pace, except for Rhys's love life.

"I suppose I have you to thank for bringing Aiden? Will's been scarce since your return." Noah winced, then ducked his head to hide it. "Not that I have anything against your brother, Rhys. It's this whole she's-my-sister thing and a wolf eager for the Lunar Fest. I've got to loosen the reins." He shrugged. "I suppose Aiden is the lesser of the evils. He's always had a thing for her."

Aiden in bed for a few days highlighted what awaited Rhys if he didn't make himself scarce. Women would be throwing themselves at him, and he wasn't in a mood to fend them off nicely. Had he not fucked things up with Ilona, his future wouldn't be so bleak.

"Who are you spending time with?" He was so up his own ass, he didn't know who his beta was fucking.

"I'll have to find someone. The Hideout's the place to be, you know this."

Rhys grinned, with fond memories of the brawls, the hook-ups, the beer on tap, and at half-price. As alpha though, he couldn't show his face there. Drunken shifters were more volatile, acting like idiots and challenging their alphas without meaning to. It was a good thing he was off to Fenneg.

"I texted Colt, Fenneg's alpha, letting him know you'll be in and out. Oh." Noah wiped his hand on his paper towel and dug in his suede jacket pocket. With one dirty forefinger, he slipped a ragged paper across the table. "Got you Ilona's addresses." He reached into his inside pocket for the boarding pass. "You'll arrive somewhere past eight. Here is your rental vehicle's waybill. I got the biggest they had available, so best of luck there."

Rhys grunted around a mouthful. An abundance of height had its cons. He stared at the printed letters confirming the arrival time. His bear grumbled his displeasure. They would miss calling her. The moment he disembarked, he would phone. A few minutes were fine, right? He hated it though, as if he had lied to her. A man was nothing without his word.

The boarding call for his flight pierced his thoughts. He downed his beer and rose, swiping his boarding pass, waybill, and the ragged paper, shoving them into his denim jacket pocket.

"Go. I've got this." Noah gestured to the table and grinned. "Best of luck, Rhys."

After squeezing his friend's shoulder, Rhys jogged to the gates with his duffel bag slung over his shoulder. When he slid into his seat on the plane, he grinned. Noah had booked an emergency row, granting Rhys extra legroom. He would have to endure an evacuation lecture, but being able to stretch his legs made it worthwhile.

The kid next to him, as tall, had set his headphones to deafening. And with Rhys's sensitive hearing, catching a nap wasn't possible. Instead, with his phone on airplane mode, he watched the seconds tick by, the minutes flip over, as each hour passed. The inflight magazine offered a range of restaurants to try, available exotic destinations from sunset beaches to skiing resorts. He read every article, hoping to keep his nerves and bear calm. What his reception would be when he knocked on Ilona's door was the main concern. Would this gallant gesture be foolhardy in her eyes?

Fuck, he hoped not. His fingers twitched with the need to hold her, to brush her hair off her temple, to breathe in the fragrance of her skin.

He was all kinds of a fool.

Yet, abandoning her wasn't in his DNA. Everything within him, on a molecular level, wouldn't walk away from her.

He nursed his soda, nibbled on the complimentary dried fruit, and listened to the bop-bop of the kid's music. There had to be something he could say to Ilona to convince her to move.

Granting her the full use of his laboratory hadn't made an impact.

Being close to Mona should have had her packing already.

Because he wanted to fuck her wouldn't go down well.

He shifted in his seat trying to ease a growing hard-on. His jeans wouldn't hide it, and his jacket wasn't long enough. Think about Noah, Jase, Will, anything but Ilona and her soulful hazel eyes, her wide smile, the sweetness of her lips. Shit…Noah, Jase, Dimitri, Mike, Jo-jo… His erection eased. He released a slow breath, ran his palms along his thighs, and gripped his knees.

The pilot mumbled something about the weather in Fenneg, the arrival time, and ordered the attendants to prepare for landing. Eagerness swept through Rhys and thumped his heartbeat. His bear knocked against the confines, as excited to see their…mate.

Striding with his duffel bag, he veered toward the car rentals, then queued as he waited to reach the counter. Minutes later, he climbed into an SUV that catered for his height. He grinned, activated the GPS, and punched in Ilona's parents' address. She would be there, of that he had no doubt. If by some reason she wasn't, he would head to her apartment.

He clipped his phone into the handsfree and dialed. Twenty-two minutes later than planned. She answered on the second ring but didn't speak. "Ilona?"

A sobbed greeting was all he got.

"What's the matter, sweetheart?" He put his foot down and raced along the highway, staying just this side of legal.

"I found my mom's photo albums, Rhys. Who keeps those?" She sucked in a shuddering breath. "I was so determined this afternoon, to finish, to be done, then this." A loud blast followed as she blew her nose. "And now, it made me realize I have all their devices to go through, whether I have to, what about passwords...?"

"I can help. Whatever you need, Lona."

Her breath caught, and she whimpered. "You're so sweet to offer."

"Sweet? Fuck, woman, I want to be there, holding you, helping you, not stuck in Inner City." He winced. It was the truth a few hours ago, but he wanted to gauge her reaction before he intruded. If he had to kill days in a hotel, he would. His bear thumped against the walls, roaring in frustration.

She sighed. "I'd love a hug, Rhys. I find I need them now more than ever."

He released the steering wheel to fist pump the air. "Feeling better?"

"A little." She hiccupped.

"Good. Have you eaten?" He turned onto the street, driving along beautiful houses, each unique, well-kept. The expensive suburb showcased wealth and class.

Her laugh was breathless. "You have no idea. Sashimi for breakfast and apple pie for lunch. Do they count?"

"Sashimi?" He arched a brow at his phone.

She sniffed then chuckled. "I had a weird craving for salmon."

The GPS intoned, "In one hundred yards, your destination is on the left."

"Where are you?" Something shifted in the background as if she was finding a more comfortable position.

"I'm sorry I was late to call." He parked the SUV, unplugged his phone, and climbed out. Taking the paved path alongside a manicured lawn, he admired the wide porch, the huge front door, and the lanterns mounted to the brick wall. "I had to wait until I had service."

He rang the doorbell—an antique thing hanging to the side and forced himself to stand still when the urge to pace, to ease his nerves threatened to overwhelm him.

She grunted as she rose to her feet, casting her shadow across the curtained front windows. "Hang on, someone's at the door."

"Did you order salmon again?" he teased, hoping his nervousness didn't reach his voice.

"I wish. I could eat—"

She gaped at him, one hand holding the front door open, and the other gripping the phone to her ear. In low-waisted jeans and a tight white T-shirt that bared her toned stomach, she had never looked more beautiful.

"Hi, Lona." He ended the call and pocketed his phone.

"Rhys." Her bottom lip trembled, then she threw herself at him.

He caught her but lifted her off her feet to better bury his nose in the curve of her neck. His bear rumbled in contentment. She smelled so good, like a sweet breeze carrying the scents of flowers and pine needles. "I've got you."

She sobbed, trembled, and tightened her hold around him, sliding a hand from his shoulders to his neck.

Filling his arms with her softness, her warmth, he rubbed his chin across her temple. "I hoped surprising you wouldn't piss you off."

She shook her head.

"Good." While stroking her back, he closed the door behind him and settled on the couch, rearranging her limbs so she sat sideways.

She offered a smile while wiping her eyes and cheeks. "I'm glad to see you."

The vice around his chest eased. He tucked a curl behind her ear and trailed his finger along her jaw to her chin. "I'm happy to see you too."

What he wanted was to kiss the tip of her red nose and settle on her lips. Wrangling his urges into submission, he tugged her closer and wrapped his arms around her.

She cuddled into him, wriggling her ass across his lap. He gritted his teeth against lust's fiery demands. Then she stiffened and leaned away.

She tilted her head. "You didn't think I would let you in."

"I hoped." He ran his gaze over her and cupped her cheek to stroke her chin with his thumb. "You've lost weight. Pizza?"

She smiled. "Bribery?"

"No, hungry." He grinned.

"Why did you come, Rhys?"

His breath hitched. "I thought we might eat first before you hit me with the hard questions."

He gripped her hips, then fell back, sprawling along the length of the couch. She squealed when she splayed across him, but he rearranged her until she nestled against his chest.

"You sounded alone, scared, sad. I was too worried to sleep." He hoped the dark circles under his eyes confirmed this.

"Oh. Where are my manners? Coffee, tea?" She twisted to meet his gaze.

"If you don't mind, I'd like to hold you a little longer."

Her cheeks flushed pink, now matching the fading glow of her nose. But she said no more, just rested her temple on his shoulder.

"Need me to do anything for you?"

"No. I tackled Dad's study and their bedroom this afternoon." She released a shuddering breath. "I was doing so well until I found the stack of photo albums." With a flick of a finger, she gestured to the bookshelf lining one wall. A few minutes later, she sketched invisible circles on his shoulder.

"Okay, spill." He laughed when she snapped her head up to meet his gaze.

"I have a job interview." She scrambled away to remove an orange card from her back pocket. The bandage around her hand snagged his focus. "It's in Inner City."

He growled and grabbed the card, blinking at the colorful lettering: Heartstone Pediatrics. Unable to stop the slow spread of a smile and the warmth engulfing his chest, he crushed her in a hug. "This is...wonderful."

"Thought you might like that." She squeezed and released his biceps with her nails grazing him through his jacket. "I'll need your help finding a place to stay."

"That's sorted. I—"

"Of my own, Rhys."

He laughed and pinched her chin. "I have cabins. You can pick one."

"Oh." Her cheeks flamed pink again. This time, he caved and pressed his lips to the faint glow, relishing the softness of her skin.

"Now explain the bandage." He leaned back to scoop her hand into his.

"I sliced my palm." She shrugged, but it was stiff, indicating there was more to the injury than an accident. "I'm doing research." On a slow sigh, she slid off him. "I tested my blood this morning, hoping to document what effect Dane's blood had on mine."

"And?" Rhys tugged her beside him to unravel the bandage.

"It's like a newborn's." She bounced, excitement flowing off her wide smile and sparkling eyes. "I mean, if we can discover the healing gene in your blood, we can help children with cancer."

His breath caught, and he stilled, staring at the neat gash across her palm. "Ilona, I—"

"I know I'm asking for much, for trust. I would never exploit shifters or—"

He silenced her with a kiss, the intense emotion flooding his chest demanding he succumb, to taste her and absorb her essence, her very soul. "It's a noble cause," he whispered, resting his temple against hers.

She blinked, her eyes wide. "You're not upset?"

He shook his head, bit his thumb, and swiped his blood across her palm. She froze, her shoulders stiffened, then she moaned in a decadent huskiness. He hardened in an instant.

"Rhys."

His name on her tongue drew a shudder from him with his nipples pebbling in reaction.

"Wow. With Dane, his blood had burned like the fires of hell." She curled her fingers and opened them while staring at her cut. "Yours... Yours aroused me. How is—?"

He dragged her onto his lap and snatched another kiss, unable to resist rubbing his lips across hers, flicking his tongue out to taste her bottom lip, to test its texture. Groaning, he delved in, swiping across her tongue, relearning the crevices of her mouth.

She kneaded his shoulders with her small hands, calling him from the depths of desire to reality. He crushed her to him, pinning his cheek to her temple on a muted growl.

"I didn't come here to make love to you, Lona, but if you don't stop wiggling that sexy ass of yours..."

Chapter Twenty-Six

A Reaction to Beat All

Finding Rhys standing on the doorstep freed more tears. The lump in Ilona's throat strangled her voice, and she garbled at him. From frozen to an explosion of energy, she threw herself into his arms. The moment he embraced her, her soul danced. She burrowed into him, needing his heat, his strength…him.

Mortification burned, but she refused to blink, unable to believe he was there, with her, holding her. What was it with bear shifters forcing their presence on her?

She sighed, having been everything he'd listed—alone, scared, sad—all that and more. But him holding her was surreal. She should be stiff-backed, fighting the comfort his presence offered, after all, she had agreed to their 'relationship' and on him being too far away to mess with her heart. Her limbs refused to obey, instead, she struggled to absorb as much of him as possible. She loved his cologne, like wild forests or a winter's breeze hinting at spring.

He growled, and she stilled, raising her gaze to meet his. Her breath caught at the dark intensity in his eyes. His words echoed in her, against her singing senses. Something about not here to make love to her, how her wiggling was driving him crazy?

At his threat, she laughed. "You'll do what? I'm not scared of you, Rhys." Wiggling again, she managed to entangle her legs in his and looped her arms around his neck. She hummed. "Better."

Make love to her? She wished he would. It wasn't in her to be the aggressor, and he had just arrived.

Scrambling off him before she succumbed to the temptation and seduced him, she strolled to the kitchen for its lighting, needing to photograph her palm post Rhys's blood smear.

He trailed her, adjusting his jeans around an impressive erection. At the sink, she splashed water on her face and used the kitchen towel to pat herself dry. Then she extracted her phone out of her pocket and took a few pictures of her palm, sending them to Evie with a text.

He leaned his ass against the cupboard while Ilona bandaged her hand. His presence thickened the air, filling it with sexual tension. There were dark circles under his eyes, and he had lost a little weight, enhancing his narrow hips and impossibly long legs. Shit, the way the denim clung to his thighs.

She bit her lip and offered her back while she made coffee. "The auctioneers will be here in the morning."

"Good." His voice was hoarse, as if from disuse. "Moving to Inner City—does that mean I can date you now?" The hope in his blue eyes speared her when she peeked at him.

Inside, she squealed like a teenager. Outwardly, she shrugged. "I don't know."

"I'm not making love to you until you agree to date me, Lona."

"What?" She faced him. "Why?"

"I want all of you, not just your body." He closed his eyes as pain twisted his features.

When his eyelids fluttered open, a desire smoldered in their depths. Her body responded, catching alight and zinging electricity from her nipples to her sex. She clenched her thighs together and tried not to show how turned on she was.

"So, no quickie?" She flashed a smile, hoping to ease the tension and burning need knotting her stomach.

"I'm serious about you. Like forever serious." He gripped the counter, and had it not been granite, she expected him to crack it.

"Forever?" Who was this man who spun a magical world around her senses, her heart? He spoke as if ancient, like time meant an eternity to him.

"I want your heart, your passion, your caring nature, the woman behind that stunning body."

Something twanged in her heart, like a musician thrumming tight bands of surgical thread. Her chest expanded on a deep breath, and she closed her eyes as heat swirled in her core.

She had to ask. "Because I look like Callie?"

He laughed. "You have the same hair color, but her eyes are greener. Your hazel eyes reveal more of your emotions. She has tons of sass I now find annoying. Your lips are prettier, and I have this fierce need to fuck you sideways, upside down, against a wall, I don't care." He lunged across the kitchen and pinned her to the counter with his hips. "Right here, right now, decide, and put me out of my misery, Lona." Cupping her cheek, he thumbed her bottom lip. "Will. You. Date. Me?" He peppered each word with a kiss.

She opened her mouth to reply, but he lifted her, sliding her ass onto the counter, then with his hips, he spread her thighs wide. He tilted his head and deepened the kiss, plunging his tongue in. The smoky taste of him, foggy Sunday mornings, sunlight-bathed terraces, coffee and croissants, flooded her. She moaned, raising her legs to draw him closer. His chest rubbing against her breasts, him stroking an earlobe while he ran his other hand up her back to crush her to him, empowered her and filled her with eager delight.

She clung to him, dueling with his tongue to dominate him as he did her. His growl rumbled through their chest cavities and traveled down her vertebrae to nestle in her pelvic bone. This was what she wanted. To feel something other than sadness, to wallow in sparkling light than miserable darkness.

Tugging on his jacket, she shoved it off his shoulders. He didn't break the kiss but let his jacket fall off one arm at a time. Joyful triumph engulfed her, and she hurried to slide her fingers under his T-shirt, searching for his velvet skin. She brushed the hair along the waistband of his jeans, and he shuddered at her touch.

He caught her fingers and leaned back. "Minx," he rasped, despite the smile curling his kiss-swollen lips.

Despair was swift to strike, and she groaned, leaning forward to press her chest to his. "I need this, you." And she did, desperately. The heavy weight of dread didn't line her stomach thanks to hot, white lust. "I'm on the pill if that matters."

He scooped her off the counter and carried her to the couch. There, he sat and spun her so her back lined his chest. With a nudge of his knees, he spread her thighs while unbuttoning her jeans.

She gasped, cupping his hand. "What are you doing?"

His answer was a kiss, luring her into the sweet depths of desire. The brush of his fingers across her labia snapped her from of the spell his addictive lips wove. Before she could protest, he swiped a finger across her clit, and set her senses ablaze. She moaned, arching into his touch, not wanting him to stop. Gripping his thighs, she pinned her back to his chest and twisted to nip his neck, needing to taste him. Every attempt to kiss him was met with air as he shifted just out reach.

She growled, but couldn't do more than glare at him, not wanting him to remove his fingers. He cupped a breast, kneading it with a gentle touch, then tweaked the nipple. She cried out. Her hips gyrated as he teased and tormented her clit, but when he returned to the same spot that rolled her eyes back, she cried out, riding his fingers with every cell in her body focused on the steady climb, on the looming ecstasy.

"Fuck, you smell so good." He latched onto her earlobe and sucked, then swiped across the shell.

She moaned at the triple assault. "Rhys..."

He growled, rolled her nipple between his forefinger and thumb, swirled the finger between her thighs, and when he nipped her neck, her world exploded. Bright joy engulfed her, shuddered through her until stars and divine bliss saturated her. He cupped her mons, peppered kisses along her neck, and massaged her breast, as if to apologize for the mind-blowing orgasm he'd given her.

As she drifted like a fallen feather to reality, his ragged breathing registered, along with the thumping of his heart against her ear. She opened her mouth to agree to date him, but all that slipped past was a sob. Along with the high, came the low, and she crashed. Blubbering in his arms, he carried her to the spare bedroom and crawled onto the bed with her. He hugged her against his chest, saying nothing, no meaningless condolences. Right then, she knew, he was a keeper.

When Ilona awoke, her eyes were puffy, and her nose clogged. Rhys sprawled beneath her warmed her, holding the cooler temperatures of early morning at bay. She twirled a finger across his chest. He slept on, his breathing steady and deep.

In the moonlight, the angle of his jawline was softened, his bearded face not so over-whelmingly handsome. This man wanted to date her. She was a fool not to agree. But her silly heart wanted no one to care for, no one to lose.

Sliding her fingers under his T-shirt, she brushed along the hairs leading up his torso to his pecs. With a smile at her boldness, she dipped to kiss a path upward. He smelled good, delicious, and she pressed her nose to his skin for a deep inhale.

His chest expanded, announcing she'd awoken him. She lifted her gaze to meet his.

"What are you doing?" His thick voice raised the hairs along the back of her neck.

She shivered, relishing the puckering of her nipples. Yup, just with his voice, he could seduce her.

His navel trembled when she placed a wet kiss there. "Making love to my boyfriend."

He stretched, and the lamp illuminated them, but she looked nowhere else but at him, at his wide eyes, at the slow smile sauntering across those sensual lips.

"We're dating?" He paused, with his long fingers wrapped around her upper arms. "You're not just saying that to get laid?"

Laughing, she rose onto her knees and crossed the distance between his stomach and his lips. "Would I lie to you?"

He didn't hesitate, flipping and pinning her to the bed. The kiss he blessed her with melted her into the soft mattress. She moaned, wrapping her arms around him as best she could.

When he trailed a kiss along her cheek to her ear, she grabbed the opportunity to breathe. "T-shirt. Off. Now."

He jerked up and whipped it off, then pressed her into the mattress again. On a hum, she scraped her nails across every inch she could reach. She savored his velvety skin beneath her fingers. With a guttural groan, he swooped in and claimed her mouth. The way he dominated her snatched her ability to breathe, to think. She ached, as if the earlier orgasm had done nothing to alleviate the throbbing between her thighs.

His hand on her bare stomach made her whimper. She wiggled, rubbing her core along his thigh nestled between her legs.

"Fuck, you're driving me wild, Lona."

Her shirt disappeared, her bra followed, but she didn't mind, not when the heat of his palms toyed with her nipples. She arched, wanting more of him, his touch. His chest left her. She flicked her eyes open to ogle him as he yanked off his boots and jeans. He wore no boxers or briefs. She gasped at that discovery. His erection twitched under her perusal. *Fuck me, James, he is gorgeous.*

A tug on her leg made her laugh when he removed her jeans, sliding them off her, but leaving on her panties. He crawled across the bed, stroking his chest along her knees, thighs, and stomach. He grinned and snatched a kiss before throwing himself next to her. He rested his hand on her thigh. She trembled, wishing she could wiggle and steer his touch to where she needed it the most. When he did nothing but lie there, smiling at her, she arched a brow.

"You're as beautiful as I imagined."

She wasn't—her breasts were too small, her hips too wide, but she shoved those thoughts aside. Her internal voice wasn't her friend.

He dipped his head, scraping his chin along her neck, her collarbone, and across one nipple. She moaned, gripping the comforter, relishing the texture of his beard. He wrapped his hot mouth around a nipple and sucked hard. Crying out, she arched off the bed as fire lanced from her breast to her core, to her clit. She ached, needed, couldn't he see that?

While he suckled and swirled his tongue, he slid a hand up her thigh to cup her mons through her panties. He growled, the sound vibrating along her chest and spreading outward.

Pinching and massaging her sex, he continued to suckle her nipples, trailing wet paths between them. Waves of merging sensations, emotions, catapulted against her nerve endings, stoking fire and anticipation.

She whimpered when he released a nipple to watch himself slide his hand into her panties.

One finger between her lips, brushing along her clit, shot her hips up.

"I want to cherish this moment, Lona, but I want you. So much you can't possibly know, sweetheart."

She nodded, biting her lip to stop herself from begging. As enticement, she spread her thighs wider, granting him more access. His breath caught, and he slipped off the bed, coming around to crawl between her legs. He looped his fingers around the elastic of her panties and peeled them off her.

Shoving his backside in the air, he arched to bury his nose, brushing it across her clit until she moaned, unable to stop her hips from gyrating. When he stroked a path from her clit to her vaginal opening, she writhed, her breathing coming in gasps. He latched onto her clit, suckling as he had done to her nipples, while dipping his finger into her channel.

The sensations were too much, too overwhelming and glorious. She crushed the linen in her fists. An orgasm crashed into her, and she called his name, thrashing, letting her body ride it, to experience a feverish, ecstatic moment.

His chest rubbed across her sensitive nipples, and his weight pressed her still.

"Your taste is nectar, Lona-love." He kissed her cheek, chin, nose, then her lips, sharing the tart flavor of her orgasm.

But with the head of his erection pressing at her weeping core, she spread her thighs wider, urging him on. He slid into her inch by inch, his body trembling where he held himself off her. His gaze locked onto hers, and something warm, dark, and intense flickered across his face. Her heart twanged again, but before she could ask, he dropped and buried his face into the curve of her neck.

He withdrew and thrust into her, groaning and grunting. She savored the sensation of his hard erection stretching her vagina and rubbing along her inner walls. Each thrust sparked a wave of heated joy through her, and she tightened her legs around his hips, urging him on with her heels digging into his sexy gluteus maximi.

Emotion bubbled up, a wave of endorphins gripped her, and she opened her mouth to confess she loved him, then bit her tongue. Tears leaked at the too-intense emotion, so she clung to him and gave him every reaction, hoping to convey what she felt for him.

As he ramped the pace, another orgasm rippled along the edges, tugging her toward that metaphorical cliff. Eager, greedy, she succumbed. He twisted to meet her gaze, and smiled, then swooped in to kiss her. He grabbed her legs, rested them along his chest, and leaned forward, changing the angle of his thrusts. Overwhelmed, her senses exploded. Screaming, she threw herself off the cliff, lost in intense joy, as if he had discovered a part of her that had never been touched.

He froze, his eyes widened, and he roared, shuddering as an orgasm tore through him. Pinning her in place, only his hips jerked. His mouth curved into the most satisfied smile she had ever seen. He released her legs, and when she lowered them, slivers of belated ecstasy rippled along her core. His moan echoed hers, and he collapsed on top of her.

"Amazing."

She nodded.

He shook his head. "No, you're fucking amazing." His grin was bright, bold, and breathtaking. "And you're mine, Ilona Devereaux Strickland."

Forcing a chuckle, she dipped her head to hide a new wave of warmth lambasting her cheeks. By doing so, she squashed her lips against his shoulder, so followed the action with a kiss.

His shiver was its own reward.

He rose, holding himself off her in a push-up. "Say it."

She met his gaze and frowned. "Say what?" That she loved him?

"Say you're mine." His expression softened and tugged at her heart threads.

She smirked. "You're mine."

He arched his back as he laughed. The sound was so joyful, she smiled in earnest.

"At last." Swooping in, he snatched a kiss that curled her toes.

Chapter Twenty-Seven

It's Done

Ilona's ringtone broke through deep sleep. She threw out a hand to slap the nightstand. What she found was a hair-covered chest and hot velvet skin. Her eyes flew open, and she blinked into Rhys's sleepy blue gaze.

"Oh." As memories flooded her, heat exploded to her hairline, and she would swear in front of a panel of her peers, that the blush traveled along her throat to pucker her nipples.

"Your phone," he mumbled, then inched closer, tugging her hips into the cradle of his.

The nightstand was empty. "But where—?"

"In your jeans." He gestured to the floor, and curled an arm around her waist, holding her close. "Call them back later."

A nuzzle at her neck, a tweak of her nipple, and any thoughts of who the caller was, slipped from her mind. She moaned, now familiar with the craving coiling inside her.

"That sexy ass of yours..." He growled and nipped her shoulder.

Her clit twanged, and she swirled her hips, trying to ease the growing fire.

"Woman."

As threats went, she wasn't impressed. Biting her lip, she gyrated on purpose and found herself face first in the pillow with Rhys spreading her thighs.

A stroke along her clit had him groaning. "You're wet for me, sweetheart."

He pressed his delicious hardness where she needed him the most. She whispered encouragement and buried her face as she shoved her ass back, urging him on. He rubbed the head of erection along her labia, then plunged into her vagina to the hilt. She cried out, relishing the sparking of her nerve endings, of the fire spreading outward.

"Harder, please, Rhys."

He obliged with a grunt, and within seconds, the cliff rushed toward her. Withdrawing completely, he waited, then thrust in, and repeat, until she whimpered into the wet spot her drooling had made. Wave after wave of intensity rushed over her, barreling her closer to the edge. He reached around her and thrummed her clit. The additional sensations made her scream and plunged her into a molten universe of stars, a kaleidoscope of colors, of sweet and wondrous bliss.

His roar bounced off the ceiling, just as he bit her shoulder.

Another orgasm hit her, so unexpected, it snatched her breath and catapulted her across the endlessness of the cosmos.

Without withdrawing, he collapsed, taking her with him. Wrapping his arms around her, he cradled her to him, feathering kisses across her temple and the crown of her head.

"Lunar, I love waking with you in my arms."

She stilled. He had said so before, and repeating it now proved his sincerity. Twisting, she cupped his jaw and captured his mouth with hers. "So do I."

His breath rushed out of him. He crushed her to him, helping himself to another kiss. "Ilona, my forever."

Tears pressed the backs of her eyes, and she smiled, dipping her temple to his chest to hide them. Gasping, she yanked out of his arms and landed on the carpet with a thud. "Shit, that was Gran."

She crawled on the floor until she found her jeans, then dug in the pockets for her phone. Sitting there, she redialed, uncaring that grinning, he had rolled over to her side of the bed to watch her.

"Hi, Gran." She waved at Rhys, trying to get him to stop smiling. "Sorry I missed your call."

"She's moving to Inner City," he bellowed.

"You are?" Gran squealed, then repeated the news to Amos, no doubt.

Ilona sighed. "Yes, I have an interview at Heartstone."

"That's wonderful," Amos called, and the video screen activated, showing Gran's happy smile and blooming cheeks, but at an odd angle.

"I'll let you go then, what with Rhys by you and lots of packing to do."

"Wait. Gran, do you want Mom's dinner set?"

"The white set with the embossed roses?" Her green eyes shimmered. "Yes, please."

"I'll ship it to you or bring it myself."

"I'd love to see you." Amos appeared on the video call.

Ilona's heart twanged again at how much he cared for her already. It was silly to be so emotional, but there it was. Rhys sprawled on the carpet, circled her waist with his arm, and tugged her into the V of his legs, his chest against her back. Warmth engulfed her. She no longer felt alone.

"We'll bring it," he answered on her behalf. "Tell Harriet to get to baking. I'm desperate for chocolate cake."

"Will do," Amos said before their images flickered off.

Rhys didn't move but continued to hold her. She layered his arms with hers and snuggled deeper into his embrace. He buried his nose in her neck and inhaled.

"Lunar, I love your scent. I should bottle it and make a fortune...if I was willing to share." He chuckled, and the sound sparked joy through her.

To wake up like this every morning, to sleep in his arms, no one could be as blessed as her. "The auctioneers are coming at nine. I'll need to call the movers too."

"We're driving to Inner City?" He arched a brow, then bent to kiss her bare shoulder and toy with a nipple, watching it pucker under his heated gaze.

"Yes, my dad gave me my car. It's..." She trailed off on a moan when he slipped his fingers between her thighs to tease her clit.

"Sentimental?" Rhys finished. His smile vanished, leaving behind something beautiful. Need burned in his eyes, but there was another emotion she wouldn't name but dared to hope for.

His talented fingers continued to swirl, rub, pinch, and torment. She trembled, wanting to arch, to close her eyes, and ride another orgasm.

"Look at me, Lona-love. I want to see you explode in my arms. I want to remember this moment for as long as I breathe."

At his sweet request, she obliged and met his gaze, not once looking away when the pleasure exploded in her, tearing a cry from her.

His nostrils flared, and the blue of his eyes darkened. He twisted and sprawled her on top of their strewn clothes. This time, every move he made, every thrust, touch, and kiss, was in slow motion, as if he savored her. His gaze locked with hers, not once breaking contact as she spiraled outward on another orgasm. When he shuddered, and his face twisted in beautiful agony, he grunted. His eyes narrowed, but he didn't close them.

She drowned in a pool of emotion, like liquid warmth and love. Her breath caught, as she allowed his soul entry into hers. His eyes shimmered like Gran's had done, but he chuckled and caught her lips in a short kiss.

"Time for breakfast?" He arched a brow. "Because if you don't cover your gorgeous body, we're not leaving this bed."

"Me? What about…?" She gestured to all of him.

He slid out of her, before rising and taking her with him. "You shower, and I make coffee?"

She nodded. "That's the best offer I've heard this morning."

"Better than my momentous lovemaking?" He snorted, despite the twinkle in his eyes. "Lies, I tell you."

"Ha ha, very funny." She laughed. "Give me ten minutes."

"Five, or else I'll investigate what's taking you so long." He ran his gaze over her and growled. "Lunar, woman, you could tempt a saint."

Shyness struck, unused to such open admiration. Her fingers twitched to cover herself despite him having kissed every inch of her. When pain lanced across her right gluteus maximus, she yelped. "Did you just—?"

"Slap that ass? Sure did." He grabbed her shoulders and spun her. "Go…shower."

When she glanced back, he was yanking on his jeans. She shut the bathroom door on him making the bed. Faced with her reflection, she gaped. Having avoided the mirror since Coedwig, where she expected to see a jagged scar, ran a long silver line. "Shit." She tilted her head to study it from all angles. This was…unbelievable. Stroking along it proved she wasn't imagining it.

"From Dane or Dimitri?" That was the real question and having access to Rhys's labs meant access to vampire blood too.

The only problem would be if the healing agent was in their saliva. Unraveling the bandage, the fine red line made her gasp. Healed, just like that. Slapping her thigh, she cursed. Of course, Rhys had shared his blood. She needed Evie to take another sample.

Ilona showered, hurrying through it, and was yanking on a T-shirt when Rhys called from the kitchen.

"What do you want for breakfast?"

Her mouth watered. "Salmon? Two portions. Menu on the fridge. Cash in the cookie jar."

His voice rumbled as he made the call. When she strolled into the kitchen, he raised his gaze to meet hers and lingered enough to spark tingles. He hung up, placed his phone on the counter, and swept her into his arms. "I'll never grow tired of looking at you, of holding you."

She burrowed into his embrace, relishing the safety his presence brought.

"Your salmon is on the way. I also called the top-rated movers in the area. They're sending someone around."

She leaned back to kiss him. "Thank you. I'll just pack the dinner set and stack it with the other boxes. There's more in the study. I'm taking Mom and Dad's medical books too."

Rhys released her. "You listen for your sushi while I lug those to the door." He bounded up the stairs before she could stop him.

Smiling, she folded a box and wrapped each plate, bowl, gravy dish with bubble wrap. One by one, she filled two boxes and slid them across the hardwood floor to the door.

"What can I bring? What furniture do I need?" She blew a stray strand of hair out of her vision when Rhys returned. Scanning the dining room table, the lounge suite, and the appliances, she tapped her chin, wondering if it would be easier to buy something in her style. "Never mind, I can shop when I'm there."

"The cabin has the bare necessities, but I'll have Noah clear and clean it before we arrive." Rhys rested his hands on his hips and grinned at her. "Aiden will be happy to see you."

"He's in Inner City?"

Rhys chuckled. "Balls deep in a woman he's had a crush on his entire life."

"What?" Ilona squeaked.

Shrugging, Rhys twirled her on the spot so he could access the filtered coffee. "The Lunar Fest means matings and hookups as long as the moon remains full. It's the shifter way."

"Oh, so this...?" She gestured between them.

"Happened way before the full moon, sweetheart, and I don't expect you to go into heat."

"What? Shifters do that?" She fanned her burning cheeks. If she did, it would explain her uncharacteristic need to sleep with him. She snorted, like humans needed an excuse.

"The women do, and it alters their scents, driving the men crazy. Pheromones?" He arched a brow as if asking for clarity. "Anyway, no boundaries between packs exist during this time, and anyone can do anyone without repercussions."

"My scent hasn't changed." She grinned.

"I beg to differ. You smell amazing, and it muddles my mind, sending me on a high." He buried his face in her neck for another sniff then leaned back to offer her a coffee. "Two sugars and cream?"

She nodded, trying to hide her shock. He knew how she liked her coffee. Either he was super vigilant or he cared to learn. Well, they had a fourteen-hour drive ahead of them. Plenty of time to learn a few things about him too.

She sipped her coffee while he watched, his blue gaze intense. With that slow sensual smile that inflamed her senses, he flicked his hair out of his face. After moaning her pleasure when the sweet caramel smokiness coated her tongue, he poured himself a cup.

"While we wait for your...strange breakfast, why don't you walk through the house for a final check?"

"What are you having?" She frowned. "I'm so sorry, Rhys. How selfish of me. I tossed out all the perishables including eggs and bacon. I can run to the local store—"

"The same as you, Lona-love. I'm a bear, and salmon happens to be my favorite." His expression softened.

"Now I know something about you." She smiled, drained her cup, set it in the sink, and abandoned him before she succumbed and kissed him. Damn, but he had a kissable mouth.

He found her in her parents' walk-in closet fifteen minutes later. Mom was far too petite for any of her clothing to fit Ilona, but she gathered her jewelry, and Dad's wristwatch collection, placing them inside an empty black handbag she had always liked. She had packed Dad's laptop and Mom's tablet, along with all their important paperwork Dad kept in a folder marked 'Important Paperwork.' Seeing it had summoned a smile.

Thankfully, before Gran had left Fenneg, she had sold the vehicles. It meant one less thing for Ilona to deal with. She followed Rhys to the dining room, set the handbag on the table, and sat to enjoy her salmon.

"You know, I never liked raw fish before or Chinese food for that matter." She moaned as she bit into a sliver of the sweetest fish she had ever tasted.

He stilled and watched her take another bite. "Lunar, woman, don't do that. I'm hard again."

She laughed. "What if I strip, and you eat pieces of fish off my body?"

He growled and lunged for her.

Squealing, she darted around the table, flushing at the hunger in his eyes. "Rhys. Stop, we don't have time—"

He caught her and silenced her with a kiss.

Groaning, she climbed him like a tree to spread her legs wide across a hard bulge. She wanted him again, as if they hadn't done it twice this morning. The taste of salmon sent her to heaven, and she sucked his tongue deep into her mouth. He rumbled, wrapping his arms around her and crushing her against him.

The auctioneer intruded, and despite the heat on her cheeks, she led the bespectacled man through the house. He mentioned an amount, and she accepted, only if he could take it all that day. When she returned to the kitchen, her phone pinging with proof of payment, Rhys was talking to a man in a gray T-shirt and jeans.

"All the boxes, except these two to this address." He rattled off somewhere in Inner City she had to assume was her new home. "Your apartment?"

"Can go in my car. Just clothes, and Carl, maybe an appliance or two."

"Carl?" Rhys growled, his shoulders stiffening.

"My cactus." She winked.

"Good, because I don't share."

"Carl doesn't mind." She grinned. "Once this place is emptied, we'll head on over. I need to stop at Amity for Evie to draw my blood." At his furrowed brow, she showed him her palm. "For research."

"No more cutting yourself." He tugged her into his arms, running his hands up and down her back to cup her gluteus maximi.

She nodded, shifting to ease the growing ache between her thighs when he massaged her. "Now, tell me, was it Dimitri's saliva that healed my scar or Dane's blood?"

He shrugged. "I'm not the doctor. All I know is bite marks heal with a swipe of their tongue. You can ask Callie or Dimitri. Maybe even Syl can tell you."

He shuffled his feet as if in a slow dance, rubbing his erection against her stomach.

She struggled to gather her thoughts. "Syl?"

"He's the head suckblood of the de Winter hold."

Chuckling, she sidled closer, swaying her hips. "Suckblood?"

"Callie's term. I like how it lowers their mysticism. They suck blood. That's what they do."

"And her term for you?"

He had the grace to snort. "Beast."

Ilona's breath caught. "In the bed, out of the bed?"

He rumbled, dipping to nip her neck. "Anywhere with you."

Men walking in and out of her house disturbed their conversation. Groaning, Rhys adjusted his erection in his jeans with a heated glare leveled on her.

"Wear a skirt for the drive." His husky command made her moan, and she folded her arms across her chest to hide her pebbled nipples.

It was two hours later before she could lock the now empty house. Rhys drove behind her to the car rentals so he could drop off his SUV. He climbed in with her, dumped his duffel bag on the back seat, and twisted to watch her.

"You know what's awaiting us at your apartment, right?" His voice dipped to a sexy drawl that scattered her thoughts and thrummed hot need through her.

"You mean after Evie draws blood?"

"Shit."

She laughed. "It won't take long, and it's close to my apartment."

"Good, because, woman, your scent is driving me wild."

She whipped a glance at him. "Again?"

He shrugged. "Full moon."

A wave of disappointment hit her. "Oh? And after the full moon?" Damn, she hoped his eagerness didn't wane with the moon.

He brushed hair off her face, ran his fingers along her neck, then across her collarbone to her upper arm. "I doubt I'll ever get enough of you."

What a sweet thing to say. She faced forward, hoping he didn't spot the burn on her cheeks and the tears in her eyes.

Chapter Twenty-Eight

Un 'Bear' able

Lunar, Rhys ached for her. The agony in his groin was distracting. And her scent had intensified, now aided by the close confines of the Jeep. The way the sunlight played across her face, the laughter in her eyes, the curve of her neck to her pebbled breasts. He loved it all. Casting a glance out the window, he sucked in long calming breaths. He loved her and had committed the moment she gave herself to him.

His bear was somewhat pacified, but still demanded he mate.

And it had been a close thing when he bit her shoulder. Thankfully, he hadn't drawn blood. She had his in her, they had made love, and now, all the connection needed was her blood in him. That was, had she been a shifter.

She did have some shifter traits in her genes with Amos as her grandfather. Rhys didn't know how humans might react to the mating call. He worried his bottom lip with his teeth, wondering how best to tell her the ecstasy she had felt when he had smeared his blood across her palm had started the mating sequence for him.

She thought Dane an ass, which was why his blood hadn't triggered a similar reaction. Fuck, Rhys would have had to kill Dane if she had found the polar bear attractive. Small wonders.

She parked the car in a vacant spot and gestured for Rhys to follow. The sunlight streamed down, making him uncomfortable, his bear forced to slow its pacing. Inside the hospital, he trailed her upstairs and into a lab, hand sanitizing as she had done.

She disappeared down an aisle, then reemerged, only to disappear again. "Evie?"

A dark head popped out of a room at the back of the lab. Her brown eyes widened. "Ilona?"

"Oh, there you are. This is Rhys."

Her friend hurried forward, a rainbow of colors in her leggings and baggy shirt beneath her lab coat. "The Rhys?"

"Yup, he…um, shared his blood." Ilona held out her palm.

"He did what? Oh." Evie grasped Ilona's hand and ran her thumb over the red line. "Fuck me, James," she whispered.

"I want you to draw my blood again and give me both vials."

"What? Why?" Evie's brow furrowed as she gathered a few things.

"I have an interview in Inner City, remember. I texted you the details."

Heat engulfed his chest, and he settled his gaze on Ilona. She had known before his arrival. Right, the business card. Watching as she gave blood, he couldn't get over what had happened since his arrival. Callie had been right to urge him to get his ass over there.

Lona was his, was fulfilling his wildest dreams by moving to Inner City, and he had all the confidence she wouldn't work at Heartstone, but at his laboratory, searching for the healing gene.

Her cause was noble, and maybe, this was the investment opportunity he'd been looking for. There was money to be made in healing, not that he planned to farm her cure to the highest bidder. Just enough to secure his…their pack's future.

As they chatted around the microscope, he waited, running his gaze over Lona's curves. Soon, he would have her beneath him, her moans serenading him, her cries and pleas urging him on, and her explosive orgasm drenching his cock with waves of heat.

He growled and offered the room his back to adjust his jeans again. It wasn't helping, and with the humidity, he had discarded his jacket.

"Honestly, I can't take you anywhere." Lona looped an arm through his, and with a small cooler bag in hand, she waved at Evie. "I'll text you when I arrive."

"You better, and whatever you discover. Nice meeting you, Rhys."

The lab door closed, but instead of heading for the exit, Lona dragged him into a room and locked the door.

"What—?"

"Doctor's restroom." She gestured to the bed in the corner, then toed off her sneakers and shimmied out of her jeans, taking her panties with it.

He groaned at the scent of her teasing him. Unbuttoning his jeans, he shoved them to his knees with his cock bobbing in eagerness. Scooping her off her feet, he pinned her to a wall, and thrust in, a growl tearing his vocal cords.

"So good." He grunted, withdrawing to thrust again.

Her head bumped against the wall, so he shuffled forward to place his hand behind her. Then thrust again. She cried out, moaning and gasping when he gyrated his hips.

"Fuck, you're breathtaking, Lona."

He wanted to admire the woman in his arms but also wanted to experience every one of her scintillating mini orgasms rippling along his length. They increased in frequency, and her mewling hinted the big one was close. So was his, with his nipples hardening, sparking fireworks to shoot to his groin. His balls spasmed, sending shivers along the length of him.

He wanted her to come first. Withdrawing, he paused, then plunged in. She arched, her face flushed, her eyes rolled back, and she cried out. Sweet heat engulfed him, barreling him toward his release. He roared but smothered it by biting her shoulder.

The taste of her blood lanced across his tongue, and another orgasm shuddered through him. Stars burst across the backs of his eyelids. He opened his eyes to lose himself in her hazel gaze. His hips twitched with smaller explosions, but instead of releasing her, he kissed her, swiping his tongue over her bottom lip, teasing hers, tracing the caverns of her mouth. He couldn't get enough of kissing her, of fucking her.

And now she was his, mated. His bear danced with joy, but sadness tainted Rhys's heart.

Lunar, how would he tell her?

He pulled out, moaning at the loss of her softness. As he watched her dress while buttoning his jeans, he settled his gaze on her shoulder where a few red droplets stained her T-shirt. "I bit you. I'm sorry."

She chuckled. "I didn't mind. Kind of like it, surprisingly."

Together, they left the hospital, and not ten minutes later, she opened the door to her apartment. Had he any control, he could have waited, and perhaps not drawn her blood.

Her home was in stark contrast to her parents'. The stacked boxes in the corner and the secondhand couch hinted at a life in transition. The green cactus was the one spot of color. He trailed her into her bedroom, placed the unfolded boxes against a wall, and stared out the window at the city skyline.

"It won't take me long to pack. Want anything to eat? We can order in."

He shook his head, then smiled at her. "The only thing I want to eat is you."

She gasped, and pink splashed her cheeks again. "This is what the Lunar Fest is like? Every month?"

He nodded. "I handled it fine, but since meeting you, the urge to mate has me in its grip."

"Mate." She mouthed the word as if testing the way it rolled off her tongue. "Well, help yourself to anything you need."

As she unfolded a box, he undid his boots, and sprawled on the bed, content to watch her dart across the bedroom.

He folded an arm under his head. "What about your lease?"

"It expires in two months. I might just leave what I don't want. The landlord can do with it as he pleases."

"So we set off for Inner City as soon as we pack the car?" Glancing at her bathroom, he considered taking a shower.

"Yup, sounds like a plan."

Leaping off the bed, he strode to the kitchen, picked up her keys, then headed downstairs to retrieve his duffel bag. Starting the long drive in clean clothes might be a good thing, although, he planned to make love to her along the way, maybe strum a few orgasms from her while stuck in traffic.

He also wanted to learn everything about her. They had started the game in Coedwig, so at least he knew her favorite color, music, movie. But he needed more. Returning to the apartment, he placed his bag on the couch and dug out a fresh set of clothes. She had filled one box and was working on another when he strode into the bathroom. While he waited for the water to heat, he watched her again, admiring the sunlight flaming her hair.

"You're making me nervous." She flashed a smile, then grabbed clothing out of the closet to fold into the box.

"I love the way the sunlight kisses your hair."

"One quickie and you're waxing poetic?" she teased, dropped the stack of jeans into the box, and sashayed toward him. His breath caught when she peeled off her T-shirt, tossing it on the carpet. She unclipped her bra and massaged her breasts. "I could do with a shower." One by one, she removed her sneakers and jeans until she stood naked before him.

He ran his gaze over her, his body tense with need. Shifters and their stamina. As a human, once or twice a day would have been all he was capable of. She captured his trembling hand and placed it over a breast. He feathered his touch around a nipple, down her belly, across her belly button to her sex. Cupping her there, he captured her gasp with his mouth, thrusting his tongue into the hot warmth as he plunged his finger between her intimate folds. Lunar, she was wet for him.

Keeping his eyes open, he thrummed her clit, rubbing and twirling until her breath hitched. Then he worked that spot until she cried out and spasmed against him, her fingernails digging into his chest through his T-shirt. Steam flooded them from the bathroom, but he didn't care if a cold shower awaited him.

She did, darting around him to switch it off. Laughing, she faced him.

The minx tormented him, and he was undecided how to take her. He wanted slow and sweet, like this morning on the floor of the guest room. She scraped her nails up his stomach, lifting his shirt.

"Off."

He obeyed, peeling it off.

She yanked at his jeans, undoing the button and slipping a hand inside to stroke the length of his cock. He arched his back, relishing the burn of need that rose with each caress.

"Off."

He removed his boots and slid out of his jeans, trembling with restraint. Her eyes widened as she trailed her gaze over him. Her fingers followed the path, tweaking his nipples, circling his belly button, and then wrapping around his cock.

He groaned again, arching his hips to thrust at her.

Her warmth and scent came closer when she cupped his balls.

He trembled, the sensation too exquisite and intense.

Letting her have her way went against his alpha genes when he wanted to toss her onto the bed and fuck her hard. What he needed was for her to be comfortable around him, even though she hadn't shown a hint of shyness despite the blushes.

She latched onto a nipple and sucked hard while pumping his length. He swayed, his knees growing weak.

"You have a beautiful body, Rhys."

He shuddered. Her saying anything in that voice of hers was an aphrodisiac to his senses.

She circled him, squeezing, stroking, pinching, and slapping, until every inch of him yearned for her touch, was eager to please her.

"Come." She tugged him toward the bed.

He stumbled forward and sprawled across it. Then she did the most amazing thing. She climbed on top of him and rubbed her sex across his length, up and down. Arching her back on a moan, she flicked her eyes open to meet his.

Color stained her cheeks, but she shuffled and slowly impaled herself.

Fiery need engulfed him. He gripped her hips, holding her in place, tempted to thrust up. His pelvis jerked, eager to do just that.

But she stilled when she was fully seated and sat upright, bending his length to a painfully pleasurable degree. Instead of fucking him like he longed to do, she captured his hand and pressed it to her sex. Ah. He grinned.

Toying with her clit sparked her hips to move, and as he thrummed her, she rubbed her channel along his length. Whimpers and gasps escaped her, and when she nudged his fingers aside, he leaned back to watch her stroke herself.

She thrashed, gyrated, bouncing her breasts while stroking him closer to an orgasm. Spots circled his vision when she cried out, his name tumbling from her lips. When she bucked then slumped, the heat from her pleasure saturated his cock. He took over, gripping her hips to thrust up. Unblinking, he watched her come apart again as lightning shot from his balls to his cock.

She threw herself across him while he fucked her, but when she bit his shoulder, his world exploded into white, hot joy so intense he spasmed, riding the wave for what felt like an eternity. He rolled her over to kiss her, pinning her beneath him as tiny sparks fired and mini orgasms trembled his body.

"Lona." He couldn't think of anything to say, how to convey what she made him feel. It was too soon to tell her he loved her.

"I bit you." Concern furrowed her brow, as if she had done something wrong.

"I've never experienced that. Bite me whenever you want to." Fuck, hell, yeah, was what he wanted to say, but he would sound like the Neanderthal she had called him.

"Is it as good as when you bite me?" She brushed his hair off his shoulders and trailed a finger along his jaw. He wanted to close his eyes and savor her touch.

"What did it feel like for you?"

"Oh, amazing. My impending orgasm goes from wow to epic." She grinned. "It's why I don't mind."

"It's the same for me." He cupped her cheeks and kissed her. His nostrils flared as he sucked in the scents from their union, memorizing them. "Come, shower. We'll stop for food when we refuel."

She nodded, then stretched to kiss him.

When he withdrew, she winced.

Laughing, he stole another kiss before lifting off her. "We should give your body a chance to recover. I'll run you a bath, then shower while you soak."

"The man of my dreams," she teased, her gaze following his stroll to the bathroom.

Chapter Twenty-Nine

THE GREAT TREK

THEY HAD BEEN ON the road for hours, her trunk laden with clothes and boxes, and the personal effects from her parents' house. Rhys snored beside her, having done most of the driving until their last stop where he had consumed three burgers, two shakes, and a slice of apple pie.

She snuck glances at him, catching his profile in the flickering streetlights. Being with him had been better than her imagination could ever have conjured. Her body ached from the overstimulation, but she wouldn't change a second of it.

Something intense encased her heart, like the weaving of a cocoon. Each silken thread whispered his name. She cared for him, might love him, and in what, days? Absurd. Though, she snuck another glance, he had proven himself, his determination admirable.

He had called Noah and set everything in place, securing her a cabin, even if it was temporary. She didn't have to worry about a bed while she found her way around Inner City. And the manner with which he had spoken to Gran and Amos hinted at a future. Sure, Rhys had said he wanted to date her, but how many men lied to get into a woman's bed?

She shook her head. No, not Rhys. He was different, in fact, too honest. And when he called her Lona-love, her heartbeat skittered. No man should have that much power over her.

Blues played on the radio, hushed to not disturb him. Her life had taken a drastic turn, not one she could have foreseen. Yet the impact she may make could be greater than that of a pediatrician.

She peeked at his denim-encased thighs and the way his T-shirt clung to his chest. Whipping her head forward, she tried to focus on the passing signs, the lights on the horizon. What they should do was stop at the motel and rest. But that way led to more lovemaking, and despite the persistent thrum of desire, her body did need a breather.

She inhaled his cologne, savoring it.

"If you don't focus, we'll have to pull over so I can spank you." His grumbling made her yelp.

"What am I doing?" Like he could know her thoughts. She was tempted to roll her eyes at his silliness.

"I can feel your gaze like a caress. Your heartbeat isn't steady, and you smell aroused." He chuckled, sitting up to stretch. "Not that I'm complaining."

"Eight hours to go. The sun has just set."

He nodded, then stifled a yawn.

"Get some more sleep, Rhys. I'll stay focused if you cover all that." She gestured to his thighs.

He laughed. "I love how irresistible you find me, Lona-love. Want me to ease the ache between your thighs before I drift off?"

She gasped, her core twanging with eagerness. "No." Softening her tone, she clenched the steering wheel. She was stronger than this. "You were right. I need time to...recover."

Meeting her gaze in the rearview mirror, she narrowed her eyes and glared. She was a Devereaux Strickland and made of sterner stuff. With a curt nod, she faced forward. Time to prove it.

"Sleep. I've got this." Digging in the pocket of the door with one hand on the steering wheel, she plugged her earbuds into her phone and chose more upbeat music. The miles sped by against an eclectic mix of sixties to eighties beats. The night sky darkened to ink black, and by the time she stopped to refuel, a few more hours had passed.

Rhys slept on. She pumped the gas, then hurried inside the store, eager for a coffee and something sweet and gooey. While she poured two grande coffees, shoving extra sachets of sugar into her back pocket, agitated talking snagged her attention. Leaving the coffees on the counter, she peered over the rows of shelves at the hooded man in front of the till. He had left his blue truck running with its lights on.

"Gimme the cash," he hissed.

Lona bit her lip to stifle a gasp. Unfucking believable. Couldn't he have waited five minutes? The clerk stiffened, his dreadlocks falling across his wide, angry eyes.

Shit.

She ran her gaze alone the aisle. Just candy bars, and oh, something gooey. Taking a few bars, she shoved them into her back pocket and crouch-walked to the next aisle. What she needed was something sharp...like a pen. She slowly peeled the cheap pen from its wrapper and crouch-crept closer to the robber.

Rhys was going to kill her for this.

She lunged, growling when a candy bar fell out of her back pocket. A kick to the man's knee brought him down, and his phone flew out of his hand, flipping into the air to skid across the linoleum floor. But she pinned him with a knee on his sternum and the pen at his internal carotid artery.

"Quit moving. Once I penetrate your neck, you bleed to death in minutes."

The man stilled.

The clerk ducked for something behind the counter.

Ilona kept her focus on the man...a youngster, no more than seventeen.

"This way lies death." She sucked in a sharp breath. "I've seen too many your age die of knife or gun wounds."

"Who the fuck are you, lady?" The boy wriggled, and she pressed the pen's nib in. He froze.

It would take a stab to penetrate his skin, but he didn't know that.

"I'm a doctor." She smiled, patting his shoulder. "Choose a different path or die young. Your choice."

"I didn't fucking ask for career guidance."

She arched a brow. "And how many old folks in your line of business do you know?"

A shotgun loading whipped her head to the clerk behind the counter. He had the damn thing aimed at her, as well.

She sighed. "Listen...," she read his name off his tag, "Tommy, did you at least call the police?"

He shook his head. "I can't. He's my brother."

"Well, fuck me, James."

All gazes spun to the door where Rhys leaned against the frame with his long legs crossed at the ankles. He folded his arms, and that slow sensual smile she couldn't get enough of crawled across his lips. She loved that he had taken on Evie's curse phrase, but now wasn't the time to moon over him.

"What are you doing, Lona?"

She glanced between the two boys. "Not saving the day?"

"With a pen?" Rhys chuckled.

At that husky sound, she swore her ovaries leaped to life.

"Hey, anything puncturing the main artery will kill." She shrugged, and pressed the pen in deeper, drawing a dark blue dot on the boy's neck. "Now, Tommy, lower that gun, and I'll release your brother."

"Better do as she says, kid."

She threw Rhys a pout. "I just wanted coffee."

The kid wiggled again. "And I wanted the money my brother owes me."

"Oh." Heat burst across her cheeks, and she jumped off him. "So sorry."

Rhys lifted him to his feet and dusted him off with his massive hands. "We all good?"

Tommy and the boy nodded, their eyes wide.

"How much do we owe you?" Gesturing to her Jeep, Rhys opened his wallet.

"And this." She darted for the coffees, tugged the candy bars out of her pocket, and scooped the pen off the floor.

Ten minutes later with the incident behind them, Rhys had yet to speak. He gripped the steering wheel, shaking his head, cussing, then chuckling around the word 'pen.'

"I damn near had a heart attack." He flicked a glance at her. "I wanted to pin you to the wall and fuck you hard."

She gasped, then shifted on the passenger seat, trying to ease the ache.

His nostrils flared, and he growled. "As soon as we reach Inner City, that I can promise you."

"Shit." She stared out the window, anywhere but at him. "I feel so bad." Guilt dipped her chin to her chest, and regret was swift to cast its bitter light.

"You apologized and gave them your number." He arched a what-were-you-thinking brow at her.

"Still." Peeling the wrapper back, she bit into the candy bar. "Want one?"

His laugh started as a slow rumble until a guffaw filled the Jeep. His cheeks darkened around his wide grin.

Joy saturated her soul at seeing him so carefree and because of her. She blinked at him, then lowered her gaze, lest he read how she felt about him. Confessing she loved the man was foolhardy and certainly not so soon in their relationship. Her breath caught. He could rip her heart out or devastate her with an uncaring word. What she had wanted was the kind of love her parents had. Scanning Rhys, with the driver's seat so far back, and those long arms, big hands, that sexy jaw, those lips, she hoped she had made the right choice.

"Yes, Lona-love, I'd love a candy bar."

She unwrapped one for him. When he took it from her, his fingers brushed hers, shooting out sparks of lightning joy that zinged along her nerve endings. Zinged? She snorted. Was that her professional opinion? What happened to her vocabulary? Stashing the half-eaten candy bar, she curled onto her side with her back to him.

He rested his hand on her hip. She sighed, contented, and let the post-adrenaline exhaustion claim her.

Rhys snuck another glance, as he had been doing since the 'incident.' He grinned, able to do so after his heart had nearly burst from his chest at the scene before him. His bear had threatened to break free, but with her skirt raised exposing a long, toned leg, her hair curling around her cheek, and the pen in her hand, he calmed.

The clerk didn't reek of fear, neither did the kid on the floor, as if they disbelieved her pen-can-be-lethal claim. A familiar warmth flooded his chest, and he stroked his thumb across her hip. Lunar, he was a goner. Just one trip had him loving her more. They said long journeys tested any relationship. It had strengthened theirs.

She slept on, her soft snores music to his ears. Despite the raging hard-on he sported, he let her rest. Inner City's skyline blurred on the horizon. They were close. Then he would wake her and taste her sweetness.

Between his shoulder and ear, he pinned his phone, not wanting to disturb her. "Noah? We're almost home."

"Oh, good. I moved your things to the cabin by the lake, figured that's where you're heading."

"Why that one?" Not that he minded. It was his favorite and the closest to the club-house. Still, Noah implied Lona and Rhys were moving in together. He would love that, but she had specified her own place. He shrugged. They would cross that bridge later.

"All the others are undergoing refurbishment."

Rhys arched a brow, amazed at how fast Noah worked. "Spending our donation?"

He chuckled. "Yup, for the necessities. Um, there have been a few changes. We'll chat when you have a moment."

That sounded ominous. Rhys opened his mouth to ask then snapped it shut. "Right."

Navigating morning traffic was on automatic as he pondered what Noah had meant. Rhys replayed the possibilities, sifting and tossing ideas until he slumped. Patience was all he needed.

Driving along a freshly scraped dirt road, he slowed the Jeep, hoping not to hit each bump. Turning left, he headed to the cabin, his retreat. Noah choosing this one for her was perfect. The exterior was darker and stank of bitumen, reaching him through the windows of the Jeep.

He switched off the engine and rubbed Ilona's hip, succumbed, and squeezed it. "Lona-love, we're home."

She stirred, twisting in the seat so his hand brushed from her hip to her belly. His breath hitched at the hiked-up shirt exposing her skin.

"What?" she grumbled, then sat up, rubbing her eyes and flicking hair off her face to peer through the window at the glistening silver lake before her. Forests lined the banks with Echon Mountain in the distance.

"This...?" She gaped, faced him, and a slow smile spread. Clambering out, she ran to the edge of the lake, where the water lapped the muddy bank. "Are you kidding me?" Squealing, she tugged off her shoes and sank her feet in the water. Mud stained the edge of her skirt, but she didn't care, dancing on the spot.

He chuckled and climbed out, circling the tinkling hood to rest his ass against the fender.

Gathering her skirts in one hand, and her sodden shoes in the other, she skipped to him, a breathtaking smile gracing lips he longed to kiss.

"It's beautiful, Rhys."

He wanted to spout she was more so. Instead, he said, "Noah moved a few of my things in until we can go shopping."

She arched a brow, but her lips still curled in amusement. "And when did he tell you this?"

Rhys tugged her into his arms, unable to resist a moment longer. "About an hour ago."

She flattened her palms across his chest and rose on her toes to kiss him. When he made to deepen it, she retreated with a shake of her head. "Shower first."

He grinned, captured her hand on his chest, and ushered her to the cabin. After opening the door, the sight before him left him slack-jawed. Where there had been an old kitchen, now stainless steel appliances gleamed, solid wood counters lined the window wall with pot and normal drawers beneath. A farm sink was placed with the best views of the lake, and in the middle was a long island housing the gas oven and electric stove.

The floors had been sanded, restained, and polished with a matt finish. Three doors led off the empty lounge, but before he ventured there, he studied Lona's face, eager for her reaction.

Her shimmering gaze was on him. "Is this...for me?"

He yanked her into his arms, needing to gather her softness against him. "Yes."

She sucked in a shuddering breath and returned the hug. Then bouncing on her toes, she squealed. "I can't wait to shop. Something leather for the living room, and we'll need a colorful rug. Oh, show me the rest."

Chuckling, he looped his arm across her shoulders and opened the guest bathroom. It reeked of new tile and grout, but when she gasped, he planned to thank Noah. What had once been dingy was now bright with white subway tiles and dark gray detailing. The finishes were new along with the sanitary fixtures. Even a towel hung on the copper rail.

To the back of the cabin were two bedrooms, a main and a guest, although, he had never used the latter, hadn't even furnished it. The wood flooring continued into it, built-in cupboards lined one wall, with mirrors as their doors. It had a fresh coat of paint in beige. He took a deep breath, loving the smell of paint.

In the main bedroom, his bed sat centerstage, perfect for his height, and dominated the spacious room. It faced the windows lining two walls. Built-in cupboards filled the one wall, with a door leading to an en suite. It used to be a shower and a toilet, but now a massive bath looked out reframed windows, a shower big enough for the two of them sat in the far corner, with the toilet shielded by a low-height wall. It too was retiled in subway white, with checkered tiles on the floor. Copper fixtures finished the look.

"Anything you don't like, we can change." He settled his gaze on her and found her staring at his bed.

"Yours?"

He nodded. "Take a shower, and I'll fetch our bags. We can unpack...afterward." Bolting, he didn't wait for her response. But when the shower switched on, he grinned, doubling his pace, eager to join her.

Returning, he dumped their bags in the corner, then stripped off his boots and socks. He peeled off his shirt as he stepped into the bathroom and paused. A new toothbrush still in the wrapper rested on the his-and-hers vanity. He tossed his shirt on top of her strewn clothes and brushed his teeth while watching her soap and rinse. Each rivulet snagged his gaze, hardened him until the only image he could hold onto was fucking her pinned to the wall.

She watched him with a hooded gaze, slowing her hands when they soaped her breasts, her sex.

"You're playing with fire, sweetheart." Unbuttoning his jeans, he dumped them on top of his shirt, and stepped into the shower, crowding her with his chest.

As soon as she placed her hands on his biceps, he growled and lunged, pinning her to the wall. The shower drenched him, and he flicked his head to clear his vision.

She laughed. "Little old me too much for you to handle?"

"Oh, ho. Is that how we're playing it?" He chuckled while running his hands where the rivulets had trickled. Her nipples pebbled under his touch. He wanted to taste but was too close to the edge to risk it. "Should you be doing that after a fifteen-hour abstinence?"

She pressed her breasts to his chest and moaned.

He growled and lifted her legs, pinning her pelvis in place with his. His cock nestled at the juncture of her thighs, and when he swirled his hips, her eyes fluttered shut. She stretched to kiss him, plastering herself against him to reach. Toothpaste met toothpaste, but her flavor dominated, and he groaned, succumbing to the need bombarding his senses. He deepened the kiss, sweeping in his tongue to claim her.

He leaned back to nip her earlobe. "What do you want, Lona-love?"

"You...in me," she gasped, scraping her nails down his chest.

He shuddered and leaned back to settle his cock at her entrance. Running a finger through her folds came away wet, the texture silkier than water. Her hips twitched when he dipped a finger in again, circling her nub. A tremor claimed her limbs, and her nipples puckered with goosebumps spreading outward.

"Please, Rhys."

He positioned himself again, gripped her hips, and thrust, plunging to the hilt. She cried out, and clamped her legs around him, holding on even as she kneaded his biceps. Her heat clenched his length, tugging him deeper. Grunting, he withdrew and thrust again. She arched, brushing her nipples across his chest.

Her shiver preceded the flood of warmth as she came. Her breath hitched with her eyes widening in amazement. Each thrust raced his orgasm closer, and when his balls tingled, and an addictive fire licked along his length, he roared, twitching as the pleasure rocked through him, blinding his thoughts. Ramping his senses, he felt every movement she made, heard her gasps, her thundering heartbeat, smelled her arousal and the scent clinging to her skin that was uniquely hers. His vision cleared, and he narrowed on her flushed face, her red hair drenched, drawing his gaze to her hazel eyes.

Emotion swelled and cinched his chest. Instead of spewing how much he loved her, he kissed her. Not sure how long he pinned her to the wall, but when the water's temperature cooled, he released her. A quick wash cleaned her, and he twisted to yank the towel off the railing.

As he soaped his hair, he watched her dry herself. She knotted the towel and sat on the closed toilet.

"Hungry?" he asked, despite hearing her stomach gurgle.

She nodded and offered a sweet smile. "I could kill for coffee."

"Same." He rinsed, spinning on the spot as the water turned cold. Switching it off, he jumped to shake off most of the droplets. She held out a towel for him. Smiling in thanks, he accepted it and patted his face and beard dry before rubbing his hair. Stepping out, he ran the towel over his legs and crotch, then knotted it at the hip.

"Shall we?" He gestured to the door.

She led the way, bending to open the mini fridges nestled under the counter. On the opposite wall rested a washing machine and tumble dryer. Noah had thought of everything.

"Salmon?" she squealed and took out a platter stacked high with the delicious pink fish.

Rhys laughed. "I'm a bear."

She moaned as she bit into a sliver, rolling her eyes in bliss. "Do you think Dane's blood has impacted my cravings?" Pushing the platter across to him, she sucked on her thumb and waited for his response.

"Could be." He popped a sliver of salmon into his mouth and chewed. His bear urged him to tell her his fears, his hopes, his heart. "We have an old healer I can introduce you to. Any questions you have, he might be able to answer."

A beautiful smile warmed her face, and she crossed the kitchen to kiss him. He looped an arm around her waist and held her close, grateful for every gesture of affection she made. "I'll make coffee, give Sans a call, then we can unpack."

She rested her temple on his right pec. "After that, we can go shopping. We need a couch, a TV maybe?"

As she danced away, his chest swelled. The idea of spending an afternoon with her on the couch watching anything shot happiness through him. Spinning, he disappeared into their bedroom to dress.

The quicker they were done, the sooner they could curl up on the couch.

Chapter Thirty

TOO SOON

RHYS HAD JUST YANKED on fresh jeans when Lona bolted into their bedroom and shut the door behind her. At a knock on the front door, she had raced across the wooden floor. Still in a towel, she was in no state to meet people.

Her cheeks flushed red, and she whipped off the towel to dig in her bag. "Um…there's a—"

"Noah." Rhys grinned, peeled on a T-shirt, and stole a quick kiss as she clipped on a bra. "Hurry, I want you to meet him." Careful to hide her nudity from his beta, he rushed out to greet him, yanking him into a barrel hug.

"Whoa. You should go away more often." Noah laughed and slapped Rhys on the back.

"This place is stunning. Are we rolling this out to all homes?"

Noah nodded. "In the process. Quite a few of our males are learning new trades. We bought a secondhand grader, and Reed is on a course to learn how to repair it when it breaks down. So, I saw you weren't alone." He sniffed. "Bear?"

Rhys jerked back and faced Noah, his jaw falling slack. "Ilona's human." He glanced at the bedroom door, his mind whirring.

"Wait, are you saying you mated a human and not a bear shifter?" Noah chuckled as if Rhys was teasing him. "I smell bear and not yours. She's a Sitka or a sun bear."

Rhys staggered and leaned against the counter. "Despite Amos being a Sitka, what you're implying isn't possible. She only has a quarter shifter blood in her."

"I'll call Sans and ask him to visit as soon as he can." Noah whipped out his phone and dialed.

Black spots circled Rhys's vision, and a wave of weakness slew his knees. He had hoped, but still, the chance had been borderline impossible.

"He's on his way." Noah nudged his head at Lona who opened the bedroom now in her jeans and a T-shirt.

Rhys stared at her bare feet, loving her tiny toes. When Noah coughed, he whipped his head up and smiled. "This is Noah, Noah this is my Ilona."

"Hi." She waved. "Thanks for this." After gesturing to the cabin, she shoved her hands into her pockets and tugged the waistband of her jeans down, flashing a fair bit of skin.

"Coffee?" Rhys threw his arm across Noah's shoulder and steered him away.

"I'm still waiting for the coffee he promised me." She hefted herself onto the counter and swung her feet. "We could be here a while."

"Right, you minx, how do you operate this?" The lights flickered across the coffee machine's screen—too advanced for Rhys.

"Easy." She leaped off, flipped the top, scooped in the coffee beans, added water until it said eight cups, then tapped a button. The grinder hummed for a few seconds before the gurgle of water and the aroma of ground coffee filled the air.

"Show off." He pressed a kiss to her temple while Noah dragged a bar stool from under the island.

Joining him, Rhys snuck glances at Noah, wondering what he thought of Lona. Having assumed the role of hostess, she searched for mugs, sugar, creamer, then placed the platter of salmon in front of them, but not before stealing a sliver. He loved her here, with him.

"We're going couch shopping, Noah." While bouncing on her toes with drying hair curling around her face, she beamed. "Tomorrow, I'll call Heartstone. Shit." With a squeal, she darted out of the house.

Rhys slid off the barstool to follow.

The bang of the car door and the slapping of her bare feet on the porch preceded her return. "Just have to text Gran and Evie." Her gaze turned molten when she trailed it over Rhys. "I wonder why I forgot."

"Sans is on his way."

She gasped as her fingers flew over the phone's keys. "I'm not ready. What if I think of something to ask him later?"

"So, take his number." Noah shrugged while eating his fourth sliver of salmon.

She smiled. "Like duh."

"Well, hello." Jase thumped the door frame and sauntered in, patting Rhys on the shoulder as he strolled past. "Nice to meet you, Ilona." He leaned his elbows on the counter and picked at the salmon.

Sighing, Rhys found a plate and added salmon to it before none were left for his...mate. Lunar, he would need to tell her soon. He had to first make sure she wasn't transitioning. "Has Callie behaved? Do I need to have another word with her?"

Ilona stilled while pouring the coffee, but he flashed her a warm smile when she met his gaze.

"Sawyer's been on her ass without getting himself killed. He'll be glad you're back. She doesn't listen to him."

Rhys snorted. "I was lucky she listened to me. Seems to me all Devereaux women are stubborn."

"Hey." Lona slid his coffee to him, already with sugar and cream the way he liked it.

"Worth it, though." He smirked, wishing he could bury himself in her again. It had to be the full moon. Although, his past festivals hadn't led him to this level of desperation. "And Aiden?"

"Hasn't come up for air, but he did ask for Will's hand in mating."

Rhys jerked back, almost spilling his coffee. "What?"

Noah laughed. "Yeah, me too. I damn near swallowed my tongue."

"Mating? As in marriage?" Lona's eyes were wide, and her lingering smile promised to dimple her cheek if she let it fully form.

"Yup," Jase answered while adding a sixth sugar to his coffee.

"Will there be a ceremony?" She cradled her cup to her chest and waited.

"Nope, the union between shifters is an intimate one." Noah sighed, then cast Rhys an arched brow when he nudged him with his knee.

Fuck, no, not now. Rhys wasn't ready to lose her.

"Quit bumping me," Noah hissed.

"Shut up," Rhys growled.

"Yeah, the pack gets informed afterward." Jase slurped his coffee unaware that the blood in Rhys's veins had chilled. "The exchange of blood has to happen followed by consensual sex under a full moon."

Stiffening, Rhys studied her expressive face, hoping she didn't put two and two together but expecting her to. She was intelligent, his Lona.

She gasped and tugged on her T-shirt's collar, exposing the faded bite mark. "Rhys?" Her voice rose at the end of his name, and her eyes widened. Then her breath shuddered out of her. "But...it makes no sense. Wait, consensual sex? I wouldn't have done it with Dane, and I didn't give him my blood. You had a drop, nothing more."

Tension thickened the air, and a breeze swept through the open door to chill the room.

"Thanks for the coffee." Noah and Jase scattered, abandoning him to his fate.

Rhys waited for their footsteps to fade and the start of a car engine. "When I swiped my blood across your palm, do you remember how you reacted?"

She nodded, but the grip she had on her cup didn't lessen.

"It confirmed we were meant to be, which I knew the moment I met you."

"I don't do matings, or insta-love, or any of that romantic crap." She winced. "Okay, I enjoy them in romance novels but not in real life, Rhys."

"Shifters do." He slumped. "I'm sorry. I lost control. I bit you knowing the consequences, knowing you didn't have a say. This is on me."

"Is it...temporary, you know, mates for a season? That sort of thing." She put her coffee mug down and splashed water on her face at the farm sink. Facing him, she held her fingers to her flushed cheeks.

"No, it's...forever."

She groaned, offering her back as she gripped the counter. "When were you going to tell me?"

"When it was confirmed. I didn't want to worry you when all I had was a drop of your blood."

She gripped the counter. "How do you know for sure it's done?"

"Other shifters smell me on you, and you on me."

"Me?" she squeaked, twisting to look at him.

"You bit me." He grinned, relieving the moment, then hardened at the memories.

She narrowed her gaze on him. "You don't seem upset?"

"To be stuck with the woman I love?" He laughed. "Nope, never, no way."

Her face paled. "What?" she squeaked and slithered down the cupboard door, hitting the floor with her ass. Sobbing, she buried her face in her hands.

Darkness twisted his soul, and he sat to tug her onto his lap. She didn't resist when he wrapped his arms around her. "Don't cry, Lona-love. It hurts me when you're sad."

"Sad?" she hiccupped, then wiped her cheeks. She wiggled until she faced him, spread her thighs on either side of his, and rose to cup his cheeks. "I love you too." Her smile was tremulous.

He jerked, banging the back of his head against the cupboard. "You do?" Grinning like a fool, he crushed his mouth across hers, unable to smother the joy barreling up his chest. Breaking the kiss, he tightened his hold, needing her softness against every inch of him. "About damn time."

"Yeah, yeah, stubborn, remember."

"Hello? Oh, there you two are." Sans hobbled into the house and assumed a bar stool, helping himself to the salmon and an unfinished coffee. "Noah said you wanted to see me."

"It's like one big family?" she whispered in Rhys's neck, the brush of her lips across his skin sparking shivers.

"Massive family." He rose to his feet, taking her with him. "There's more."

"More?" She arched to meet his gaze.

"Your cravings, Lona."

"What about them?" Her eyes widened, she gaped, then beamed. "It's linked to Dane's blood? I knew it." She punched her fist in her palm.

"Sans, this is Amos's granddaughter, Ilona."

The older man slapped his thigh. "Well, I never."

"The few shifter doctors we have form a community." Rhys led her to the stool and lifted her onto it, sliding the small plate of salmon across to her. "Lona's grandmother is human, Sans. Is it possible for Lona to transition?"

"Well," he smacked his lips after a sip of Jase's coffee, "she has the shifter genes from Amos. It would have to take a dose of alpha blood as a catalyst."

"And vampire saliva?" She stoked her scar, now but a silvery line.

"And my blood?"

"Are you saying she has had two alpha blood coursing through her veins?" Sans shook his head. "Sorry, my dear, at the next full moon, you will shift. The first time is more painful the older you are."

Rhys growled and wrapped his arm across her collarbone to hold her against his chest. "Anyway to ease it?"

"More of your blood will help strengthen the connection. You mentioned cravings, give into them. You'll feel a pressure in your chest, as if something wants out, then your skin will ripple like shifting sand dunes."

"What?" Fear darkened the green of her eyes. "Do you know what I will shift into?"

"Amos is bear, as is Dane and Rhys. Odds are, so are you. It's hard to know for sure though. Like a melting pot. Look at George, a polymorph in a wolf pack." Draining the mug, Sans thumped it down. "If that's what you needed me for?"

"There's more. Ilona, ask away."

She clasped Rhys's arm pinning her to him. "I'm reeling. Do you mind if I gather my thoughts then find you, doctor to doctor?"

Sans grinned. "Followed Amos's footsteps, did you? Well, I'll be hog swaddled. Sure. Rhys's got my number."

She reached across the counter to pat his arm. "I'll treat you to apple pie."

"I'll hold you to that." Sans grinned, slid off the stool, and scampered out.

"Want to talk about it?" Rhys pressed a kiss to her temple.

"No, let me mull it over. Right now, I need to focus on something mundane. Let's go couch shopping."

He stared into her shimmering eyes and stole a kiss. "Leather, you say?"

She nodded, slipped from his arms, and hurried to their bedroom. "Want me to bring your boots?"

"Please." He grinned and succumbed to an air fist pump. She wasn't leaving him.

Chapter Thirty-One

REVELATIONS

"Just using the bathroom." Ilona shut the bathroom door and slid down it. Her mind reeled, while her heart leaped and danced. She couldn't focus on any of the revelations from the past hour.

"Fuck me, James, Evie," she whispered as soon as her friend answered the call. "I'm his mate, I'm a bear, and he loves me."

"Oh." Squealing followed then halted. "Wait, what?"

Tidal waves of emotion crashed against Ilona's heart, only to recede and another to form. Air was scarce, and she struggled to inhale without asphyxiating herself. "I'll text you the details. I don't know how I feel about this."

"Which part, girl?"

"I love him," Ilona smiled, "so only two out of three to deal with."

"And love conquers all, or they wouldn't sing about it all the damn time. So, which one is the worst of the two remaining? Becoming a shifter or that you're his mate?"

"I don't know."

"Well, figure it out. As a shifter, we have access to your blood without needing to ask permission. Wacky doctor tests on herself. That ain't news." Evie bit into something crunchy and chewed.

"Apparently, becoming an animal is super painful." Ilona stroked her scar and rested her hand over her thumping heart.

"So? Like women don't give birth and live to tell the tale. Is it the mating thing? Did he go on one knee? What's the story?"

Trust Evie to dumb it down, which was why Ilona had called her. If anyone could help her see reason, it was her bestie.

"He didn't ask, just lost control...um...during sex, and made the mating permanent." Ilona bit her lip. "Part of me is on cloud nine that he loves me, has married me. The other part wants to crawl in a hole and hide." She squeezed the bridge of her nose and sighed. "I should be pissed, right?"

"You're asking me? Honey, I'm still trying to date Eric. What if I wrestle him to the floor and chloroform him? In which country is that legal?"

Ilona chuckled. "Well, you could move here and choose a shifter yourself. If that's possible, I mean, with you being human." She frowned. How had they gotten onto Evie's rollercoaster love life?

Rhys called her name, and Ilona whispered, "I've got to go. I'll text later." She scrambled off the floor and used the toilet because she did need to. While washing her hands, he rapped on the door. "I'm done."

With two fingers, he pushed the door open and leaned against the frame. "You okay?"

She bit her lip. Lying wouldn't solve anything, but how could she put into words the pendulum swing of her emotions. "I don't know. I love that you love me, Rhys. Just...all the other stuff."

He tugged her against him, and his strength soaked into her limbs. Sighing, she snuggled deeper, almost feeling as if she had come home. "Did you want the grand gestures, the rings, the white wedding? Anything for you, Lona-love."

"A proposal would have been nice." She titled her head to rest her chin on his chest. He dipped to kiss her, a brushing of his lips across hers, nothing more. "Gran might insist on a wedding."

He tucked a curl behind her ear, stroked her jaw, and pinched her chin, holding her still for another kiss. "She might ask for a double wedding."

Ilona laughed. "Oh, no, let's not do that."

"We'll have the best cake."

She groaned. "I'd love a slice of cake."

"Or apple pie?" He released her to cup her cheeks, holding her still for one of his devasting kisses, deep, penetrative, thorough, snatching her breath again. "I love you, Lona."

She smiled. "You're just lucky I love you too. I should be losing my shit here."

"I'm grateful you aren't." Capturing her hand, he pressed his lips to her knuckles and led her to an SUV parked out front. "Noah brought my car."

She settled in the front seat. The interior carried the rich scent of Rhys's cologne. While putting on her shoes, she had shoved her bank cards in her back pocket. She couldn't expect Rhys to pay... "Let's talk finances."

He jerked back and flicked a startled glance at her. "What about them?"

"You don't have a day job, so how do you survive?"

"Most shifters have work, but some serve the pack. Those with steady income help where it's needed."

She gaped. "So, any money I earn would—?"

"Go to our family, then to the pack. We also receive donations and have made investments." He gripped and released the steering wheel. "All new. I haven't been alpha long."

"So, you wouldn't mind if I bought things?" She placed a hand over his white-knuckled fist on the gear shift. "My parents made me independently wealthy. Whatever I want or need has been taken care of."

His eyes bulged. "We'll need to invest."

"Dad already did. I'll show you his documents. Maybe there are investments you might consider worthy."

He nodded.

"I'm asking because some couples have joint accounts and others share living expenses but not their full earnings. Since my 'marriage' was a surprise, we haven't had a chance to talk about this."

"I won't lie, Lona, money is a sore point. Alrik, the last alpha, squandered what we had. I'm trying desperately to feed and house my people unable to help themselves. The incident with George's brothers highlighted a serious need. As you saw, your cabin was upgraded, and is the first of many."

"Well, we'll see how much disposable income I have and where we can plug holes." She patted his hand. "With your big ass, we'll need to buy an expensive leather couch." She grinned at his snort. "On me, of course."

He flipped his hand and laced his fingers through hers, lifting it to kiss her knuckles. "I don't deserve you."

"Yup, that's the attitude right there for a successful marriage."

"Mating." He chuckled.

"You say potato..." She grinned, letting him navigate traffic to park outside a massive furniture warehouse.

Laughter followed as he tested couch after couch. The TV was a quick choice, the largest they had, but the couch? In the end, she put her foot down when he sprawled her across his lap. A three-seater, a two-seater in brown leather and with overstuffed cushions. For an extra fee, they would deliver that day.

When Rhys stopped outside a diner, her heart leaped to choke her.

"You did say apple pie." He winked and climbed out the car, circling the hood to open the door for her while she struggled to control the urge to cry.

"I did, and damn, I love you for it."

After cinnamon-apple-golden goodness with double whipped cream, they returned to his pack's land. She didn't know how big it was, but he parked outside a two-story building with a massive wraparound porch.

"This is the clubhouse, with bedrooms for those in need. It's my office, so to speak. Let's see who's around." He ushered her up the wooden steps and into the well-lit confines sporting haphazard furniture, a few desks, and stairs leading to the next floor.

"Rhys, and this must be Ilona, welcome." A woman hurried to hug Rhys and offer Ilona her hand for a shake.

"Ilona this is Madison. She runs the school."

While clasping the woman's hand, Ilona gaped. "You have a school? How big is your land?"

He shrugged. " A few hectares, I think."

Madison laughed and brushed chestnut-colored hair off her face. "Rhys never was one for geography."

"I know where Fenneg is." He circled an arm around Ilona's waist and tugged her against him.

"Uncle Rhys." A little girl burst through the open front door and threw herself at him.

He laughed and picked her up, tossing her into the air as another man hovered at the door. His black attire was stark against his pale skin. "Lona-love, this is George."

So, this was the polymorph? Brown hair and eyes and with the cutest nose, the girl blinked at Ilona.

She beamed, tugging and yanking on the girl's pink skirt. "I want one just like this, but Uncle Rhys won't let me." She added an exaggerated pout. "He's a meanie."

"Uncle Rhys." George wagged a little finger at him. "Pink's bootiful. Gabe says so."

"Be-you-tee-full," Madison said, but her gaze lingered on the man at the door.

George pouted. "That's what I said."

Rhys chuckled. "Are you going home now, cupcake?"

"Yup." She grabbed his beard and yanked him down for a kiss on the cheek. "See you tomorrow." Wiggling, she forced him to release her. With a wave, she slid her hand into the stranger's and out they went.

"Um...that man?" Ilona gestured with her thumb. "Suckblood?"

"Not you too." Madison threw her hands into the air.

Rhys laughed and grabbed Ilona's hand. "Call if you need anything, Maddy." He ushered Ilona to the car and lifted her in. "She's in love with him. Maybe. And yes, he's a suckblood. One of Dimi's men."

"At some point, you have to break down the packs and holds for me," Ilona said when Rhys settled into the driver's seat and started the engine.

"It's not that complicated. Each city has a pack and, therefore, an alpha." He smirked. "Now vamps are little more arbitrary. The holds report to the Drimari Council which metes out justice, or so I'm told. And any number of holds can exist in a city. Inner City has five, governed by a king, and in this case, Syl of the de Winter hold. Got it?"

She frowned. "Coedwig has vamps?"

"Nope. The town's too small for their liking." His blue eyes turned molten. "I want to test out our couch and the TV."

She studied his eagerness, the way his gaze lingered on her lips. "Maybe the couch first," she rasped. "Who knows how long it will take you to master the TV."

He grinned. "Good point."

"I've never seen him like this."

Ilona shrieked, startled awake to find a woman in her bedroom. "Who...?" Fear choked her, and she sliced a glance at the closed bedroom door, then at the sealed windows. "How did you—?"

"Callista de Winter." The woman beamed, and with a flick of her fingers, light engulfed the room. "Well, to be fair, I'm ex-human, now a suckblood." One moment she sat in the leather cub chair, the next she gripped Ilona by the shoulders. "Let me have a look at you." With a familiar emerald gaze, she studied Ilona's face, humming at intervals. "I can see Aunt Mona in you."

Ilona gasped. "You know my gran?"

"I used to when my parents were alive. I must have been about six when I last saw her, though." Callie chuckled. "Kind of makes us cousins."

"Wait, what did you mean when you said you've never seen him like this? Who?" Ilona's mind was reeling, what with Callie confirming they were related as Rhys suspected.

"Why, Rhys, of course. The last time I saw him, he didn't hear a word I said, then chewed me out. I liked that about him, the big old teddy bear." Callie flicked a dismissive hand. "Since we met, he's been uber polite, like I might rip his head off. Then he returned from Coedwig with fire."

"He did?" Ilona squeaked.

"Sure thing." Callie grinned. "I can see why. You're gorgeous."

Ilona cupped the side of her face, trying to hide the scar.

Callie brushed her hand away. "The idiot loves you. What does it matter what you look like? Besides, it's faded. Dimi said he had to lick you." With a curt nod, she settled on the edge of the bed. "Vampire saliva works wonders."

Ilona blinked. So it is in their saliva? "Where's Rhys?" She patted the bed beside her, finding a lingering warmth.

"A busted water main or something." Callie grinned, unrepentant. "I wasn't going to wait for the teddy bear to bring you to meet me. George told me about you, and I came right over."

With another flick, Ilona wore head-to-toe pajamas. Gasping, she fingered the silk of her instant-clothing. Her door swung open to a tall man wearing a stiff smile.

She blinked at him, dazed by his silvery eyes and good looks.

He growled, "he's on his way back." Then he was gone, like vanished.

"Well, that's my cue." Callie rose. "Make Rhys bring you for a visit. Oh, before I forget." With a click of her fingers, a pink skirt draped across the foot end of the bed.

Ilona gaped at it. What the hell? Did suckbloods have magic? Like the man had done, Callie vanished as the front door opened.

Clambering off the bed, Ilona hurried to the living room. She slumped at the sight of Rhys. Questions burned her tongue, but they would have to wait. He was drenched, his jeans and T-shirt clinging to him. He squelched as he tip-toed in. She rested her ass on the back of the couch and smiled.

He stilled while peeling off his shirt. "Hey, I didn't want to wake you."

She shook her head and sauntered across to him to unbutton his jeans. His breath caught, and his shirt slipped from his finger before he gripped her hips and threw her over his shoulders. She squealed, and when he slapped her ass, heat pooled in her core.

But when he tossed her onto the bed, he stared at the pink skirt.

"Callie was here." He cursed, stomping his feet as he paced. "I'll fucking kill her. I wouldn't put the burst pipe past her."

"She was here with some guy."

"Probably Gabe." Yanking off his boots, Rhys dropped them then peeled off his jeans. His penis bounced free, and her breath caught with her mouth drying. "If you look at me like that…"

"You'll what? Threaten me without following through?"

"Oh, ho." He tugged on the edges of her pajama pants and dropped them on the floor. Then with a jerk, buttons flew across the room, gaping her top. His nostrils flared, his gaze darkened, and he crawled onto the bed, spreading her legs wide. He paused in a full push-up. "Lunar, I love you."

"So when threatening doesn't work, sweet-talking is your go-to tactic?" But she ruined her serious tone by dragging him down, needing his chilled skin against hers.

He grunted and buried his face in her neck, nuzzling her.

She wrapped her legs around his hips, shifting until his erection rubbed against her labia. Arching on a moan, she tightened her arms and tangled her fingers in his wet air, inhaling his cologne.

"Just love me, Rhys, and don't stop."

He growled, rose to meet her gaze, and at last, she recognized the intense emotion lighting his eyes—love for her.

"Always, Lona-love."

CHAPTER THIRTY-TWO

THE BREAKTHROUGH

THREE WEEKS LATER, ILONA had settled into a routine she enjoyed. The interview with Sarah Olson had gone well, with Ilona spending her mornings at the hospital. She adored the children but didn't want to commit full-time. Afternoons were spent in Rhys's lab, studying her blood, and the effects known diseases had on it. Her and Evie co-researched, passing notes via text or email daily.

Some days, Ilona wore the skirt Callie had given her, swishing around the wards like a fairy with orange hair. As long as she made children laugh, her day was complete.

When her phone rang, she answered without checking caller I.D.

"Fuck me, James." Evie's cursing had become their normal greeting. "I'm sending you images, then I'm packing. You got one crazy woman moving to Inner City."

Ilona squealed. "For real?"

"Sure. Check the images, and I'll call you when I land. I'll need a ride." The call ended, and Ilona paused to stare at the screenshots of printouts. It took her seconds to realize what she was looking at.

She spun on her heel and rushed into the hospital, taking the steps two at a time to reach Sarah's office. Without knocking, she burst in to shove her phone at the dark-haired doctor in a headless bunny suit.

"What is it? Something to do with your research?"

Emotion barreled up Ilona's throat and burned behind her eyes. She wanted to squeal, to dance, to kneel and pray.

"It's...delta thirty-two." A slow smile spread across Sarah's face, warming her brown eyes. "We should have known. Is this your blood? Or...?"

"Mine. I have a mutation. I'll get sick, but it won't kill me." Leaning across, Ilona flicked to the next photo. "That's Rhys's blood I couriered to Evie."

"Two markers, and with his off-the-charts RBC, it explains so much." Sarah handed Ilona her phone. "But how to test it?"

"Evie's on her way to Inner City. She's been working through known diseases when she stumbled on this. We can throw cancer at it and see what happens."

"What you're saying is it's too soon to test on children. You're right. We need to be sure. Share those images with Philip...I mean, Dr. Olson. See what he thinks. The more doctors we have backing you, the better."

Ilona nodded.

As she left, Sarah called after her. "Well done."

Ilona couldn't remember how she got home, but she snapped out of her daze when she parked outside the clubhouse. Excitement ran roughshod over her, and her cheeks hurt from the grin she still wore. Climbing out of the Jeep, she sprinted up the steps and across the porch.

When she burst through the front door, Rhys leaped to his feet, his eyes wide in alarm. "What is it?"

And like a lovesick fool, she wept great sobbing tears. "We found it."

He swept her into his arms and shushed her. "Breathe, calm, I've got you. Now tell me slowly, what did you find?"

"The genetic marker behind your miraculous healing."

He gaped, then laughed. "I knew you could do it, Lona-love."

"The what now?" Noah asked from behind the desk.

"What makes shifters heal so quickly. If we can reproduce it, we can heal children, maybe even eradicate diseases." Throwing back her head, she laughed for the sheer joy of it. "I've got to phone Amos, Sans, and Dr. Olson. Oh, Noah, do we have a place for Evie? She's moving to Inner City."

"I can find a small cottage." He thumped Rhys on the shoulder and kissed Ilona's cheek. "Congrats." As he strolled away, he mumbled, "you'd swear they were having cubs."

Shaking her head, she said to him, "how much money is in big pharma?"

Noah whipped to face her. "I don't know, tons?"

"Exactly. Of course, we won't charge a fortune. That would be silly. Besides, I'm getting ahead of myself. Now the real work starts. We need to test against all viruses, bacteria, any mutations."

Rhys steered her through the door and into the sunlight. "After this, focus on helping the suckbloods procreate."

She nodded. "Started, but with this discovery, the answer has to lie in their genes. I'll narrow my efforts." Pressure grew in her chest until she thought she might explode. A low growl trembled through her, and she stilled. "What was that?"

"What was what?" Rhys arched a brow as he clipped her in the passenger seat.

"I heard a rumble. Felt it here." She tapped her sternum.

He grinned. "Might be your bear."

She snorted. "You say that when I have indigestion."

"The full moon is in one week, my love. Then I'll teach you how to hunt." He rubbed his palms together. "Nothing tastes as delicious as salmon fresh from the lake."

As he circled the hood, the rumble intensified, and something rippled under the skin of her forearm. She blinked at it, fighting the rising panic churning her gut. From ecstatic to horrified was a harsh swing, even for her.

Rhys climbed into the driver's seat while humming a jaunty tune she didn't recognize. "How do you want to celebrate?"

She shrugged, unable to think when her skin rippled again, this time on both arms.

"A hot bath, bubbles, champagne?" Each option he matched with a kiss across her captured knuckles.

She flashed a smile. "Though, where would you find champagne at this hour?"

As he drove them home, he spoke of fetching a bottle or two after he ran her a bath.

Minutes later, she stood in their bedroom blinking at the steam rising from the bathtub with Lily of the Valley wafting from the bathroom. Her senses had heightened, more so after every time she bit him during sex. The cacophony from the forest was almost deafening. And her olfactory more enhanced, picking up the salmon in the fridge.

Making love had taken on a breathtaking intensity. The sweep of his hands ignited her nerve endings. His cologne clinging to his skin saturated her nose. His thumping heartbeat synchronized with hers. More than this, she sensed when his emotions altered if they were deep enough. And often, it was his uncompromising love engulfing her.

He stripped off her clothes and shoes, then led her to the bathtub. With a kiss to her temple, he hurried out, intent on buying champagne.

She faced the mirrors above the vanities. "If you plan to come out, can we do it now and get it over with?"

The presence huffed. Then something bumped against the inner walls of her soul, demanding release. Pain lanced outward like a spreading acid burn. She gasped and gripped the vanity's stone, curling her spine as another wave hit her. Her skin rippled, and a thousand needles pricked, pinched, and caught alight. She screamed, as each hair extended, her bones snapped, and reformed, like logs in a bonfire. With her eyes squeezed shut, she dared not peek at her reflection.

This couldn't be happening.

She was human.

Was.

Her vision blackened as something shook her skeleton and trembled her teeth in her jaw. The agony was excruciating, too much for her to handle. With that, she slumped into blissful darkness.

Awaking, she stared at the tiled floor, trying to recall how she got there. Rising onto her hands and knees, she rocked, gathering her strength to stand. But all she could manage was to lift her head enough to catch her reflection.

A roar escaped, bearing a wide mouth and tons of teeth that had no place being in her mouth. She plunged forward onto her front paws again.

Paws.

Her long claws tapped the tiles, and where her hands were supposed to be, brown paws flowed into hairy front legs.

Her bear.

She slumped, sat on her padded ass, and peeked at the Sitka brown bear in the reflection. She shifted to the right. So did the bear. Then to the left. The bear did the same while something inside her snorted. Ignoring the other presence, she yawned, exposing her elongated incisors.

Now what?

Forcing herself to walk, she staggered and lurched, unused to moving on four legs. She bumped against the door, the bed, and the couch, trying to reach the front door. But before she made it, a shadow fell across the floor.

"Lona?"

She growled, baring her teeth.

Move, Rhys. But he didn't hear her. He placed bags on the counter, then yanked off his boots, all the while complaining about her stubbornness and impatience.

"What were you thinking? I wanted to share this with you, be there as you transitioned."

It's a matter of dignity.

As he stripped off his shirt and jeans, he went on about how something could have gone wrong, how beautiful he found her bear. Naked, he urged her to follow him outside. As she padded onto the porch, he changed into his bear, and a wealth of emotion crashed into her.

His alpha waves rolled across her senses, urging her to submit. She snorted. Instead, she raised her nose to sniff, picking up the earthy scents of sand, water, wind, then the sweetness of the salmon in the waters and honey nearby.

He nudged her with his head, almost toppling her. She growled a warning, but he chaffed, as if he laughed. Then he danced around her, urging her to move, to bat him with a paw.

Having never been one of those nature girls content to rough it in the wild, finding the sun on her face, the cool breeze ruffling her hair, and the feel of the dirt beneath her paws, there was nothing to compare it to.

She gave her bear free rein and loped after Rhys's bear, as he led her along a worn path through the forest. When she bumped against trees, plunged through bushes, her bear chaffed, stumbled to her feet, and continued, wanting to chase Rhys, enjoying the challenge. She burst into a clearing with soft moss and clover lining the forest floor.

He returned to his human form, and waited, with his hands on his hips. "Come now, Lona-love. Change back. Your bear can have another go when we head home."

Her bear roared, unhappy with the suggestion, but Rhys squared his shoulders. Authority rolled off him, like a heady breeze addictive and compelling. Her bear cowered. New agony stormed through Ilona, as her bones popped into place. She crumpled to the ground and curled into a whimpering ball.

He sprawled beside her and wrapped his arms around her. "The first time is hard on everyone, Lona-love, worse for those who are alone."

"Will it always hurt this much?"

He kissed her temple. "No, just in the beginning. Your human body will adjust."

She nuzzled his shoulder, loving the scent pouring off him, like sunbaked rock. Moaning, she pressed her nose to his skin and inhaled. Heat uncoiled in her core, igniting her senses. She groaned, her hips twitching with a need so powerful, she almost orgasmed just by rubbing her thighs together.

"What now?" she cried out, pushing up to meet his gaze.

"The fun begins." He chuckled and cupped a breast. Fire exploded outward, from her puckering nipple to her belly. "Your first on-heat."

"Oh." She gasped, fascinated by the bobbing of his erection. "This is how it feels?" The urge to climb on top of him gripped her. She could spread her thighs and ride his hard length. Shuddering, she raised her gaze to the afternoon sky, searching for control, for calm.

"It's futile." His nostrils flared, and his eyes fluttered shut on a growl. "Just...use me, please."

She stretched her hand then hovered it above his erection resting on his stomach. "Are you sure?"

"Ilona."

Laughing, she layered herself on top of him, whimpering at his heated skin against hers. Then with deliberation, she impaled herself on his hard length. Lightning exploded across her vision, and she cried out, gyrating her hips as she rode him. He gripped her hips to thrust up, meeting each of her downward strokes.

The need to consume him, to have every inch of him merge with her, to know his every thought, his desires, exploded within her, and she screamed, arching her back as pleasure crashed over her. He flipped her over and pounded into her, chasing his orgasm, then as a tremor claimed his body, he sank his teeth into her shoulder.

Joy skittered along her veins, hardening her nipples until they pinged, and her clit twanged like a too-tight elastic. She cried out, riding yet another wave she hadn't anticipated.

He slumped over her, his weight pressing her into the soft clover. His slow rumble merged into a full-bellied laugh. "I fucking love you, Lona."

She smiled, running her hands along his shoulders. "I love you too."

"I was prepared to wait forever for you."

She blinked back the tears. "Thank you for not giving up on me."

"Oh, Lona-love, you mean the world and more to me." He kissed her cheek, the tip of her nose before brushing his mouth across hers. "My forever."

ABOUT THE AUTHOR

Sevannah Storm is a fiction writer who immerses herself in fantastical worlds both magical and science fiction. She has a flare for the creative, having studied art and interior architecture, and spends her time drawing, oil painting, and writing. An avid reader from an early age, Sevannah finds her inspiration from various sources: games, novels, music, and the land of make-believe. The unique versus the practical has brought on numerous debates.

In her spare time, she does Pilates and rereads novels that snatch her breath away. Having embraced the social media world, you can find her on most platforms.

Her home is a land south of Wakanda, where animals roam free. Born in Zimbabwe, she grew up in South Africa. The crisp blue skies with cotton-candy sunsets expand her heart and soul, encapsulating a sense of freedom.

Words she lives by: "Know your pothole and dodge it. Don't work in a pencil factory if you're a vampire."

Sevannah loves to hear from her readers. You can find and connect with her at the links below.

Website/Newsletter:

https://www.sevannahstorm.com/

Facebook:

https://www.facebook.com/sevannah.storm

Instagram:

https://www.instagram.com/sevannah.storm/

Twitter:

https://twitter.com/sevannah_storm

Thank you for taking the time to read *The Healer*. If you enjoyed the story, please tell your friends and leave a review. Reviews support authors and ensure they continue to bring readers books to love and enjoy.

Stay tuned for sample chapters.

THE HUNTRESS

THE BLOOD OF LEGENDS 1

CALLIE IS A SASSY detective, known for her attitude and her ability to endanger her partners. While investigating a senator, she stumbles upon suck-bloods (her word) and a canister, embroiling herself in a diabolical plot older than her grandfather. Trying to stop her dying sister from an unlikely conversion, she falls for an ancient suck-blood and discovers that she's more than human.

GABRIEL is centuries old but has withdrawn from society, preferring to spend his years avoiding vamp politics and reading ancient Greek texts. Asked to rescue Callie as a favor, he doesn't expect her to tempt him with her scent, her delicious blood and her honor.

When another vampire abducts her, Gabe must use his allies and their skills to find her before she suffers through a conversion dooming her to an eternity of enslavement. The passion between them is potent, their love empowering as Callie learns that controlling everything won't bring her happiness. Gabe discovers that to truly live he must lose his heart. What follows is the merging of vampire and human, of lust and love, of honor and forgiveness while preventing the suck-bloods and beasts from fighting a war they didn't start.

CHAPTER ONE

BRAVERY VS. STUPIDITY

CALLIE TREMBLED IN THE darkness, unable to hide, not when they could hear her heart pound and scent her fear on this blustery night, not when she clung to the side of a building twenty levels up. Focusing on her breathing, keeping it shallow and as silent as possible, she tried not to hyperventilate. To them, she had to sound like a wheezing geriatric. She should have stayed away, but stubbornness was one of her *many* faults.

On top of it, she'd lost her gun when she'd first stepped onto the building's ledge. Her purse as well. Shoving the gun down the front of her gown to nestle between her breasts might have been a better option. The image of her captain lambasting her for losing her weapon *again* was enough to consider suicide. Thoughts of impending doom niggled her, tempting her to leap onto the moonlit balcony, throw herself at their feet and demand they end her life now.

She shrugged. Despite the paperwork losing her gun would entail, it didn't matter. Not at the moment. Therein lay her fear.

Balancing on her bare heels on a narrow ledge to eavesdrop? Insanity at its finest. She inched toward the balcony, rethinking her *genius* plan to climb onto the ledge and cling to the glass façade as if her fingertips were octopus tentacles. She wasn't *that* desperate for leads, was she?

Something suspicious was happening tonight, which explained why she was at Mayor Duhamel's ball, dressed like a sequined mannequin with enough make-up on to disguise a rhino. She stared at her manicured toes hanging over the edge. The chilly wind plucked at her burgundy gown, trying to rip her away from the building's embrace. She tightened her grip on the glass as if she could resist the wind's incessant nagging. Her cheeks stung, and if these bastards didn't hurry, she'd suffer from frostbite, or at the very least, she'd look like a happy cherub for days. Typical selfish suckbloods. Her fellow officers would show her no mercy. She grimaced—they'd torture her for sure.

"The drop-off is happening tomorrow evening," a sexy voice rumbled.

It was smooth like decadent dark chocolate. So sex-on-a-stick sexy he had to be a suckblood.

Drop-off?

"I want no surprises," said the suckblood.

"I don't expect any. They know better than to disappoint you," yet another sexy male voice reached her.

Shit! How many were there? She could take one, and only if she was properly armed, which she wasn't. The dagger strapped to her thigh was all this disguise allowed. Much good a single weapon would do her now.

"Good," said Suckblood One.

"Are you sure you want to do this alone? It doesn't sit right with me." Concern was clear in Suckblood Two's voice.

"I'll take a few guards with me, but I need you to hold the fort, so to speak." The first one's chuckle was deep, husky...alluring. "It's not as if I can't defend myself."

Callie nodded. They were excellent fighters, able to resist human weapons with ease. She'd developed her personal arsenal after years of dealing with suckbloods and beasts. The boys at the precinct mocked her for it but, in truth, her battle-readiness had spared many lives, including her own.

If Dad saw her now, though. She winced, imagining the shake of his head and the silly smile he donned when she'd done something brave or idiotic.

"Fine. Should I assist the woman off the ledge?" asked Suckblood Two.

She snorted at his question, confirming their awareness of her presence, and she didn't like the eagerness in his voice. He sounded ravenous.

"Her scent is delicious, but I need a drink, not nourishment. Do as you see fit."

"She does smell good," said Suckblood Two, as if the bouquet of her blood mattered. Oh, fuck!

Suckblood Two's appearance at the balcony's railing made her grip on the glass slip. Tall, at least six-foot-four, with blond locks falling below his collar gave off a Viking-of-old vibe. His broad shoulders with matching biceps strained his sleeves in his expensive-but-struggling tux barely containing the visceral magnetism pouring off him.

His face was another matter—square jaw to a pointy chin with a dimple for added effect. An unnecessary effect. He was a stunner without it. How did they recruit converts? One look at him made her believe they trawled the fashion runways. To be beautiful forever would tempt Narcissus himself.

"Admiring the view?" he said.

A smirk curled his upper lip, yet she sensed no hostility, leaving her to stare into his entrancing blue eyes.

The wind whipped at her again, snatching her from the mesmerizing depths of his seductive eyes. She hadn't admired the view until now.

"Yes, stunning," she said, proud of herself for managing to string two words together.

"I could join you...?"

"It's a free world last time I checked," she said, her hair blowing around her face.

She wouldn't flick it out of her eyes, unwilling to remove her fingers from the glass.

"Or you could join me?" His voice cut through the wind.

Unable to see him, she huffed like an asthmatic hippo, trying to shift her hair. With the help of another gust of wind, she cleared her vision.

"For a scotch?"

She scowled. How did he know her preferred drink? She hadn't indulged tonight, so the scent of it didn't cling to her.

"Have we met?" She snorted at the naïve question.

Such a face wasn't easy to forget.

Said face burst into a charming smile she didn't appreciate. He offered his manicured hand as if beckoning her to trust him. Since the jig was up, she should accept his assistance. Besides, he might—and that was a humongous might—reveal more about this drop-off.

She slid her bare feet from heel to heel until her fingertips could brush his. He extended his arm and grasped her hand, his grip warm, firm. With a sharp tug, she tumbled into his arms.

Sprawled across the front of him, with her fingers curled over his tuxedoed shoulders, she drew in a shuddering breath. Despite having her feet back on something solid, she wasn't grateful. Concern furrowed her brow, instead. Her responses to men were never this instantaneous, but she expected it from a suckblood. She hoped he wasn't one. It would be nice to meet an attractive *human* man for a change. One who couldn't manipulate her with his pheromones.

"Your name?" He glided his hands up her bare back, drawing her into the warmth he emanated.

She shivered, goosebumps rippling from her spine to her thighs. After burrowing his nose in her neck, he inhaled her scent, shameless in his appreciation.

"Callista," she said.

"Ah, beautiful beloved huntress of Zeus." He chuckled.

Of course he knew what her name meant. Damn suckbloods. Overeducated arrogant bastards. Was that supposed to impress her? Okay, it did! But that didn't mean she had to *succumb* to his seductive ways.

"Yes." Her instincts screamed, demanding she flee.

She ignored them for now. This man had information about the package. Not that she had any idea what *it* was.

Disappointment dampened her mood. She should've known crashing this event wouldn't garner evidence—only raise more questions and create new crimes to investigate. Her compiled files on the various patrons attending tonight needed a few secrets to unlock the investigations further. She was desperate for closure.

He gathered her hand in his distracting her from her thoughts and brushed his lips across the pulse at her inner wrist. The sensation was too good to be natural.

His head shot up. He scowled, but it didn't detract from his dazzling handsomeness—it made him brooding, which was downright breathtaking.

"I must abandon you, sweet Callista. Rest assured, I will find you."

"Why?" She claimed her hand back.

She fought the urge to rub her wrist along her outer thigh to erase the memory of his kiss. He was too close for her senses or her instincts to handle, not to mention for her peace of mind.

Smothered by his presence, she raised her hands palm up, placed them on his chest, and pushed. He didn't budge, but she did, stumbling backward from the force she applied. She suspected she'd surprised him and thus gained her freedom. She'd felt his strength—iron-like and indomitable—beneath his tuxedo. He could have held her against him for as long as he pleased, and there wouldn't have been a damn thing she could do about it.

"Because you smell delicious." He smiled.

What had she expected? Typical suckblood, thinking with his stomach. The poor man was hungry, like she gave a damn. "So?"

He blinked, tilting his head to the side. "Don't I smell good too?"

She arched a brow, her suspicions confirmed. He *was* using his pheromones on her. His sheer beauty swayed her more than his cologne. Since he waited for her to respond, she leaned in to sniff him, her nose brushing along his Adam's apple, which bobbed at the contact. Citrus, bonfire, and earthy undertones combined to form a mind-numbing enticement, yet her knees remained unaffected.

She stepped back, resisting the temptation to place an open-mouthed kiss to his throat. Her knees were fine, but her lips weren't. They tingled, made demands of her, needing his skin's warmth. She forced a shrug, and his horrified expression was worth it. But when it morphed into a fascinated one, she sighed. It was official. Her evening wasn't going as planned. She should leave now and chalk it up as bad luck.

"You smell good. Your cologne suits you. Now, if you'll excuse me, I see scotch in my future."

Spinning on her bare toes, she made a beeline for her pumps she'd left in the back corner of the balcony. If only she'd thought to leave her purse there. What the hell had she been thinking? Climbing the side of a building while clutching her purse—idiotic. Not to mention, she couldn't bring herself to leave her gun unattended. Well, it sure lay unattended now, wherever it had landed. Hopefully, it hadn't hit someone on the head when it fell.

She sensed his gaze caressing her as she slipped on each shoe. At least he missed her wince as she squished her toes into unnatural shapes. Nerves had her fluffing her hair and sliding her damp palms down her velvet-covered thighs before entering the crowded, unbearably hot hall, vowing never to do something so stupid again. She hadn't gotten much for her crazy death-defying balancing trick.

There was a drop-off tomorrow? Hell, there was always a drop-off. What she needed was a location. Inner City was huge, so she'd appreciate any clue. This wasn't the movies. This was real life where information didn't magically fall into her eager hands—she had to fight for every morsel, every titillating secret.

Her targets had taken their champagne glasses to the balcony's seductive privacy. She'd raced here in the hopes of hiding behind a potted plant or in the shadows. There'd been neither with the balcony illuminated by Chinese lanterns. No one would speak of sensitive matters with her leaning against the railing admiring the cityscape. Now, while she hesitated at the door, a few men assessed her. None were panty-dropping gorgeous enough to match the first suckblood's voice.

Not that she could sweet-talk *him* into revealing the drop-off's location. If she guessed his current position, he was amid a group of desperate women, their body language blatant with intention. Lust's stench emanated from that side of the hall—oily, wicked...tempting.

Callie spun on her steel-tipped heels to weave through the dancing couples to the bar. She claimed a barstool with a deep groan, relief instant with her weight off her toes. Her killer heels were doing just that, killing her. Smothering a borderline hysterical giggle, she flicked her hair off her face, hating the frustration that pounded at her patience. Disappointment ate at her, at the disastrous outcome of a promising evening.

"Scotch, neat," she said to the bartender, not bothering to meet his gaze.

A tumbler of the burnished liquid glided across the glass counter and into her line of vision. She scooped it up and threw back the finest malt she'd tasted in a while. Peppery, smoky, and smooth, it flowed down her throat, bursting her innards into flames of false courage. She should've started the evening with this.

"Are you acquainted with Leonardo?" a gentleman asked. "You seemed cozy."

She stiffened, assessing the man...Devlin Carter. Needing the time to compose her thoughts and a poker face, she took a careful sip from her refilled glass.

He was tall, cresting six feet, and filled out a tux like no forty-year-old should be able to. Gray streaked his temples, adding to his distinguished appearance and his sensual appeal. Not that he tempted her—his nefarious deeds were well documented. Okay, only by her, and she never made it official. The very-much-human senator had a thick case file of his own. She'd been investigating him for years.

"Leonardo, Senator?" She opted for ignorance, arching a brow in query.

"That answers my question." He grinned.

His cold blue gaze traveled her bared leg and settled on her adorned foot. Oh, yes, the foot fetish. She fought the urge to twitch her toes under his unashamed depravity.

"You don't strike me as his type."

"Their type is human." She twirled the amber liquid in her glass before raising it to her lips again.

"Touché. Does he know you're in law enforcement?"

Knowing who she was, or at least, what she did, didn't bode well. Her instincts skittered along her nerves, worse than when she'd stepped onto the ledge. Something about Carter had her skin crawling. That something was slimy and dangerous.

"He didn't ask. I didn't offer." Her reply was sharp.

She sighed. Her miserable mood called forth her worst manners. Not to mention, he had her at a disadvantage. Somehow he had known she was police. She must have given herself away. Maybe her shifty gaze, distrusting everyone, her stiff shoulders and over-vigilant stance screaming she didn't belong here. She'd ruined the evening with her subconscious behavior.

She tried not to grimace at his delighted smile. He was enjoying their conversation, very much aware of how he put her on the defensive.

"So why crash James's party?" Carter gestured to the bartender, who served him a tall blonde beer with a thick head.

Beer? An interesting choice at a ball.

"I felt like dressing up." She tapped her unpolished fingernails on the glass countertop. "Listen, Senator, you're not one to waste time, nor to beat around the bush. Mind telling me the purpose of this conversation?"

Her bluntness made him chuckle. Thankfully she hadn't pissed him off. If that happened and her captain found out, she would be issuing parking tickets for a year.

"He's enamored with you," Carter said, not answering her question.

She shook her head. "Ah, so if we were on a first-name basis, I could spy for you?"

"Spy is such a nasty word, and I didn't ask you to," he said, licking the beer foam off his lips.

"My apologies, Senator." She flicked her hair back in an exaggerated manner and giggled, batting her eyelashes hard enough to hurt. "What I meant to say was that we could discuss over coffee the merits of suckblood-feeder relationships and the impact of this on the psyche."

If he found her sass offensive, he didn't show it. A consummate diplomat, he gave a deep belly laugh that sounded authentic. "Yes, something like that. I've heard horrendous stories of their sexual prowess. It's enough to harm my ego."

"Yours?" She admired his form, stopping to study the pin on his lapel—a large, winged bird embedded in flames.

It was solid gold and crafted by a master jeweler, she didn't doubt. She couldn't imagine him shopping at the local stores.

"Can anything harm your ego, Senator?"

"He's interested, mark my words, my girl." Carter shifted closer as if intending to share something for her ears only. "When he comes for you, pay attention to anything unusual. I don't trust these...suckbloods. Never have and never will." He flicked his two fingers, his business card pinched between them. "Here's my private number. Call me if you find anything useful."

She took the card and slipped it into her cleavage. She didn't want to accept it, but she sensed he'd stay with her until she did. He sauntered away to bombard other guests with his bombastic personality. Goosebumps prickled her skin in an instinctual warning that he wasn't a man to trust.

She didn't intend to have another scotch, but the interlude with Carter and his false happiness highlighted the sadness staining her heart. No matter the circumstances, the distractions, the environment, or the company, her sister's terminal illness circled the edges of her mind. Scotch wouldn't solve her problems, despite its aged smoothness. Her bed beckoned, and she planned on flopping onto it in a most unladylike manner.

Facing the hall, she caught a glimpse of her scowling captain bearing down on her.

So much for her best-laid plans...

Get it here: